A W

Jackie didn't like the woods. Having grown up in the city, he had a natural distrust of the forest. In all the fairy tales his mother had read to him, and in the one scary movie that he had ever been brave enough to watch on TV—without his parents' permission—it was in the woods that bad things had happened to people, especially children. Little Red Riding Hood, Snow White, Hansel and Gretel—all had been in danger as soon as they had entered a forest. Walking through one now, Jackie could understand why.

The woods were creepy. In addition to the shadowy light, the air was filled with strange rustlings and creaking noises. The trees leaned every which way and the thick interconnecting weave of leaves and branches overhead reminded him of a spider's web. When the breeze blew through the leaves, they danced as if long-legged creatures were scurrying over them. At any moment he expected some furry, bug-eyed thing to drop down on a gluey long thread and snatch him off his feet to devour him . . .

Books by R. Patrick Gates

THE PRISON*

GRIMM MEMORIALS*

FEAR

JUMPERS

TUNNELVISION

DEATHWALKER

*Published by Kensington Publishing Corporation

GRIMM MEMORIALS

R. PATRICK GATES

PINNACLE BOOKS
Kensington Publishing Corp.
http://www.kensingtonbooks.com

PINNACLE BOOKS are published by

Kensington Publishing Corp.
850 Third Avenue
New York, NY 10022

All Kensington Titles, Imprints, and Distributed Lines are available at special quantity discounts for bulk purchases for sales promotions, premiums, fund-raising, and educational or institutional use. Special book excerpts or customized printings can also be created to fit specific needs. For details, write or phone the office of the Kensington special sales manager: Kensington Publishing Corp., 850 Third Avenue, New York, NY 10022, attn: Special Sales Department, Phone: 1-800-221-2647.

Pinnacle and the P logo Reg. U.S. Pat. & TM Off.

First Pinnacle Books Printing: June 2005

10 9 8 7 6 5 4 3 2 1

Printed in the United States of America

For Corey Briscoe Gates and his cousins—Jackie, Jennifer, Devin, Sara, Melissa, Adrian, Shea, and Sylvia. Fairy tales are real, kids. You can be living one and not even know it, and only you can decide if it has a happy ending.

Author's Note

This book would not have been possible without the inspiration of the following: Mother Goose, the Brothers Grimm, and *The Uses of Enchantment: The Meaning and Importance of Fairy Tales* by Dr. Bruno Bettelheim. I would also like to thank Christopher Schelling for his support of this book, and my uncle, Verne (Bucky) Roy, for his detailed information on undertakers' gurneys and crematoriums.

*For every evil under the sun
There is a remedy or there is none . . .*

*Ye parents who have children dear,
    And ye, too, who have none,
If you would keep them safe abroad
    Pray keep them safe at home.*

—Mother Goose

Once upon a time . . .

—the Brothers Grimm

CHAPTER 1

There was an old woman and what do you think?

They're coming!

The old woman sat on the bar stool and listened to the low, gravelly voice.

SHE'S *coming! The one* I *was waiting for.*

Her long white hair, speckled with blotches of charcoal gray, hung over her face as she sat, her head down, staring into the glass of tequila on the bar in front of her. With a hand that trembled from palsy, she reached for the glass, clutched it, and warily brought it to her mouth, spilling only a few drops. As the glass reached her lips, she tipped her head back and downed the fiery liquid. The strength of the tequila made her want to gasp, as it always did. And, as always, she swallowed the fire in her throat, fighting the burning liquor back into her belly.

Can you hear them? They are your funeral march.

She pushed away the voice, listening beyond the murmuring thoughts of the other bar patrons, beyond the rush of mental images in the street and town outside until, finally, she could hear them. She squeezed her eyes shut and concentrated. She could feel the Machine start in motion. An image formed on her eyelids.

Can you see them? You'll never have them.

An orange Saab wavered blurrily, then shrank into focus. It hovered in her mind's eye and rippled slightly as if seen through great heat. In the car was a family: woman, man, two children—a boy and a girl. The boy was blond and cherubic with wide blue eyes. The girl was older, hair darker, eyes brown. The children were in the backseat. The girl was reading to the boy. The man was driving. He was tall with longish, dirty blond hair. His complexion was red with a fresh scrubbed look.

The old woman fixed their images in her mind, then dismissed them. She turned to the mother, a small, brown-haired woman with wide, almond-shaped brown eyes and a swollen pregnant belly. The old woman took a deep breath. "I can almost taste her," she mumbled. "Fe, fi, fo, fum, I smell the blood of a pregnant mum," she said out loud.

The bartender, who was washing glasses a few feet away, looked up at her. "Excuse me, ma'am?"

The old woman opened her eyes and looked at the bartender. He started to smile at her and stopped. The back of his head went suddenly cold with fear. For a split second, he could have sworn that *something had happened* to the old woman's face. He could have sworn (he would convince himself later that he had had something in his eye) that her face had *sagged*, almost melted, for just a second, then it had snapped back into place.

"Give me another," she said in a cracked, ancient voice. The bartender shook his head clear and quickly poured another tequila, straight up, for her. Just as quickly, he backed away from her and went to the other end of the bar. She downed the drink as she had the one before it.

"She's the one, Edmund," she murmured to the air. "The one *we* were waiting for," the old woman said dreamily as the tequila burn left her high and slightly dizzy. "She's the one . . ."

* * *

At the intersection of Main Street and Route 9 in downtown Amherst, the orange Saab stopped at a red light. Suddenly its engine stuttered, and skipped, then shuddered loudly and shook until it stalled

"Shit!" the blond-haired man at the wheel exclaimed, giving a guilty glance toward the children in the backseat.

"What's wrong with it, Steve?" the woman asked.

"If I knew that, Diane, I'd be a mechanic instead of a teacher," he said with a sigh. He got out of the car and went to the hood and opened it. Heat vapors rippled upward from the hot metal. Steve stared at the engine and swore under his breath. Cars were lining up behind the Saab as the light turned green. Several cars began beeping when he didn't move his vehicle. The horns fueled a resentful anger in him. He furiously motioned for the cars to go around, but when the light changed, each car had inched its way forward in anticipation and now they were too close together to do anything.

Diane Nailer got out of the car with the difficulty of the very pregnant and looked at her husband's face getting redder than normal. "That bad, huh?" she asked. He merely grunted. She reached in the car, pulled the passenger seat forward, and told her children, Jackie and Jennifer, to get out.

"Are we there yet?" Jackie piped up as he slipped out of the car. His big blue eyes blinked sleepily.

"No, honey," she said and looked up. "Here comes a policeman, Steve. Maybe he can help."

The cop, a baby-faced, slim-built young man, immediately went to the rear of the Saab. "Let's get it out of the road," he said with an air of authority that belied his years. "You steer and push from the driver's side," he commanded Steve, who did as he was told. Together they pushed the car around the corner and to the curb.

"There's a Sunoco garage down the street," the cop said, pointing south along Main Street, "but you can't leave it here too long or I'll have to ticket it."

Steve nodded, smiled, and thanked the policeman for his help.

"I've got to pee *real* bad," Diane whispered urgently to her husband as he rejoined her and his stepchildren on the sidewalk.

"Okay," Steve said, putting his arm around her. "They must have a restroom at the gas station. Let's go kids."

"Can we get ice cream?" Jackie asked, as he took his stepfather's hand and walked alongside him.

"We'll see, Jackie, we'll see."

A half block away, in Roosevelt's Bar and Grill, the old woman pushed the hair back out of her eyes and looked up. Seated across the end angle of the bar from her was an old man dressed in black, as she was. His hair was whiter than hers, and his eyebrows were youthfully black and so thick that his tiny eyes were hidden, but otherwise their features were nearly identical. The old man smiled at her and his leathery face cracked into a thousand hideous wrinkles.

You're going to fuck it up, Eleanor! His voice was grating.

Eleanor smiled tightly. "Go away, Edmund. You're dead."

The old man faded.

A waitress returning empty glasses to the bar heard her and laughed uncomfortably.

Eleanor got off the bar stool, rising to her full six feet, picked up her large black bag, and shuffled out of the bar. As she walked past the waitress, she let loose a barking burp in the waitress's direction that made the latter jump. The old woman started to laugh, then grabbed at her chest as a needling pain shot through it. She staggered to the door quickly as the pain spread, seeping into her arms.

* * *

With Jennifer and Jackie on either side of them holding their hands, Steve and Diane strolled arm-in-arm down the steaming sidewalk. She was seven and a half months pregnant, just big enough so that she appeared to be waddling when she walked and had to lean against her husband to support her unbalanced frame. Near the entrance to Roosevelt's she had to pause and rest next to a maple tree growing out of a rectangular prison of dirt encased in sidewalk. The heat was making it hard for her to breathe. The hot weather had bothered her all summer as she got bigger and bigger, but lately it was becoming unbearable. She shook herself free from Steve's arm and Jennifer's hand and sucked in the stifling air. She held her hand to her heart and thought, Good day for a heart attack.

"Are you okay, honey?" Steve asked with concern. Diane leaned against the tree, fanning herself with her left hand, and nodded.

"Mom, look!" Jackie shouted, pointing to the alleyway next to Roosevelt's Bar and Grill where a long, gleaming black, wing-finned hearse was parked.

"It's Batman's station wagon," he said with a giggle.

"Oh, *gross*," Jennifer exclaimed. "It's a hearse."

"What's that?" Jackie inquired

"It's a car they use to carry dead people to the cemetery in," Jennifer explained. Jackie stopped laughing.

Diane looked at the hearse and giggled nervously to herself. If I do have a heart attack, I won't have to go far, she thought and immediately felt a chill.

Opposite them, the door to Roosevelt's burst open with a loud bang that made them all jump. Eleanor stumbled through the door of the bar and leaned heavily against the wrought-iron railing lining the short walk that led to the sidewalk.

Diane fell back against the tree and stared. The old man who had just walked out of Roosevelt's was the spitting image of her late father; he could have been his twin. As the old man met her eyes, Diane almost swooned. It *was* her father. But then he smiled and the light changed; he returned to being a man who merely looked a great deal like her father. She pushed her fists into her groin as her weakened kidneys suddenly threatened to let go and she grabbed at Steve's arm.

"Honey, I've *got* to go," she pleaded. He stood mesmerized for several moments, staring at the old woman, then pulled himself away to help his wife cross the street to the gas station. The children followed, but the cherubic-faced boy lingered, giving the old woman a distrustful look, as if he didn't want to turn his back on her.

"I need more time," the old woman muttered as she watched the little boy run across the street. A wave of pain enveloped her suddenly, wracking her body with shuddering torture. She clutched at her chest and fished in her bag. Staggering sideways to the hearse she leaned against it to steady herself. She found what she was looking for, a small, black pillbox, and struggled to open it with feeble, trembling hands. She fumbled a tiny pill from the box and shoved it under her tongue. She closed her eyes and leaned against the hearse. After nearly a minute, the old woman sighed and straightened.

You're out of time, Sister.

"I'll be all right," she whispered, defiantly. "Got to get home." She staggered around the car, leaning heavily on it, and was barely able to pull the driver's door open. Gasping for air and struggling with the door, she managed to get in, her head lolling against the top of the seat as she stopped a moment to rest. The nitroglycerin pill she'd taken was doing little for her. The pain in her chest was like searing heartburn, only a thousand times worse. With an immense effort, she closed the door and started the engine. Grinding the gears, she forced the shift into first, pulled out without a glance at the oncoming traffic, and drove away.

* * *

Two hours later, after the Saab's fan belt had been fixed, they'd had ice cream, and were driving to Northwood, Jackie spoke up and voiced his opinion of the old woman.

"That old woman near the gas station was creepy," he said to his sister, Jennifer.

Jennifer smiled thoughtfully. The old woman had reminded her of her grandmother. "I thought she looked nice."

In the front seat, Diane was lost in thought and seemed not to hear the children, but Steve had to chuckle to himself when he heard Jackie call the woman old. To Jackie, he supposed she was old, but she couldn't have been more than twenty-five; probably she was more like twenty. He felt himself getting hard as he remembered how beautiful she was; how she had stared at him as if she could see right inside him; and how she had fondled her breasts with her left hand as she stared.

CHAPTER 2

I went to the wood and got it.

The drive from Amherst to Northwood was a pleasant one, full of sights to keep the children occupied. They drove through the campus of the University of Massachusetts, past the towering, but half-empty, library and the abstract, concrete block architecture of the Fine Arts Center.

As they turned onto Route 116 the surrounding countryside changed suddenly from the modern, urban-style buildings of the college campus to rolling green fields occasionally dotted with ramshackle barns and houses alone against the sky. Except for the humpbacked and breast-shaped hills along either side of the road, the area could have easily been in some Midwest farming state; the contrast between urban and rural was immediate and shocking. Shimmering green ravines cut into the hilly fields here and there along the sides of the road for miles as it wound through the countryside, leaving the vast, towering structures of the university behind like a mirage of some fabled and magical city.

In the distance, the tall, rounded mound of trees and red shale cliffs that make up the summit and western face of Mount Sugarloaf jutted boldly into the bright blue, early September sky. Beneath the open red wound of the cliff face the sleepy towns of Northwood and Deerfield nestled together. On the other side of the mountains, the Connecticut River flowed through the town of Sunderland.

"Look, kids," Diane said, pointing ahead. "There's Mount Sugarloaf. You can see it from our new house. There's a road going up there and at the top they have a little park with a picnic area."

"Oh, Mom, let's go up there! Can we, now?" Jackie asked excitedly.

"Not today, honey. We've got to get in our new house and get settled. School starts next Wednesday, you know."

Jackie grimaced as if to say, Don't remind me. Next to him, Jennifer smiled at her little brother's frown. Unlike Jackie, Jennifer was looking forward to going to a new school and making new friends.

At the blinking red light at Bloody Brook Square, in the middle of Northwood, they turned left onto Route 47 and traveled for two blocks by rows of white Colonial houses until they came to a street sign on the right that read: Dorsey Lane. Steve turned the car onto the tree-lined road and drove to their new home, a large, two-story Colonial identical to the only other house on Dorsey Lane, which ended in a cul-de-sac after the Nailer house.

Steve pulled the Saab into the driveway and turned off the engine. "Well, kids, this is it. We're here."

The house had been white at one time, but years of weather and little upkeep had turned it gray. Its windows were blind with reflected clouds and shadows cast by several large maple trees growing close to the house. The trees spilled over the roof, their branches like monster arms reaching to gather the house in and carry it off somewhere to be eaten. At least that's what Jackie thought as he and Jennifer climbed out of the backseat, after Steve and Diane got out.

They had been there before, when Steve and Diane were looking at the place, but that had been back in June and, bored to death by the process of house viewing after seeing five houses in two hours, Jackie and Jennifer hadn't paid much attention to it.

As they got out of the car, Steve went to the mailbox at the end of the driveway and got the key that the real estate agent had taped to the inside for them. Steve took the key and unlocked the front door. He whistled as the door swung open. The hallway and front rooms, visible from the door, were filled with cardboard boxes and plastic-wrapped furniture.

Steve turned to Diane who was standing behind him, smiled, and rolled his eyes. *"We* have got a *lot* of work to do, babe. Maybe it's not too late to forget all this and move back to Boston."

Diane laughed and patted his shoulder. "Oh, come on, it's not that bad. We'll be done before you know it."

"What do you want us to do, Mom?" Jennifer asked. At ten, and very aware of her mother's condition, she was always ready to help.

Diane reached down with some effort and grabbed Jackie by the collar of his shirt as he tried to crawl between her legs and slip into the house. "Hold on, cowboy. You stay with your sister. I think the best help you can be, Jen, is to keep this little monster out from under our feet while we unpack everything."

"But, Mo-o-om, I want to stay with you," Jackie whined.

"I know, honey, but we've got a lot to do. You go with your sister and play. You can explore the woods behind the house, okay? Just don't go too far."

Jennifer took Jackie's hand and began to lead him away, but he resisted. "No-o, I want to stay with you, Mummy. There's *trolls* and *ogies* and *witches* in the woods," he pouted, on the verge of tears.

Steve squatted in front of him and took him by the shoulders with both hands. "Hey, big guy, come on. What's this? We need your help here. There aren't any trolls, or 'ogies,' or witches around here. Where'd you get that idea?"

Jackie looked at his sister. "Jen said so. She was reading fairy tales to me in the car and she said they're real. She said we'd probably find trolls and ogies in the woods around the new house cuz this used to be a 'chanted forest. She said the witch in 'Hansel and Gretel' used to live in these woods."

"I was just fooling around," Jen said sheepishly. She shot her brother a dirty look.

"Well you can just fool around in your room for the weekend after we move in," her mother scolded. "I don't know how many times I have told you not to tell him wild stories. You know how he gets."

Jennifer looked at her shoes and mumbled, "I'm sorry."

"Listen, big guy," Steve said confidently to Jackie, "There are no such things as witches, trolls, or 'ogies,' or anything like that. They're all make-believe. And if they are make-believe, and not real, then they can't hurt you and you don't have to be afraid of them. Do you remember what I told you about being scared of things?"

Jackie pouted and shrugged.

"Come on, you remember. I said fear is ignorance. People who are afraid are ignorant. Do you remember what ignorance means?"

Jackie mumbled, "That's when you don't know nothin'."

"Right. People get scared when they don't understand something. Once you *know* something, there is no reason to be afraid of it anymore. Your knowledge is strength. Now, since you *know* there are no such things as trolls or witches, or as you call them, 'ogies,' or monsters of any kind, you don't have to be frightened by the woods."

"How do I know there's no such things?" Jackie asked, gazing with intense sincerity into his stepfather's eyes.

Steve had to laugh in spite of himself at Jackie's seriousness. "You know because I told you so, and your mother told you so. And even though Jen told you those stories were real she doesn't believe them and she knows that they aren't real. Don't you, Jen?"

Jennifer nodded slowly, looking sincerely repentant.

Jackie regarded her with suspicion and Steve with doubt. "If you won't believe us, then go and check the woods for yourself. All you'll find are a lot of trees and a neat place to play."

Jackie looked warily in the direction of the trees. He had been maneuvered into feeling now that he had to go and look.

"Yeah, I think that is a good idea," Steve went on. "You and Jen explore the woods around the house while your mother and I unpack stuff. That way you'll *know* there's nothing out there so when your little brother Stevie is born you can tell him that there is nothing to be afraid of. Once we make a dent in the unpacking and get things arranged a little, you two can come in and put your stuff away."

Steve stood up, gave Jackie a pat on the head, turned him around, and guided him to Jen. She took his hand and led him around the corner of the house to the backyard.

Jackie looked fearfully at the trees that bordered the yard and, to him, loomed overhead like fairy-tale giants. Jackie paled at the image his mind had conjured. He was gifted with a wild imagination that didn't need much prodding to shift into high gear.

"Are there really trolls and ogies and witches, Jen?" he asked his sister. "Tell me the truth."

Jennifer looked at him and rolled her eyes. "You know you are such a queebo. Thanks for getting me in trouble." Jackie looked despondent. "First of all, it's *ogres,* not *ogies,* stupid, and (exasperated sigh) what did Steve just get done telling you? I can't believe that you are going into the first grade; sometimes you are such a stupid, queebo wimp."

"I am not," he retorted vehemently.

"Are to."

"Am *not!*" he reiterated, tears springing to his eyes, his mouth twitching on the verge of a bawl.

Jennifer looked at him and clucked her tongue in disgust. "Okay, okay, you are not. Just don't start crying on me."

They rounded the rear corner of the house and went into the backyard. Very near the house grew the three huge maple trees that had appeared so threatening to Jackie from the front. Under the far tree, in a sand-filled square area, a swing and kiddie slide had been set up. The rest of the yard was dotted with several smaller birch trees that refused to grow straight and slanted at odd angles. In between the trees the grass was long, with an occasional bare spot here and there where dirt or ledge showed through. The property stretched a good twenty yards behind the house until it met a large field of goldenrod and strawgrass that ran another half an acre to the woods.

Upon seeing the play set, Jackie immediately ran to it and began swinging. He kicked his feet hard and made the swing arc higher and higher. One of the posts of the swingset had rusted free of its cement anchor and jumped off the ground with a loud groan at every kick of Jackie's legs.

"Jackie, stop it," Jennifer protested. The irritating metallic *ka-chunk* of the swing post had the same affect on her ears as nails scraped across a blackboard. Jackie grinned wildly and pumped his legs harder, making the awful sound louder.

Jennifer walked away from him. "Okay, be a jerk, I'm going to explore the woods. You can stay here if you want to, but if there were such things as witches and trolls, I bet they'd like that sound. I bet that noise would bring them running."

Jackie immediately stopped swinging and looked around. "I thought you said there was no such things?"

Jennifer stopped, shrugged, and smiled slyly.

"I'm telling Mom, Jen," he threatened. "She told you not to tell stories anymore."

"I didn't say anything," she answered smugly. "I said *if* there were such things." She smirked and walked away.

Jackie watched her go. Suddenly, the shadows under the tree seemed to get darker. He looked up at the tree above him. In his wild imagination its many branches resembled a canopy of snakes, writhing in the breeze. A bird flitted abruptly from one branch to another, startling Jackie. Without hesitating a moment longer, he leapt from the swing and ran into the field after his sister.

Jennifer was admiring a spray of buttercups that filled a shallow ditch in the middle of the field when Jackie called to her. He had nearly caught up with her but was now squatting in a small clearing a few yards away. As she reached him, she saw that he was crouching next to a large anthill. She leaned over and saw what had fascinated him: two red ants were struggling to pull a large, dead spider up the side of the anthill.

"Oh, *gross!*" Jennifer spat out, making a face. She turned away and headed for the woods.

Jackie giggled with delight at having grossed his sister out and ran after her, crawling his hand up her back like a large arachnid.

"Cut it out, Jackie, or I'll leave you in the woods."

Jackie scuttled his hand down her arm and ran ahead of her, laughing.

"I'll get you for that, Jackie!"

He ran to the edge of the woods and stopped. The sun passed behind a cloud and he was swallowed by a gray-blue shadow. The trees loomed darkly and the undergrowth was thick with the musty, biting odor of rotting leaves. A grayness seeped from the woods, tainting the air and chilling the back of Jackie's neck. He stepped back, ready to retreat, when Jennifer walked by, ignoring him, and skirted the edge of the trees looking for an opening in the underbrush. Not far away she found a narrow path between two crooked birch trees.

"I don't want to go in the woods," Jackie said uneasily.

"Fine. Stay here then, wimpy," Jennifer said tauntingly and went into the woods.

Jackie hesitated a moment and looked around. The trees leaned very close here. He turned to go back to the house, but he imagined that the grass of the field was longer than it was before. Visions of what might be hiding there ran quickly through his head. His imagination made up his mind for him and he ran after his sister.

The change in lighting was sudden and dramatic. Jackie plunged from sun-filled daylight to shadow-filled twilight. It took a few moments for his eyes to adjust and he was in a small panic until they did. He held his breath and stumbled forward until he caught up with Jen, who was poking with a stick at a toadstool growing at the side of the path.

"If you ate one of these, you'd shrivel up and die," Jennifer said wickedly.

Jackie eyed her doubtfully, but kept clear of the fungus. He didn't like the woods. Having grown up in the city, he had a natural distrust of the forest. In all the fairy tales that his mother had read to him, and in the one scary movie that he had ever been brave enough to watch on TV—without his parents' permission—it was in the woods that bad things had happened to people, especially children. Little Red Riding Hood, Snow White, Hansel and Gretel—all had been in danger as soon as they had entered a forest. Walking through one now, Jackie could understand why.

The woods were creepy. In addition to the shadowy light, the air was filled with strange rustlings and creaking noises. The trees leaned every which way and the thick interconnecting weave of leaves and branches overhead reminded him of a spider's web. When the breeze blew the leaves, they danced as if long-legged creatures were scurrying over them. At any moment he expected some furry, bug-eyed thing to drop down on a gluey long thread and snatch him off his feet to devour him at its leisure in the treetops.

Jackie walked faster, staying right behind Jennifer and stepping on the heel of her sneakers whenever she slowed down to look at something.

"Jackie, you gave me a flat," she said, suddenly angry when he caused her sneaker to slip off her foot.

"Sorry," Jackie said in a small voice, all the while keeping a wary eye on the surrounding trees.

Jennifer fixed her shoe and straightened, then pointed ahead just past where the path ended in a tangle of bushes and undergrowth. "Look, there's a road," she said and started off through the thick patch of laurel and lilac toward it. Jackie stayed right with her, glad that she had seen the road. On the road he would definitely feel safer.

They broke from the brush and walked onto the road. It was dirt covered and just wide enough for a single car. Jackie looked down the road and was surprised to see the roof of their new house through the trees, which were sparser as the road, the opening of which could barely be seen through overgrown bushes, connected with Dorsey Lane. A bird was sitting on the chimney. The image vaguely reminded Jackie of something that made him uneasy, but he couldn't remember what it was.

"Let's see where it goes," Jennifer said, heading off up the road.

Jackie watched her go, then looked back at the house. It was much closer than he thought it should be—to him it felt like they had walked miles into an unknown wilderness—but still was too far away for him to risk going to it alone through the threatening trees. He turned and reluctantly followed his trailblazing sister.

The road wound serpentine through the woods. It curled around thick trees and made sharp sudden turns that would be difficult for a car to maneuver. Neither of them noticed the fresh tire ruts beneath their feet. After following the twisting road for five minutes, it opened up wider and began to run straight. Ahead, they could see a clearing; the road went up a dusty, curved incline and continued out of sight.

"Jackie, look at this," Jennifer said, staring into a thicket of bushes at the side of the road. Lying against the stump of a tree that appeared to have been blasted by lightning was a large, old wooden sign. There was printing on it, but they couldn't make out what it said until Jennifer pulled back the bushes to completely reveal it and read the faded black printing on it out loud:

GRIMM MEMORIALS
EDMUND GRIMM, MORTICIAN
COFFINS MEMORIAL STONES
BURIALS CREMATIONS.

"This is a place that burns dead people," Jen said in a spooky voice.

A chill ran down Jackie's arms, making the downy hair stand on end with goosebumps. He looked up. Through the tops of the trees, he could see a tall, square spire of a house with a single window in it. He had the strange feeling the window was staring at him. Into him.

"Gotcha!" Jennifer cried loudly and suddenly as she grabbed her little brother by the arm. He let out a gasping shriek and turned tail down the road, running as fast as his short legs could carry him.

CHAPTER 3

Fe, fi, fo, fum . . .

The big black hearse, its motor barely running, was parked in front of the rambling, many-gabled, gray Victorian house. The old woman, her face still pale and a line of sweat bubbling on her forehead, sat with her eyes closed and head back. Her chest moved imperceptibly with every weak, shallow breath that rattled in her throat and whistled from her nose.

She didn't know how she had made it home. The pain in her chest had spread to her entire body, setting it on fire and pulling a red veil of torture over her eyes. She remembered driving, swerving from side to side on the highway so badly that it was a wonder a cop hadn't pulled her over. She had driven by instinct more than anything else. She didn't remember passing through the town square, or turning onto Dorsey Lane, and she barely remembered steering the hearse up the winding, tree-lined road through the woods surrounding the big old house. Now she sat in the car, her muscles so tight with pain that she could barely stretch out her hand to turn the ignition off.

I could die right here, she thought. It would be an end to the intense pain she was feeling, but she was not ready yet to die. If she had anything to say about it, it would be quite a while before she would succumb to death.

But only if she could get out of the car and into the house.

Eleanor, a voice hissed in her ear through the open driver's window. She tried to turn her head but the pain running amok in her chest, arms, and neck wouldn't let her.

Eleanor, the voice hissed again. The rattle of her laborious breathing grew louder for a moment. Her eyes fluttered and her gaping, gasping mouth worked silently. She opened her eyes and blinding sunlight made them water. She managed to turn her head a little and look at Edmund's face peering with concern through the window at her.

You're fucking it up, Eleanor, he said with a laugh so hollow, it sounded like it came from the depths of a tomb.

Eleanor tried to shake her head, no, but the pain had made her neck rigid. With a superhuman effort she moved her left hand to the door handle and pulled on it. The door swung open, nearly spilling her out, but she held on to the wheel. Grunting painfully with every move, she swung her legs out of the car and stood, leaning heavily against the car door.

Another wave of pain flowed through her, turning her vision dark for several seconds. When it cleared, with swirls of light popping around the edges of her sight, she saw Edmund standing a few feet away. A dull, hot breeze blew, and his body rippled with it as the air passed through him.

How do you like it? he said in a voice as gritty as graveyard dirt. *It's not pleasant, is it?*

Using the door as a crutch, Eleanor staggered around it, then leaned against the fender and slid to the front end of the hearse. From her pocket she took the little black box that held her nytroglycerin pills. In her right, she held a bottle of tequila. She took a swig before tugging the box open and scooping one of the tiny pills out and into her mouth, where she pushed it under her tongue with her finger.

You're going to fuck it all up as usual, Edmund chuckled.

"Shut up," Eleanor said between clenched teeth. When the pill was dissolved, she took a deep breath, stood straight, and pushed herself away from the car, lurching across the dirt driveway to the front porch stairs.

You'll never make it, Edmund gloated.

She grasped the stair railing and braced herself against the shock of pain she expected. Surprisingly, there was no unbearable wave of pain; the pills were finally working and the torture was actually subsiding. She was going to make it. Moving slowly, she went up the steps, across the porch to the massive double oak doors, and unlocked the left side.

Eleanor pulled herself through the doorway and shuffled over the black marble floor of the entrance hall. To the left, a wide staircase went up the wall to the secondfloor landing, which ran the length of the room and had an ornate oak railing with diamond-cut balusters. Directly ahead was a large, dirty white marble podium with an open book on it. At the top of the exposed, dusty yellowing pages was the legend: *Guests of the dearly departed.* Dark, heavy oak furniture decorated the room solemnly: a large sofa between two closed paneled doors (one of which had *Crematorium* printed on it in gold letters, the other *Chapel*) against the back wall; a black, Boston rocker in the far right corner; and a long mirrored coatrack along the right, next to another door. The walls were dark oak paneling and bare.

Eleanor made it to the sofa and fell heavily on it, landing on her side with her legs dangling off the end. The black leather cushions squeaked loudly as she landed on them. Her head hung back and her mouth gaped open, gulping at the air.

The pain that had started in her chest, spreading from there to the rest of her body, returned to its starting point. With every beat of her heart she could feel the pain diminishing. After several minutes, though she felt lightheaded, she could again breathe normally.

She stood and wandered around the room, touching the

furniture as if she had never seen it before. She stood for a long time in front of the mirror, then went through the door next to it.

The room was dark and she stood just inside the door for a while, allowing her eyes time to adjust. She was in the main waking room. The windows were heavily draped with thick, black velvet curtains. Around the room, on risers, were set showcase caskets that were dusty, their linings moldy. At one time Grimm Memorials had been the Connecticut Valley's leading mortuary, but in the past five years it hadn't had even one funeral.

Eleanor looked at the little-used room as if she couldn't remember what it was for. She crossed the floor and opened a door at the other end of the room, but didn't go through it. The smell of wood and stone wafted out to her from the large room that had been Edmund's carpentry and masonry shop. She breathed deeply of the scent and it seemed to clear her head. She looked around as if she had just awakened.

She turned quickly and bustled back the way she'd come, back into the entrance hall and to the door marked Crematorium to the left of the sofa. She leaned against the door, breathing heavily, and listened to the faint sobbing coming from the other side. She started to reach for the handle, but stopped. She didn't think she could make it down the stairs and back up again in her weakened condition. She needed rest first, and nourishment.

She pressed her face to the crack of the door and sniffed deeply. Behind the spicy, lacquered smell of the wood was another smell, strong and mouth-watering. "Later," she whispered to the door. Her stomach growled loudly in protest and she patted it. Moving slowly, she pushed away from the door, went around the stairs and through another door to the kitchen.

She went to the refrigerator and opened it. There were a couple of foil-wrapped packages inside and a plastic pitcher, half-full. Eleanor grabbed the pitcher, popped open the triangular spout, and drank greedily and noisily from the container. A thin dark drop of the liquid dripped from the corner of her mouth and rolled down her chin to her neck.

She finished drinking, recapped the pitcher, and put it back in the fridge. She stood with the freezer door open for a while and let the cool air wash over her.

She straightened suddenly and turned away from the refrigerator. Voices, *children's voices,* drifted through her mind. She went to the back door, opened it, and sniffed at the air. Yes, there were indeed children nearby and from the sound of their thoughts in her head she knew it was the little boy and girl she had seen with their parents in Amherst.

The boy was very afraid. Though she knew it would be easy to grab them both, now was not the time. If she tried now, and did fail, she'd never get another chance. Besides, she still had much to do before she'd need this boy and girl, and their lovely pregnant mother. The Samhain Harvest of Dead Souls and Halloween were still a month away, and with them living so close now, she could afford to wait until the time was right.

"Fe, fi, fo, fum, I smell the blood of a little one," she said, and cackled softly to herself at the promise of delicious things to come.

CHAPTER 4

There was a little boy and a little girl . . .

Diane was unpacking dishes in the kitchen when Jackie ran in, slamming the aluminum screen door behind him. He was out of breath, panting loudly as he leaned against the wall. His face was flushed and there were a few red scratches on his cheek and forearms from plowing through the bushes at the end of the dirt road and into the backyard.

"My word! You look as if the Wicked Ol' Witch of the West herself were chasing you," Diane exclaimed.

Jackie gulped air and crossed to the table where Diane was stacking dishes to be put on the shelves. "Can I have a drink?" he gasped.

"It'll have to be water," Diane answered, picking up a glass and going to the sink. She looked over her shoulder at her son. "So, how come you're so out of breath?"

"Just runnin'," Jackie said, sliding along the table to the sink and taking the glass. He gulped it, downing half the glass quickly.

"Whoa! Slow down or you'll choke," Diane warned and grabbed his arm, forcing him to take the glass from his lips. "So did you find any trolls?"

Jackie shook his head.

"Where's your sister?"

"In the woods," he said into his glass, as he raised it and drank from it again.

"Go and call her. I want you two to go upstairs and get washed. It's peanut butter and jelly sandwiches for supper."

Jackie finished the water and went to the back door, but before he could open it, Jennifer came in. When she saw Jackie she said "Boo!" and laughed at him.

Jackie's lips tightened and he muttered, "Very funny."

"I've never seen you run so fast," Jennifer said with a giggle.

"Oh shut up," Jackie pouted angrily.

"Jen, what did I tell you before about scaring your brother? Now, knock it off and get upstairs and wash for supper. Move it," Diane ordered, motioning with a nod of her head.

The house had eight rooms, four up and four down. Jackie and Jennifer went out of the kitchen via the front hall, which connected the kitchen, living room, and dining room, with the front door and the stairs to the second floor. The fourth downstairs room was off the kitchen and unfinished, used primarily as a storage room by the previous inhabitants.

They gave the two front rooms a cursory glance—Steve was in the dining room on the right, assembling the large, dark pine table—and went upstairs. The right side front and back rooms were closest to the top landing. The bathroom was between them. Jackie went straight to the bathroom, but Jennifer turned away and started down the left side of the hallway that ran the length of the second floor with a closet at the other end between the other two rooms.

When Jackie saw what she was doing, he followed her, asking, "What are you doing? Mom said get washed."

"We're going to have to pick out our rooms, you know. We can each have our own room here because there's one more bedroom than at our apartment," she told Jackie. She opened a creaking door and went into the left front room. It was a dimly lit, dull, square room with faded yellow wallpaper covering its walls. The shades on the windows were torn and the hardwood floor needed varnishing. The crib, changing table, bureau with fairy-tale figures painted on it, and several large boxes were stacked in the center of the room.

"What do you think of this room?" Jennifer asked.

"It's nice," Jackie replied. "All the baby's stuff is in here."

"That don't mean nothing," Jennifer told him. "Look, Mom's makeup table is in here, too, and Steve's typewriter."

"What do *you* think of this room?" Jackie asked his sister.

"It's beautiful."

"Then I want this room," Jackie said quickly.

"Well, okay. I guess you can have it," Jennifer said in a generous tone of voice.

Jackie eyed his sister suspiciously. "I changed my mind," he said after a moment. "I don't want it."

"That's okay," Jen said and went into the opposite room. It was a little smaller than the front room and a lot darker. A huge maple tree growing outside the window blocked all the sunlight. The walls were bare plaster painted a drab tan color with a green-leaf, stenciled border running around the top of the room. The room was half-filled with boxes stacked in uneven piles.

"This room is nice," Jen said with mock admiration. Actually she didn't like it; it was too small and dark. She wanted her room to be big and full of sunlight.

"You really like it?" Jackie asked.

"Oh yes. Very much," she answered teasingly.

"I want this room," Jackie said with a mischievous smile on his lips.

"Okay, this room is yours," Jennifer said, hiding a smile behind her hand. She started out of the room.

"Hey!" Jackie cried. "I thought *you* wanted this room."

"Oh, that's all right. If you want that room I guess you can have it. After all you did give me a piece of gum on the ride up here." She went out the door and down the hallway to where the bathroom was situated at the end of the hall between the rooms at the other end of the house.

Jackie hurried after his sister. "I changed my mind again," he said, running past her. "I don't want that room."

"Jackie! You can't keep changing your mind."

"Can to!" he yelled gleefully over his shoulder as he raced by her. She chased him into the right front room and was blinded by the bright sun pouring in the windows. This room had been recently redecorated. The walls were covered with a tasteful, peach-flowered print wallpaper. The woodwork was a highly polished, dark rich brown, as was the hardwood floor. All the beds were piled in here; headboards, frames, box springs, and mattresses, were leaning in stacks against the back wall.

Jennifer cooed, "Oooh! This room is beautiful," and meant it.

"This is my room!" Jackie piped up, running over and tagging the wall as if that were the magic talisman for ownership.

"Jackie, you just want this room because I like it," Jennifer reprimanded.

"No sa. I just like it best. You said I could choose my room, so I am. I want this one."

"But you keep changing your mind. That's not fair."

"I won't change no more. This is the room I want," he answered.

"You're sure?"

"Yeah."

"And you won't change your mind anymore?"

"No."

Jennifer smiled. Now she had him. She had already decided, after a quick glance inside when they'd first come upstairs, that she wanted the right back room. Not only was it as large as the front room and just as sunny, that end of the house having the southern exposure, but its windows had a clear view of the field and the woods behind the house. The room she and Jackie had shared in the old apartment in the

North End of Boston had looked out at the brick wall of another building next door and the alleyway that ran between the two buildings. She had known that Jackie would fight her for whatever room she wanted because he never missed an opportunity to tease her and be a pain, but this time she had outsmarted him.

"But that isn't fair," she said, feigning disappointment. "The other rooms are lousy compared to this." She went across the hall into the back room. Its walls were done in gray barnboard paneling and the floor was covered with a worn, blue wall-to-wall shag carpet. "This room is gross," Jennifer lied.

Jackie beamed with pleasure. "Too bad," he taunted. "But you sa-a-id I could pick *any* room I wanted."

"Oooh, you're a creep," she said with disdain, playing her plan to the hilt. "Okay, take that room, but see if I ever talk to *you* again. And while you're at it, get out of my room. Even if it is crummy, you're not allowed inside." She pushed him into the hall and turned her back on him.

Jackie went into the front room, trying to think of something good he could get out of Jennifer in exchange for the room. The truth was that he didn't care what room he got (Actually, he was kind of scared at the thought of sleeping in a room *all by himself!*) He just liked bugging his older sister. And now it looked like he'd be able to bargain the room for something of hers that he wanted.

He started back to Jennifer to offer her the front room for her boom box and found her staring out the back window with a funny look on her face.

"It's so private. I can see right into the woods," she murmured. "No more brick wall or dirty alleyway."

Jackie joined her at the window and looked out at the trees and the backyard. A large shadow waved over the yard and the field as a great cloud passed in front of the sun. From the joy on Jennifer's face, Jackie knew he had been duped.

"You know," he said, a mischievous grin twitching at the

corners of his mouth, "I can't take that other room from you. Since you like it so much, I'll take this room and you can have the other one."

"Oh no you don't!" Jennifer cried loudly. "You can't change your mind again."

"But I just want to be fair," Jackie said sweetly.

"No, no, no!"

"Hey, what's going on up here?" Diane's voice came from the stairs. She appeared in the doorway with a pile of towels in her arms.

"Mommy, I want this room," Jackie exclaimed. He ran to her and wrapped his short arms around her pregnant belly, looking up at her cutely. "Can I have this room, Mom? Please?" he asked in his best pleading whine.

"No," Jennifer shouted. "He said he wanted the front room. He's just saying that because he knows I want this room."

"No sa-a," Jackie said in an accusing singsong.

"Oh, don't lie, Jackie," Jennifer pouted.

"That's enough," Diane interrupted in a loud voice. "What makes either of you think you can just *claim* the room you want? Steve and I have already planned out the rooms. This is going to be the baby's room. The room across the hall is going to be our bedroom. The other front room will be Steve's study, and the other back room will be your bedroom."

Jennifer looked shattered. "I thought you said we could have our own rooms," she said with a hint of anger in her voice.

"I'm sorry, Jen. I know I said that, but it can't be that way right now. We don't have enough room," Diane said sympathetically, but firmly.

"But why?" Jen asked, flapping her arms in exasperation, her voice whining. "We have more rooms than the old place, and some of my stuff is already in here. See?" she said pointing to her bureau.

"The movers put that there by mistake. They put everything in the wrong rooms and didn't even follow the directions we gave them. If we hadn't had that trouble with the car on the way here, we would have had them straighten it out, but now we have to do it ourselves. Your stuff has got to be moved into the other room. I'm sorry, hon, but it'll only be until Steve can fix up the room off the kitchen and put his study in there, then you can have your own room. You know he's working on his poetry and he needs a study to get it done by the contest deadline next month."

Jennifer fought back tears and ran out of the room, Jackie following behind. She knew that Steve was trying to win some poetry writing contest that would win them a lot of money and get him a job at a college, and if her mother said she could have her own room eventually, then she knew she would, but she had so been looking forward to her privacy that her disappointment ballooned out of control. That, combined with the fact that she was tired and hungry from the long drive, made her overreact.

She ran down the hall to the room Diane had said would be hers and Jackie's. She slammed the door behind her, but Jackie opened it again, slipping inside and closing the door quietly behind him.

Jennifer was sitting on a box near the window, crying softly into her hands cupped over her face. Jackie went over to her, seemed about to touch her shoulder for a moment, then thought better of it and sat on a smaller box opposite her.

"She gives him everything," Jen sobbed, her voice sour with resentment. "We never get anything anymore."

"You can choose your side of the room first," Jackie said, softly and eagerly, wanting to soothe his sister.

"Whoopee," Jennifer said drolly as she dried her eyes, then raised her hand and made halfhearted circles in the air with her finger. She got up from the box and stood in front of the window. The maple trees pressed against the house, pushing their thick-leaved branches against the glass, leaving Jen with only a spotted view of the field and woods. She placed her hands on the window and frowned a little. It was better than a brick wall and an alley, and in the late fall, winter, and early spring, she'd have a clear view of the woods. It wasn't so bad after all.

A tiny flash of rainbow-colored light caught her eye and she looked at the ring her grandmother gave her, which she never took off. Sunlight was refracting through the perfectly oval diamond set into it. The ring, and the light, made Jennifer think of her grandmother, Diane's mother, whose great Italian bear hugs and chuckling, throaty laughter had been like rays of sunshine in Jennifer's life. The light had gone out two years ago. That was when Grammy, senile from the effects of Alzheimer's disease, had to be put in a home. The sorrow Jackie and, more so, Jennifer felt at seeing their grandmother disintegrate mentally—to the point where she no longer remembered who anyone was—is rarely experienced by children so young. The death of their natural father followed soon after. One would expect that neither she nor Jackie would be able to sustain such emotional trauma, but they did and were stronger for it. It was something inside them, something they couldn't control, a boundless energy for survival.

"Okay," she said to her brother, turning away from the window and fighting the threat of new tears at the thought of her grammy. "I'll take that side of the room." She pointed at the right half and watched Jackie's face carefully.

Jackie paled when he saw that he had the side next to the closet. Visions of trying to sleep next to that door, with who knew what horrible monsters might be lurking inside, appearing there as soon as the door was closed and the light was put out each night, quickly passed through his mind, but he said nothing.

Jennifer let him squirm for a while, then took him off the hook and told him she'd take the side next to the closet.

CHAPTER 5

Jerry Hall, he was so small . . .

An hour later, as they were sitting down to their supper of peebee and jay sandwiches, chips, and warm lemonade, there was a knock on the front door. When Steve opened it, he was greeted by the warm spicy smell of hot tomato sauce and melted cheese. Holding a large square pan of deep-dish pizza out in front of her like a Roman offering, a short, round woman with dark hair and eyes smiled up at him from a glowing face and said in a corny cowboy accent, "Howdy, neighbor!" Standing behind her was a tall, blond-haired man wearing madras shorts, a red and white soccer shirt, and oval-shaped, rose-tinted glasses.

He smiled and nodded at Steve. "I'm Roger Eames," he said, shoving his hand past his wife's head to shake Steve's hand. "This is my wife Judy." Judy said howdy again. "And this is my daughter Margaret." A brown haired curly head peeked out from behind her father's leg and flashed him a quick smile before looking inside the house with a child's natural curiosity.

"We thought you might be hungry after your busy day," Judy said. Her voice was nasally pitched and slightly irritating to the ear, taking some time to get used to.

"Oh, this is great! Come on in," Steve blustered. "Honey, look at this. This is great." He ushered them into the dining room where Diane, Jen, and Jackie oohed and ahhed over the heavenly smelling pizza. Steve made quick introductions, then the peanut butter and jelly sandwiches were tossed in the fridge to be eaten for lunch tomorrow.

Judy cut the pizza and doled out mammoth pieces to everyone before putting one of the biggest pieces on her own plate.

In between mouthfuls of pizza, which she gobbled and swallowed rapidly, even though it was piping hot, Judy told Steve and Diane about her family. They had moved to their house at the end of Dorsey Lane seven years ago, just before Margaret was born. Roger was a campus police officer at UMASS, while Judy worked at a nursery school.

Diane and Judy hit it off as soon as they discovered they were both Italian. Steve and Roger drank beer and made occasional comments, but Diane and Judy carried on like old friends. Eventually, Diane was able to get a word in edgewise and told Judy and Roger about herself, Steve, and the kids. She explained that Steve was starting a new job after Labor Day at the Northwood Academy as health and English instructor and head football coach. She also mentioned, almost casually, Steve thought, that he was a finalist in the Dickinson Poetry Competition, first prize of which was $100,000 and a three-year term as poet-in-residence at Emily Dickinson College.

Judy was impressed by that, but didn't let it keep her quiet. She soon launched on a long discourse about her daughter Margaret, the pluses and minuses of living in Northwood, and who was doing what to whom in and out of bed according to the small town's gossip machine, a prominent cog of which Judy obviously was. On the more delicate matters, she had a comic way of humming and gesturing to get her point across to Diane without the children understanding what she was saying.

Eventually, she got around to the Halls, the family that Steve and Diane had bought the house from. "Every time I think of them, I want to cry," Judy said, her voice full of emotion.

"We met them at the closing," Steve said, a little uncomfortable with Judy's exaggerated demeanor.

"They seemed nice, but quiet, kind of sad in a way," Diane added.

"They have every right in the world to be sad. I'm surprised the real estate agents didn't tell you. They were probably afraid you wouldn't want the place if you knew. I bet you could get out of it if you wanted to, since they didn't tell, but it really has nothing to do with the house itself, just something that happened to Joe and Mary's little boy." Judy stopped her chattering and paused thoughtfully, as if working out all the legalities in her head. Diane was hanging on her every word, waiting with anticipation and dread for Judy to tell her what horrible thing had happened to the Hall's little boy.

Judy put her hand to her mouth and waved at her husband. "You tell them, Rog, I can't," she blubbered, her voice full of emotion.

Roger looked at Diane's frightened face, then at the faces of the children, which mirrored her fear. "I don't think we should be discussing this in front of the kids. I don't want to scare them."

"What?" Judy exploded. "Of course we should. They *should* be scared. Maybe it'll save them." Her voice was full of indignation.

"My God!" Diane cried, unable to keep quiet any longer. "What happened?"

"The Hall's little boy Jerry . . ." Roger started.

"Was abducted by some madman or a cult," Judy finished for him.

"Now, honey, you don't know that. That's not what the police said." Roger argued.

"I don't, huh? The police don't know what they're doing. They say Jerry ran away because his father beat him, but we never saw any evidence of it and we were friends with them for two years. What about that body they found in the river last year? It had been carved up like a Thanksgiving turkey. That's what Mrs. Lyman said and her husband was one of the guys who found him. He was water-skiing and skied right over the body. It was a little boy who'd been missing from somewhere in Vermont. There's been a whole slew of child abductions in western New England and upstate New York dating all the way back to the 1930s. Every year more kids have turned up missing. One year, might be two missing in Vermont, the next year one in upstate New York. There was a thing about it on 'Good Morning, Springfield' on channel 4 a couple of weeks ago. A writer who's been researching the story traced the beginning to 1931, that's when a kid in southern Vermont, and two from Troy, New York, disappeared. Over the more than fifty years since, children have continued to disappear from western Massachusetts, western Connecticut, Vermont, and eastern upstate New York. And this writer said that the center of the abductions was in western Massachusetts, and that's where the person, or cult, was operating from. For *over fifty years no less!*"

"That's incredible!" Diane exclaimed.

"And they've found only *one* body, the boy in the river, in all those years. None of the children missing from within that area since 1931 had been found until last year. And he was found dead and mutilated," Judy added with a knowing nod.

"Judy, that's a lot of conjecture. There's no way all those disappearances can be attributed to one person. I'll bet more than half of those so-called abductions *were* runaways, or were kids stolen by a divorced parent," Roger said.

"Excuse me! Did I say *one person?* No, I said it could be a cult, too," Judy raved, her temper flaring. "What about the two kids missing in Springfield, and the ones in North Adams

and Belchertown? And now, little Jerry Hall right here in Northwood. *Right here on our street.* All of them missing in the last twenty-five years. *Don't* tell me they were runaways. And that little boy all mutilated in the river. *His* parents weren't divorced," Judy huffed.

"Don't get so upset," Roger cajoled. "I didn't say that there isn't something going on, just that to try and say it's been happening for over fifty years is absurd. The police or the FBI would have investigated it if that were the case, no matter what some writer who's just trying to make a buck and sell his book says."

"I think it's true and it just goes to show how truly inept the police and the FBI really are," Judy said, and sniffed, dismissing Roger's argument and turning to Diane. "I walk to the corner with Margaret every morning and wait for the bus to come, and I'm there every afternoon when she gets home. *I'm* not taking any chances. Who knows what kind of monster is out there?"

Later in the evening, after Roger had changed the subject so as not to tempt further his wife's volatile Italian temper, and they had eaten all the pizza, plus a bag of oatmeal cookies for dessert, Diane retired to the kitchen to do dishes, with Judy volunteering to help. Roger offered his help with unpacking and moving furniture, and he and Steve went upstairs to get the beds put together and the bedrooms set up.

Jennifer, Jackie, and Margaret sat in the living room, watching snowy reruns of "Bewitched" on television. Halfway through the show, just after Darrin had been turned into a jackass by Endora, Margaret ended her shy silence and spoke up in a soft, clear voice. "I know where a real witch lives," she said.

Jennifer, who was glued to a 501 jeans commercial barely heard what Margaret said, but Jackie sat up and looked at her. He hadn't been paying much attention to the tube; he was more concerned with worrying about what Mrs. Eames had said at the supper table. Her comment, "Who knows what kind of monster is out there," had intrigued and terrified him, as did any mention of monsters and such things.

"What did you say?" he asked Margaret.

Jennifer turned away from the screen and looked at Margaret also. "Did you say a *witch?*" she asked.

"Yes," Margaret said timidly.

"Really? Where?" Jackie asked in a frightened voice.

"In the woods right behind your house," Margaret replied.

Jackie eyed Margaret doubtfully, then his sister. "Did you tell her to say that, Jen?"

"No way!" Jennifer pleaded innocence. "I was only kidding you before. She's lying," Jennifer said with a sneer.

Jackie didn't know what the difference was, but kept quiet.

"I am not," Margaret declared. "Jerry Hall told me there was."

"You mean the Jerry who used to live here?" Jackie asked, his voice barely above a whisper.

Margaret nodded.

"Then Jerry was lying," Jennifer said matter-of-factly.

"How do you know?" Margaret asked defensively.

"Cuz there are no such things as witches," Jennifer said. "Even Jackie knows that and he's only six years old."

Margaret didn't have any answer for that and got up and walked out of the room. Soon after, she and her parents left and it was time for Jennifer and Jackie, who was already nodding off, to go to bed.

When they were washed, had brushed their teeth, and were lying in bed, Steve and Diane came in to say goodnight. Diane sat on Jackie's bed and arranged his pillow. "Do you guys remember what Margaret's mother said at supper about the boy who used to live here?" she asked, looking first at Jackie, then at Jennifer. Jen nodded. "Do you remember, Jackie?"

"Yeah," he said. "A monster got him."

"Not a *monster,* dopey," Jen said with ridicule.

"Quiet, Jen," Diane said quickly. "Not the kind of monster you're thinking of, Jackie. There are no such things as monsters like in the movies or in books, but there *are* people who have monsters inside them. Do you know what I mean?"

"They're bad?" Jackie tendered meekly. He didn't like having this conversation with his mother. It was bad enough that he had nightmares about monsters and spent a good deal of his waking time daydreaming about monsters, but to have *his mother* start talking about monsters as if they were real was too much. (And to make it worse, ones that were *inside* people—how could you tell who had a monster in them?) He felt very afraid, too, because she was so serious; she wasn't fooling around now like she often did with him.

"Yes, honey, they're bad and they like to do bad things to children," Diane said taking his hand.

"You mean like the witch in 'Hansel and Gretel'?"

"Sort of, but there are no such things as witches. These bad people look just like everyone else. They might drive by and ask you to go for a ride with them, or offer you money or candy if you'll go with them. But if you do, no one will ever hear from you again."

A dread chill sank into Jackie's bowels like a load of worms squirming inside him. *No one will ever hear from you again!* The words were the most fearful his mother had ever spoken. They conjured horrible images in his mind of being dragged off into a deep dark hole to become supper for some creature of the night. But his mother was talking about *human* night creatures.

"So I want you to promise me that you will never—either of you," she added pointing at Jennifer, "talk to, or go *anywhere* with a stranger, *ever!* I don't care what they say. Even if they tell you I'm in the hospital dying, or that Steve or I said it was okay to go with them, you stay away from them. Do you hear me?"

Jackie squeaked out a scared yes, and tried to pull his

hand free of his mother's. She'd been squeezing his hand tighter and tighter as she spoke and was hurting him. She realized it and let go of his hand and stood up.

"Remember what I said." She leaned over and kissed Jackie's forehead, then went and did the same to Jen. Steve followed suit and they left, Diane pausing in the doorway to glance back at her children.

When they were gone, Jackie sat up in bed and looked across at his sister in the dark. "Jen?" he whispered.

"Hmm?"

"Do you think that boy Jerry really told Margaret there was a witch in the woods?"

"Be serious," Jennifer scoffed.

"But if there is, maybe she's the one who took Jerry and the other kids."

"Jackie," Jen said sitting up and looking at him, "how many times do you have to be told? There are no witches. There are no werewolves, no Frankenstein, no vampires, no mummies, no ogres, trolls, or monsters of *any* kind. They are *all* make-believe. There are only creepy people, like Mom said. But they can't hurt us if we stay away from them."

"But an old lady could be a witch and you wouldn't even know it," Jackie countered.

"Oh, I give up," Jennifer said, flopping back on the bed. "Believe what you want, but leave me alone and go to sleep."

Jackie lay in bed watching the shadows cast by the moonlight filtering through the trees outside the window. He lay very still and kept his entire body, except for his head from his nose up, under the covers, even though it was a warm night. He didn't know where he had come by the knowledge, but he was sure that if he slept this way, no monsters that might be hiding in the closet, or under the bed, or in the tree outside the window, or in the shadows themselves, could get at him. He was safe.

When the pattern of shifting leaf silhouettes finally became familiar to him and he was certain that there were no monsters lurking in the room, Jackie closed his eyes and sank into a deep sleep. Sometime after midnight, thunderstorms rolled up the Connecticut River and the skies above Northwood strobed with lightning. Balls of thunder rolled across the sky, leaving crackling retorts to mark their passage. Then the rain came, heavy chilling sheets of water that cooled the muggy land.

In the midst of the lightning flashes and thunder shots, Jackie came awake within a dream and began to walk through it.

His eyes were half-opened as he pulled back the covers and swung his legs out of the bed. Wearing only his underpants, which is what he always wore to bed, he padded on bare feet to the window and stood looking out. The lightning flashed brightly, creating a perfect snapshot of the backyard, the field, and the woods. In the snapshot was a boy running. Behind him was a figure emerging from the woods, chasing him. The lightning flashed again and Jackie saw that the boy wasn't running, he was hopping, and the reason he was hopping was because—the lightning flashed again and the boy was in the backyard, swinging on the swing; at the edge of the field stood a dark figure shrouded in shadows—*he had no arms or legs.*

Jackie woke with a start as a report of thunder cracked through the night. Another bolt flashed and he saw that the field was empty. He couldn't quite remember what he had seen there in his dream. A pair of lights flashed between the trees to the right and he saw headlights moving on the dirt road through the woods. Jackie ducked away from the window instinctively, as if the headlights were eyes that might spot him. Another flash of lightning and peal of thunder sent him scurrying into Jen's bed where he snuggled close to his sister for protection. The next morning he remembered nothing of his dream, the lights in the woods, or of getting into Jen's bed.

CHAPTER 6

Humpty Dumpty sat on a wall.

Thirteen! Edmund crowed.

"The magic number," Eleanor whispered as she drove.

Thirteen innocent boys! he said, as if it was the largest number known to man. *You'll never do it.*

Leave me alone, she snapped, anger creeping into her voice. She stepped on the brakes and slowed the hearse to a halt at the end of the dirt road. She looked to the right, through the tall lilac bushes, at the Nailers' house.

"Got one little kitten already sitting in my lap," she murmured, took a swig from a bottle of José Cuervo, and licked her chapped lips. "Twelve more to go."

You're going to die!

Eleanor sighed and stepped on the gas, pulling out onto Dorsey Lane. "Edmund, Edmund, go away, come again some other day. Little Ellie wants to play," she sang and giggled.

Edmund had always been a worrier. Ever since their birth—six seconds apart—he had always been the one to think of the worst that could happen. Right out of the womb, she had felt his primitive distrust of first the doctor, then their mother, and she still remembered it; as she also remembered their childhood, listening to his constant paranoid thoughts endlessly intruding on her own. It wouldn't be until much later in life that she would be able to block him out at will.

In infancy, he was always certain that their mother, whose growing madness they could hear, would murder them in their sleep, or forget to feed them, or drop them over the second floor railing, or down the stairs, or out a window. Since Edmund was the first to discover and master their special gift—which they would later come to call the Machine—he fed these images to Eleanor long before either of them could talk, conjuring thoughts so realistic that she soon became as frightened as he was paranoid.

A car cut in front of the hearse unexpectedly, pulling Eleanor's mind back to the present. She had just gotten off the highway at the Amherst exit and was very near the street she wanted. Ahead, in the beam of her headlights she saw the green reflecting sign for Lincoln Street. Twenty yards down on the left were the university's apartments for students who were married.

She guided the hearse into the parking lot and parked in the deepest shadows outside one of the rear units. She turned the engine off and looked at the second-floor window of the unit to the left. The light was on in the window. Eleanor looked at the dashboard clock. After midnight—too late for that light to be on.

The window belonged to the bedroom of a five-year-old boy, Davy Torrez, one of many children that Eleanor had been watching for a few weeks. She'd enticed him and teased him with her thoughts, learning all about him as she did so. She knew that his favorite color was red; his favorite TV show was "Alf"; and his favorite food was pizza. She also knew his deepest desires and innermost fears.

Eleanor closed her eyes and began to breathe very deeply. Grunting softly, as if coaxing a bowel movement, she pushed her thoughts outward. She envisioned them fleeing her head, passing through the windshield, floating on the night air, through the bedroom window, and opening a tiny portal into Davy Torrez's mind without him feeling a thing.

He was awake. His mother was in the room with him. He had had a bad dream about being chased by a witch, like in the fairy tales his father had read to him before bedtime. (Eleanor smiled at the intricacies of the Machine's workings.) His mother had heard him cry out and came to comfort him. He cried that he was afraid to go back to sleep. Good mother that she was, Davy's sat on the bed to read him nursery rhymes, which she promised would bring happy dreams.

"Humpty Dumpty sat on a wall," Davy's mother read, but Eleanor heard different voices: her mother's and Edmund's.

"Humpty Dumpty had a great fall."

The words filled her mind with memories. She saw her own mother reciting the rhyme, as she had done many times before her death. She had always claimed that they were descendants of the Brothers Grimm and loved telling fairy tales and reciting rhymes, acting out all the parts in her own mad world, mixing nursery rhymes all up with fables and fairy tales and creating weird surrealistic stories. Anyone watching or listening would have marvelled at her creativity and storytelling powers. But Eleanor and Edmund, the Machine tuned to their mother's mind, seeing and hearing everything that sailed in the ocean of her thoughts, knew that when telling one of her stories, Mother was completely unaware of their existence. She *lived* the stories, and unless they forced their thoughts very loudly upon her, she was oblivious to them. She might start a story for them—she *did* have moments of clarity, of sanity, though over the years those became fewer and farther between—but she lived the story for herself. Their mother *was* quite mad, but Edmund needn't have worried about her. The only harm she would ever do would be to herself.

Eleanor and Edmund were four years old at the time. Edmund had been the first to discover the workings of the

Machine; he had a natural talent for it. Within weeks of birth he instinctively knew that he could invade other people's minds, hear their thoughts and make them *see* his, even when not consciously trying to do so. It wasn't until much later, when she was nearly two, that Eleanor finally grasped some idea of what the Machine could do. Before that, Eleanor had been barraged with thoughts from every person within a three-mile radius. It had caused her great headaches and distress. It was only with Edmund's help that she survived those years until she learned how to use the Machine and could be selective in the voices she wished to hear, blocking out all others. Only then did she come to understand, at first instinctively and later intellectually, that the Machine was really an extension of themselves, their egos, and their subconscious minds collecting and affecting the thoughts of everyone, except their father's, within a three-mile radius, even when Edmund and Eleanor were asleep.

Edmund had been manipulating Mother on a regular basis to get her to give them whatever they wanted. Soon after they were born Edmund had begun invading her mind whenever they needed anything and had demanded incessantly, at first in images, later in words, that she serve them. Edmund was very adept at playing her. Eleanor didn't realize until after her mother's death that the power he had over her, combined with her intruding thoughts, had driven their mother crazy and led to her death.

Eleanor remembered that for a week before her mother's death, nightmares about her mother had tortured her. She'd dreamt that her mother was being devoured by spiders and snakes, and being ripped apart by animals. On the night that her mother dived headfirst from the second-floor window, Eleanor awoke from a viscious dream where her mother was being torn to shreds by a pack of wolves. In the darkness she saw Edmund's eyes shining as she heard her mother's diminishing scream, stopped by a soft thud and a *snap!*

"Humpty Dumpty had a great fall," Edmund whispered in the dark.

"And all the king's horses and all the king's men," the memory of Edmund's voice faded and became the voice of Davy Torrez's mother, "couldn't put Humpty Dumpty together again." She closed the book and put it down next to the bed.

"I bet I could put Humpty back together, Mom. I'm real good at puzzles," Davy said.

"Oh, I'm sure you could," his mother agreed.

"Can you read it again?" Davy pleaded.

"I've read it four times now, that's enough. Time for bed, it's after midnight."

"But I'm afraid of the nightmare witch."

"You won't have any more nightmares. You're just going to dream happy dreams about Mother Goose and all her happy rhymes. That's what they do; whenever you read them you always have happy dreams," she told her son and tucked him in.

Davy looked suitably impressed with this knowledge and decided that, if his mother said it was true, then it was. His father was always making stuff up, but his mom always told the truth. He snuggled down in the bed. Eleanor felt Davy's mother's lips lightly upon her forehead as mother kissed son goodnight. Memories of her own mad mother faded and Eleanor sat up straight.

Before you die, you'll face the truth! Edmund said from behind her.

Eleanor looked in the rearview mirror. He was lying in an open coffin in the back of the hearse. "I'm not dying," she said solemnly. She took another swig of tequila. "Watch and learn, brother. Watch and learn." Eleanor streamed fully into Davy Torrez's sleeping mind like a moonbeam through glass. She flooded his sleeping senses with feelings of calmness and security. She brought warmth with her, like being immersed in a hot soapy bath, and a teasing, tickling feeling that pulled the sleeping boy deep into the subterranean layers of sleep. He sank in the pleasant sensations she bathed him in and soon reached the level of dreams.

Eleanor began to work feverishly. Whispering softly to herself, she conjured images to dance through Davy's mind. She constructed dreams lasting no more than a minute apiece, but each packed with illusions in a frenzy of activity in his brain. Eleanor was filling Davy's dreams with all the Mother Goose characters his mother had just read to him about. He frolicked with the dish and the spoon, and laughed with the dog when the cow jumped over the moon. He watched Mr. and Mrs. Jack Sprat devour a ten-pound ham between them, and searched Old Mother Hubbard's bare cupboards with her. But the best dream of all was the one where, he, Davy Torrez, was *the only person in the world* who could put Humpty Dumpty back together again. All the king's horses and all the king's men couldn't put Humpty together again, but five-year-old Davy Torrez *could*.

He woke suddenly from that happy dream, laughter spilling from his lips, and heard a sound. A shadow passed over the window for a moment and he heard again the sound that had woke him; it was a heavy, slow whooshing sound, like a lot of air being moved around. He looked at the window and saw the tip of a huge, brown-feathered wing stroking the air, and caught a glimpse of a bright yellow bonnet.

Davy's eyes widened and his smile stretched into a gape of wonder. He jumped from the bed and ran to the window. He stifled a shriek of excitement as Mother Goose touched down in the parking lot below his window. She was not alone. All the nursery rhymes were cavorting around her: Wee Willie Winkie, Little Boy Blue, Little Miss Muffet, Mary Mary Quite Contrary—all of them were there. Davy gasped with joy as he took it all in. When he saw Humpty Dumpty sitting on a wall in the middle of the parking lot—it didn't matter that there had never been a wall there before—Davy squealed with delight.

I must be dreaming, he thought, and pinched himself on the arm. He winced and realized he was *not* asleep. Mother Goose and all her children were really out there!

He started to call for his mother, but something, a feeling, an unspoken voice, kept him from doing it. *She won't see us,* it seemed to say. *We're here only for you.*

Davy realized the voice must be that of Mother Goose. He waved to her and she lifted a beautiful, brown-dappled wing and waved back. Her long orange beak opened in a smile and her big blue eyes twinkled. *Come out and play with us,* she said.

On bare feet, Davy padded out of his room, into the kitchen, and out the back door. His parents, sleeping in the room at the other end of the hall opposite the kitchen, never heard him go. They never saw him again.

Davy stepped out onto the walk outside and giggled ex- citedly as Jack and Jill walked by; Jack with his head wrapped in brown paper, smelling of vinegar, and Jill, carrying a dented pail. Ole King Cole was sitting on the hood of a Chevy sta- tion wagon. He was holding a pie that chirped and seemed to float in his hands. He chuckled merrily at it as if it were tick- ling him. Running around the station wagon was Little Bo Peep crying for her sheep.

Davy looked around in wonder and laughed with pure happiness. He walked into the parking lot slowly, twisting his head constantly as he tried to see everything. The fingers of his right hand were planted in his mouth and he giggled around them.

A loud shriek made him whirl around suddenly. Little Miss Muffet was being chased down the sidewalk by a tiny spider. On the small square lot of brown grass that tried to grow between the buildings, an old-fashioned lace-up boot as big as a house was sitting. It had windows in its heel and a door on the ankle. A stovepipe stuck out from the top and puffed little clouds of white smoke. All over the apparition, children swarmed, laughing and crying, running and fighting. Sitting on the doorstep was an old woman, head in hands, wondering aloud what she was going to do.

Near the fire hydrant across the way, Simple Simon and the pieman were discussing the latter's wares when they were interrupted by Tom Tom the Piper's Son, who burst between them, squealing pig in arm, and ran past Davy, who was by now bouncing up and down in uncontrollable excitement.

He ran into the parking lot, laughing wildly, and went straight to his favorite rhyme. "Hiya Humpty," he said boldly to the eggman perched high atop an eight-foot brick wall running the length and middle of the lot. Humpty Dumpty waved, but lost his balance. Rolling on his rounded edges, he fell off the wall, his eyes wide with surprise as if this had never happened to him before, his thick red lips forming a perfect O. He hit the pavement and shattered.

Davy clapped his hands and ran to the wall. This was just like his dream. *He was going to put Humpty Dumpty back together again!* He reached the mass of shells and stopped. The yolk, a massive quivering bubble of bloody yellow and white slime, oozed from the shattered remains.

This wasn't like his dream.

He bent over and picked up a piece of shell a little bigger than his hand. An eye, red-rimmed and malevolent, stared out at him.

This was definitely *not* like his dream.

He dropped the piece and turned away. Bloody yolk squished between his toes. It was cold and clammy and had the rank smell of egg salad gone bad.

Suddenly Davy heard a scream and looked up. Little Miss Muffet was screaming bloody murder—with good reason. The tiny spider had swelled to the size of a car. Its pincerlike mandibles opened and closed with a clicking, whining noise like machinery working. They closed on Miss Muffet's head quickly as she stumbled and her skull popped like an over-ripe melon.

Davy looked away from the sickening sight and saw that

the shoe house was in flames. He could hear the screams of the children being roasted alive inside. The old woman was standing nearby holding a gas can and matches.

He heard a rapacious growling. Old Mother Hubbard was being attacked by her starving dog. She was trying to crawl into the bushes near one of the buildings but the dog danced around her, lunging every few seconds to rip a chunk of flesh from her tattered bleeding body. He wolfed the meat down and immediately went back for more.

Elsewhere—Davy seemed to be able to see everything at once—Jack Be Nimble *wasn't,* and impaled himself on a giant candlestick. The hot wax melted into his skin and the flame set fire to his clothes until he was screaming and lurching about atop the candle like a flaming rodeo rider astride a burning bronco. In the corner of the lot, Little Jack Horner sat eating his Christmas pie, but when he stuck in his thumb, he pulled out a punctured eyeball that bled down his arm. Nearby, Peter Peter Pumpkin Eater was crushed beneath his wife's giant pumpkin prison. Trapped between an old black El Dorado and a beat-up Volvo, Little Boy Blue was being trampled to death by an enraged bull. On the sidewalk the little dog was tearing the cat and its fiddle to pieces. Peter Piper nearly tripped over them as he staggered about, a pickled pepper caught in his throat, his face turning blue. Simple Simon was strangling the pieman and Jill was battering Jack's wounded head with the bucket. At the other end of Humpty's wall, Mr. and Mrs. Sprat had turned cannibal and were going at each other with knives and forks, slicing and eating. Behind the burning shoe house, Mary Mary Quite Contrary was being strangled by monster vines from her garden.

Davy tried to run, but his feet stuck in the inch-thick gluey yolk beneath him. A hand suddenly closed on his right ankle, then another on his left. He looked down to see Humpty Dumpty's disembodied hands clutching his ankles in a vise-like grip. He reached down and tried to pull the hands away, but another piece of eggshell slid over and leaped at his face. On it was Humpty Dumpty's mouth, fierce and snarling with razor-sharp fangs gnashing inches from his skin.

Davy's laughter and joy rapidly turned to tears and fear. He struggled against the hands holding him and cried to his mother for help. His voice barely seemed to have left his lips when it died, lost amid the bedlam of the rioting rhymes. Surely his mother would hear the tumult and come and save him, but no light came on in her bedroom window. No lights came on anywhere; it seemed the cacophony around Davy was one that only he could hear.

Panic began to explode in him but was quelled by a reassuring sight. Mother Goose was waddling toward him. She *had* to still be good, Davy hoped fervently. His hopes were quickly murdered. As she came closer, Davy saw that her feathers were molting, leaving huge bare spots that festered with pus-leaking sores. Her eyes were runny, and her beak was decomposing, showing glimpses of a blackened, fungus-covered tongue.

Davy sucked in air, preparing to scream, but a hand shot out from under the feathers of Mother Goose's breast and clamped over his mouth. Another hand shot out and clamped on his arm. He felt himself being lifted off his feet as all around him the demented nursery rhymes began to fade.

Eleanor embraced him, wrapping her arms around him as if he were a long-lost lover, and carried him to the hearse.

CHAPTER 7

Poor little kittens have lost their mittens.

Davy Torrez woke in darkness, hanging in midair. He was groggy and nauseous. He had a horrible taste in his mouth and his stomach felt cramped like something tight was wrapped around it. He realized it was an arm around him, carrying him like a sack of potatoes, and remembered the old woman lying on top of him in the back of the hearse and putting a smelly cloth over his mouth. After that he could remember nothing until now.

He felt like he was moving downward, as if the person carrying him (his dopey mind conjured an image of the old woman) was walking downstairs. Every few seconds there was a slight bump, and he jiggled in her arms. Hot sweaty air was pushed around his face with every jolt.

He heard a door open, and cool, moist air flowed over him raising goosebumps on the flesh under his cotton pee-jays. There was the sound of heavy, shuffling footsteps on stone as he again felt himself moving through air, sideways this time.

A dim light came on and Davy found himself staring at a square metal drain set into a stone floor next to two black-shod feet under a long black dress. He tried to lift his head to see more, but his muscles were stiff and he could barely move.

Panic flooded him and he tried to scream, but couldn't; his mouth didn't want to work. He was swung around and hoisted higher as Eleanor regained her grip on him. In that instant he saw some of the room around him: stone walls—one with a large arched metal door set into it; a large metal pool table; a big star within a circle painted on the floor a few feet away with an upholstered reclining chair set in the middle of it; a wooden podium near that, and a flash of iron bars.

He heard a rusty scrape, then a tinny rattling and the long creepy squeak of old hinges. The bottom of a door made of bars came into his vision just before everything blurred. He landed on his right side like a dropped laundry sack, and banged his head on the stone floor. He realized he had been thrown in a cage as the door creaked and slammed shut behind him. This was followed by the rattling of the key in the lock.

Davy's eyes adjusted to the poor light in the cage slowly. As they did, he saw a face, a very white, almost bluish face, glowing ghostly in the dark about three feet opposite him. There was another boy in the cage. His eyes were closed. Davy's eyes, now more accustomed to the poor light, took in the rest of the cage. It was very large, the ceiling being high above him. On the side that was in his line of vision, Davy saw blankets and a bowl and cup near the boy. In the rear was a bare porcelain toilet with a chain hanging next to it.

Something strange about the other boy made Davy peer closer. At first glance, when he'd not been able to see clearly, he had thought that the boy, who appeared to be naked, had a blanket partially over him. As Davy looked again, he saw that he was mistaken.

Davy felt a scream building so loud that his head might burst from the force of it if he ever let it out.

The boy opposite him was naked and had no arms and no legs.

They had been cut off.

Perfectly straight suture scars showed like miniature train tracks across the end of each stump.

Another line of train track scars ran vertically for several inches between his legs.

A hot, prickly wave of sweaty nausea rolled over Davy's entire body, and his mind went numb with cold fear. The suppressed scream swelled. Out of the corner of his eye, Davy saw the old woman's face at the bars, looking down at the little quadriplegic with a sad smile on her face.

"Poor little kitten has lost his mittens," she said quietly. "Too bad."

The scream began to spill from his lips. The cold fear turned to freezing terror when she reached through the bars and prodded the little boy's pallid flesh. "Pease porridge hot, pease porridge cold, I think I'll let your juicy meat get nine days old," she mused softly, then looked directly at Davy. "The better for stew," she said and laughed wild, cackling laughter that came straight out of Davy's worst nightmares.

The scream erupted from him in all its force. At that moment, Davy Torrez's five-year-old mind collapsed in terrified shock and crawled into a deep dark hole at the bottom of his brain where nursery rhymes didn't come to life, and he didn't see dead boys with their arms, legs, and peepees cut off, or hear the laughter of his nightmare witch and know that, no matter what his mother said, she was *real*.

CHAPTER 8

There was an old man . . .

Steve was up early, waking at 5:30, a full half hour before the alarm was set to go off. It had always been that way with him on important days—first day of school, first day of a job; he could barely sleep the night before and woke with time to spare in the morning.

He got out of bed carefully, not wanting to wake Diane, and pushed in the alarm button on the clock. He wanted to let her sleep as long as possible; sleep was becoming a rare thing for her the bigger and more uncomfortable she got. He tiptoed out of the room and down the stairs to the kitchen.

They were pretty much settled in, though it had taken them a week to do it; the fact that they had spent Labor Day weekend at the Eameses' house for endless cookouts had something to do with it. Steve put a small pot of water to boil on the stove and spooned instant coffee into a large stoneware mug. He didn't really feel like eating, he was too nervous, but he knew if he didn't he would pay for it later when he couldn't do anything about it. He made two pieces of toast and forced them down with the coffee.

When he was finished, he put more bread in the toaster and poured two bowls of Cheerios, placing them on the table for Jackie and Jennifer's breakfast. He went upstairs to wake them and get them ready for their first day of school also.

By 7:45 he had showered, shaved, dressed, and managed to get the kids fed and dressed and into the Saab to be taken to school. He and Diane had decided last week, after hearing Judy Eames's frightening story, that he would take them to school the first day and she would pick them up. That way they could both become familiar with the route and put themselves at ease. It would be an easier parting, too, than just seeing them to the bus stop.

Though he and Diane had been married only ten months and he had dated her for just a few months before their marriage, he felt a strong emotional bond with her children. He knew he was a surrogate father, filling the space left in their lives when their real father died in a car accident only the year before Steve met Diane, but he didn't mind. He liked being a father.

It had not always been so. At one time, fatherhood was something that scared the dickens out of Steve Nailer. He had seen what it had done to his own father: the responsibilities, the financial pressures. Of course, he knew it had been worse for his father, who was uneducated and worked as a night custodian at Jordan Marsh. Raising a family on one income, especially a janitor's wages, was very hard. The fact that he never let his wife work (or she *wouldn't* work, he never really knew but suspected the latter) had put a great burden on Richard Nailer; too great a burden and it had broken him. Steve grew up listening to his father's constant warnings against getting married too young and taking on the crushing responsibilities of raising a family. Until he met Diane, Steve had heeded his father's advice. Now, he wanted to prove him wrong and put his ghost to rest forever.

The Pioneer Valley Regional Elementary School wasn't that far, a mile and a half down Route 47. In a safer time, Jackie and Jennifer would have walked to and from school, but not now. Steve dropped them at the schoolyard's front gate and gave them strict instructions about waiting at that spot after school for their mother to pick them up. He also reminded them of what he and Diane had been drilling into them ever since the first night in the new house: Don't talk to strangers and never go with *anyone* who isn't your mother or father. The children promised to obey and got out of the car. He watched them walk across the playground blacktop and go up the steps and into the large brick building before driving off.

Now came the hard stuff: first day on the job, first time back in the classroom in six years. He was glad it was only a half-day orientation for students. He would only have to conduct a homeroom, take roll call, and assign seats and lockers. The rest of the morning would be spent in the auditorium riding herd on the kids while they got scheduling cards and listened to windy greeting speeches by the headmaster and dean of students.

Northwood Academy was a coed commuter prep school and Steve was glad it was. His first job had been at a boys' boarding school. One week a month he had been required to live in the dorm and supervise the students. It had not been a pleasurable experience. After that, Steve had vowed never to teach in a private school again—the pay was usually poor and the duties teachers were required to perform without compensation were too many. But when his advisor at Northeastern University in Boston recommended him for the job at Northwood, he saw that it paid better than most private schools and gave him the advantage of being close to Amherst for the poetry competition; so he had decided to take it.

He'd started his teaching career as a physical education instructor and football coach. He had been a good quarterback as an undergrad at Fitchburg State Teachers College and coaching supplemented his income. But within four years Steve was burnt out and desperate to get away from teaching. It wasn't the teaching itself that was getting to him; it was teaching high school.

At that level he felt like nothing more than a glorified babysitter. As far as he could see, the structure of secondary education was unproductive—it put adolescents in a restrictive environment that dared them to rebel. Since the period of adolescence is one of rebellion anyway, high school only ensured what it most wanted to avoid by treating the students like children to be constantly watched and disciplined.

He decided to quit his private prep school position and, with money saved plus a low-interest federal loan, moved back to Boston and enrolled in Northeastern University's Fine Arts Graduate School, where he could pursue his first love in life, poetry (something his father had made fun of), and teach at the college level.

Within five years he had a doctorate in poetry, having written his dissertation on American poets, but couldn't find a college teaching position. There was a glut of Ph.D.'s at the college level in New England, and having married Diane shortly after graduation, he couldn't afford to just pull up stakes and move elsewhere unless he was guaranteed employment. Inheriting an instant family in Jackie and Jennifer, and Diane getting pregnant a mere two months after their wedding, had forced him to accept the Northwood job.

To be honest, though, he had to admit that the job itself was a reason for accepting, too. Except for teaching health and coaching football (a throwback to his old phys. ed. days), he would be teaching an advanced course on Shakespeare and a poetry writing seminar.

The headmaster, Dr. Samuel Plent, assured him that next year he would move into the English department full time. He'd have to keep coaching football, but he didn't really mind that, and sometimes even enjoyed it. Of course, if all went well with the poetry competition and he got the position at Emily Dickinson College, he could kiss Northwood Academy good-bye.

* * *

"Keerist! You've spent more time in school, taking *poetry* classes no less, than you have teaching. And you've *never* taught health before." Joe Conally leaned against his desk and slapped Steve's rolled-up resume against his leg. "I go away for a month before school starts and Plent pulls something like this. Well, I can tell you he isn't going to get away with it."

"I *am* certified in Massachusetts to teach health," Steve said defensively. The new job was definitely not getting off to a good start; not when his boss, Conally, the athletic director for the academy, greeted him with a charge of incompetency.

Conally put Steve's resume on the desk and sized him up. "I'm going to be perfectly honest with you, Nailer. You're not my pick for the job. You see, you're the victim of a power game perpetrated by our *esteemed* (he made the word sound dirty) headmaster, Dr. Plent. We need a *full-time* phys. ed./health instructor and football coach, not a part-time English teacher who's winging it as football coach because he happened to play a little ball at some rinky-dink Division Three state college. But, on the other hand, the English department needs a part-time teacher, so good Dr. Plent decides to kill two birds with one stone and shaft the athletic department as usual. It's perfect as far as he's concerned; he only has to pay one salary, yours, and that must be pretty cheap, Ph.D. or no Ph.D., with your lack of experience."

Steve winced as Conally's words hit home. His salary was a paltry eighteen thousand dollars a year, and even with another four thousand dollars thrown in as the stipend for coaching football, he was making only thirty-two grand, which wasn't much to raise a family on and pay for a house. Though Diane planned to go back to work as a real estate agent when the baby turned two, the cost of day care would eat up a lot of whatever she managed to make.

Conally smirked as he saw from the expression on Steve's face that he had hit a nerve. "The way this procedure is supposed to work is that I do the preliminary screening of candidates and then recommend three *qualified* people to the headmaster, which is what I had already done before I went on vacation and you came into the picture. Plent was supposed to review my choices and meet with me to pick the final candidate. As soon as I go away—he promised me he would wait until I returned to make the choice—he hires you as a favor to some old college buddy. I don't even get to interview you and my choices are thrown out the window. And let me tell you, Nailer, they were a *lot* more qualified for the position than you. Now I'm told that you're it, whether I like it or not. Well, I don't like it. Nothing personal, but I can't let Plent get away with this. I'm going to file a grievance with the board of regents for an appeal on your hiring."

Steve closed the door of the athletic director's office behind him, fighting the urge to slam it as hard as he could. He leaned against the wall and put his hand over his eyes, squeezing them shut, fighting down the old panic swelling inside him.

"What am I going to do?" he muttered to himself. He had almost demeaned himself in front of Joe Conally—had felt the bottomless panic opening up in his gut like a sinkhole in a torrential rainstorm—and begged for his job. He had just managed to keep himself under control, swallowing the pleading words as though they were a belch of searing heartburn that tasted like vomit in the back of his throat.

Instead of shaming himself, he had stood and very quietly said, "I guess you have to do what you have to do," before calmly (at least he hoped he had appeared calm) walking out the door.

The corridor stretched away in front of him and to the left and right. He broke into a cold sweat as another wave of panic flowed through him. Like a man with vertigo at the edge of a steep precipice, Steve swayed, all sense of balance lost. A cold hard stone of nauseating anxiety settled into his stomach.

It's happening to me, he thought frantically, just like it happened to Dad. The cost of running the house, the monthly mortgage payments, food bills, the money he still owed on his school loan—all flashed through Steve's mind as the specter of unemployment toyed with his fears. And when he thought of having to bear the full brunt of the cost of Diane's having the baby, without *any* paid medical plan to help (something Plent had promised), he felt like his intestines were being twisted into a barbed wire knot.

Never take on responsibilities for anyone but yourself. Steve's father's voice floated through his memory. The old man had been right, Steve thought, grimacing as he tried to control the sick panicky feeling rolling around in him.

Only a rich man can afford the luxury of a family. The rest of us joes have to break our backs and kill ourselves for the rest of our lives if we want one. It's just not worth it.

"It's going to kill me just like it killed him. Why didn't I listen to him?" Steve whispered soundlessly.

The morning didn't get any better. The kids in his homeroom, thirty freshmen, were pumped up for the first day. He spent most of the hour-long extended homeroom period just getting them to settle down while he tried to take attendance, arrange seating, and assign lockers. Before he knew it, it was time to line everyone up alphabetically and march them off to the auditorium. He spent the rest of his first day walking up and down the aisles telling students to be quiet, to pay attention, to stop fooling around, and all the other things teachers bark at students when they are riding herd on them.

By the time the dismissal bell rang at 11:30, sending the students rampaging for the buses, Steve was exhausted. The only good thing about the morning was that he had been so busy that he'd had little time to worry about Joe Conally's threats.

At 12:30, after he'd turned in his homeroom attendance,

had a short meeting about lesson plans with the English department head, and waited half an hour to see Dr. Plent only to be told that Plent couldn't see him until next week, Steve packed his plan book and grades register in his briefcase, along with a copy of *Macbeth,* and left school.

Diane was waiting at the end of the drive for him when he got home. She had made plans for them to go out and celebrate his first day on the job. The last thing he felt like doing was celebrating, but he couldn't tell her that, couldn't tell her he had failed. He told himself that in her condition it was better for her not to know, but in reality he was afraid if he admitted his impending failure to her, *the nagging* would start.

Steve guessed that the nagging had been the worst of it for his father. His mother was a cold person to start with, but when she put her mind to it she could be as vicious as an angry wasp, stinging again and again. "If you had half the ambition of *my* father, you'd be able to make something of yourself," she used to say, spraying words like bullets. "I could have married David Wellsley. *He owns* his business, but no, I had to marry you, *Mister Loser."* The clincher was one that she had started using shortly before his father's death and which Steve was certain had driven him to suicide: "I'd be better off with you *dead* so I could collect on the insurance and get out of this dump."

Though she sometimes nagged him, Diane was never as bad as his mother had been to his father; but then he had never failed Diane before. After his father's funeral, Steve, who would soon turn eighteen, walked away from his mother and never saw her again. As far as he knew that had been fine with her because she never tried to get in touch with him.

Diane waved as he pulled in the driveway. She waddled to the car and Steve managed a smile for her as she got in. She mistook it as him making fun of how big she was and punched his arm playfully.

How are you going to support another mouth to feed if you lose your job?

"Hi," Diane said, as he leaned over and kissed her cheek quickly. "How did it go today? Think you'll survive?"

"Yeah," he said with a shrug and avoided her eyes. "The kids were a little crazy, first day and all," he added as he backed the car out of the driveway. "It went okay. They'll settle down eventually."

In Northwood Center, Steve parked the car at the Bloody Brook Cafe. Northwood didn't offer much in the way of fine dining, you had to go to Amherst or Northhampton for that, but Judy Eames had told Diane that the food at the cafe was good and inexpensive.

Steve was helping Diane out of the car when he noticed a long black hearse drive slowly by. He saw the young woman who was driving was the same woman who, outside of Roosevelt's Bar and Grill, had fondled herself and stared at him like no woman had ever stared at him before. He let go of his wife's hand and stood up. Diane toppled back into the car with a look of surprise on her face, but Steve didn't notice. The young woman was staring at him again with that look. Without taking her eyes from him, she put her index finger to her mouth and ran her tongue over it.

Steve flinched as he felt her tongue glide over his suddenly erect penis.

She licked her lips and opened her mouth, sliding her finger into it.

Steve was engulfed in ecstasy. In seconds he was ready to climax.

Abruptly, she pulled her finger from her mouth and the sensation of having his cock swallowed disappeared. She drove off, leaving strange, *old*-sounding laughter and a very frustrated Steve behind.

"Thanks a lot!" Diane said angrily. She was sprawled on the front seat, her head near the stick shift where she'd landed when Steve let go of her.

Dazed and not really sure if what he thought had just happened had really happened, Steve reached for Diane and helped her up and out of the car. When she was standing next to him, he quickly put his hands in his pockets and adjusted his erection so that she wouldn't notice.

"Sorry, babe," he said sheepishly. "I lost my grip."

"Oh sure! It's because I'm too fat!" Diane said in a pouting voice.

Steve knew that tone of voice. It was one that he had gotten used to since the start of Diane's pregnancy. It was her I'm-feeling-sorry-for-myself voice. She fell into it whenever the rigors of being pregnant began to wear on her. Steve was usually able to counter her mood by getting her to laugh at something, or by reassuring her that he loved her. This time, though, he was too distracted and disturbed by what had just happened to react to his wife.

His penis was throbbing from the touch of the young woman's lips and tongue, making him very uncomfortable. He knew what had just happened was impossible. She could not have given him head in those short seconds; she could not have even touched him with any part of her body because she was a good ten fucking feet away in a passing car. The erection that wouldn't die insisted differently. He tried to think it away and could not. The ghost of her mouth wouldn't let him. He craned his neck this way and that searching for the hearse. It was nowhere to be seen.

As they went into the cafe and a waitress was seating them in the small nonsmoking section, Steve thought he saw the hearse pass by again, but couldn't be sure if it had stopped. Diane was still angry and pouting, but Steve excused himself from the table as soon as they were seated and headed for the bathroom, leaving her at the table. He went back to the front of the cafe and looked out but could not see the hearse or its seductive driver anywhere. He'd have been doubting that he had ever seen her if it wasn't for the boner in his pants that kept reminding him. He shook his head in puzzlement and went to the men's room.

Diane watched Steve cross the room and go to the front door. She knew she was being crazy, but lately since the move, she had begun suspecting Steve of being interested in other women, and sometimes of actually having an affair. She had no proof, but lately he'd been acting strange—like just now outside. She had seen the erection in his pants, and though she didn't see anyone else around, she was sure he had caught sight of some nice young thing that he was more interested in looking at than in helping her out of the car. It seemed she had noticed him doing that a lot lately, or imagining that he was. She had even thought she caught him eyeing plump Judy Eames.

When she really examined her feelings she realized she was probably just being oversensitive because she was pregnant. She was able to trace her suspicions to a dream she had had the second night in the new house. In the dream Steve had come home to tell her he was running off with one of his students.

Since then, her paranoia had grown, and because she was pregnant and prone to fits of irrationality and emotionalism, she had been unable to deal with it realistically. To make matters worse, she had read in an article in *Cosmopolitan* that, while a woman is pregnant, her husband is more likely to stray. Steve was usually a doll, but any man could put up with only so much. She knew her attitude was hard on him sometimes, but then she told herself she had a right to be bitchy; she was the one going through all the pain and discomfort, not him. If he couldn't keep his hormones in check until after she had the kid, then didn't that say something about how little he valued their marriage?

She was just getting herself good and steamed when she felt a light tap on her shoulder. She turned, half expecting to see Steve, but found herself looking up at the tanned, blue-eyed, dimpled face of her father. Her *late* father. She gasped, catching saliva in her windpipe, and choked.

He sat in the chair next to her and patted her back softly until she was done choking, then he took her hand. His fingers were like ice and their coldness soaked into her flesh quickly. Her hand grew numb. Diane looked into her father's eyes and the numbness spread up her arm. When he spoke, the numbness flooded up her neck and into her head.

"Don't worry about him," her father said in a mellow, reassuring voice, enriched by the strong hint of an Italian accent. He nodded in the direction Steve had gone. "Worry about yourself. Take care of yourself; take care of the baby. You don't need him. He and his lover can take care of the other children. You take care of yourself and the baby." His words were thick and soothing like warm honey poured down a sore throat. She drank them in greedily; it was just what she wanted to hear.

Her father leaned close and placed his left hand caressingly on her swollen belly. "Nothing must hurt this child," he said. "Don't let *him* (a jerk of the head indicated Steve) put his *thing* (he made the word sound diseased) in you or he'll hurt the baby." His gnarled hand was lightly drawing patterns on her stomach.

For a moment, as if from far away, Diane thought she heard a voice chanting in a strange rhythmic language, then the fetus in her kicked hard at the cold hand. He withdrew it, but kept smiling.

"Promise me," he said, running an iciclelike finger down her cheek, "that you won't let him endanger the baby. Promise me," he insisted again so demandingly that she felt compelled to answer.

"I do," she said, losing herself in his eyes. "I promise."

CHAPTER 9

Tweedle-dum and Tweedle-dee

Sunlight glowed like a flurry of solar flares in the windows of the cars in the mall parking lot. Eleanor pulled the hearse into the lot and found a spot as close to the mall entrance as she could. She rolled up the windows and locked the doors before getting out. Dressed in her usual black garb from head to toe, and standing next to the sinister hearse, she looked like the Angel of Death.

Though there were people walking by, no one noticed Eleanor; the Machine continued to cast reassuring images into their minds, and nothing could be traced to her. One person might think she looked like a short woman with a cane, leaning on an old Buick; another would see her as a young man in a business suit standing next to a sports car. She and the hearse remained unseen as they truly appeared.

The mall wasn't crowded, which was fine with Eleanor. She didn't want a lot of people around; the more people the more interference and the more energy she would have to expend keeping others from seeing her activities. Normally she wouldn't have thought twice about it—the Machine could handle it easily—but her poor health had taken its toll on her powers and she didn't want to overtax them. After her last heart attack, she hadn't regained all her strength.

Several times in the past few days she'd had bone-shaking attacks of palsy followed by periods in which she remembered nothing. The most recent episode had begun last night and had ended in the morning when Eleanor found herself lying on the kitchen floor with the last of Edmund, still wrapped in foil from the freezer, clutched in her arms. Her fingers had been raw and bleeding from deeply embedded slivers and she couldn't remember the last ten hours.

When she had unwrapped the foil to reveal Edmund's frozen head and it spoke to her, she knew she was losing control. She was running out of time, losing her mental faculties, hallucinating, exactly as Edmund had just before his final, fatal heart attack.

"I'm waiting for you in Hell," his severed head had said to her, and she heard him laughing in her mind now.

Edmund's dead! she told herself in a scolding tone. His laughter rang from her head and echoed across the parking lot, mocking her. "That's your guilty conscience," she whispered, "not his ghost." But she went quickly into the mall before she heard any more laughter.

If it wasn't for her physical deterioration, she would be doing fine. The Machine was holding up well under the onslaught of her failing body and continued to weave an intricate web to catch her prey. It had led her to the restaurant downtown when she'd been on her way to the mall. She knew then, as the Machine always let her know, it was time to plant some seeds. Things were going according to plan; she just hoped the plan didn't outlive her. Halloween, the Festival of Samhain and the Harvest of Dead Souls was still over a month away. With the help of the Machine, a little tequila, and her nitroglycerin pills, she'd make it.

She pushed through the heavy glass doors and passed under a wide arch, *Welcome to Pioneer Mall* written on it in seashells embedded in stucco. The sign forewarned of the tackiness found in the rest of the mall. It was a long V-shaped building with the main entrance at the joint of the V. The left side of the V was done in the style of an old Western town, complete with a horse trough that was a drinking fountain, a stage coach that was really a popcorn stand, and metal tumbleweed sculptures that looked like they were made out of rusty wire clothes hangers placed here and there throughout the length of the mall. In the point of the V, where Eleanor now stood, was a large fountain that flowed over a wooden trellis to create a small waterfall that in turn filled a wishing pool, the bottom of which was covered with algae-green pennies and assorted coins.

The right side of the V was done in a New Orleans French Quarter style with balconies over the stores, an outdoor cafe, and a life-size plastic replica of a Dixieland band that was wired for sound and played "St. John's Infirmary" over and over again.

Eleanor scanned both lengths of the mall from a small wooden platform that overlooked the wishing pool. From what she could see on the Western town side, pickings were slim. The youngest child she could see was a boy who looked to be at least twelve, probably older. As he came closer, a telltale spot of acne on his chin told Eleanor that no matter what age he was, he was too old for her purposes.

She turned and scanned the other end of the mall. No children in sight. Eleanor frowned and her shoulders hunched as if a great weight were settling on them. In the past, when Edmund was still alive, the mall had always been a good place to snatch a child if they were desperate. They'd only used it twice—Edmund was careful about abducting children too close to Grimm Memorials—but it had come in handy when they couldn't get the young ones they needed for their monthly rituals through their usual black market connections, or hadn't the time to travel far enough to abduct one without arousing suspicions locally. Today, the Machine had told her that she would find what she needed at the mall, and the Machine was rarely wrong.

Eleanor looked at several middle-aged women strolling among the stores and had to admit that prospects didn't look good. She was starting to wonder whether her physical problems were affecting the Machine after all when a hot tingling flash ran through her body and she heard small voices in her head. Stepping out from behind the life-size Dixieland band was a mother with two children, twin boys dressed alike in jeans and blue sweaters, by her side.

"Michael, leave it alone. Mark, get over here." The mother spoke with the tired exasperated tone that mothers of twin boys, or hyperactive children, always seem to have. The mother sank wearily onto a wrought-iron and wooden bench in front of the Dixieland band. By her feet, she placed two large gray plastic bags with the *ZAYRE* logo on them in red letters.

The boys paid no attention to their mother. The one she'd called Mark wandered away and climbed on another nearby bench to inspect the contents of a wire trash barrel next to it. The other one, Michael, was busy kicking the plastic shin of the black banjo player as mournful horns belted out "St. John's Infirmary," for the two-hundredth time that day.

Though she reprimanded her children constantly, the woman's voice was not harsh, nor was her demeanor one of anger; she saved anger for when the boys pushed their mischief beyond the point of tolerance. If they weren't destroying something, or trying to kill each other, she reprimanded them only mildly. Otherwise she would have been run ragged and screamed herself hoarse, or gone right into the nut house, very soon after they had entered the terrible twos. They were four now, but still full of hell.

"Michael!" Now her voice was raised a pitch and contained a tone of ire. Michael had chipped the paint on the leg of the banjo player. "Get over here right now."

The boy stopped kicking the statue. He knew that tone of

voice from his mother meant that a swat across the fanny was soon to follow if he didn't listen. Frowning, he sauntered over to his mother and climbed on the bench next to her. He stood up and hung his arms and head over the back as though he were in stocks. "Mom, I'm hungry," he whined, keeping an eye on his brother who, as yet, had found nothing interesting in the trash.

"We'll go home soon," she said from rote. It was her standard answer.

The boy started to whine, "But I'm hungr—" and stopped in mid-sentence. He stared at something behind them. "Mommy, look," Michael said, pointing.

She didn't bother to look up. She figured (in fact, would have bet on it) that Michael was pointing at something Mark was doing. "Mark, knock it off," she said, using the I-mean-business tone of voice.

" 'S not Mark, Mommy," Michael said.

Her first thought was one of relief that something, *anything,* had caught their attention and arrested their hyperactivity long enough that she might have a few quiet moments. Usually, nothing but MTV could hold their attention longer than a few seconds. When they continued to be quiet, she became curious as to what they could have found so fascinating.

She looked up. Michael was standing on the bench, smiling goofily, and jiggling his left leg the way he always did when he was excited about something. She half turned to look at Mark on the other bench, but he had given up his perusal of the trash barrel, leaving it for some other fortunate kid to plunder, and had climbed down. He was smiling and staring at something behind her, also.

This must be good, she thought. This I gotta see. She turned and had to clamp a hand over her mouth to keep from laughing outright.

* * *

"I know who you are," Mark said to the rotund twins standing near the tables of the sidewalk cafe a few feet away. "You're Tweedle-dee and Tweedle-dum. You're twins like us."

"We are not," said the one on the left. He was dressed in an ill-fitting blue suit with short pants that were too small for him and wearing a blue cap with a stubby visor in front.

"We are too," the one on the right responded. He was dressed identically to his brother.

"Who is who?" Mark asked, delighted to be inquiring of someone else what people were always asking Michael and him. His brother was standing beside him now, all smiles and awe. When Mark asked his question, Michael just nodded his head and continued gazing goofily.

"I'm Tweedle-dum and he's Tweedle-dee," the one on the right explained.

"I am not. *I'm* Tweedle-dum and *he's* Tweedle-dee," the twin on the left argued.

"You are not."

"I am too."

"Are not."

"Am too."

Mark and Michael looked at each other and giggled. Tweedle-dum and Tweedle-dee were arguing just like they always did. Mark stepped forward and, mimicking his mother, cried, "Why are you boys fighting?" Michael found this extremely funny and began laughing hysterically.

Tweedle-dum and Tweedle-dee stopped fighting and stared at Mark, at each other, then at Mark again. "Tweedle-dum and Tweedle-dee resolved to have a battle," the left twin said, slapping his brother on the back of the head and then stepping forward. "For Tweedle-dum said Tweedle-dee had spoiled his nice new rattle." Here he indicated his brother, who held up a large candy-striped rattle with a crack and a hole in it.

The loud sound of flapping wings made Mark and Michael turn at the same time. A huge crow, as large as a ten-speed bicycle, flew low over their heads, causing them to duck. Tweedle-dum and Tweedle-dee jumped into each other's arms

"Just then flew by a monstrous crow," the right twin said in a frightened voice, "as big as a tar barrel, which frightened both the heroes so, they quite forgot their quarrel."

The crow landed a few feet behind the comical twins. In fear, they ran forward away from it and over to Mark and Michael, who were delighted to be closer to them. They jumped up and down, scrutinizing the twins who were exact replicas of the picture in *Alice in Wonderland,* a book their mother often read to them.

"I wasn't scared," one of them said to Mark.

"You were too," the other one accused.

"Did I look scared?" the first asked of them both.

They looked at each other, giggled, and nodded their heads yes.

"I told you so. I told you so," the other cried gleefully

"You were scared, too."

"Was not."

"Was too."

"Was not."

"Was he scared, too?" the one near Mark asked them. Mark and Michael looked at the other brother, Michael still giggling uncontrollably, and nodded their heads in unison.

"I was not!"

"Nyah, nyah, were too, were too."

The fat, funny twins began slapping at each other again, eyes closed, hands flailing wildly. Mark and Michael watched with happy fascination. Michael, who was a natural daydreamer, was in a state of ecstasy. Mark, who was more pragmatic, never believed the porcine duo were *really* Tweedle-dum and Tweedle-dee. He figured they were just guys dressed up like them, like at Christmas they had Santa Claus at the mall, and at Easter when they had the Easter Bunny. Even though he didn't believe it, he still thought it was neat, especially the big crow, which had looked so real, but could no longer be seen anywhere.

The fight ended when both of them punched each other in the nose at the same time. They looked stunned for a moment, then burst into tears, their voices whining like ambulance sirens. The sound hurt Mark's and Michael's ears. They ran forward and tried to comfort the bawling twins. After a few moments, they were successful in quieting them.

"I want my mommy," the one standing next to Michael pouted.

"Me, too," his brother echoed, looking hopefully at Mark.

"Will you take us to our mommy?" they both asked at the same time.

Michael readily agreed. He believed completely in the existence of these fairy-tale characters and was happy to go anywhere with them. Mark figured they had a display on the other side of the mall, like Santa's Village at Christmas or the Bunny Trail at Easter. He didn't mind going along because free candy usually was handed out at these displays. He just hoped it wasn't those gross lime green lollipops he always got at the doctor's office.

Mark and Michael took the hands of Tweedle-dum and Tweedle-dee and started walking away. Mark turned back a second and shouted, "We'll be right back, Mom."

"Okay, boys. Be good," she answered from the bench.

Ten feet away from Michael and Mark's mother, near an array of wooden tables with colorful striped umbrellas in the middle of them, meant to simulate a French sidewalk cafe, a tall, silver-haired woman stood in a fullflowing, sequin-dappled ball gown. In her hair, which was the color of spun sterling and was piled high atop her head, was pinned a diamond-studded tiara that sprayed rainbows of light like faded watercolors on the walls, tables, and floor around her. The gown was a beautiful shade of aquamarine and made of crinoline and silk. What made the twins' mother laugh was that in her hand, the woman held a wand that dripped with sparkling dust, and on her back, sprouting up behind her head, were a tremendous pair of fairy wings.

No wonder the boys were so fascinated, she thought. The wings looked so real. And when she looked at the dust falling from the wand, she could swear that she could see images wavering like pictures of magical possibilities. A trick of the light, she told herself, but she was feeling strange, like the one time in college she had tried mescaline. She felt exhilarated, but out of breath, and mentally intoxicated, a sensation that made her think that she could do anything and all things were possible. It was a good feeling. She hadn't felt that way in a long time—at least four years.

Michael got off the bench next to her and ran to his brother's side. She could see that they were both very excited. She smiled and wondered what the occasion was for the mall to be putting on a display like this, which was usually reserved for holidays or sales promotions. Then she remembered seeing that the video store in the mall was advertising a sale on Disney's *Cinderella*. That explained the fairy godmother outfit.

She was going to get off the bench to bring the twins to meet the woman when the latter's wings suddenly began to buzz. The woman seemed to grow taller, rising up as she left her feet and glided over to the bench, hovering an inch or two off the floor.

The twins' mother was dumbfounded. She looked over the woman's head to see if there were any wires, but could detect none. As the woman landed next to the bench, she could feel cool air from the beating of the woman's wings.

"Hello, Linda," the woman said in a musical voice.

"How do you know my name?" Linda asked. The woman was exquisitely beautiful in the classic tradition of such high-cheekboned icy beauties as Grace Kelly and Ursula Andress. Her eyes were large and such a deep blue that they reflected everything. Linda felt in awe to be so close to her.

"I'm your fairy godmother," the woman answered, her words rich in tone as if many people were speaking at once.

"My . . . what?" Linda had to laugh.

'I know a lot about you," the woman said, smiling.

This must be a gag, Linda thought to herself. Someone I know has put her up to this, or else I'm on "Candid Camera." She turned to look around and see if any of her friends were nearby watching, getting a kick out of this, or if there were a hidden camera with Allen Funt waiting to pounce, but she suddenly found that she could not look away from the strange, beautiful woman.

The woman's wings stopped beating and the cool breeze from them died. "How . . . how do you do that?" Linda asked, craning her neck to see the wings. There were still no visible wires, nor anything else that might reveal a trick.

"It's very easy, really. I just think about it and it's done. It's a lot like riding a bicycle, it becomes second nature after a while," the woman explained amiably.

"Oh my God," Linda exclaimed as the woman turned to allow Linda to see the wings more clearly. They appeared to be absolutely real. The back of the gown was cut low, revealing the wings sprouting from small fleshy bumps on the woman's shoulder blades. The wings themselves were like framed and veiny sheets of mica-smoked glass. "They're *real!*"

"Of course they're real," she said with a smile, turning back to Linda. "All fairy godmothers have wings. I thought you knew that."

She reached out her hand and touched Linda's shoulder lightly. Her words echoed in Linda's head like a soft, soothing lullaby. The more they echoed the more sense they made. "I've come to help you with the children, dear. Isn't that your secret wish, to have help with the boys? I've come to grant that for you." Her hand moved up Linda's shoulder and caressed her cheek.

Yes, that would be nice, Linda mused, but thought she had spoken out loud. She realized suddenly that her lips weren't moving. The funny thing was that when her fairy godmother spoke, Linda didn't remember *her* lips moving either, yet she heard her voice clearly.

Just relax, Fairy Godmother said soothingly. This time Linda looked closely at her mouth and confirmed that her lips never moved. The voice was a sensation in her mind, like listening to stereo headphones where the sound seems to come from the middle of your head. The still-rational part of her brain tried to explain the phenomenon away by insisting that the woman was a ventriloquist.

Yes, something like that, Fairy Godmother's voice spoke up inside Linda's head. But never mind that now, she added. You're tired, aren't you? The children wore you out.

Linda immediately felt an immense exhaustion, worse than the weariness she usually felt from chasing the boys about. It permeated her being, making her head feel as heavy as a bowling ball. She looked up into her fairy godmother's eyes and saw that they were big enough for her to fall into. "Yes," Linda said aloud, softly. She was swimming in the deep sparkling blue of those eyes.

Very tired.

Linda's arms and legs felt as though they were encased in wet concrete. She felt giddy and her vision became blurred.

I'll take the children. You rest.

That sounded to Linda like the best suggestion she had ever heard. The woman's eyes continued to swallow her up as her bowling-ball head got heavier and heavier and her eyelids slid closed. Moving slowly, Linda lay back on the bench, putting her feet up, and curling into a fetal position. She fell into a deep sleep. The last thing she heard was her son Mark saying something. "Okay, boys," she heard someone else say with her voice. "Be good."

* * *

Eleanor led the boys, one on each hand, out of the mall to her car. As they exited through the glass doors she could sense that Mark, the boy on her right, thought something was wrong. She slipped into his mind and distracted him with an image of the hearse as a huge coach driven by twelve beautiful white stallions. She led the boys to it and opened the back while they patted the horses and gazed enthralled at the coach's velvet finery. She called them to her and, in the guise of Tweedle-dum and Tweedle-dee, held out an ether-soaked cloth to each boy, making them appear as rare and beautiful flowers which she invited them to sniff. When they were quite unconscious, she piled them into a coffin in the back and closed the lid.

As Eleanor got in the car, she smiled at a mall security guard strolling past. He smiled and tipped his hat to the kindly, small woman he saw in her place and walked by. Within minutes he wouldn't remember seeing her at all.

Several hours later, the same security guard would finally notice the twins' mother lying all curled up on the bench in front of the Dixieland band. He would walk by her three times during the afternoon and not until early evening would he actually see her. When he did, he would find her very hard to wake.

At first, the security guard, whom everyone called "Murph," figured she was a drunken bag lady. It had happened before, and just last summer a young guy from the university had OD'd on the bridge by the waterfall. But the more Murph looked at this woman and inspected her bags filled with children's clothing, the more he realized she wasn't a bag lady at all. It was obvious that she was a mother. Murph just hoped her kids hadn't been with her because now they were nowhere to be seen.

An ambulance was called and an E.M.T. revived her with an ammonia capsule broken under nose. She sat up straight, blinked several times at the medic, looked at the small crowd of security men, police who'd come with the ambulance, mall officials, and shoppers, and spoke to them with her mind the way she had with her fairy godmother. She was disappointed when she got no response.

"Where's my fairy godmother?" she asked, impatient with these clods who couldn't read minds. Several people, mostly the shoppers, but several of the cops and security men, too, laughed loudly until they saw that she was serious.

"Where's my fairy godmother?" she asked again, a kernel of panic present in her voice. When no one answered her, she stood up and grabbed the E.M.T. by the shoulders and shook him. "Where's my fairy godmother, damn you, *she's got my children!*"

Initially, officers from the sheriff's department treated Linda as though she were a drunk. They put her, screaming for her children and fairy godmother, in the ambulance and sent her off to the local detox tank at Amherst Hospital. They realized there was more to it when they called the woman's husband and found out that their children had been with her.

When the hospital reported that the woman was alcohol- and drug-free, Deputy Sheriff Ken Vitelli thought it sounded like another child abduction. He was head of the investigation into the Hall and Torrez boys' disappearances. Linda Lafleur's losing her kids in a shopping mall seemed to fit the pattern.

The sheriff didn't agree. During questioning Linda Lafleur admitted to having taken hallucinogenic drugs in college and said that she thought she was having a drug flashback at the mall. She also admitted that she and her husband smoked pot on occasion. A neighbor came forth to tell police that Linda Lafleur had complained to her on several occasions that her twin boys were driving her crazy and, jokingly at the time, had said she'd sometimes like to wring their necks. The sheriff figured the Lafleurs for drug dealers. His theory was that she had had a drug flashback that, combined with her children's hyperactive behavior, had driven her to kill the children and dump their bodies before she ever got to the mall. When one of the boys' sneakers was found on the Hadley River bridge (thrown there by Eleanor when the Machine told her to do so), the county prosecutor, looking for a sensational case along the lines of Hedda Nussbaum/Joel Steinberg trial to boost his political aspirations, readily agreed. The sheriff's department began dragging the river, and Linda Lafleur was arrested and charged with the double homicide of her two children.

CHAPTER 10

Dance to your daddy . . .

Steve parked the car in the driveway and got out. He immediately went around the car and helped Diane get out the passenger side, then went and unlocked the front door. Neither of them said anything; neither had spoken for the past hour. Their lunch had passed in heavy silence with them picking at their food and avoiding looking at each other.

Steve hadn't been able to stop searching for the young woman from the parking lot. He felt certain that she would return; his aching, boner-that-wouldn't-die kept the hope alive. But she did not return, no matter how much he wanted her to.

Diane noticed Steve's looking everywhere but at her and remembered what her father told her. She was in a minor state of shock from having seen him alive again and all through lunch felt as though she'd just wakened from a dream; a dream that had seemed so real, but was just bizarre enough that she knew it couldn't possibly have happened. Her father was dead. Dead many years. He couldn't come back. Could he?

Suddenly Diane wasn't sure. She had never been one to believe in the supernatural, or the kind of weird-phenomena stories that paint the headlines of the gossip rags, but after her father's visitation, leaving her exhilarated and very frightened, anything suddenly seemed possible. All the strange things she used to laugh at while standing in the checkout line at the supermarket and reading the headlines of those newspapers (ALIENS HOLD TOP GOVERNMENT POSITIONS; WOMAN MARRIES BIGFOOT—GIVES BIRTH TO MUTANT) became possible—more than possible. An unshakable feeling began to grow in her that her father *had* come back; and he had done so to warn her.

He must know that something bad is going to happen to the baby and he came to warn me and protect it, she thought. She looked at Steve unlocking the front door and remembered what her father had told her. Would Steve (could Steve?) cheat on her, or hurt the baby? The rest of what her father said came to her as if in answer: *Don't let him put his thing in you.*

Diane suddenly knew, irrevocably, that the reason her father had warned against letting him put his thing in her was because Steve had caught some kind of disease, maybe even AIDS. Here she'd been thinking that she was just having a bout of pregnancy paranoia in thinking that Steve was fooling around on her, and all the time it was true.

He wouldn't do that; that's crazy, a small part of her still insisted, but after her father's visit, Diane found it too easy not to believe it anymore.

Steve got the door open and went inside, hanging his coat in the hall closet. Diane followed him in and went down the hall to the kitchen. She tossed her pocketbook on the kitchen table and went to the sink. From the right hand cabinet, she took a bottle of Tylenol and a drinking glass. She scooped two pills out and into her mouth, following them with water. The faint beat of a headache was starting in the back of her head. From the way it throbbed with every pulse of her heart, she knew it was going to swell into a doozy.

Steve came down the hall, stopped in the kitchen doorway, and watched Diane as she rested a moment against the sink. His penis, throbbing maddeningly against his shorts, had remained semi-erect since the incident in the parking lot. Now, ogling his wife's swollen belly and equally swollen breasts, he felt it growing fully hard again.

Though Diane thought her body was fat and ugly and growing fatter and uglier with each passing day, Steve found her pregnant belly and milk-laden breasts extremely sexy. He crossed the kitchen and snuggled up behind her, reaching around and caressing her belly with his right hand while lightly grabbing her breast with his left.

Diane pulled away immediately and went to the table, picking up her pocketbook and coat. "I have a really bad headache. I'm going to go lie down for a while," she said to Steve without looking at him. She left the kitchen through the front hall and went upstairs.

She had been lying there for only a short while when Steve came into the bedroom. He closed the door and the window shades, then began undressing. Diane rolled over on her side away from him. He lay on the bed next to her, wearing only his T-shirt and boxer shorts, and snuggled up against her, putting his arm around her and cupping her left breast. She patted his hand and put it off her.

"I told you I have a headache," she said quietly. She moved away from his body and the uncomfortable feel of his hard cock in her back.

"That's okay," Steve said gently. "We don't have to do anything." He sat up and leaned over her. "Do you want to practice your breathing?" They had been enrolled in a Lamaze birthing class at Mass. General Hospital in Boston, finishing the course just before they moved. They were supposed to be practicing once a week the special breathing she would do to get through labor contractions, but they had been very lax.

"No," Diane murmured, softening.

Steve put his hand on Diane's ankle. "How 'bout if I massage your feet?"

A feeling of guilt washed over Diane like a cold sweat. Could this kind, gentle man cheat on her?

Steve began massaging her feet, rubbing the instep and heel of each foot hard with the ball of his palm. It sent delicious tingles all the way up her legs. Steve gave the best foot massages and she let herself be rubbed limp by him now. Deliberately, he worked every inch of both her feet, then started on her ankles and moved up to her calves. By the time he got to her thighs, running his hands alternatingly light and heavy up under her maternity dress and over her inner thigh and crotch, she was breathing heavily. Her panties were moist and clung to her labia, outlining them like an orchid for Steve to see under her hiked-up dress. Though she had left her clothes on when she lay down, she had removed her bra. Steve could see that her nipples were hard and excited.

Sliding his hands up over her crotch sensuously slow, he began unbuttoning her dress. When he had it laid open to her waist, revealing her ballooning breasts, he smiled and sighed. He cupped her breasts with both hands and leaned over, licking each hardened nipple lightly. He glided his tongue over her skin to her belly and down to her extra-large pink panties. He slid the bottom of her dress up higher, piling it on her stomach and slid a hand between her legs as he kissed her thighs. His fingers quickly sought out and rubbed the warm wet object of his desires through her flimsy underwear.

Don't let him—

The words came out of nowhere like a gust of wind behind her eyes. She stiffened just as Steve's gently probing fingers slid her panties down and found her clitoris, rubbing it softly, sending electric thrills through her bowels.

—put his thing in you—

The words settled in her mind like a heavy snowfall blanketing all else. Steve's fingers searched deeper but the electric pleasure of his touch was cooling under the white noise of her father's voice.

—or he'll hurt the baby!

The words became an irresistible command. With a groan

of anguish and pleasure, she pushed Steve away just as he was slipping a finger into her.

"No, I . . . I don't feel like it. I . . . don't feel good," she stammered. The voice in her head was rolling around like thunder, causing her headache to swell its beating so that now she felt like there were bass drums pounding in unison at her temples. "My head hurts," she whimpered tears springing to her eyes.

"Okay. It's okay, babe," Steve said, pushing away the feeling of resentment that had at first rushed in upon him when Diane pushed him away. He got out of bed and went around to her side, sitting next to her and leaning over, hugging her firmly with both arms. "It's like I said. We don't have to fool around. It's okay."

Diane put her head back, covered her eyes with her hand, and began to sob. She began trembling and the pain in her head throbbed stronger, almost to the point of nausea. For one fleeting moment, she thought of blurting out to Steve what had happened at the restaurant, but the pain became so unbearable in that instant that she nearly fainted from it. The next moment, when she thought that if she did tell Steve he'd think she was crazy, the pain let up until it was completely gone.

Without consciously thinking it, Diane knew that if she ever told Steve, or anyone, about seeing her father, the pain would come back and this time it would kill her, baby or no baby. She also knew, like an unwritten law, that she must keep her promise to her dead father and protect the baby.

Diane let Steve prop several pillows behind her head and shoulders, and a couple under her knees. He then tucked her in with just a sheet over her. He stepped back and slid off his T-shirt and shorts. His erection didn't appear to have been dampened by her rejection.

"Steve, don't, please," she said in a tired voice.

"Hey, it's *okay*," he said slowly, a hint of annoyance in his voice. "I'm not going to do anything. I just want to cool off. It's muggy today." His hard-on throbbing, he climbed back into bed next to Diane. "Are those pillows helping your head? Does it feel any better?" he asked.

"No," she whined, lying. At the sight of his rigid penis, she had felt another flash of excitement which was quickly answered by a stab of immense pain in her temples. Immediately, the hot, pleasurable itch between her legs and in her nipples, disappeared. When it did, so did the pain.

"Do you want anything?" Steve asked, lying with his head propped up on his bent elbow.

"No," she said softly.

Steve slid closer. "Is it okay then if I just rub your belly and talk to little Stevie?" He placed his right hand on the lower part of her stomach and began massaging in big gentle circles. As he did this, he leaned close and kissed her belly just above the navel, through the sheet. "Hello, little Steve," he said, pressing his mouth into her belly through the sheet. They'd known they were having a boy since the fifth month of her pregnancy when she'd had an amniocentesis done.

Diane's skin grew hot from his breath as the sheet muffled his words. She could feel his voice vibrating in her stomach, and felt the baby move, responding to his father's voice.

"This is your daddy speaking," Steve said, and wet the sheet with his tongue. At the same time, he began rubbing her belly below her navel, widening each stroke so that he was soon rubbing the top of the inverted triangle of her pubic hair that felt like steel wool under the sheet. "I'm waiting out here for you, little guy," Steve went on, moving his lips up her belly and closer to her breasts while his left hand pulled the sheet slowly down. "Your momma's not in a good mood today," he pouted, his lips grazing the underside of her left breast. The sheet slid over the nipple and his tongue darted out, flicking snakelike at it. The aureole tightened and the nipple became erect. "Her lips say, 'No, no, no,' but her nips say, 'Yes, yes, yes.' " He giggled into the cleavage of her breasts.

"Steve, stop it!" Diane shouted suddenly. She yanked his hand from between her legs and flung it off her. Pulling the sheet up tight to her neck, she turned away. The feelings he was arousing in her had brought the pain back like a boomerang. When she pushed him away, she pushed it away.

Steve was miffed. He looked at Diane with a mixture of puzzlement and anger on his face. Diane had been increasingly moody throughout her pregnancy, and her sex drive had decreased considerably, but she hadn't shut him off totally, unlike the horror stories he'd heard from other guys whose wives wouldn't even let their husbands touch them for nine months, much less make love to them. At times, she had even been quite amorous, but lately, ever since the move, Diane had been colder than usual while he had become hornier.

It was obvious to Steve that his advances were arousing her, he had felt the viscous wetness oozing from her widening vagina, had seen her nipples blossom rigidly. For some reason, she was fighting it. Though he could think of nothing he had done (the girl in the hearse popped into his head, but Diana couldn't know about that—he wasn't even sure if she was real), he surmised that she was angry with him for something.

She'll get over it, he thought spitefully to himself. Normally, he would have talked to Diane and found out what was bothering her, but with the possibility of losing his job hanging over his head—not to mention the possibility of losing *his mind* due to the strange young woman and her phantom lips—he felt he was justified in not bending over backwards to make her feel better. As far as he could see, *he* was the one who needed a little TLC.

Frustrated beyond words, Steve exhaled loudly and rolled over onto his stomach, trapping his throbbing erection beneath him. While trying to seduce Diane, he had been able to avoid thinking of the young woman in the hearse. Now, her inviting, seductive image came back to him, again refusing to let his hard-on soften.

Next to Steve, Diane wept silently, her face turned well away so that her husband couldn't see. She was a maelstrom of conflicting emotions: lust, jealousy, fear, paranoia. She didn't know what to think or believe. She only knew that if she didn't obey her father's voice, the pain would return, and something bad would happen to her unborn child. That sense of doom was devastating and kept her thoughts jumbled. Whenever she tried to concentrate and straighten out the jigsaw puzzle of her thoughts and emotions, her father's face loomed; she felt his ice-cold touch on her belly again, and heard his voice echoing through her brain, leaving her feeling as though she might lose her mind. To escape, she slipped into a deep sleep, floating down until she reached the REM stage and her eyes flitted back and forth rapidly behind her closed lids.

Cloudy scenes and images arose in her mind's eye and solidified. She dreamt she was in Haymarket Square, the outdoor produce market in Boston where her father had had his fruit stand for twenty years. She was walking the narrow blacktopped alley that ran between the stands, which sold everything from fruits and vegetables to mussels and stuffed pot roasts. The chatter of the merchants bickering with fat Italian women wafted to her as if over a great distance, even though she saw them within arm's reach as she walked by.

Her father's stand was at the end of the row, just past the Camella Brothers' seafood stand. She could smell the pungent odor of shellfish and garbage as she approached the end of the row. The odor had always reminded her of the smell of the nursing home where her grandmother had been sent when she lost her mind to senility. It was a smell like week-old tuna fish, stale urine, ammonia, and death.

She could see her father's fruit stand, a large wooden cart with a big, bright red Prince Spaghetti Sauce beach umbrella over it to protect the produce from the sun. The cart was loaded with wood-slatted baskets that were filled with apples, pears, strawberries, peaches, tomatoes, green beans, heads of lettuce, and loads of zucchini.

All the produce her father sold was grown on her Uncle Sal's farm, northwest of Boston, in the tiny farming community of Bolton. They were trucked fresh daily every summer morning into Boston and her father's stand at Haymarket Square. A few hours later, after breakfast, Diane would walk down Hanover Street, under the overpass of I-95, and visit her father who had already been there since 4 A.M. unloading the day's fruit and washing it before arranging it on his stand for sale.

As she came around the seafood stand, breathing through her nose so as not to smell the stench from it, she started to shout, "Papa, I'm here," but stopped. He wasn't standing there by his cart, haggling with some old padrone over the price and freshness of his zucchinis, as she had expected to see him.

"Papa? Where are you?" she called to him.

"Right here." His voice came from behind her. She whirled around and there he was a few feet away, dancing with an old, white-haired woman dressed in black. At first glance, Diane thought it was her grandmother let out from the nursing home for a visit, but as her father twirled the old woman around, Diane saw that it wasn't.

Diane blinked and rubbed her eyes. Everything had suddenly changed. Haymarket Square had dissolved and was replaced by a thick green forest, the kind one might read about in a fairy tale. Deep within the forest she caught a glimpse of a small, shining white cottage with a thatched roof. She turned around. Papa's fruit stand was still there, but the forest had sprung up around it and ferns now framed it making the fruit look deliciously tempting. All the other stands were gone, as were the nearby expressway, Faneuil Hall, and the buildings of Government Center that usually dominated the skyline.

"Papa, what's happening?" Diane asked, as she turned back to her father and his dancing partner.

"We're dancing, little one," he remarked. "Come dance with us." He laughed boisterously.

"But the woods . . ." Diane began and stopped, suddenly unable to remember what it was she wanted to say.

The old woman dancing with her father turned a familiar face toward Diane as she waltzed. Where have I seen her before? she wondered. As she stared at the old woman, she suddenly realized who she looked like: the wicked queen disguised as the old woman who offers Snow White the apple in the Disney classic. It was crazy that a person could look like a cartoon character, but the woman not only looked like her; Diane suddenly knew, as one can truly *know* something only in the mystery of a dream, that the woman actually *was* the wicked sorcerer queen of the movie.

The old woman smiled at her, showing brownish gray, bad teeth. She winked and stepped away from Diane's father. For a moment, the two of them appeared soldered together. Diane could almost hear a tearing sound as the old woman pulled herself free from Papa.

The old woman approached Diane, reaching out a gnarled, claw-fingered hand. Diane backed away, but the old woman reached past her and picked an apple off Papa's cart. "Protect the baby," the old hag whispered, offering the apple.

Diane took it and the old woman placed her ancient hand on Diane's stomach. Her touch felt strange and uncomfortable, like ice, yet warm, almost melting. Diane wanted to pull away immediately but could not. The apple the old woman offered mesmerized her. It began to pulsate and glow as if it were alive. She stared at it and the apple's skin became transparent.

As if looking at the fruit through an X-ray machine,

Diane looked inside and gasped at what she saw. Instead of a core and seeds, there was a tiny fetus inside the apple. She knew immediately that the fetus was her unborn child.

She brought the apple closer and felt a shriek build in her throat. Besides the fetus, the apple was filled with maggots and they were squirming all over the helpless baby. A shriek erupted from Diane's throat and she tried to throw the apple away. It felt glued to her hand.

Diane looked pleadingly at the old woman but she was laughing and pressing her wrinkled hand against Diane's belly. Diane tried to call to her father for help, but he was disappearing into the forest, being swallowed up by the trees and bushes that grew rapidly around him.

"Protect the baby," he managed to say before ferns grew into his mouth and vines wrapped around his head, pulling him into the forest until he was gone.

Diane felt a sharp pain in her stomach and a searing, burning sensation. She looked down and tried to scream at what she saw, but couldn't. It was as if a hand were clamped tightly over her mouth. The old woman's fingers were piercing Diane's abdomen, sinking into her pregnant flesh. The hag pushed, and her whole hand slipped inside Diane's stomach with a gurgling, sucking sound. The woman's hand delved deeper until it had searched out her womb and clutched at the baby.

"This is me," the old woman said, and burst into the most horrid, cackling laughter that Diane had ever heard. She struggled to escape the dream and wake up.

Steve was dozing on his back, his erection pushing against the sheet he had pulled over himself. When Diane began whimpering in her sleep, he knew she was having a nightmare. She'd had them before and always whimpered like that when she got so scared that she would try to scream in an attempt to wake herself up. The cruel irony of this reaction was that she was never able to really cry out, only whimper deep in her throat as if her screams were being muffled by invisible hands. Usually when she did this, Steve would gently shake her awake and hold her until the dream was forgotten and she could sleep again. Now, though, he listened to her whimpers and made no move to rescue her from her nightmare. On the edge of sleep himself (due to the several beers he'd downed at lunch) and still angry at Diane, he exacted a small measure of revenge on her by letting her sleep on, tortured by her nightmares.

It wasn't long before Steve himself was dreaming. He saw himself in a field, lying naked in tall grass. Bending over him was the seductive young woman who'd nearly given him a psychic orgasm outside the cafe. She was fondling his penis and blowing on it gently before sliding her lips over its head and swallowing the shaft in one slow, sucking motion.

In the ecstasy of this dream, Steve heard Diane's tiny cries as little moans of passion in the young woman's throat. Her head bobbed up and down, faster and faster, giving him the best head of his life. He began to build to what he felt was going to be the *ultimate* climax. Eyes closed, he arched his back, reached out with both arms and dug his fingers into the ground around him as he rose higher and higher toward the pinnacle of ecstasy.

The ground around him felt strange; slippery yet sticky once it got on his hands. He opened his eyes and turned his head, groaning as his balls felt as if they were going to explode with built-up sperm. His fingers were wet with dark, purple blood. He looked at his other hand and realized at the same moment that he was no longer in the field, he was back in his bedroom. There was something swinging overhead but he ignored it because the young woman's head was pistoning on his cock now at an unbelievable rate and he was at the point of no return. Any second now his orgasm would explode with so much jism that he thought he could fill the room with it and drown.

Suddenly she pulled her face from his crotch and looked up at him, smiling. Her teeth were disgustingly bad and caked with decaying meat. He winced at the thought of those diseased-looking teeth touching his cock. She looked above him and he followed her eyes. Swinging from the light fixture was a man in a T-shirt and boxer shorts, a rope around his neck, his face purple and bloated, the eyes bloodshot and bulging, the tongue swelling from the mouth like a partially inflated balloon.

It was his father, just as Steve had found him on the day the old man had decided to take his wife's advice and die. There was one important difference, though, between this scene and the way Steve remembered it: There was a large blood stain on the front of his father's boxer shorts and blood ran down his legs to his feet, dripping off his bare ankles and toes.

Steve looked back at the young woman bending over him. The breath went out of him when he saw what she was holding in her cupped, bloody palms. A severed penis and testicles sat in a pool of blood in her hands. He looked down at himself and realized they were his.

"That's what women and the responsibility of a family will do to you, son," his father said, his words thick and wet around the obstruction of his swollen, dead tongue. "They emasculate you; whittle away at your balls until you're nothing but a sniveling bleeding *cunt!*"

Steve jumped into wakefulness, sitting straight up in bed. His hands were protectively clasped over his nuts. It was just a dream, he thought thankfully to himself. The burning, gnawing desire in his cock made him realize just how close he had come to having a wet dream. He felt foolish and flushed hotly like a kid going through puberty and embarrassed by what his body was doing to him.

Next to him, Diane was sleeping fitfully, apparently still bothered by bad dreams. He looked past her at the clock radio on the night table. It read 2:15 P.M. Steve reached over and shook Diane's shoulder. "Di, wake up. You've got to get the kids at 2:30 when they get out of school."

Diane jumped and moaned softly and rolled over onto her back. "What?" she mumbled through a bad case of cotton mouth.

"Get up. You've got to pick the kids up at school in fifteen minutes. I'm going to take a shower and do some work." Steve got up from the bed and left the room.

Diane struggled to open her eyes but felt as though the lashes were tied together, top to bottom. "Can you go pick them up?" she asked the empty room, not realizing that Steve had gone. "Steve?" she struggled up on an elbow and managed to force one eye open. Someone was sitting on the bed. "Steve, why didn't you answer me? Will you go get the kids for me?"

No answer.

Diane squinted at the figure. Her eyes crossed with the effort and the figure doubled then shrank back into focus. Her father was sitting on the bed. He tossed a round, red object into the air and caught it.

"Go back to sleep, *Filia Mia*," he said softly. "Everything is fine."

His voice was like a lullaby, closing Diane's heavy eyelids and singing her into a bottomless sleep before her head even hit the pillow.

CHAPTER 11

Jack be nimble, Jack be quick . . .

Jennifer and Jackie stood at the playground gate watching the late bus leave the yard and head down Finch Street to Route 47. Their bus had been one of the first to leave, but they had remained behind waiting for their mother to pick them up like Steve had told them to. The last bus pulled away at 2:40 P.M. Twenty minutes later, Jackie and Jennifer were still waiting.

"I'll bet she's too busy with Ste-e-ve," Jackie said with emphasis on his stepfather's name. He was still helping Jennifer carry a grudge over the fact that she couldn't have her own room.

"I don't know," Jen said and added, "I hope there's nothing wrong, like she's having the baby early or something."

"Maybe you should call and make sure," Jackie said uneasily. It hadn't crossed his mind that anything might be wrong, but now that he thought of it, whenever his mother stressed something as much as she had about the importance of her picking them up that first day—when they would rather have ridden the bus—then he knew that she would do it unless something really serious came up.

Jennifer looked back at the school. Going in and asking a

teacher if she could use a phone to call for a ride home would make her look like a stupid little kid. But there was another reason Jennifer didn't want to go in and call: She was afraid that if she did, she would find out that, like Jackie said, their mother was too occupied with helping Steve in his study (or that they were *fooling around* like she'd heard them doing a few times) and had completely forgotten about them. That would be worse than her having the baby early or anything else; it would confirm what Jen and Jackie had begun to fear lately, that their mother cared more about Steve and his baby than she did about them.

Jennifer turned away from the school and surveyed the short length of Finch Street that ran by the school and out to Route 47. She knew they were only a few miles down the highway from home and that they could walk it easily. "I think we should start walking," she said to her brother.

"But Steve told us to wait for Mummy no matter what."

"I know, but if we start walking she'll see us and stop. Anyway, the car might have broken down again and she might need help," Jen replied.

"I don't know," Jackie hesitated. "What if the guy who's stealing kids tries to get us?"

"We'll just tell him to get lost. He can't do anything to us if we won't go with him."

Jackie looked down the street, then back at the school. "Why can't you just call her?" he asked his sister.

"Because they don't let kids use the phones," Jen lied. She turned and walked out of the schoolyard and down the street. Reluctantly, Jackie followed.

Finch Street was nice and shady. A wide, bumpy concrete sidewalk ran past hedges and stone walls with tall white Colonial houses behind them. Overhead, the leaves of the maple trees, which lined both sides of the street, rustled softly in the warm afternoon breeze. The bustle of traffic from the nearby highway was just loud enough to be reassuring.

This was a new experience for the two city-born and bred Nailer children. Even Jackie, who remained distrustful of their new home, especially the woods, had to admit that he liked this tree-lined street. Everything was so much quieter here than in the city, but not too quiet like it was around the new house. He liked that. Here was a neighborhood where he didn't have to worry about the woods and what was in them, or of getting run over if he stepped off the curb like in the city. Jackie found himself wishing they had moved to Finch Street with its many houses, a real neighborhood, rather than to where they had. Their house on Dorsey Lane was too isolated and alone. It felt like one of those houses in the middle of the woods in a fairy tale where bad things always happen to the children.

Things were different on Route 47. When riding in the car, Route 47 was a nice, rural highway, part of which was populated with Colonial houses like those found on Finch Street, the other part with tobacco fields, and barns that had every other board in their walls pulled out at an angle so as to dry and ventilate the curing tobacco. But walking on Route 47 was another story; it was a fearsome experience.

They walked on the left shoulder, heading east. To their right, cars roared by, buffeting them with turbulence. With a deep drainage ditch running just off the side, Jackie and Jennifer had only five feet or so of shoulder upon which to walk. Jennifer walked, protectively of her younger brother, on the traffic side with Jackie holding her hand and walking a little behind her, wincing at every speeding car and truck that flew by.

For Jackie, the trucks were the worst. They came charging down the road like raging dinosaurs, their engines roaring, their grills gleaming like teeth. When one approached, the sound of its engine got louder and louder until the metal monster was right on top of them, bellowing in their ears and shaking them with wind like invisible hands. Sometimes the driver would blow his horn in greeting, or warning, which only served to scare Jackie even more, making him jump each time and break out in a cold sweat.

They walked a mile, looking hopefully and fearfully at every oncoming car—hoping it would be their mother, fearing it would be the monster in human form their mother had warned them of. At a mile and a half they came to a narrow dirt road that crossed from the highway over the drainage ditch and went into the woods. A bent, iron pole carried a faded green street sign that read: DORSEY LANE EXT.

"Dorsey Lane Extension," Jennifer read aloud, correctly interpreting the abbreviation of *extension*. "This must be the other end of the road through the woods near our house," she cried excitedly. "If we take this through the woods it will take us right to our house."

Jackie didn't like it. "I think we should stay on the highway," he told Jen as she started down the road. "Mom's prob'ly on her way now."

"Don't be such a chicken shit," Jen teased.

Jackie's eyes widened at her use of a swear word. "I'm going to tell Mom you said that."

"Oh, come on! Don't be such a little fink all your life. We'll walk through the woods and sing a song." She started singing to show him: "Over the river and through the woods, to Grandmother's house we go."

"But Grammy doesn't live out there. She's in the hospital," Jackie said, refusing to move.

"It's just an example, stupid. Come on. If Mom was coming, she'd be here by now."

Jackie looked wistfully down the road and had to agree with her. There wasn't a car in sight that looked like theirs.

"We'll be safer in the woods, too. If we see a car coming, we can hide. No crazy guys can get us then," Jen argued further.

Jackie gave one more hopeful glance toward the highway, didn't see the family Saab approaching, and ran after his sister. A short distance down the road, he suddenly stopped and knelt on the road's surface. He began picking up handfuls of small white pebbles, filling his pockets with them.

"What are you doing?" Jennifer asked, coming back to him when he stopped.

"I'm getting stones to drop so if we get lost we can get back to the highway," Jackie explained as he stood, pockets bulging with pebbles.

"Who do you think we are, Hansel and Gretel?" Jen smirked.

Drop a stone.
Walk ten steps.
Drop a stone.

Pretty soon, Jackie realized he was going to run out of stones very quickly at the rate he was dropping them. He lengthened the number of steps between stones to twenty then thirty. When he ran out of stones he stopped in the road and knelt to look for more.

The road was different here deep in the woods. Instead of sand it was covered with a hard-packed mix of leaf mulch and clay dirt with no stones in it. Jackie searched in vain while Jen stood at the edge of the road, peering into the woods. When Jackie saw what she was doing, he stood and looked nervously over her shoulder.

"What are you looking at?" Jackie asked Jen. He couldn't see anything.

"Nothing," she replied.

"Then what's the matter?" Jackie asked.

"Nothing," Jen replied. "I was just listening to something. Be quiet and you'll hear it, too."

Jackie listened but heard nothing unusual. There was the rush of the wind in the trees, and the sound of birds, and once in a while the faint sound of a large truck on Route 47, which ran roughly parallel to the road in the woods. Jackie was about to say he heard nothing when he noticed that the tree branches overhead were still; there was no wind. "What is that?" he asked, moving closer to his sister.

"That's the Connecticut River," Jennifer explained. "I heard Steve say that it runs right by our house, a couple of miles back in the woods. By the sound of it, we must be close. Let's go find it."

"No way! I'm not going in the woods."

"What's wrong?" Jennifer asked, exasperation with her brother's baby attitude showing in her tone of voice.

"I just don't want to. We got to get home. Mom's prob'ly looking all over for us and we're gonna be in big trouble."

Jennifer gave him a withering look, but she knew he was right. If their mother *had* shown up looking for them they were going to be in *major* trouble, especially her, since she had talked the reluctant Jackie into it. She knew she could expect no help from the little twerp either; he'd blame everything on her just to save his own skin.

"Oh, all right, you queebo wimp. Let's go."

Jackie ignored her name-calling, glad that she wasn't going to drag him into the woods, in search of a *river,* no less! What if they fell in? He didn't know how to swim. *They'd drown!* He shivered at the thought of it and started following Jen down the road again, looking for anything to drop as markers. Not watching where he was going, he promptly bumped into his sister.

"What are you doing?" she asked with a cold stare.

"I'm all out of stones," he replied looking back, trying to see the last one he'd dropped.

"Duh!" Jennifer said with disgust. "We're on a *road,* stupid. Besides, we're practically home. Look. There's that house we found the sign for: GRIMM MEMORIALS."

The place where they burn dead people, Jackie remembered Jen telling him. He looked to where she was pointing and could see the very same turret window of a tower on an old Victorian house through the tops of the trees ahead that he had seen on the first day in the woods with Jen.

"Let's go." Jennifer started off down the road in the direction of the house. Jackie had to run to keep up with her.

The road, which had been fairly wide and sunny through most of the woods, got very narrow, and the thick overhang of trees blocked out the sun more and more the closer they got to Grimm Memorials. The rush of the Connecticut River, still hidden in the woods to their left, was louder.

The road rose, then dipped suddenly and went through a thicky overgrown gully. The bushes were as tall as some of the trees and hung over the road like menacing spirits. The ground became muddy and Jackie could see several large earthworms squirming in it. In the middle of the gully, an open wooden bridge spanned a ten-foot-wide stream flowing to the river.

"Look," Jennifer cried, her eyes lighting up with mischief as she gave her brother a sly, teasing look. "It's a troll bridge. You have to pay the troll to get over."

Jackie stopped in his tracks. "You mean pay the *toll,* don't you?"

Jennifer laughed tauntingly. "You pay whatever lives under the bridge. Now, what do you think lives under a *troll bridge?"*

Jackie looked at the bridge, then at his sister. His breathing speeded up and his throat went dry. "Cut it out, Jen. 'Member what Mom said."

"I'm only kidding," she said nonchalantly, then froze, staring intently at the bridge.

"What's wrong?" Jackie asked, frightened by her theatrics.

"Did you see that?" she said mysteriously.

"Cut it out, Jen," Jackie pouted.

"For a minute there I thought I saw . . ." Jennifer paused for dramatic effect, then screamed the rest wildly as she galloped over the bridge, "a *troll!"* She reached the other side and went up and over the gully's edge, disappearing into the woods.

Her sneakers had thudded on the wood of the bridge so

loudly, like gunshots to Jackie's ears, that any hope he'd had that if there was something under there it might be asleep, quickly disappeared. His heart hammered in his chest, his fear growing, as he looked at the bridge.

The forest grew suddenly quiet; the birds stopped singing and the sound of the river seemed far, far away. A cloud passed over the sun, deepening the shadows created by the overgrown bushes and trees. The bottom of the gully became a murky place, and to Jackie's eye the murkiest part was the bridge.

Jackie looked up at the tower window of the house where they burned dead people and shuddered. It was easy to imagine it as the baleful eye on the jutting head of some great monster lying in wait in the woods ahead. Imagining this kind of thing was normal for Jackie, but feeling, in a deeply instinctive way, that it was somehow *true* was definitely more than his overactive imagination at work.

Jackie stepped back out of sight of the window peeking through the tops of the trees. He looked back the way they'd come, but no matter how much he wanted to get away from the bridge and that house, he knew he couldn't go back that way by himself. Going all the way through the woods and facing Route 47 without Jen was out of the question.

He turned to the bridge again. He knew Jen was only teasing him and that there was nothing to be afraid of—he could tell himself that at least. It didn't help the fact that, as usual, she had succeeded in scaring him. Knowing that he was in view of that cyclopean window didn't help, either. He looked beyond the bridge, scanning the top of the gully where the road twisted away out of sight. He figured Jen was hiding up there now, spying to see what he would do and getting ready to jump out and frighten him one more time when he got safely across the bridge.

"There are no such things as trolls," he said softly but with little conviction. A thought, like a foreign voice popped up in the back of his head. Quietly but clearly it said, *Don't let the troll hear you say that.* He immediately looked up at the window of Grimm Memorials as if the thought had somehow come from there. A chill seeped into his bowels and he found himself reaching instinctively for his penis the way he always had, since infancy, when he was frightened or nervous.

"Come on, Jackie. We haven't got all day," Jennifer called from not too far away, by the sound of her voice.

Trying to keep from looking up at the window, Jackie walked slowly forward to the edge of the bridge. The smell of the wood was fragrant, but nauseating at the same time; the spice of the wood was sweet, yet it was diseased with the damp scent of mildew and rot. The boards were old but looked safe enough.

Jackie stared at the dark cracks between the boards, straining to see if anything was moving under there and fervently hoping there wasn't. Did the dust swirling lightly on the boards indicate the presence of something huge just beneath, its anxious breathing barely contained as it lay in wait for him, or was he just imagining it? He had a sudden urge to look at the window of Grimm Memorials but fought it.

Just get across the bridge and away from here, he thought.

There's something under the bridge!

One of the boards had moved. Right in the middle of the bridge, a lone board had popped up and down as if some monstrous thing had rubbed against it from beneath. Deciding to take no chances, Jackie walked upstream a little way, keeping his eyes on the underside of the bridge. He went as far as he could through the thick brambles growing at the stream's edge and saw for himself that there was nothing under the bridge. As if on cue, the birds started singing again, the sun came out of the clouds, and the roaring sound of the nearby river returned.

What are you afraid of? There are no such things as trolls. The thought, like an adult voice, reassured Jackie. "You're right," he said aloud in answer to himself. He took a deep breath. Should he charge across the way Jen had? What if he slipped and fell? Splinters! No. He'd show Jen he wasn't a queebo wimp. He'd take it nice and easy, like he was enjoying it.

He started across, hands in pocket, head down—no matter how brave he was feeling, he still didn't want to look up at that window again. He remained calm and didn't walk too fast, but kept right in the middle of the bridge. He found himself glancing nervously at the sides and mentally scolded himself. Hadn't he seen with his own eyes that there was nothing under the bridge? And "seeing is believing" was something he'd heard his stepfather say more than once.

To keep his mind off it, Jackie scanned the other end of the bridge. There was a large, gnarled oak tree that grew out of the top of the gully bank, half its roots exposed like strange wooden intestines. He made the tree his goal; if he could make it to there he was safe and only had to worry about Jennifer jumping out at him. When she did, he wouldn't move a muscle. He'd show her!

A board behind him creaked loudly. Jackie immediately told himself that it was because he had just stepped on it, but he quickened his pace anyway. Water splashed nearby, maybe from under the bridge. A fish, Jackie reasoned. Twenty steps to go to safety. More water splashed, definitely from under the bridge this time. This didn't sound like any fish; it sounded like legs slushing through deep water.

The next board he stepped on pushed *up* under his foot as if something underneath was straining to break through. A low growl from under the bridge chilled him to his bowels, making him so terrified that he almost went to the bathroom, numbers one *and* two, right there.

Jackie broke into a run. His facade of bravery was over. At the first thump of his feet on the boards, there was a tremendous bellowing from under the bridge. The boards beneath him shuddered with the volume of it.

"Pay the troll! Pay the troll!" a monstrous voice demanded.

It sounded like a cross between an elephant and a dog, if either of those animals could talk.

Jackie's feet felt like they were no longer attached to his body. The tree of safety seemed to be farther away than it was before. Directly beneath him, something wet and heavy slapped against the wood nearly knocking him off his feet. Somehow he managed to maintain his balance and run on, his legs moving as if he was running under water.

Something grabbed the side of the bridge. He looked. It was a gigantic hand, its skin blue-gray like that of meat gone bad. It reached up from under the bridge and slapped down on the boards a few feet in front of and to the side of him. A monstrous head, as big as a tractor trailer tire, emerged. Its eyes were huge beneath three horns sticking out from a tangle of greasy long red hair at both temples and from the middle of its forehead. Its mouth was as large as a manhole cover. Inside, it was studded with spiked teeth several inches long that still held the reeking remains of dead flesh from its last meal. Its nose was flat and caked with snot, wet and dried.

"Pay the troll," the creature growled. The rest of it was rising from under the bridge now. Jackie couldn't pump his legs anymore; the connection between his legs and brain had been sabotaged by fear. He stopped and stared in horror as the creature, nine feet tall, emerged. Its hair hung to its scabious shoulders, and swinging from its chest were two huge, veiny blue breasts with dark purplish black nipples.

"Pay the troll! I've got to feed my baby," the creature cried.

It's a mummy troll, Jackie realized. For one terrifying second, the troll looked like his mother, then his bladder let go and he wet his pants good before he got it under control again by clutching at his crotch and pinching off the flow. The hot liquid on his legs stimulated them and he leapt forward in a mad dash to get by the creature.

The troll's arm, two yards long, swept toward him. Its

hand was four-fingered, each finger ending in a rapier claw. There was another claw, which was more of a spike, jutting from the heel of its palm.

We'd love to have you down for dinner, the she-troll said, her strange, horrible voice suddenly inside his head. Her words left a residue behind, like a light mist that got thicker and thicker, making Jackie sleepier and sleepier. All of a sudden it seemed like a good idea to just lie down and give up.

The she-troll's hand clutched at his ankle and he was jolted awake. He yanked his foot away, kicking it forward the way a halfback does to avoid a hand tackle from behind. One of its clawed fingers caught on the cuff of his blue jeans, ripping through it as he jerked his foot away.

"Je-e-en!" He screamed for his sister with all his might. Behind him, the bridge groaned and creaked as if under a sudden great weight. Jackie looked back. The troll had climbed onto the bridge. Her arms and legs were covered with a thick reddish hair like that on her head. The hair from her crotch grew over her stomach and up over her ribs. The shape of her body, with its long spindly arms and legs and swollen bulbous torso, reminded Jackie of a picture he'd once seen of a tarantula.

"Come back little boy," the troll roared. The air moved around him and he could feel her voice vibrating in his bones. "You forgot to pay the troll." She grinned, yellow saliva running from the corner of her mouth, dripping from her chin, and snaked out both arms for him as she lunged forward.

Jackie timed his leap to avoid her but guessed wrong. She managed to wrap one hand around his left shin. He screamed as he felt her claws dig into him and the horn spike in her palm pierce his leg to the bone. She tripped him up, sending him sprawling forward on his chest, his hands outstretched, on the dirt at the edge of the bridge. Immediately, the troll began dragging him back.

"Come pay the troll," she said sloppily through a mouth

watering hungrily with gobs of saliva. "Treat me to dinner," she added, chuckling and gurgling.

Jackie clutched at stones and at the wooden end of the bridge but could find nothing substantial to hold onto to keep himself from sliding inexorably back. The pain in his left leg was excruciating. He could feel hot blood flowing over his ankles, soaking his socks and filling his Reeboks. With panic and the pain in his leg threatening to take his senses away, Jackie realized he had one chance to save himself. Using the last of his quickly failing strength, Jackie pushed himself painfully to a standing position and pressed his good foot down on the leathery arm grabbing his leg. He stepped on it with all his might, scraping the troll's arm harshly against the splintery old boards of the bridge.

The troll screamed horribly as daggers of wood pierced her inhuman flesh. Jackie glanced back for a second and saw that a long, spiked splinter had impaled the monster's wrist. Green blood bubbled from the wound, flowing in abundance over the troll's hand and down its arm. Howling in anguish and rage, the troll let go of him.

Jackie scrambled off the bridge on his belly, dragging his mangled leg behind him. He struggled to his feet, nearly passing out from the pain, and hopped headlong up the embankment on his good leg. At the top of the gully, he lunged right into his sister, Jennifer.

"*Run!*" he screamed at her, his face pale with fear.

She laughed at him.

"*Run!*" he screamed again, pointing back at the bridge.

She kept laughing.

Jackie looked back in mortal terror that quickly turned to confusion. The bridge was empty behind him. "The troll . . ." he mumbled.

"You pissed your pants," Jennifer cried and laughed harder, pointing at the wet stain that covered his crotch and ran down both legs to his knees.

Jackie looked at his sister and teetered on his feet as if his balance had suddenly deserted him. The pain in his leg swelled and shot through his entire body making him cry out. His face paled, draining completely of color. The pain knocked him down and he landed hard on his fanny. A wave of nausea washed over him forcing him to turn away and lose lunch in the bushes at the side of the road.

Jennifer stopped laughing and looked with concern at her little brother. "Are you okay?" she asked.

Jackie let another wave of nausea pass before he could speak. "My leg . . . The troll . . . it came out . . . it almost got me. It cut my leg." He pointed at his leg where the troll had grabbed him, puncturing his skin with its claws, but the rips in his jeans and the soaking blood were gone. He grabbed his pant leg and pulled it up. His leg was okay. The flesh was untouched; there was no pain now, no blood bubbling out of the holes in his flesh because there *were no holes in his flesh any longer.*

"You have got the craziest imagination. Can't you tell by now when I'm kidding you?" She put her hand on Jackie's shoulder. She was quickly realizing that she had pushed him too far.

"I knew you were kidding," Jackie said, his face gray, his voice trembling with emotion, "but the troll was there anyway! It kept saying, 'Pay the troll! Pay the troll!' over and over again." Tears rolled down his cheeks and dripped from his chin. He began trembling, his teeth chattering uncontrollably.

Jennifer sat next to her brother and hugged him. "You dope," she said with a mixture of fondness and amusement. "That was no troll saying that, it was *me*! Just me. I'm sorry. I didn't realize you were so scared."

CHAPTER 12

There once was an old woman sat spinning

Eleanor Grimm rested her head against the glass of the tower window. She was exhausted. She hadn't had a day this busy since Edmund's death. Below her, in the little clearing of trees near the old wooden bridge Edmund had built nearly twenty years ago, she watched the girl named Jennifer take her crying brother back to the bridge, forcing him to look under it to show him there was nothing there.

Eleanor smiled weakly and her lower lip began to quiver. She never ceased to be amazed with the Machine. She didn't know how, but once she made telepathic contact with someone, the Machine kept that contact going even when Eleanor was out of range or asleep. The Machine could keep dozens of people dancing to her thoughts, both conscious and subconscious, like marionettes until she had no further use for them.

What had just happened at the bridge had been of extreme importance for her plans. She'd been trying to decide what would be the perfect moment and the best way to establish contact with the boy and girl who had moved into the house at the end of her road. She had plenty of time before Halloween, but she wanted to be sure she had her hooks deep into them by then. Her little game with the boy had achieved some contact, and had served to test his willpower.

The funny thing was that without the Machine, she would have missed them out there all together. She had been feeling very sick; the chest and arm pains had returned and though the nitroglycerin pills had helped, she still felt like there was a half-ton weight sitting on her chest. She had been on her way to lie down, after putting the twins in the cage with Davy Torrez when she'd found herself climbing the narrow stairway to the tower room before she even realized what she was doing. When she got there and heard the thoughts of the children in the woods, and identified them, she understood that the Machine had arranged it all, including preventing their mother from picking them up at school so they would be forced to walk home and choose to go through the woods, directly by Grimm Memorials. The rest had been up to her.

She'd always had a special way with children. Edmund's powers may have been stronger—his derisive laughter echoed through the house—and he was certainly smarter than Eleanor, but he didn't have the knack with children that she had. Eleanor had discovered that children are much more survivalist than adults. In Edmund's case the Machine worked against him. He was too eager and children seemed to be able to sense that in him, because he wasn't patient enough to entice and coax and dig inside a child's mind to find ways to win its trust, or find its secret fear.

It was Edmund who had sought out the black-market baby-and-children dealers to supply them with fresh meat for their rituals. For their daily diet, they mostly depended on flesh taken from clients of the mortuary. They became very adept at stripping a body of its meat, yet making it presentable for viewing at a wake. Edmund resorted to letting Eleanor lure children only when they had exhausted all other sources, including an organization of perverted professionals known as NAMBLA, which stood for the North American

Man/Boy Love Alliance. This organization ran a series of "boy houses," which were really meat markets for men to buy young boys for their sexual pleasure. Edmund joined the group and was one of their best customers, paying thousands of dollars a year for boys until he died. Unfortunately, for Eleanor, they didn't allow women to join or make purchases. Instead she had to rely on her own ingenuity, and had done very well for herself.

Eleanor loved seducing a child's mind. She seemed to draw as much nourishment from probing the depths of a young child's mind as she did from devouring its succulent, sweet flesh. The fact that, due to her mad mother's influence, she knew all the well-known fairy tales and nursery rhymes, and in many ways was still a child herself, made it easy for her to slip inside a child and draw it to her like a moth to a flame. She loved luring a child with a happy image pulled from the child's mind, then toying with the image, playing on the child's joys and fears. Edmund and she had learned early in life the pleasure of inducing fear and pain. The intense fear children generated, which could never be matched by an adult, brought her near orgasmic pleasure.

Eleanor shivered suddenly and the quivering in her lower lip became more pronounced. Her hands began to tremble and her teeth chattered even though it was very warm in the tower room. Below, the girl and boy continued on their way and were now passing the front of the house. The girl kept looking up and talking, but the boy kept his head down and walked quickly past. Eleanor listened to their contrasting thoughts go by and head off down the road through the woods toward their home.

The boy might be trouble. She hadn't expected him to react the way he had on the bridge. He was supposed to just give in, like all the other children always had. Since the first time she'd seen him outside Roosevelt's Bar in Amherst, she'd sensed something in him that she'd never found in other children: an acute awareness of danger that amounted almost to a sixth sense. She'd have to find some very special way to catch him, but she was sure the Machine would come up with something when the time was right. It had never failed her before.

You should have taken him now while you had the chance! Edmund's voice echoed out of the gloom around her. *But then you never were too smart.* He laughed at her.

Smart enough, Eleanor thought. I'm still alive and you're dead, aren't you, Edmund? No answer.

Everything is going according to plan, no matter what Edmund thinks (and he's dead, anyway), she told herself just before a white-hot light exploded behind her eyes. A severe, bone-rattling tremor ran through her entire body and she began to shake to the point of vibrating, as though she were strapped to a reducing machine. Another burst of light exploded in her brain, spreading through her head, down her neck, and through the rest of her body, sending her spinning down into the bottomless pit called unconsciousness.

"What's he doing?" she whispers to Edmund in the darkness. They are in the casket elevator that runs between the chapel on the first floor and the crematorium in the basement. It is their favorite hiding place. She looks at her brother peering through the crack of the elevator door's hinges. He appears to be no more than five or six years old and suddenly she remembers.

He's gonna 'balm her, *Edmund says in her head. She crouches beside her brother and peers through the crack also. They are looking at the crematorium, which also functions as the embalming room. On the metal embalming table, with its gutters, drains, and specimen-collecting bottle, is a naked woman. Her skin is tinged a pale, cold blue. Next to the table stands their father wearing a full-length white smock and rubber gloves.*

Is she dead? *Eleanor silently asks her brother. She doesn't know why, but she doesn't want her father to catch them hiding there.*

Of course, stupid, *Edmund replies.*

Father bends over the corpse, grasping the woman's shoulders with both hands. Slowly he slides his hands down her arms, then over her belly and up until he is squeezing her dead breasts. His hands work her breasts roughly, kneading and pulling, tweaking the pale nipples and rolling them between his fingers, pinching them so hard that Eleanor winces in the darkness.

Father is breathing heavily. Beads of sweat dot his forehead though it is cool in the room. His right hand leaves its breast and slides down between the dead woman's legs while the left one continues to maul her other breast.

His right hand begins to slide faster and faster between her legs. Father's breathing speeds up, matching the rhythm of his hand. With a suppressed giggle, Eleanor notices that the front of father's apron is sticking out as though he had something hidden under it.

Suddenly, Father stops his stroking and bends over the woman's head. He grasps her face with his right hand, puts his lips to the dead woman's and kisses her passionately. He steps back and, with one quick motion, tears the smock from his body. He is naked underneath. His long, wrinkled penis juts out from his body and bobs up and down. His breathing is loud in the room, drowning out all other sounds. He climbs onto the table, sitting on the corpse's chest. He grabs her head and holds it up, letting the lower jaw fall open. Inching forward, he pushes himself into the cold dead mouth.

When it is over and father has covered the body and gone upstairs, Edmund and Eleanor let themselves out of the elevator and go to the embalming table. Edmund pulls back the sheet and looks at the woman's face. It is bruised and mottled and the mouth hangs open far too wide for a normal mouth. He reaches up and tries to close it, but it falls open again and a trickle of thick white fluid runs out one corner of it.

"Let's play like daddy did," Edmund says softly to Eleanor. "You be the dead lady."

It was dark when Eleanor woke. From where she lay on the floor, legs spread-eagle, her left arm trapped under her, her right one splayed out to one side, she could see stars winking through the room's sole window. She didn't know how long she'd been out. The attack had been a bad one. Her mind was still foggy and she could barely remember what she had dreamed, something about her father and Edmund. The Machine was playing the thoughts of those caught in her web so faintly she had to strain to hear them.

She pulled her arm out from under her. It was numb and she rubbed it until needles and pins made her wince. She looked out the window. The moon wasn't out yet, which told her it was early evening, and the fact that she hadn't soiled herself meant that she hadn't been there more than a few hours.

After much effort, she sat up in the darkness. Her legs were stiff and they throbbed with the pain of arthritis. After much hard rubbing and massaging, she was able to loosen up her legs enough to get to her knees and crawl to the window. Grunting, she forced it open and stuck her head out, breathing deeply of the cool night air.

As her head cleared, the Machine grew louder. The thoughts of the twins in the crematorium cage swelled to a cacophony drowning out all the others. Thoughts of food were prominent in their minds, overriding even fear for the moment. Eleanor smiled to herself. She just *loved* the way kids' minds worked.

It took Eleanor forty-nine minutes to get down to the kitchen from the tower room at the top of the house. Her legs felt rubbery and, for several seconds when she first stood, they felt completely liquid. She walked a step at a time, steadying herself on the walls and clinging to the stair railings with both hands as she descended three floors.

The hungry thoughts of the starving twins in the crematorium filled the Machine, pushing out everything else. Her ears began to throb and the throbbing became a pounding pain in her head. She had to stop several times and sit on the stairs for fear that the thundering voices in her head would make her pass out. Every thought was a slashing pain between her temples, cutting her brain to pieces.

A memory came with the pain and she saw herself, two years old, experiencing the same thing that was happening now. The voices of her demented mother, stoic father, and domineering brother had become a tumultuous riot of torturing noise in her mind. It had been building for a long time because, unlike Edmund, she had not yet learned how to tune out the thought-voices in the Machine. Eventually, it became a matter of keeping her sanity, of *surviving*, that forced her to learn how to do it.

Do it now, she willed herself. Through the pain, she imagined that the booming thoughts were a wall. She pictured herself pushing against the wall until it slid back a few inches. The thoughts diminished slightly. She pushed again. The wall moved. The voices grew quieter. The pain in her head slowed its frantic beating. The thought-voices were at a low level now, manageable. Just behind the hungry children's demanding thoughts were the troubled minds of the Nailer family members.

She pulled herself to her feet and staggered down the last steps to the second floor. Eleanor smiled weakly. Once again the Machine had shifted gear, running on according to plan. It was good that the Machine ran even when there was no one at the controls; Eleanor had barely been at the controls at all lately.

The next flight of stairs was much easier to manage. Eleanor was feeling stronger now, drawing new strength from the Machine. She made it all the way to the first floor and the kitchen with only one stop.

In the kitchen, Eleanor took a huge stainless steel pot from the cabinet and placed it on the stove. From the refrigerator, she took a can of lard and several large aluminum-wrapped packages and placed them on the kitchen table. Above the stove, on a rack, hung a meat cleaver, which she retrieved and placed on the table next to the foil-wrapped packages.

She scooped a good amount of lard into the pot and turned the burner on underneath it. As it began to sizzle, she unwrapped the packages, picked up the cleaver, and went to work chopping their contents for stew. As she chopped, several small fingers flew from the table and rolled on the floor. She left them for the dog.

As soon as they heard Eleanor on the stairs, the twins in the cage stopped the whimpering they'd been soothing each other with since their capture. When she opened the door and entered the crematorium they retreated to the back of the cage and hugged each other tightly. Davy Torrez, who, in shock, had remained curled up in a fetal position in the same spot in the rear left corner of the cage, didn't move. Davy's mind had decided to opt out for a while and take a little vacation away from the horrors of his situation. But now, as Eleanor approached, and he felt her evil presence like a cold draft in his head fear began pulling him back to reality and made him aware once more of his surroundings.

Eleanor carried a tray into the room and placed it on the large metal embalming table. Steam rose from the bowls on the tray and filled the room with the succulent aroma of stewed meat. It set the boys' mouths to watering. The twins disengaged themselves from each other's arms and moved cautiously forward, sniffing like animals lured to a hunter's fire. Against his will, Davy Torrez's mouth watered, too, but at the same time the smell of the stew (pease porridge hot!) made his stomach queasy.

On the tray were three large bowls of piping hot stew, bread, a pitcher of milk, glasses, and a box of Devil Dogs. Before opening the cage and placing the tray of food inside, Eleanor removed a small packet of powder from her dress pocket and dumped it into the pitcher of milk.

Normally, she wouldn't have had to drug the children, she could have relied on the Machine to keep each child in a blissful dream state, but in her weakened condition she wasn't at all sure the Machine wouldn't break down at some point. The weakness of the Machine when she had awakened from her latest palsy attack had frightened her. She decided it was safer to keep the captive children quiet with small doses of ground sleeping pills or tranquilizers mixed in their daily milk than risk them coming fully awake to the reality of their situation and wasting away in shock the way Davy Torrez was, and the way the Hall boy before him had.

Edmund had been a connoisseur of drugs, both legal and otherwise, and had always kept a well-stocked supply of every drug he could get his hands on. As she dropped the sleeping powder into the milk, Eleanor caught Davy Torrez watching her, but he immediately closed his eyes and feigned unconsciousness again.

"Eat, little ones, eat everything," Eleanor cooed.

Davy opened his eyes. He couldn't get out of his mind the image of the little boy with no arms, no legs, and (Oh Mommy!) no peepee. The boy was no longer in the cage.

The better for stew!

"Eat up like good little boys, and your mommy will be here soon to take you home," Eleanor cooed to the twins. They needed little encouragement to eat and attacked the food voraciously.

Davy Torrez looked up at her with renewed terror in his

eyes and something else—revulsion. He felt her thoughts enter his mind with a message the twins couldn't hear: *Eat or you'll be in the stew next!*

The twins paused from their eating as Eleanor left the room, but didn't stop for long. Hunger had overwhelmed fear for the time being and they filled their bellies, oblivious to anything else.

DON'T EAT THE STEW! Davy wanted to scream at them. IT'S MADE OUT OF A LITTLE BOY WHOSE ARMS, LEGS, AND PEEPEE WERE CUT OFF! But his mind was setting off on that long dark road again. The few moments of horrifying reality it had just witnessed had convinced it to go back to the safety of deep shock and forgetfulness. Don't eat the stew, he thought, weakly, one more time and went under.

The twins ate everything on the tray.

CHAPTER 13

Girls and boys, come out to play.

Jackie sat at his desk in the middle of the third row, copying letters from a primer. The tip of his tongue stuck from the corner of his mouth as he practiced his printing, but his mind was not on his work; the events of yesterday kept intruding. From the moment he'd tried to cross the troll bridge, he'd felt as though he'd been thrust into a living nightmare. Jen's proving to him that there was no troll under the bridge, and that he had caught his foot on a tree root, had done nothing to make him feel any better. If anything, he felt worse. He knew what he had seen had not been his imagination, but then, what was it?

It had taken Jen a long time to calm him down after they'd left the gully. If he hadn't been so embarrassed about wetting his pants, he would have run right home and told his mother what Jen had done to him. Instead, he traded not telling on her for her help in sneaking him into the house and hiding his incontinence.

They had no trouble sneaking into the house; Diane was taking a nap and Steve was working in his study. Neither of them said anything to their parents about not being picked up at school. Jennifer told Jackie not to bring it up because then they would be questioned about how they got home and they'd get in trouble, not to mention that his parents would find out about his "accident." Jennifer took Jackie's pants into the laundry room right away and washed them with a load of dirty clothes that were piled next to the washing machine. Jackie had crept upstairs to their room and put on a clean, dry pair.

After that, they'd hung around; Jen reading in their bedroom and Jackie sitting in front of the television with the Care Bears and then the Smurfs on, but not really watching them. No matter how he tried, he wasn't able to rid himself of the image of the troll, or the memory of the pain in his leg, or the nauseating, paralyzing fear in his stomach. Several times during the afternoon he'd felt sick enough to puke but fought it down. Around four, his mother got up and started making supper.

The meal was a quiet one; his mother and stepfather didn't say a word to each other throughout dinner. Jackie could sense a tension between them that had never been there before. He was also acutely aware, as was an angry Jen, that both parents were oblivious to having forgotten to pick them up at school. After all their lecturing about safety, it seemed that neither of them cared how they had gotten home, or what might have happened to them on the way.

Jackie had picked at his food listlessly throughout dinner, bothered by his parent's indifference and unable to forget the horrifying events of that afternoon. When dinner was over, Steve immediately left the table and went back to his study while his mother cleared the table and loaded the dishwasher, completely ignoring him and Jen.

Jennifer had finished her meal and was about to go in the living room and watch TV when Jackie lost it. He'd done his best to hold it in, to try and forget what had happened, but when his parents never even offered an explanation of not picking them up at school, Jackie feared they no longer cared. And if they didn't care, who would take care of him?

Unable to control his tears, he tried to hide them by bending his head over the table as the tears flowed down his cheeks and dropped off his face onto the vinyl tablecloth.

Jennifer had quickly glanced at their mother, but her back was to them as she rinsed glasses before putting them in the dishwasher. Jen turned back to him and whispered fiercely, "What's wrong with you?"

Jackie gulped hard, but wasn't able to answer her without letting all his tears out.

"Stop it!" Jennifer hissed, but Jackie hadn't been able to help it. The horror of what had happened had tortured him until he could hold it in no longer; the floodgates had opened.

"What are you two up to?" their mother had asked then in a tone of voice that said she didn't want an answer, she wanted them to stop whatever it was they were doing.

An uncontrollable, tearful sob that had been building with Jackie's silent tears began to emit from his compressed lips in a high-pitched whine.

"Cut it out," Jen said, low and threatening.

Like air leaking from a punctured balloon, the sound from Jackie had continued, getting louder as it wheezed out of him.

Their mother whirled around from the sink and glared at them. "What are you doing to him?" she asked accusingly of Jen.

Jackie hiccuped and sneezed and snot ran out his nose and onto his lips. Unable to control himself any longer he opened his mouth and wailed loudly.

"What's wrong with you?" his mother had snapped, making him cry all the harder. She had never snapped at him like that before when he cried.

His mother had seemed suddenly to realize that, too. She shook her head and passed a hand over her eyes. "I'm sorry, Jackie," she said with emotion and an apologetic look at both of them. She came to the table and pulled Jackie into her arms. In return, he had buried his face in her neck thankful for some affection at last. "What's wrong, hon, did something happen at school today?"

"He's okay," Jen had piped up nervously. "He's probably just overtired."

"Yes, or maybe you were scaring him again?" his mother asked suspiciously. A guilty look immediately crossed Jen's face. "How many times do I have to tell you? You know what his imagination is like.

Jackie cried louder then because he really hadn't wanted to get Jen in trouble.

In defense, Jennifer had let her anger and frustration out, saying what both of them had felt. "He wouldn't have been scared if you had picked us up at school today like you said you would. We had to walk home because we missed our bus waiting for you, and you don't even care. We could have been kidnapped by the crazy child-killer and it would have been all your fault." Jennifer had burst into tears then herself, pushing away from the table and running upstairs.

"I told . . . Steve to pick you up," his mother had mumbled vaguely as if she couldn't quite remember.

Jackie had decided then and there to spill his guts and tell his mother what he saw in the woods, but she abruptly got up, put him down, and left the room, going upstairs also. Seconds later, Jackie heard her arguing loudly with Steve about why he hadn't gone after them when she'd asked him to. Jackie was left sobbing in the kitchen, blaming himself for causing everyone so much trouble.

Jackie pressed his pencil so hard on the paper while practicing his G's that the lead snapped, bringing him out of his thoughts.

"Alright, children," Mrs. McDuffy announced in her PAY ATTENTION voice. "It's five minutes to our afternoon recess. Time to put our desks in order."

Jackie swept the erasure crumbs off his desk and lifted

the top, placing his paper and pencil inside. Two rows over, Betty Boone was talking to Timmy Walsh. Jackie closed his desk top and watched Betty. He thought she was cute and had a crush on her.

From the front of the room, Mrs. McDuffy cleared her throat and gave Timmy and Betty a look of warning. Timmy immediately closed his mouth and Betty turned around, facing the front of the room. Mrs. McDuffy was not one to be disobeyed. As Betty turned, she saw Jackie looking at her. She made a clucking noise and stuck her tongue out at him in the ultimate little-girl put-down. Jackie looked away, his face hot with embarrassment.

The recess bell rang and Jackie pushed himself out of his seat. He shuffled out from between the rows of desks and chairs and ran with the other children to the door. "No running," Mrs. McDuffy commanded loudly. The children heeded, at least until they were out the door, then they ran shrieking and laughing into the schoolyard.

Afternoon recess was the only break in the day that Jackie wished were over sooner. The reason was that after recess came the reading hour in Mrs. McDuffy's class. Jackie loved reading and was the best reader in A group. The class was divided into three reading groups: A group, superior readers; B group, above average; and C group, average. Jackie was such a good reader that Mrs. McDuffy sometimes let him read to the B and C groups as an example of good reading.

The playground was bathed in sunlight and filled with chattering, playing children. Jackie made his way through the groups of girls talking and playing jump rope, and boys roughhousing and teasing the girls. He went to the jungle gym near the chainlink fence that ran around the perimeter of the school's grounds.

Jackie climbed quickly and easily to the top of the gym and sat there, legs anchored securely around the top two crossbars. From this perch, he scanned the playground for his sister. As of that morning, she had still been mad at him for getting her in trouble and hadn't said a word to him on the bus (Steve had informed them the night before, after his argument with Diane, that they should take the bus to and from school from now on).

The schoolyard was huge, encompassing softball, baseball, football, and soccer fields at the far end, which the nearby regional high school and middle school used, but the children let out for recess from the elementary school were confined to the area directly in front of the school. First, third, and fifth grades had the first morning and afternoon recess; second, fourth, and sixth grades had the second. Being a regional school, the recesses had to be staggered due to the large number of children attending.

Jackie scanned the column of kids still exiting from the fifth-grade door. He couldn't see his sister. Suddenly she appeared at the door and Jackie waved his arms frantically at her, shouting her name across the playground. He was sure she saw him—she looked right at him—but she turned away and went to the other end of the yard to where a crowd of girls from her class were standing around talking.

Jackie sighed and slumped down on the bars, letting his butt hang between them. Jen was obviously still angry with him, and that really bothered him. Jennifer was his only friend. In Boston, his mother had never let him play outdoors without Jennifer, and since there were no kids in the neighborhood his age, he always ended up hanging around with her. Things hadn't changed much now that they were in the country because he couldn't seem to make friends with any of the kids in his class.

He knew his failure to make friends was his own fault, but he couldn't help it. Yesterday, the first day of school, he'd started talking to a classmate and without meaning to, had started telling him a fantastic story about UFO's flying over his house. When the kid had called him a liar, Jackie had insisted it was true. The kid had told others in the class and soon everyone knew and was looking at him strangely.

It was ironic (though Jackie didn't know what irony was, he still had a keen sense of it) that now that he had a true story to tell about the troll, no one would believe him. It was like the story of the boy who cried wolf; no one would believe him because he had lied before. Even if he hadn't lied, he couldn't blame anyone for not believing him; the more he thought about it, the more trouble he had believing it himself.

A sudden squeal of surprise and excited laughter behind him tugged him away from his self-pitying thoughts. Betty Boone and Timmy Walsh were standing under a couple of elm trees near the fence, about fifteen feet away. Jackie strained to see what they were looking at, something up the street, but the trees blocked his view.

Above the noise of the children in the playground, Jackie realized he could hear another sound. It was a flute, trickling a melody on the wind. The sound grew louder and the figure producing it came into view down Finch Street heading for the schoolyard.

Jackie couldn't believe his eyes. The man playing the flute was tall. His pointed felt cap with a feather stuck in its red band made him appear even taller. The feather was yellow, the hat was green, as was the rest of his fringed leather outfit. Jackie looked around at the other kids in the playground to see if they saw it, too, but they were playing and going on as though they heard or saw nothing. Only Betty Boone and Timmy Walsh, besides Jackie, saw. Jackie called to them but they didn't hear him. They were too enthralled with the music.

Jackie looked at the flute player and at first thought he looked like Robin Hood, what with his pointed felt moccasins and green tights on his legs. It wasn't until he saw what was tagging along behind him, that Jackie understood who he really was. He played his flute, pranced around on the asphalt, and right on his heels, following every step and gyration of his body, every note from his flute, their tiny eyes glistening blackly, their needle teeth protruding over their lower jaws, came a mega-hoard of rats.

Betty and Timmy cheered and called to the Pied Piper. They ran to the gate at the end of the playground. Jackie felt a sudden intense fear. He crouched, then climbed down into the center of the jungle gym, where he was protected by the dome of bars. From this secure position, he watched the Pied Piper play Follow the Leader with the ocean of vermin all the way to the schoolyard gate.

Betty and Timmy pushed the gate open and rushed out to meet him. At the same moment, the Piper stopped playing and the rats disappeared. Betty and Timmy laughed and clapped their hands. The Piper put the pipe to his lips again and began to play a new song. Now it was Betty and Timmy's turn to dance to the piper's tune. Like marionettes they jumped and spun, dancing and laughing to every note the Piper played.

Jackie trembled with terror. The same intense feeling of unreality, of watching a dream inside his head, that he had felt on the troll bridge, washed over him. He crawled out from between the jungle-gym bars and walked toward the fence. Betty and Timmy were dancing down the street, following the Pied Piper.

Jackie dashed to the fence. "Betty! Timmy!" he cried.

The Piper blew a long, trilling note as he turned and looked at Jackie. He winked, lowered the flute from his lips, *and disappeared;* the Piper, Timmy, and Betty—all gone.

Jackie climbed to the top of the fence and searched the area where they'd just been. The street was empty. He could see nothing.

Jackie climbed down from the fence and ran to the open gate and out to the street. He searched in both directions. A short distance away on the right, just turning a corner of the schoolyard fence, was a tall, hunched figure in black carrying a large black laundry sack. The sack was moving as if something, or someone was inside it.

Timmy and Betty! Jackie opened his mouth to cry out for

one of the teachers to come quick, but the words never left his mouth. The hunched figure stopped at the corner and turned around. Jackie couldn't tell if it was a man or a woman. All he could see were the eyes looming huge and staring. Those eyes bore into him, seemed to crawl right inside his head and, like Mrs. McDuffy cleaning the chalkboard, erase all that he had seen.

By the time the bell rang to end recess, Jackie was back on the jungle gym and didn't remember a thing about the figure carrying the sack, which he had been certain contained Timmy and Betty. By that time, the whole incident with the Pied Piper was no longer a part of his memory.

When all the children were back in class, Mrs. McDuffy took a head count, discovering that Timmy Walsh and Betty Boone were missing. Teachers were sent to search the playground and school grounds and the children were questioned. None of them had seen anything.

When Timmy and Betty were not found in a search of school property, the sheriff was called in and each child in the first grade was questioned individually. When it came time for Jackie to be interviewed, he could tell them nothing. For a moment, he thought there was *something* that he had seen, that he should tell the sheriff's men about, but for the life of him he couldn't remember what it was. He also started to tell them about what had happened to him the day before in the woods near Grimm Memorials but now that incident seemed very fuzzy, and he wasn't sure if he had just dreamed it; everything was hazy and vague in his head like a dream fading and soon forgotten.

After the questioning, and some digging into the Walsh boy's and Boone girl's backgrounds, the sheriff's men decided they were dealing with a dual case of parental abduction. Both children's parents were divorced and their mothers were on welfare. In the case of the Boone girl, her father had abducted her once before, and Timmy Walsh's father had fought for custody of his son during divorce proceedings. An

APB was put out on both children's fathers, warrants for arrest were issued, and the public was assured by authorities that there was no connection between the two abductions and recent sensationalist media reports concerning the disappearance of children in the area.

CHAPTER 14

Old Mother Hubbard . . .

Eleanor opened the passenger door of the hearse and hefted the black sack onto the front seat. The ether-soaked rags she'd thrown in with the two children were doing their job and her two captives had stopped squirming. They would be sleeping for quite a while.

She closed the door and leaned against it. Her breathing became difficult and her heart was pounding loudly in her chest. A needle of pain slid through her left breast and she clutched at it. When the pain passed, she moved as quickly as possible to the other side of the car and got behind the wheel. She opened her pocketbook, removed her pillbox, and slipped one of the tiny pills under her tongue. While she waited for the pill to bring relief, she rested her head against the back of the seat.

A man in a business suit walked by, but didn't glance once at the odd-looking long, black hearse, or her, seemingly passed out behind the wheel. Eleanor watched him pass and listened to his mundane thoughts about some business contract he was worried about losing. She smiled. She hadn't even had to think about it; the man never saw her or the hearse, and neither would anyone else because the Machine had taken care of the situation by reflex, just as it had told her which two children in the playground had backgrounds that would make the police think their disappearance was a family matter.

The pill began to work and she took a deep breath. She leaned forward, started the hearse, put it in gear, and drove off. On the way home, Eleanor pulled into a Cumberland Farms store on Route 47. As she got out of the hearse, a sheriff's department car pulled in next to her.

Deputy Sheriff Ken Vitelli got out of his car and smiled at Eleanor. The petite old lady in the white lace dress and shawl reminded him of his favorite aunt, Lucille. He tipped his hat to her and nodded when she sweetly returned his smile. As she went into the store, he realized that her car was a Nash Rambler, the exact same kind of car his Aunt Lucille had owned.

"Imagine that," Deputy Vitelli mused aloud at the coincidence. He circled his patrol car and took a closer look. It was amazing; the car was just like Aunt Lucille's, right down to the fuzzy white steering wheel cover and the rosary beads hanging from the mirror. As he marvelled at it all, he noticed the black sack on the front seat. Poor lady, he thought, has to lug her laundry out to do it.

Deputy Vitelli went into the store eager to meet the old woman. He wanted to get a closer look at her and ask her where she had gotten the car, in the off chance that it was the same car his aunt had owned. Who knows, maybe the old woman had known his aunt! But once inside the store, he couldn't find her. The only other person in the store, besides the pimply faced young clerk, was a very fat woman of about thirty loading her arms up with Yodels, Devil Dogs, Twinkies, and candy bars.

Vitelli went outside. The Rambler was gone. In its place was a small white Toyota. He started over to look at it when he got a call on his radio to go to the Pioneer Valley Regional Elementary School to check out a report of missing children. As he got in his car, he gave the Toyota one last look and shrugged his shoulders. He didn't know how the old lady had gotten past him, but she had. He drove away, never noticing that the same black sack that had been on the Rambler's front seat was on the front seat of the Toyota.

Inside the store, Eleanor carried her armful of groceries to the counter and piled them there. She added a jar of Skippy peanut butter and several loaves of bread and stood, head bent, breathing deeply while the clerk rang it up.

"That'll be twenty-two dollars even," the clerk said picking at a pimple on his chin and glancing with ill-concealed disgust at the woman's obesity.

Eleanor rummaged in her bag, then held out her empty hand. The clerk took the twenty-dollar bill and two ones he saw there and put them in the cash register. Later that evening, when the manager came in to tally the register receipts, he would accuse the clerk of stealing twenty-two dollars and fire him.

Smiling to herself, Eleanor carried her groceries out of the store and placed them on the floor of the hearse below the sack on the front seat. The pain in her chest was returning. She knew she was doing too much, but it couldn't be helped. She took a bottle of tequila out of the glove compartment and took a swig. She sat back, trying to relax, and waited for the pain to subside, but it didn't. Though it didn't get any worse, it also didn't get any better; it just kept on at a steady, consistent hurt. After several minutes, when she realized the pain was not going to go away, she started the hearse and pulled out of the store lot.

She parked the hearse behind the house, close to the kitchen door and out of sight of the road. After a few moments of rest during which she finished the half-pint of tequila and dropped another pill *(bomb pills* is what Edmund had called the nitroglycerin tablets), she clutched at her bags of groceries and carried them in the kitchen door. The black sack remained unmoving on the seat.

Eleanor came out and retrieved the sack, dragging it inside with great pain and difficulty and left it by the refrigerator. From outside, the sound of loud barking startled her. She went to the back door and looked out. Mephisto, Edmund's massive St. Bernard/Pit Bull mixed mongrel was lunging wildly against his rope tied to the gnarled oak by the cemetery fence.

"Alright, alright," she called through the screen. "Old Mother Hubbard's coming to fetch her poor dog a bone." Mephisto lay down and whined, licking his chops in anticipation, as if he understood what she had just said. She shuffled to the refrigerator, pulled out a foil-wrapped package, and carried it outside.

Mephisto stood in anticipation as Eleanor approached. He worked his tongue over his teeth noisily, drool dripping from his jaws as he watched Eleanor peel off the foil. When she tossed his meal to him, he caught it in midair. He turned, holding the small, severed forearm tightly in his mouth, and trotted back to the shade of the oak tree where there still remained a pile of gnawed finger bones from an earlier meal. The small hand, sticking out of Mephisto's massive mouth, jiggled as he walked away and appeared to be waving.

Smiling, Eleanor waved back.

CHAPTER 15

What are little girls made of, made of?

The new captives were still unconscious from the ether when Eleanor wheeled the upstairs portable gurney out to the kitchen. It was a narrow metal table on wheels that collapsed flat on the ground, and lifted to an upright position with the aid of hydraulics. A body could be strapped to the gurney and be stood straight up by one person to be moved with ease through doorways. It, and another just like it that was kept in the crematorium, had been bought by Edmund to replace the ancient hoist their father had used to lift dead bodies into caskets, or onto the embalming table, or to lift caskets into the chapel elevator, or onto the conveyor belt that fed them into the crematorium's blast furnace.

She released the lever that collapsed the gurney to the floor, and slid the black sack onto it. It was relatively easy, with the help of the hydraulic legs on the gurney, to pick up the bodies so they could be pushed into the chapel. There the sack could be rolled into the elevator, and lowered with a minimum of effort.

When the sack was in the elevator, she closed the door and pressed the button sending it down to the crematorium. She followed by way of the stairs, resting at the bottom before she wheeled the second gurney out of its storage cabinet and pushed it over to the elevator. She removed the boy from the sack first, rolling him out, sliding him onto the table, and strapping him up. She pushed the gurney over to the cage where she unceremoniously collapsed it and dumped the body inside with the drugged twins and unconscious Davy Torrez.

Behind her, the girl in the elevator moaned, a sign that the ether was wearing off. Eleanor returned the gurney to the elevator, strapped the girl in, and lifted her body to the embalming table. Since the girl was waking up, Eleanor took the precaution of muzzling her with heavy gray duct tape over her mouth; she didn't need the girl's screams (and oh how she would *scream!*) distracting her during the ritual. When she was finished with the tape, she secured the child's arms, legs and head with the leather restraining straps that Edmund had rigged to the table just for the special rituals.

As she tied the girl down, the dream-memory she'd had in the tower flashed in her mind. This was the very same table the dead woman had lain upon; the very same table upon which she and Edmund had watched Father perform his secret perversions; and the very same table where Edmund would later teach Eleanor the life-extending rituals which had drawn him to occult worship while away at school.

From a nearby shelf, Eleanor retrieved a pair of scissors and began cutting the girl's clothes from her body. When the girl was naked, goosebumps rising on her cold skin, Eleanor ran her hands lightly over the pale, succulent flesh, and her mouth began to water.

Eleanor removed her own clothes quickly then laid out the necessary instruments for the ritual on the metal instrument tray attached to the side of the table. From the storage compartment next to the elevator, she removed the electric embalming aspirator, which she wheeled to the table's side. After lighting the hundreds of candles placed strategically around the room, she opened the large book on the wooden podium set in the middle of the pentangle. She was ready to begin. As she read an incantation from the book and prepared to make the first incision, she thought of how much parts of the Rituals of Sacrifice were like the embalming procedures she had first watched her father teaching Edmund a long time ago.

She was eleven at the time. Unlike their mother, Eleanor and Edmund's father was oblivious to their powers and untouchable by them. He was a hardheaded New England undertaker of little intelligence. Neither Edmund nor Eleanor had been able to penetrate that hardheadedness; neither to project their thoughts, nor to hear his.

When their mother died, Father hired a series of nannies to care for them, but none stayed more than a week. After the eighth one left, crying hysterically about the children being possessed, Edgar Grimm decided he would care for the children himself.

When Edmund realized he couldn't control his father he took a different tact, convincing his father that he was a dutiful son who wanted to be just like his dad. His father responded by letting Edmund watch him as he performed the mortician's craft.

Eleanor was cleaning the front waking parlor one afternoon when Edmund and Father disappeared into the crematorium to embalm a body that had just come in. Eleanor was never allowed in the crematorium during embalmings, only to clean up after, and she resented being left out. That day she decided to slip into the chapel elevator and lower herself to the crematorium to watch through the same hinge crack where she and Edmund had watched father abusing corpses.

On the table was a naked old man, completely bald, his skin tinged a pale white-blue and mottled with age spots and dark, purplish blood clots just under the surface of his flesh. His head was turned to one side and his right arm was raised as though he was pointing at something of interest on the ceiling. One of his legs was rigidly bent, also.

The first thing Father showed Edmund was how to massage the body, loosening the effects of rigor mortis in the muscles and joints so that the body could be positioned with legs straight, arms crossed over the chest, and head raised, turned slightly to the right. Father worked a long time at this with obvious enjoyment.

Next, he set the features of the old man's face. Two thin metal picks with tiny-toothed clamps on the ends were stuck into the corpse's eyeballs and the lids drawn over them and held together by the clamps. He then pierced each side of the dead man's upper and lower jaw with needle injectors to which were attached a very fine threadlike wire that was almost invisible. When the wire ends of top and bottom were twisted together the corpse's mouth was drawn closed and held shut. Father then pushed the wire ends between the teeth and sewed the cadaver's lips together with an invisible stitch of catgut.

With the facial features set, Father explained that the arterial embalming—replacing the blood supply with embalming fluid—could begin. Using a scalpel, Father sliced through the flabby dead skin at the man's neck, armpits, and groin until he had exposed the major veins and arteries of the man's body. Drainage forceps were injected into the veins and laid out to the gutter at the edge of the table so that the blood would run off when the displacement began. Father then hooked up the injection needles and hoses of the electric aspirator to the exposed veins and began pumping a mixture of formaldehyde and water into the veins. Immediately, a thick, sludgy flow of dark blood began to run from the drainage forceps and into the gutter where it collected in the large glass jar at the bottom of the table.

Again Father massaged the body, this time, he said, to be sure all clots were washed out of the cadaver, and another stronger solution of embalming fluid was pumped into the body. Eleanor remembered marvelling at how the embalming fluid, which was treated with a red dye, brought a healthy pink tinge back to the dead flesh. After the three vein areas were sutured closed, Father demonstrated the process of cavity embalming.

Using a large-bore injection needle, which Father called a *trocar,* hooked up to the electric aspirator's vacuum pump, he inserted it into a small cut he had made just below the cadaver's navel. When he turned on the electric aspirator, a foul mixture of blood and waste was drawn from the dead man's intestines and bowels. When this part of the corpse was sucked dry, Father hooked the trocar and hose up to the formaldehyde pump and filled the cavity with an extra-strong solution of formalin, in order to (as Father put it) *cook* the man's entrails and insure the destruction of microorganisms that might present a health threat.

Eleanor had found the whole process fascinating, as had Edmund. She would return to the elevator many times over the years to watch her father perform embalmings, and other, more perverted acts on dead people he had been hired to prepare for burial. And later, after Father's death, she would share the mortician's duties with Edmund as the business thrived and they handled nearly every burial in the Amherst-Deerfield region. But the thing Eleanor enjoyed most was the ritual of sacrifice that Edmund taught her, which was built around the embalming procedure and rites of ancient occult worship that he had discovered while away at school.

With cadavers they were hired to prepare for wakes and burials and which supplied their daily diet, they used the same ritualistic procedures, but instead of formaldehyde they used boiling water circulated through the body so that the meat would still be edible and the body would be completely drained of blood, which they refrigerated for later ingestion but sometimes drank straight from the body. The rest of the corpse was stripped of edible meat and flesh from the neck down. When the body was clothed and made up, no one knew that little remained under the clothing of the person that once was. Edmund even did research into ancient Egyptian embalming practices and adopted their method of severing the brainsteam at the back of the head and inserting a hooked wire up through the nose and into the brain (a most delectable delicacy and important ritual offering), snagging it and drawing it out whole through the nasal passage.

The only difference between that procedure and the ritual she now performed on the girl (Edmund would have called her an *innocent,* because she was untouched by puberty and therefore seen as *clean* spiritually) was that this girl would be skinned alive first, as Eleanor was now doing, and most of her meat would be left on her for the altar, according to the ancient rites.

As she worked, Eleanor whistled softly to herself, oblivious to the girl's tape-muffled screams. Betty Boone's eyes bulged from her head, and her faint screams sounded like a faraway horse whinnying in pain.

CHAPTER 16

See-saw, Margery Daw . . .

No one wanted to talk about the disappearance of Betty Boone and Timmy Walsh, and that bothered Jackie. Something had happened that day, something *bad,* but like a forgotten sentence on the tip of his tongue, Jackie couldn't remember what. He thought that by talking about it, and asking questions, he could jog his memory and it would come to him. For some reason, it seemed very important that he remember. A week and a half had passed since they'd turned up missing at afternoon recess and all anyone would say—from the teachers on down to the kids in first grade—when he brought it up was the official line: that they had been taken away by their fathers and would return as soon as the police caught up with them.

He had tried to talk to his mother about it, but she had become more and more withdrawn, staying in bed all day and coming down to the kitchen only occasionally to make supper, which recently consisted of peanut butter sandwiches. There was little else to eat in the house since she wouldn't go out shopping; sometimes they went for days without a hot meal. Steve had gone out and picked up a few things—frozen pizzas, SpaghettiOs—a few times when he had gotten sick of peanut butter, but in the past few days he had skipped supper altogether. Two nights in a row Jackie and Jennifer had made suppers of Cheerios and milk for themselves.

Steve was no comfort to Jackie, either. In the past he'd always had time for Jackie. He'd always had an interest in what he had to say and in what he was doing. They had grown close before they'd moved, but now Steve kept putting him off with the excuse that he had to finish his poems for the competition deadline less than a month away. He'd begun secluding himself in his study, and now that he didn't even come out for supper, Jackie and Jennifer saw him only in the mornings, leaving as they came downstairs for breakfast.

Though Jackie often brought the matter of Timmy and Betty up with Jen, she tired quickly of his questions to the point where she had begun avoiding him, as she was doing now, sitting with Margaret Eames on the bus home after school. Jackie sat behind them with a freckle-faced boy from second grade whom he had managed to make friends with recently. The boy was a quiet loner in desperate need of a friend, who accepted Jackie's overtures with shy enthusiasm.

"You better not sit with my brother, Billy," Jen said, leaning over the seat, to Jackie's friend. "People will think you're wacko."

"Shut up, Jen," Jackie shot back.

"Seen any *trolls* lately?" Margaret asked with a cruel grin on her face.

Jackie's mouth dropped open and he looked at Jen with such an expression of betrayal that she blushed and had to look away. Jackie had made his sister promise—she'd crossed her heart and *hoped to die!*—not to tell anyone about that incident, especially the part about wetting his pants.

"Don't worry. I didn't tell her *everything*," Jen said tauntingly. She felt bad about betraying her oath to Jackie, but not knowing what to do to rectify the situation, she did the opposite and worsened it.

Margaret sat up, her curiosity piqued. "What?" she asked greedily.

Jennifer glanced sidelong at Jackie, her face hot with guilt, but she forced a smile. "Oh, nothing."

"What? What?" Margaret implored, grabbing Jen by the arm.

"She said, *nothing!*" Jackie said forcefully.

Margaret gave him a dirty look between the seats. "I think you're weird," she said, shaking her head at him in that snotty little-girl manner as though to say he was more than weird, perhaps the weirdest person to have ever lived. "I think you like to make up stories to get attention," she said accusingly.

"What about you? You said there was a witch in the woods," Jennifer said, seeing her opportunity to make up to Jackie. Margaret looked at her with surprise at her turnaround.

"Yeah," Jackie said, delighted with his sister's coming to his aid. "What about the witch in the woods?" Jackie asked, with *nyah-nyah* emphasis to the words. "Huh, Dumb Ol' Margaret?"

"Don't call me that," Margaret pouted. Jackie had been calling her that since having seen the name in the Sunday comic strip, "Dennis the Menace."

"I never said there was, Jerry Hall did," Margaret said defensively.

"Oh sure," Jen said with exaggeration, "Blame a kid who isn't here to defend himself."

"Yeah," Jackie concurred enthusiastically.

"He disappeared!" Margaret answered.

Jackie stopped smiling at the mention of that fact.

Margaret, sensing his mood swing, jumped on the opportunity. Giving Jackie a slit-eyed stare and speaking in a low, creepy voice she said, "Right after he told me about the witch, he disappeared. I'll bet the witch got him!"

Jackie paled at the thought of it, but Jennifer laughed.

"See. That proves you believe there's a witch," she said victoriously.

"Yeah," Jackie echoed, less enthusiastically than before.

"Well, I don't believe there even is a bridge in the woods. I think both of you are liars," Margaret rallied.

"I can prove there's a bridge by showing it to you. Can you show me the witch?"

Margaret hesitated a moment. "Yes," she said doubtfully.

"Hah!" Jennifer scoffed, but Jackie shivered all the way to his bowels.

"Make sure you come over to my house as soon as you can, Margaret," Jen said as the bus approached their stop. Her words dripping with sarcasm. "I can't wait to see the witch." Jen purposefully spoke loud enough for half the bus to hear. The kids Jen's age and older laughed, but a lot of the younger kids, including Jackie, remained in a frightened silence, holding their breath, eyes wide at the factual mention of something the adult world said was make-believe.

Margaret's face flushed red with embarrassment and she nearly leapt from the bus when it stopped at the end of Dorsey Lane and the doors opened. Her mother Judy was waiting there, stuffed into too-tight jeans that caught every nuance of bulge and pocket of cellulite on her fat thighs. The bright red T-shirt she wore only emphasized the obesity of her upper body. She grabbed Margaret by the hand as soon as she was off the bus and waited until Jackie and Jennifer had got off before leading the three of them down Dorsey Lane.

Judy frowned on the fact that neither Diane nor Steve Nailer met their kids at the bus stop each day. Judy didn't believe a word of what the *Northwood News* said about the disappearance of the Torrez boy, or of Betty Boone and Timmy Walsh. *She* knew it was the cult of Satan worshippers she'd heard about on the local TV station's version of the talk show "Geraldo." When she'd called Diane and informed her of that opinion, she'd had a rude awakening about the person she was beginning to consider her best friend. Diane Nailer hadn't even seemed to care, saying only, "Anything's possible," in a weary voice before hanging up. Judy was outraged by her response, especially when she heard Jennifer telling Margaret about how she and her brother had had to walk home on the first day of school.

Judy was all ready to go over and give Diane Nailer a good piece of her mind when her husband Roger stopped her, joking that if she gave a piece of her mind to Diane she wouldn't have enough left for herself. Since then, Judy had taken it upon herself to walk Jennifer and Jackie halfway home, to the driveway of her house, then watch them as they went the rest of the way to their house. It had occurred to her that she was doing *exactly* what Diane wanted her to, which was to walk *her* kids home every day. If that were the case, it only made Judy hate Diane more. She could not now understand what she had ever found to like about her that first weekend they had moved in down the street.

Margaret walked quietly at her mother's side, not looking around. Jennifer and Jackie walked behind them, Jennifer with a gloating grin on her face and Jackie with a scared, uncertain one on his. Jackie didn't like what Margaret had gotten them into—but then neither did Margaret.

Though she had no proof of it, Margaret was pretty certain that the witch in the woods Jerry had told her of was really the old lady she'd seen on two occasions driving by in the funny-looking, big black station wagon with the fins on the back. Each time she'd seen the woman she'd felt a chill down her arms and, not knowing why, had made sure the woman hadn't seen her.

Margaret hadn't really believed Jerry Hall when he'd told her about the witch, whom he said had visited him in his dreams, telling him to come play with her in the woods. After he disappeared, though, she began to wonder. Just to be on the safe side, she promised herself never to tell anyone what Jerry had told her; after all, if a witch *had* gotten Jerry, it had happened right after he had told Margaret about her. To Margaret it seemed logical that the reason the witch got Jerry was because he told. Margaret's problem was that, like her mother, she couldn't keep a secret and had blurted out the story to Jackie and Jennifer on their first meeting, much to her regret now.

Margaret had no desire (just in case Jerry had been right) to go anywhere near that old lady's house, but now her pride was at stake. She just had to prove Jennifer, the know-it-all, wrong.

While her mother remained at the end of the driveway watching Jennifer and Jackie walk home, Margaret went up to her room and changed from her candy-striped dress (her mother liked her to look like "a little lady" for school) to jeans, a sweater, and her pink Nikes.

"Where do you think you're going?" Judy Eames demanded of Margaret, who was trying to slip out the kitchen door.

"Over to Jen's," Margaret replied, hands against the screen door, ready to push it open and bolt.

"Why don't they come over here and play?" Judy suggested. She didn't like Margaret being over there. Any woman who didn't care about the safety of her own kids wouldn't care about hers.

"We're coming over here after. Jen got a new doll that she wants to show me first," Margaret lied, avoiding her mother's eyes.

"Why doesn't she just bring it over here?"

Margaret had to think fast. "Uh . . . because her mother won't let her take it out of the house."

Huh! Judy thought angrily. That woman cares more about her daughter's *doll* than she does about her daughter! Before she could say anything else, Margaret was out the door.

"I'll be right back," Margaret called.

Judy started to call her to come back, but stopped. Instead

she went out to the front of the house to watch Margaret. When she got to the living room window, she felt a jolt of panic yank at her guts. Margaret was gone! Before her panic swelled any further, she remembered that Margaret and the Nailer kids had taken to using the path at the edge of the woods that ran behind the two houses. As quickly as her size allowed, she ran back to the kitchen and out the door. As she reached the path behind the scraggly laurel bushes at the edge of the yard, she saw Margaret's bouncing curls take a right into the Nailers' backyard.

Never hurts to be too safe, she reminded herself. She started back to the house but had to stop a moment to catch her breath. I *have* to start a diet, she thought, then remembered the leftover carrot cake in the bread box that she had made for last Sunday's dinner. Tomorrow, I definitely start my diet, she promised the diet gods, then headed for the house and a date with the carrot cake and the latest episode of "General Hospital."

CHAPTER 17

See, see! What shall I see?

"So, you decided to show up," Jennifer said, coming out the back door of her house and confronting Margaret on the steps. "Don't try telling me that your mother wants you home right away, either."

"Well, she does," Margaret said, a little taken aback by Jen's guessing what she was going to say.

"I knew it," Jen gloated. "I knew you'd be a chicken shit."

"I'm telling your mother you said that," Margaret threatened.

"Figures you're a *fink,* too, *chicken shit!*"

"I am not. Stop calling me that!"

"I'll stop if you show me your big bad witch."

"I never said I wouldn't!" Margaret shouted at her. "I just have to get home right after," she added with an angry pout.

"Great! Then let's go," Jen challenged.

"Where's your weird brother?"

"He's a worse chicken shit than you are," Jen said, laughing.

"Stop calling me that," Margaret demanded. She turned her back on Jennifer and marched across the yard in the direction of the woods. Laughing again just to irk Margaret, Jennifer followed.

Jackie pulled aside the curtain and watched Jennifer and Margaret cross the backyard and enter the field. He shivered at the thought of going into those woods again and was glad that he had refused to go, no matter what names Jen called him.

As he watched them wading through the tall grass, a strange feeling came over him. The further Margaret and Jen got into the field, the grass reaching higher and higher around them, the more it appeared they were moving without legs. The illusion stirred a feeling of déjà vu in Jackie. He found himself thinking about Jerry Hall, and didn't know why.

The sun flickered between clouds for a moment and the flash reminded Jackie of lightning and the sense of déjà vu grew stronger. No matter how hard he tried, he couldn't quite remember why the field and lightning seemed familiar. The dream he'd had the first night in the house remained in his subconscious, where it toyed with his perceptions and memory.

For one panic-stricken moment, he was certain something bad was going to happen and had a powerful urge to warn Margaret and Jen not to go into the woods. He tried to open the window, but the wood was swollen with dampness from frequent recent rains. After several tries he gave up, deciding it was just as well. Margaret and Jen, but especially Jen, would have just laughed at him again and called him names. Still, he was worried for Margaret and more so for his sister, though he would never admit it.

The woods were dangerous. He was sure of it. He had finally, begrudgingly, accepted the fact that he had *not* seen a troll that day, but instead what Jen called "Anna Lucy Nation," which Jackie conceived in his six-year-old mind to be a person that was like a dream that appeared to be real but wasn't. Nevertheless, he still mistrusted the woods. Instinctively, he knew that somehow the woods had something to do with him seeing Anna Lucy Nation.

As he watched Jen and Margaret go off in pursuit of a witch, Jackie wondered with dread if the witch had turned Anna Lucy Nation into the troll.

The afternoon air was of the cool brisk kind common to New England autumns. It went into the lungs clean and left a thin trace of vapor when exhaled. The strawgrass, tops long and furry with seed, waved lazily in the breeze. The woods were just beginning to take on subtle shades of the fiery colors they would burst into within a few weeks.

Margaret and Jennifer crossed the field quickly, their feet squishing in the soggy ground so that their sneakers showed a waterline around the bottom by the time they reached the trees. Neither spoke; Margaret took the lead with Jen following

Jennifer was beginning to feel a little sorry for Margaret. She knew Margaret was going to have to admit sooner or later that there really wasn't a witch and that she had lied. Jennifer debated whether or not to take pity on her and give her a chance to get out of it. As they entered the woods, she decided she'd give her a break.

"You don't know how lucky you are not to have a little brother," Jennifer said to break the ice.

Margaret didn't say a word.

"Sometimes he's okay," Jen went on, "but most of the time all he does is fink on me and get me in trouble."

Though Margaret still refused to answer, she softened a little and looked at Jen, a shy, appealing smile starting at the corners of her mouth.

Encouraged, Jen continued. "And what an imagination on that kid. He's always thinking dumb stuff is real, like when you told him about the witch. He nearly died. That was a good joke. It's just too bad he didn't come with us now so we could scare him really good," Jen said with a smile at her good deed for the day.

Margaret looked hopeful, but wary. She knew an out when she'd been given one, and she was tempted to take it. She would have liked nothing more than to just go home and forget all this; she was scared—hadn't been this scared since the day Jerry disappeared. She didn't trust Jennifer, though. She had shown Margaret on the bus just how fast she could turn on her. Being an only child, Margaret couldn't understand why Jen had done it. Besides, Jen was so snotty, that just once Margaret wanted to show her up good.

"It was no joke," Margaret said in a cool voice.

"Aw, come on!" Jen smirked. "Look, you don't have to keep this up for my sake. I know you were only trying to scare my little brother. Don't worry, I won't tell him. We can even make up a really good story about finding a gingerbread house and seeing a witch. We'll even tell him we got chased. That ought to scare the pants off him."

"I wasn't telling a story," Margaret kept on. She was dead certain that if she took Jen's lure and said she'd made it up, Jen would turn on her again, calling her a liar. She would run right home and tell Jackie, and tomorrow she would tell everyone on the bus. Margaret gave Jen a steely gaze of defiance. "There *is* a witch and *I'll* show you where she lives."

Jennifer smirked at Margaret and shook her head. With a flourish, she swept her arm in front of her indicating to Margaret to lead on. Already, the wheels of mischief were turning in her head. She didn't know what Margaret hoped to prove by sticking to her stupid story—if she thought Jen was as easily frightened as Jackie then she was dumber than Jen had thought—but if that's what she wanted to do, then Jen would have to teach her a lesson.

Margaret led the way along the path until it reached the dirt road. Pushing through the bushes and tangle of undergrowth at one end, she crossed to the road, walking in the direction of Grimm Memorials.

So that's her game, Jen thought, a superior look playing across her face. She's going to try and scare me by telling me that the witch lives in that old house with the crematorium that Jackie is so afraid of. A plan quickly hatched in Jen's mind. Letting Margaret get several feet ahead of her, Jennifer ducked into the woods just before they came to the rising curve in the road that led to the front yard of Grimm Memorials. Moving as quickly as possible through the thick growth, she circled ahead to find the right spot from which to jump out and scare Margaret.

Margaret got all the way to the crest of the curve in the road, where it widened out into the dusty parking lot in front of the ominous-looking house, before she noticed that Jennifer was no longer behind her. She went back a few steps, searching the surrounding woods and the stretch of road beyond the curve. Jen was nowhere to be seen.

"Come on, Jen, I know what you're doing and I'm not scared." Margaret stood in the road for several minutes, waiting, *hoping,* that Jen would come out. She knew that Jen was just trying to frighten her; the problem was that she was succeeding. Suddenly, Margaret had a very bad feeling about this.

"Jen come out," Margaret demanded, a slight tremor to her voice.

There was a sound behind her. Margaret turned, but the road was empty, the bushes unmoving. All she could see was the big, gray house waiting ahead. She heard the sound again and realized it was coming from the house. On the first-floor side, facing her, she could see an open window. From it came such strange sounds. There was singing and barking and moaning and talking spilling from that window.

With a last glance look around for Jennifer, Margaret started toward the window.

The going was tough. The woods Jen was trying to sneak through often became a flood plain for the nearby Connecticut River and remained boggy year-round. Her sneakers were soaked within minutes, and for a moment she worried about catching hell from her mother—if her mother had been normal, which she wasn't of late. Jennifer didn't know what had gotten into her, but it constantly bothered and angered her.

Her foot went into soft mud up to her ankles suddenly, intruding on her thoughts. She yanked it out and it came free with a puckering sound. "Oh, shit," she swore under her breath. This was turning out to be a really lousy idea. She knew she had to be close to either Grimm Memorials or the road, but the bushes and trees were so thick she couldn't see more than a few feet in front of her.

She stopped against a tree whose leaves had turned a bright reddish purple early and tried to clean the mud from her shoe with a stick. From far to her left, much farther than she would have thought, she heard Margaret calling her. I must have gone further than I figured, Jen thought. Margaret had sounded much too far away.

All of a sudden Jen was very uncertain as to where she was. She'd thought she was roughly parallel to the road about twenty yards into the woods and pretty close to the Grimm place. Her sense of direction had seemingly deserted her. The trees and bushes felt as though they were closing in on her. She began to sweat and the sweat dried in the cool air, leaving her chilled. She had an urgent desire to go crashing through the bushes, shouting for Margaret to find her, but fought it back. After all, she was not a *child* like Jackie. Taking several deep breaths to calm herself, she started off in the direction Margaret's call had come from.

Almost immediately the bushes and trees thinned out and she was encouraged that she was nearing either the road or the house. She ducked under a low-hanging limb and pushed through a thicket of dogberry bushes and hanging vines before stumbling into a clearing.

Jennifer's mouth dropped open in a loud gasp of astonishment. Where the road should have been, there was a narrow meandering path. And where Grimm Memorials should have been, there was a small, white-roofed cottage.

It can't be, Jennifer mulled in disbelief. She stepped out of the woods, onto the path, and approached the cottage warily. Her disbelief soon changed to wonder and a smile broke over her face.

The cottage was made of gingerbread.

Margaret approached the open window from an angle so as not to be seen. At one point, still many yards from the house, she decided to heed her instincts and get away from the place, but at that moment the sounds coming from the window changed. She thought she could hear children's voices; one of them sounded like Jerry Hall's. Forgetting her sense of impending danger, she went on running to the side of the house and pressing herself against the old wood boards. Moving slowly, she slid along, her back against the house, until she reached the window.

The sill was level with the top of her head, low, but not low enough for her to see inside. She stood on tiptoes, but still couldn't see over the edge of the sill, only the ceiling and the top part of a wall. Soft light reflected on the ceiling, flickering as though from many candles. Grasping the sill with both hands, Margaret lifted herself until she could peer over the edge and into the house.

The first thing Margaret noticed was a terrible smell coming from the room. Against the wall opposite her was what looked like the altar at the Catholic church in town that

Margaret and her mother went to every Sunday, only something was different. It had a huge cross suspended over it, but something must have happened to it, one of its cables must have broken because it was hung upside down. The Jesus on the cross was different, too. She couldn't see it clearly in the poor light of the room, but something wasn't right; the skin wasn't the right color, and a thick dark liquid dripped from it.

What she saw next paralyzed her. The old woman she had seen driving the funny black station wagon was on all fours in the middle of a big red circle with a star in it at the foot of the altar. The woman was naked, her flabby wrinkled body covered with strange squiggly lines and symbols drawn in the same red color as the circle and star on the floor. The talking, moaning, and singing were all coming from her open mouth, but Margaret hardly noticed. Her eyes were riveted to the huge black dog mounting the old lady from behind.

Margaret screamed and the dog and the old lady looked at her. Her grip on the windowsill slipped and she fell hard on her rump on the ground below the window. Instantly, she was on her feet and running for home.

This is just like a fairy tale, Jennifer thought, as she approached the gingerbread house. The closer she got the more details she noticed: The roof was coated with a thick layer of buttercream frosting; the gingerbread walls were trimmed with chocolate icing; the windows were of clear rock candy and the front door was made of pure milk chocolate. Around the cottage ran a candy-cane fence. The walkway that started at the fence's front gate and went to the front door was made of chocolate chip cookies.

This is crazy, Jennifer thought. This is like something Jackie would make up. She looked around, past the house, at the surrounding area. Everything was shrouded in fog. Like looking through a steamed-up windshield, the area in front of her, including the fence, yard, and cottage, was clear, everything else was fogged up.

Where's the road, Jen wondered, and the big house? "This is like a weird dream," she mumbled aloud, touching her face to be sure she was awake. A scary thought suddenly crossed her mind: if this wasn't a dream, if this was *real,* then maybe Margaret's story about a witch was real. In the fairy tale a wicked old witch who ate children lived in the gingerbread house in the woods; why not in this one?

Looking at the cottage in a new light, Jen decided she didn't want to go any closer. She just wanted to get out of there. She took a step back, then turned around to go back the way she'd come. There was nothing but fog behind her— a wall of impenetrable fog, and it was pressing in on her, blowing in her face, seeping into her nostrils and mouth, filling her lungs, her brain, until she forgot her fear and turned back to the gingerbread house.

She went through the gate and up the cookie walk to the front door. She raised her hand as if to knock, but instead broke a piece of chocolate off the door and ate it.

"Nibble, nibble, gnaw. Who is nibbling at my little house?" a soft voice cried from within.

Jen let out an intoxicated giggle. "The wind, the wind; the heaven-born wind," she answered.

Footsteps approached from inside and the chocolate door swung open.

Eleanor rushed to the window, Mephisto hot on her heels, and watched Margaret run down the road, disappearing around the bend. Mephisto lunged for the window, desiring to give chase, but Eleanor grabbed his collar, pulling him back. She closed the window. There was a better way to take care of that little troublemaker—letting Mephisto run her down now would only make a bad mistake worse.

Eleanor was worried. She hadn't known Margaret was at

the window until she'd heard her scream. She hadn't heard her thoughts, hadn't heard her approach. Something had gone wrong with the Machine.

Eleanor had been well aware of Jennifer, and now, as she turned away from the window, she realized the two girls must have come together. Why had the Machine picked up one and not the other? It had created a splendid lure for the Nailer girl, who was an integral part of Eleanor's plans. She had watched it all unfold in her mind like a movie as she was performing the Ritual of Defilement with Mephisto. She still saw it in her mind's eye as Jennifer approached the back door, a blank look on her face.

Suddenly, for one awful moment, everything went black in Eleanor's head. She heard no thoughts, had no thoughts of her own, saw no workings of the Machine: *There was no Machine.* White light pulsed in her head while a wild, rampaging pain broke across her chest like a huge wave, staggering her. She was on the verge of collapse when, like a merry-go-round that ends one song and begins another, the Machine returned, cranking up again. The lights stopped flashing in Eleanor's mind, the pain diminished, and the calliope continued.

Jennifer was at the back door. Eleanor had no time to worry about Margaret now. She'd have to hope that having made eye contact with her was enough. If it was, the girl would forget; either way, Eleanor would take care of it later. She rushed out of the chapel, just closing the door behind her before Mephisto could follow, and hurried, her flat, veiny breasts slapping against her belly, to the kitchen.

Jennifer was picking a piece of imaginary chocolate from the door and eating it. Out of breath and gasping, Eleanor spoke the words she'd heard so many times as a child when listening to her mother tell the story of Hansel and Gretel, her favorite fairy tale. The girl, almost completely in the Machine's control now, giggled out the correct response and Eleanor opened the door.

"Grandma!" Jennifer cried with delight and rushed into Eleanor's naked embrace.

Margaret ran until she could no longer draw a breath to power her flight. She had reached the path but could go no farther without stopping to catch her wind. She collapsed against a mossy mound by a tall oak tree and gulped air into her hungry lungs. She looked fearfully back at the road, which was still in view behind her. She dragged herself out of sight to the other side of the tree.

What am I running from?

The thought shot into her head, and like a student who knows the answer on a test but blanks out when asked it, she couldn't remember.

And where is Jennifer?

She couldn't answer that either. Something came to her: Jennifer had been playing games, trying to scare her. That was why she was afraid; Jennifer must be chasing her.

What are we doing in the woods?

She had no idea. Margaret didn't like this feeling. She felt the way she did upon waking from a nightmare, only she hadn't been sleeping. Not wanting to see if Jennifer was really chasing her, Margaret leapt to her feet and sprinted all the way down the path to her house.

Jackie was sitting in front of the television watching "The Real Ghostbusters" cartoons when he saw Jen in the hall, on her way upstairs. Jumping up, he followed her to their room.

"What happened?" Jackie asked, as soon as the door was closed. Jennifer didn't answer. She sat on her bed, staring at the ring her grandmother had given her for her seventh birthday.

"Jen? What happened?" Jackie repeated, sitting on the other side of her bed.

Jennifer stirred and seemed startled, like one awakened from a daydream. "What?" she asked, a slight frown upon her face.

"What happened? In the woods? With Margaret?" Jackie asked sarcastically.

"Oh," Jen said softly, and looked again at the ring on her finger. "Nothing," she replied.

"What do you mean, nothing?" Jackie nearly exploded.

Jennifer gave him a disdainful look. "I mean, *nothing*. She was lying. Now quit bugging me."

"Oh," Jackie said. He gave a loud, immense sigh of relief. All the while Jen and Margaret had been gone he had told himself just that, over and over again. He was very glad to be proven correct. He gave Jennifer a curious look—she was staring at her ring again—then shrugged his shoulders. It was time for "Teenage Mutant Ninja Turtles," and he never missed them if he could help it.

When Jackie was gone, Jennifer went to the window and looked out at the forest. Grandma is back and she's all better, she thought with excitement. It was incredible, but true. Grandma had explained it all so well; how Diane and Steve had convinced a doctor that she was senile with Alzheimer's disease so they could put her away. But she had escaped and followed them, always watching Jen and Jackie to be sure they were safe. She'd had the gingerbread house in the woods built special just for them—a secret magical place where they could escape from their uncaring parents. It all seemed feasible to Jennifer; all believable because deep down inside she wanted to believe it more than anything. She never once thought about the times she had visited Grammy in the nursing home, only to find her drooling and staring into space. She didn't remember how, the last time she'd seen her, Grammy was so bad she didn't know who Jen was. And the impossibility of a house actually being constructed of ginger-bread and candy didn't matter, either. Grandma had said it was true, so it was. When Jennifer had looked into Grandma's enormous eyes, she had accepted everything, and known exactly what she must do.

CHAPTER 18

Curly locks, Curly locks, wilt thou be mine?

An hour after her daughter left, when "General Hospital" was over and the carrot cake gone, Judy Eames roused herself from the living room couch and went to the back door, peering out for Margaret. She pushed the door open and leaned out into the cold air, searching the backyard and edge of the woods for her daughter. When she called her, she was surprised to hear an answer from upstairs. Judy went up to her room and found her lying on her bed, staring at the ceiling.

"I didn't hear you come in," Judy exclaimed. "When did you get home?"

"Awhile ago," Margaret answered listlessly, not looking at her mother.

"Do you feel okay, hon?" Judy asked. She placed the back of her hand against Margaret's forehead, checking for fever and found none.

"Yeah," Margaret answered, sliding her head out from under her mother's hand.

"Are you tired?"

"Yeah."

"Okay, hon. You take a nap before supper." Judy started

out of the room, then stopped. "Oh, how was Jennifer's new doll?"

"What?" Margaret looked confused.

"Jen's new doll; the one you went over there to see."

"Oh yeah. It was nice," Margaret lied, her voice a monotone. She had no idea what her mother was talking about. She agreed with her only to get rid of her. All she wanted to do was sleep. But when her mother was gone, Margaret couldn't sleep. The rest of the afternoon she lay as she was, eyes open, staring at the ceiling, sometimes at the wall. When her mother peeked in to check on her, Margaret closed her eyes and pretended to sleep, but then opened them again, resuming her staring when she was alone. She moved again only to answer her mother's call for supper.

Throughout dinner, she played with her food, moving it around her plate with no apparent interest in eating it. She paid attention to her parent's conversation only when her father spoke of the new patrol dogs the campus police had just bought. The mention of dogs sparked something in her; some memory she couldn't quite grasp. Her father noticed it was the only time she looked her old self and tried to follow up on it.

"So where's Puffin tonight, Margy? I haven't seen her around," he said, referring to Margaret's orange cat.

"I don't know," Margaret answered dully, losing interest again as soon as the subject was changed. "I'll go look for her later."

"Honey," Judy said with concern, "if you're done, why don't you go right back to bed. I'll bring up some aspirins for you."

"What's wrong with her?" Roger asked when Margaret had gone upstairs.

"I think she's coming down with something," Judy said. She got up from the table, placed her dish in the sink, and took a bottle of aspirin from the cabinet. After pouring a glass of milk, she took it and the aspirins up to her daughter.

Roger Eames finished his dish of shepherd's pie and poured himself a cup of coffee from the pot on the stove. He made a mental note to look in on his daughter before going to bed. He would later fall asleep during the eleven o'clock news, wake during the weather, and go to bed, forgetting to look in on his daughter. He would regret it the rest of his days because dinner was the last time he would see her alive.

The brat will remember and tell someone.

Edmund was standing at the top of the crematorium stairs. Eleanor had just finished feeding and drugging the boys in the cage and was carrying the empty tray back to the kitchen. She ignored the ghost of her brother.

She'll tell and they'll come to investigate. Then you'll join me.

Eleanor climbed the stairs, walking right through the apparition blocking her way. A chill swept over her and a sinister chuckling rang in her ears, but she did her best to ignore it, telling herself it was the wind because Edmund was dead and the dead stayed dead.

Though she had probed Margaret's mind after finishing with Jennifer, and found that she remembered nothing, she couldn't be sure that would last. Edmund's warning (*It's not Edmund, it's your guilty conscience,* she chastised herself again) had raised serious doubts. No, she decided, it was too risky; something would have to be done.

She needed another sacrifice for the next ritual and, though ideally it should be a newborn infant, any prepubescent innocent would suffice. Besides this would save her the trouble of hunting for an infant, which would have been difficult and time-consuming. With her health and the Machine failing her, she decided to go for the bird in the hand and take care of two problems at once. She didn't like taking another child so close to her house and so soon after having snared Jerry Hall, but it couldn't be helped. Besides, Halloween and the Harvest of Dead Souls, when she would perform the sixth and final sacrifice for Samhain, was only two weeks away. She'd just have to gamble that the Machine could keep suspicion away from her that long. After that, she didn't care.

She went into the kitchen, feeling her way in the darkness, and went to the back door. She opened it and went out into the cold night. Mephisto whimpered from his tether at the oak tree, but she ignored him. She stood at the cemetery gate, facing in the general direction of Dorsey Lane and Margaret's house. The clear fall sky was studded with stars and pink around the edges, heralding the coming dawn. Eleanor looked at the sky and slowly raised her arms in a beckoning gesture.

"Curly locks, Curly locks, wilt thou be mine?" she said softly and closed her eyes.

Margaret woke at 5:30 A.M., a half hour after her father left for work and a half hour before her mother's alarm would go off and she would rise to get Margaret ready for school. A sound woke Margaret. She sat up in bed, listening for it again. A dog barked far away. In a mad rush of images she remembered everything she had seen through the window of the house in the woods yesterday afternoon. That was the last thing she could remember. Since then she'd felt as though she'd been sleepwalking with no knowledge of what she'd done or where she'd gone while asleep.

With the memories came another sound: a cat's frantic meowing. *Puffin!*

Margaret threw the covers back and swung her legs out. She glanced quickly around the room for her cat, who usually slept on her bed. Pufffin was gone. The cat's cry came again from outside, followed by the dog's angry barking.

That horrible dog is after Puffin, Margaret thought frantically. As quickly as possible, she put on her jeans, a sweatshirt, socks and sneakers, and ran out of the house.

She ran headlong over the dark path behind her house and the Nailers'. She slowed her speed only when the path turned into the thick of the woods and the gray light of dawn was swallowed by the trees hanging on to the shadows of the night. Margaret stumbled several times and fell once, landing painfully on her knees. When she pushed through the overgrown bushes where the path intersected with the dirt road, one of the branches left a nasty scratch across her left cheek.

She paused in the middle of the road, her eyes slowly adjusting to the near darkness as she checked in both directions for Puffin. There was no sign of her. From the direction of Grimm Memorials the sound of barking followed by a strangled mewling, spurred Margaret on. As she ran, what she'd seen the old woman and the dog doing ran through her mind again.

Though Margaret couldn't quite comprehend what it was that the old woman and her dog had been doing, she knew it was a *bad thing*. They had been naked and that made it ten times worse than a bad thing. She reasoned frightfully that if the dog could do such a bad thing to that old lady, then what might it do to poor Puffin? A chill ran down her spine at the possibilities.

The dog's barking became a horrible snarling and growling and the cat's pathetic cries could no longer be heard. As she rounded the bend in the road and came into view of the house, Margaret realized that the sounds were coming from behind the house. She could just imagine poor Puffin up a tree, the ferocious dog lunging up at her, *or worse*.

I have to save her! That thought overcame her fear at being so close to the house and she ran up the drive to it and started around, being very careful not to look into any of the windows.

The backyard was made up of two sections; the front part consisted of a scraggly, crabgrass-infested lawn that stretched between the house and an old, rusted, wrought-iron fence that surrounded the second section—an ancient, overgrown ceme-

tery. Thin old tombstones, sculpted headstones, and simple
stone crosses stood, some crooked, some nearly hidden by
the long grass that was testimony to the graveyard's long dis-
use. The gate hung at a skewed angle at the cemetery's entrance. A worn dirt path ran from the gate across the yard to
a screen door at the back of the house. To the far right of the
cemetery, an old run-down barn was being swallowed by the
encroaching forest.

Margaret peered cautiously around the corner of the
house, surveying the yard and cemetery. Puffin was nowhere
in sight. On the far side of the cemetery, near the other corner of the house, the huge black dog was tied by a frayed
rope to a tall, leaning oak tree. The dog was lunging frantically against its leash, snarling and trying to get at something in the tall grass near the cemetery fence.

"Puffin!" Margaret breathed anxiously. In a sudden fit of
motherly concern, not caring whether she'd be seen from the
house, nor whether the ferocious dog might break free,
Margaret ran across the backyard determined to save her cat.

"Little girl!"

The shrill voice came from behind her, followed by the
squeak and slam of the screen door opening and closing.
Margaret stopped in her tracks and whirled around. The old
woman she'd seen through the window was walking toward
her.

At first, Margaret was frightened. She nearly ran from the
old lady, but, as the woman came closer, Margaret realized
there was something different about the old woman. It wasn't
just that she now had clothes on—a long, neck-to-ankles
dress and high black orthopedic shoes—she actually looked
changed, not ugly or threatening the way she had when
Margaret had spied on her through the window. Now her face
was cherubic, red-cheeked and smiling. Her pure white hair
had a cloudlike softness to it. Her blue eyes, slightly magnified behind a thick-lensed pair of glasses made her look owlish
and cute. Margaret was immediately disarmed.

Maybe it's not the same lady. The thought insinuated itself in her mind as invisibly as a parasite. *Maybe I didn't see what I thought I saw,* crawled in right behind it.

"Did you lose a cat, little girl?" The old woman asked. Her voice was high-pitched, squeaky and friendly.

"Yes, ma'am. Did you see it?" Margaret blurted out.

"Oh yes," the woman chuckled sweetly. "She's in my kitchen having a bowl of milk. She went too close to my dog and I got worried. Old Mother Hubbard's cupboard is bare, you know."

Margaret giggled. She liked this old lady. The woman made her feel warm.

"Come see," the woman coaxed, motioning for Margaret to follow her inside. "Your kitty likes my milk, but Old Mother Hubbard's poor dog needs a bone." When Margaret came closer, the old woman put her arm around her shoulder. "So you're Margaret," she said softly.

"Yes," Margaret replied, but her voice sounded faraway. When the old woman touched her, the back of her head tingled warmly. She exhaled and forgot to inhale for several seconds. Her mouth became dry and she felt light headed. She smiled sleepily and let herself be led inside.

The old woman steered Margaret to a seat at the kitchen table, then went to the cabinets over the sink. As soon as the old woman's hand was no longer touching her, Margaret's head cleared a little and her breathing returned to normal. She looked around the room for Puffin but didn't see her. Nor could she see any bowl of milk in the room.

"Where's my cat?" Margaret asked politely.

"She's around here somewhere, probably off exploring my house. Cats are curious, you know," the old woman said reassuringly. She opened the cabinets and took out two clay mugs. "Curiosity killed the cat, you know. Would you like some cocoa?"

Margaret nodded. "But where's the bowl of milk you gave her?" she asked.

"It's right there." The old woman pointed to a half-full bowl near the stove. Margaret could have sworn there was no bowl there when she had looked a moment ago.

"Cocoa and cookies for breakfast, how does that sound?" the old woman asked and answered herself "Mmm, good." She opened a large ceramic pot on the counter and scooped cocoa into the mugs. She carried them to the stove where she put them down and lit the gas burner under a large cast-iron teakettle. The gas ignited with a quick sound, like air being sucked through a rolled tongue. The old woman looked at Margaret and winked.

Margaret smiled back politely. She had obviously been wrong about this woman and had nothing to fear from her, but now all she wanted was her cat. Outside the dog continued to snarl and bark ferociously. Margaret didn't like the sound of it.

"I've seen you spying on my house," the old woman said in the same sweet tone she might use to say she had seen Margaret in church. The old woman crossed to the table and sat opposite Margaret. "You were peeking in my window yesterday, weren't you?" Her eyes seemed to be pushing from behind the thick lenses at Margaret, and she felt another wave of hot numbness slide over her scalp.

"What did you see when you looked in my window, Margaret?" The woman's voice was soft and purring.

Margaret tried to think hard, but for the life of her she couldn't remember what she had seen. Even the dog's wild barking outside couldn't jog her memory. "I . . . I don't know," Margaret mumbled. The old woman's eyes started to recede. "Nothing, I guess," Margaret added.

The old woman smiled. "That's good" she cooed. She rose from the table and went back to the stove, removing the kettle from the burner and pouring steaming water into the mugs. "Let's have our cocoa."

"Did you know Jerry Hall?" Margaret blurted out. She didn't know why she had asked that.

"The little boy who used to live at the end of the lane? Oh, yes. We became *good friends*," she said happily, as she replaced the kettle on the stove.

"Jerry told me something about you." Margaret again spoke before she knew what she was doing.

The old woman looked slowly over her shoulder at Margaret and gave her a small, sly smile. "Yes?" she asked, turning and coming to the table with a mug in each hand.

Though goosebumps had risen on her arms, her bowels felt suddenly liquid, and she knew she shouldn't go on, Margaret found herself speaking words as though compelled to. "He told me you were a . . . a *witch!*"

The old woman smiled, her eyes twinkling merrily, and chuckled. Margaret felt as though a great weight had just slid from her shoulders. What had she been afraid of? She reached out and took the offered mug with both hands. "That's silly, I guess," she added, embarrassed. She brought the mug to her lips, blowing at its contents the way she always did before drinking something hot.

"Oh no, it's not really," the old woman said. She placed her mug on the table and stepped to Margaret's side. "It's *true*," she said with that same merry chuckle to her voice.

The words hit home as Margaret took a tentative sip from the mug. Something tickled her lips and she felt a hair in her mouth. She coughed and pulled the mug back, looking into it. The mug wasn't filled with piping hot cocoa. Swimming in the steamy, dark red water were big clumps of orange fur.

The old woman's chuckling exploded into a shrieking cackle. Margaret looked up at her and gasped. In her hand, holding it by the bloody scruff of its neck, was Puffin, her bleeding pink body completely skinned of fur. As Margaret's gasp swelled into a scream, the old woman's other hand shot out and clamped on her throat cutting off her scream and her breathing.

"Now," the old woman wheezed, her foul breath washing over Margaret's face, *"you're mine!"*

* * *

In the cold gray light of morning, Mephisto watched expectantly as Eleanor approached him. "Mother Hubbard's brought her poor dog a bone," she said, as though talking to a baby, and threw Margaret's dead cat to the ravenous canine. She stood and watched for several minutes, enjoying the sight and slobbering, crunching sounds of Mephisto's feast.

At six o'clock, the alarm went off at Judy Eames's bedside and buzzed until it exhausted itself and fell quiet. Judy slept on. It wasn't until 9 A.M. that the ringing of the telephone would finally wake her. It was the nursery school where she worked, calling to see if she was coming in. She was an hour late. Judy groggily told them she couldn't make it, her daughter was sick, and hung up the phone. She stared at the clock on the nightstand, wondering if Roger, knowing she would be staying home with Margaret, had turned off the alarm. But when she checked it, she found the alarm button was still on and the alarm had wound down.

How did I sleep through the alarm? she wondered. She had never done that. She tried to get out of bed, but flopped back exhausted. The thought that she was coming down with whatever had put Margaret under the weather yesterday crossed her mind, explaining her oversleeping. She certainly felt like the proverbial truck had hit her.

What about Margaret? she worried suddenly. If she felt anything like Judy, then the poor kid was probably still sleeping. Judy just hoped Roger had checked on her before he left for work, but even so it was time for her to take some aspirin, have her temperature checked, and eat some breakfast.

She forced herself out of bed, pulled on her robe, and staggered out of the bedroom and down the hall to Margaret's room. She was surprised to see her daughter's bed empty, but upon further thought figured she must have had a twenty-four-hour bug.

Sure, now she's given it to me, she smirked. It was typical of Margaret, even if she was still feeling a little under the weather, not to want to miss school. She'd have to be practically dying to *want* to stay home. Still, with all that had been going on in Northwood lately, Judy worried that she had gotten off all right. She decided to call the school to check on her when the phone rang.

"Hello, Mrs. Eames. This is Pioneer Regional checking our absentees. Is Margaret home sick today?"

Judy nearly collapsed. Her worst fear had just come true: *Her daughter was missing.*

CHAPTER 19

I'll tell you a story . . .

The sunlight was blinding as Jennifer walked out of the school building at afternoon recess, but she barely blinked. She'd been waiting all day for afternoon recess and it had seemed to take forever to get here. She walked with purpose across the yard, ignoring the group of girls from her class who were sneaking down to the football field to have a butt. In the past, she had accompanied them, but today she had something more important to do—an errand for Grandma.

She pushed through the third-grade horde and made her way to the far end of the playground where the first-graders played on the swings, seesaw, and jungle gym. She kept her eyes peeled for Jackie and saw him playing Hacky-Sack with a group of boys near the first-grade entrance to the building. She walked in the opposite direction, skirting the fence to be sure he didn't see her. Near the gate, behind the jungle gym, she found who she was looking for.

He was a small first-grader, even smaller than Jackie. He was standing alone by the fence, watching two boys flip for baseball cards, when Jennifer approached him and spoke to him. He was a shy boy and shrank from her at first. Something about her eyes stopped him, drew him back. Her voice was strange, too, rhythmic, like the drumming of the rain on a rooftop.

As she came close and put her arm around his shoulder, he realized she was telling him a story.

There were two tall policemen, wearing dark glasses, waiting for Jackie and Jennifer at the bus stop when they got home. They identified themselves as being from the sheriff's department and asked the two Nailer children several questions concerning the last time they had seen Margaret Eames and whether they had seen her that morning on the bus or at the bus stop.

Jennifer told the officers of playing in the surrounding woods with Margaret after school the day before, adding that neither she nor Jackie had seen her since. Jackie kept quiet, intimidated by the sheriff's men, and nodded along with Jen's account. He gave her a strange look when one of the officers asked what they were doing in the woods and Jen replied, "Just playing."

When the two men finished with their questions, one of them went back to the Eames' house, which had two sheriff's department cruisers in the driveway, while the other one walked them to their house.

"Has something happened to Margaret?" Jackie asked as they walked along.

"Nothing for you to worry about, son," the officer replied with a smile.

Jackie opened his mouth to speak again, but Jennifer pinched his arm, making him yelp. The officer looked at them with mild reproval and led them up their driveway to their front door. He knocked several times and rang the doorbell twice in growing annoyance before a sleepy-eyed Diane Nailer, dressed in a rumpled neck-to-toe flannel nightgown, answered the door.

The officer took one look at Diane's enormous stomach

and yawning mouth and his annoyance quickly changed to embarrassment. Nobody had told him she was pregnant. "Uh, sorry to wake you, ma'am. We just wanted to make sure your kids got home okay." Diane yawned again and nodded, opening the door. Jackie and Jennifer went inside and Diane closed the door on the officer without another word.

As the officer walked away, he thought she had been rather indifferent. He knew that Deputy Sheriff Vitelli had questioned her earlier in the day, so she knew about the disappearance of the Eames girl, but now she hadn't asked about it. To him that seemed strange; he thought she would at least want to know if there were any more news about the girl. He'd want to know if a kid on his street, a playmate of his daughter's, had disappeared, but she had seemed not to care.

Maybe she hadn't said or asked anything so as not to alarm her children, he reasoned. That certainly made sense; he'd had to stop talking at home about the several disappearances of children in the area because his own kids were scared to death. Satisfied with that explanation, the officer went back to the Eameses' house.

"What happened to Margaret, Mom?" Jackie asked as he took off his coat. She was starting up the stairs, intent on returning to bed. Jennifer was in the kitchen with her head in the refrigerator.

"Who knows?" his mother groused. "The little brat probably ran away." She continued up the stairs and went into her bedroom, slamming the door behind her.

Jackie went into the kitchen where Jen, still wearing her coat, was downing a glass of milk. "Jen, how come you didn't tell that guy about the witch Margaret took you to see yesterday?"

"What are you, crazy? There was no witch. You think I want people to say I'm as weird as you are?"

"Mom said that Margaret ran away."

Jen laughed sarcastically.

"What?" Jackie asked.

"If you believe that then you're dumber than I thought." She put her empty glass in the sink and headed for the back door.

"What do you mean? Where are you going?" Jackie asked, following her.

"I'm going out." Jen paused at the door.

"Where?"

"In the woods." Jen said and went out the door.

Jackie jumped, catching the screen door before it could close. "Hey! What happened to Margaret?" he yelled at Jen's back. She either didn't hear him, or ignored him, and continued into the field and the woods.

Jennifer sat on a tree stump at the edge of a path on the other side of the road from the one that ran behind her house. Grandma had shown her this path, which ran parallel to the river behind the row of Colonial houses on Route 47, yesterday. Further on, the path dipped through a wall of bushes and hanging vines and came out on the beautiful glen where Grandma's gingerbread house was. Jen couldn't wait to go back there, but she had something to do first—something for Grandma.

Sitting there, waiting, Jennifer marvelled again at how wonderful it was to have her grandmother back. Now she didn't care whether her mother or Steve seemed indifferent and uncaring. Grandma would always be there.

The sound of voices from down the path brought her to her feet. She could just see the tops of three, then four, small heads—three brown-haired and one red—bobbing along the path between a tangle of blueberry bushes. The little boy she'd told the story to at recess was in the lead and he had brought some friends just as Jen had told him to. Jennifer smiled; Grandma would be pleased.

"Is this the bozo who told you that nutty story?" the red-haired boy asked contemptuously of Jen's small friend when they reached her. The latter nodded shyly.

The redhead turned on Jen. "What are you, some kind of weirdo? Why'd you tell my brother that Goldilocks and the Three Bears live in these woods?"

Jennifer grinned slowly, looking at each boy in turn, lastly fixing her gaze on the redhead. "Because it's true," she said convincingly.

"You're loony tunes, baby," the redhead said, smirking. The other boys, except for his brother, giggled.

"And what's your name?" Jen asked, stepping closer and bending to the redhead's eye level.

He stared right back at her, undaunted. "I'm Jimmy's brother," he said, indicating the boy from recess, "Jeff."

"Well, Jeff," Jennifer said, straightening and glancing at the others, "how would you like to see for yourself where Goldilocks and the Three Bears live? I can show you."

The other boys looked at each other, wide-eyed. Here was an impressive boast and they looked to Jeff, their leader, for his reaction.

For the first time Jeff seemed unsure of himself. "You're crazy, or you're putting us on," he said. He looked around at his brother and friends for agreement, but got none. "This is some stupid joke, right?"

"Why don't you follow me and find out for yourself?" Jen replied. She turned and started up the path, not looking around to see if they were following her. Jimmy was the first to, after a triumphant I-told-you-so look at his older brother. The other two boys followed him. Reluctantly, redheaded Jeff, the skeptic, brought up the rear.

The path went through the same boggy floodplain Jen had struggled through prior to discovering Grandma's house. The narrow path was muddy and pockmarked with puddles. Jen and the four boys made their way carefully, watching where they were stepping and not talking except for an occasional griping remark from Jeff about the stupidity of the venture.

As they approached the cluster of hanging vines that marked the entrance to Grandma's glen, Jeff stopped and refused to go on. "This is a wild-goose chase," he said petulantly. "Come on, you guys, let's go home. She's just pulling our legs."

The boys looked at each other but no one moved.

"Okay. You jerks can follow her and get all muddy out here, but I'm going. And Jimmy, Ma's gonna kill you when she sees that you wrecked your new sneakers."

Jimmy looked down at his mud-caked Nikes and frowned. The other boys followed suit, wondering what their own mothers would say about their muddy feet.

Moving quickly, Jennifer went back to Jeff, stepping in front of him, blocking his way. "But, Jeff," she said soothingly, "it's just ahead. You can't turn back now." As she spoke to him, she placed her hand on his shoulder and squeezed it lightly. The boy stiffened suddenly as if a mild electrical shock had just coursed through his body. He stared into Jen's hazel eyes and felt his mind go numbingly cold. His head nodded in agreement as if it were disconnected from his body and controlled by someone else, like the bobbing head of a marionette on a string.

"Let's go on," Jennifer said softly. She turned and continued on the path. Jeff followed on her heels without a glance around at his brother and his buddies. They looked at each other, a glance of uncertainty passed between them at Jeff's sudden change of heart, then followed also.

The house was just as Jennifer had described it to Jimmy at school: long and squat with a bulky, heavy thatched roof on top, its long straw spilling over the sides almost to the ground. At the closest end, a great stone chimney climbed the side of the house, jutting well above the thatched roof. From it, a steady stream of gray smoke rose and drifted lazily away through the treetops. At the front of the house was a small oval wooden door with a tiny round window in it. On either side of the door, nearly hidden by the overhanging roof straw, were two more small round windows.

"Wow!" the two friends of Jimmy and Jeff exclaimed at the same time. Jimmy smiled with delight, but Jeff remained silent.

"Wait till you see inside," Jennifer coaxed. She, too, marvelled at what Grandma had done with the gingerbread house, but she didn't question how. Grandma had told her she was going to do something special with the house for the company Jen was bringing, and that was good enough for Jen. She waved the boys on and led them to the small front door. She pushed it open and a warm, sour smell, like boiled cabbage, emanated from within.

"Look, it's just as I told you," Jennifer said happily as she led them inside. The boys oohed and ahhed as they walked through the door and into a tiny, wood-paneled kitchen. A hand-hewn square wooden table sat in the middle of the room to the left of a wide open hearth with a fire going under a large black kettle. Around the table were three stools of varying size from small to tall, each one at a spot where a bowl was sitting on the table with wooden spoons by their sides. Wisps of steam rose from the contents of each bowl.

Jennifer went around the table and sat on the first stool which had the largest bowl in front of it. "Someone's been eating my porridge," Jen intoned in a deep voice. The boys, except for Jeff, giggled. She moved on to the next bowl as they watched with rapt attention. Now she spoke in a falsetto, saying again: "Someone's been eating my porridge." At the third bowl, she spoke in a high, squeaky baby voice: "Someone's been eating my porridge, and they ate it all up!" The boys laughed loudly at Jennifer's antics, which brought a small smile even to Jeff's serious face.

Leading them from the kitchen, Jennifer brought the boys into the next room at the back of the small house. Its floor was covered with a red and green braided rug upon which sat two rocking chairs, one large, the other a little smaller. A third one lay in a broken heap. Jen followed the story to a tee, sitting in each chair and proclaiming, "Someone's been sitting in my chair," like a ritual chant, until at the third chair she cried like a baby over the broken pile.

The boys cracked up with laughter until Jeff pointed at a ladder that went up through the ceiling at the back of the room. "I bet Goldilocks is up there," he said. The other boys looked at him wonderingly.

Jen smiled and nodded. "Let's see," she said, and went to the ladder. She began climbing up.

The upstairs room was small, the underside of the thatched roof squeezed between the wooden support beams and pressed low over their heads. Continuing on in the Goldilocks mode, there were three beds in the room: one large, one medium, and one small. The first two beds were empty, the bed covers rumpled. Jennifer paused by each one and recited the proper words. There was obviously someone in the third bed. The blankets were pulled up and tucked around a blonde-haired head, hiding the face.

"Goldilocks," Jeff whispered excitedly, his eyes gleaming.

"Someone's been sleeping in my bed, too," Jennifer squeaked in her baby bear voice, "and here she is!" She grabbed the covers and pulled them back, throwing them to the floor.

The boys stared at the figure in the bed with anticipated delight, which soon turned to horror. Though it had long, golden hair, the thing in the bed was not Goldilocks. The thing in the bed was barely recognizable as having once been human. The body was devoid of skin except on its face, where it was a bluish gray color and very loose, wrinkled like the skin of a dried apple. Even so, little Jimmy thought he recognized it as that of a girl in one of the other first-grade classes at school. Exposed muscle and cartilage showed on her arms and legs where the skin had been flayed away. The stomach was a hollow cavity, empty of entrails and revealing the top edges of the hip bones and the base of the spine. Her chest had been flayed open, the ribs exposed and the heart and lungs removed. A mass of tiny flies and insects flitted over the rotting corpse and a stench like chicken bones left in a garbage can for a month rose from it, causing the boys to gag and back away from the bed. Only Jennifer continued to smile.

A low growl came from behind them. Jeff turned and gasped at what he saw. The three bears were hunched in the corner. A tall, ferocious grizzly bear was the daddy, a black bear, nearly as tall, was the mother, and a little brown bear with a mouth full of long, nasty teeth was the baby.

Papa Bear roared loudly, shaking the rafters of the thatched roof and revealing double rows of daggerlike teeth. Mama Bear licked her chops hungrily. Baby Bear yawned, showing his razor-sharp teeth, also. Together, the three started slowly toward the boys.

They were petrified with fear. Jimmy, in front of the others, wet his pants. His brother, Jeff, soiled his, the odor mingling with the stench of the flayed corpse in the bed. The other two boys burst into tears. Suddenly, as if they had all been seeing triple and now their eyesight was returning to normal, the boys saw the three bears waver and begin to slide together. First Baby Bear was absorbed into Mama Bear, then Mama Bear was sucked into Papa Bear. Finally, like a holograph that shifts images with the changing light, Papa Bear turned into an old woman. She cackled loudly and threw a heavy nylon net over the screaming boys.

"I brought you some company for tea, just like you asked," Jennifer said to her grandmother, smiling sweetly and completely unaware of the horrors the boys had just seen. In her eyes, the boys were sitting down to tea and cookies in a corner of the room. "When can I bring Jackie, Gram?" Jen asked pleadingly.

Eleanor patted Jennifer's head. "All in good time, child. All in good time."

CHAPTER 20

Old woman, old woman, shall we go a-shearing?

Eleanor closed the cage door on the four sniveling boys Jennifer had brought her. She was very pleased. Despite the constant pain in her arms and chest, things were going well. There were less than two weeks to go to Halloween and she needed only five more boys. Since she was fairly sure she could take Jennifer's brother Jackie any time she needed him, the count was down to four.

She went to the embalming table and brought a tray of peanut butter sandwiches, milk, and an assortment of junk foods back to the cage and placed it inside. A quick compelling thought from her was enough to make the four new boys forget their predicament for the moment and become hungry enough to devour everything on the tray. The twins and Timmy Walsh, who hadn't eaten for a day, needed no prodding.

She looked at Davy Torrez lying in the rear corner of the cage and bit her lip. He looked worse every day. His color was bad, a sign that shock was taking its toll on his health. As far as she knew, he had neither eaten nor drunk since his capture. Nor had he used the toilet, soiling his pajamas instead until he stank so bad the other boys stayed away from him. If he kept this up, he'd be dead by Halloween and she'd have to look for another. She couldn't have that. Though it had been awhile since she'd heard any thoughts from him, Eleanor probed his mind and felt only the barest glimmer of a response. She sighed. There was nothing more she could do. Little Margaret was waiting for her. It was time for the Third Ritual of Preparation.

Deep in the protective subconscious hole Davy Torrez had dug for himself, faint echoes of the witch's probing reached him. With it came memories: his mother reading to him; his father playing catch with him. He smiled at these, his thin pale lips barely moving, but then more recent memories came unbidden.

He relived all the nightmare turns his life had taken recently—the Mother Goose rhymes running riot in the parking lot outside his home; the boy in the cage with no arms or legs *(What else? I don't know but he'll never go pee-pee again);* the witch's wrinkled old face grinning at him, her mouth stretching open to reveal wasted teeth waiting to sink into his trembling flesh *(good for stew!)*

Davy sat bolt upright. His eyes flew open, and he became vaguely aware of his surroundings. He was still in the cage, still a captive. Across the cage seven other boys were wolfing down sandwiches and packaged pastries and drinking tall glasses of milk. The hazy memory of the witch pouring a white powder into the milk pitcher came to him and he suddenly understood what it meant: That powder would put them to sleep.

Don't drink the milk! Davy wanted to yell at them, but he couldn't get his voice to work or his lips to move. He was too weak. *Don't drink the milk or it'll put you to sleep,* he thought again, much fainter this time. It was no use. He was drifting again, hovering on the edge of consciousness.

* * *

Eleanor led a naked Margaret into the crematorium and told her to sit in the high-backed wooden chair she had placed in the middle of the pentagram after moving the heavy recliner out of the way. She made a quick mental check of the boys and found them all in deep, drugged sleep. That done, she wheeled the metal instrument cart over and placed it to the side and behind the chair.

Eleanor looked over the tools and picked up a large, rectangular-shaped, barber's electric shears. She plugged the shears into a wall socket next to the cage and turned it on. It hummed to life, buzzing like a swarm of attacking bees.

The shears removed the hair from Margaret's head as easily as a wet rag clears dust from a tabletop. Starting at the base of her neck, Eleanor pushed the shears up and over the top of Margaret's head, letting the long brown curls fall on the floor and roll down the girl's naked chest to her lap.

From the instrument cart she next took a thick roll of heavy, gray, duct tape and began winding it around Margaret at the waist, chest, and neck, securing her body to the chair. She next applied the tape across Margaret's forehead, strapping her bald head tightly to the back of the chair so that it was immovable. Throughout, Margaret never made a sound nor moved a muscle. She remained staring straight ahead.

When Margaret was securely strapped to the chair, Eleanor removed a large, glowing hot, stoneware bowl from the crematorium oven and placed it in the middle of the pentangle. It was inscribed with strange symbols and runic letters. Carefully, she picked up all of Margaret's shorn locks and dropped them into the bowl one at a time while she knelt over it, mumbling as if in prayer. Flames shot up with each lock and little black globs of burnt hair floated out of the dish toward the ceiling.

Eleanor stepped back, held her hands up, palms outward, and finished chanting. She crossed herself with the sign of the five-pointed star and began removing her clothing. When she was naked, she went to a shelf on the other side of the crematorium furnace and removed the neatly folded skin of Betty Boone and a Ball jar filled with a dark, gluey substance.

She placed the skin on the embalming table then unlatched the top of the jar. She removed the glass and rubber stopper and dipped her finger in. The stuff was purplish black as she held it up in the candlelight. She brought her fingers to her lips, tasted it, and smiled.

The liquid, which was rubbery and stale, was hard to work with, but Eleanor didn't seem to mind. She scooped the stuff out with her fingers and painted it on Margaret's naked head and body carefully, being sure to make each symbol precisely. When she was done and there were thirteen symbols in blood painted on her head, eyelids, lips, and unformed breasts, Eleanor again tasted the contents of the jar, leaving a bloody smear down her chin. Licking the stuff from her lips, she painted corresponding symbols on her own face and body.

When she was done, she replaced the jar on the shelf and unfolded the skin, which had grown leathery. As though putting on a mink stole, she draped the skin of Betty Boone over her head and shoulders and proceeded to dance around the pentagram six times, her body gyrating wildly as she sang a song that had no discernible melody or understandable words. On her last turn around the table, Eleanor snatched a mortician's electrical bone saw from the instrument cart. She finished her dance where she'd started it, directly behind Margaret's chair. She plugged the saw into the same socket she'd used for the shears and with a flick of the switch brought it to life. It whined, a hard mean sound that set Eleanor to cackling merrily.

From the twilight edges of dreamless unconsciousness Davy Torrez became aware of a sound like a dentist's drill magnified a hundred times. The sound pulled him reluctantly to consciousness again and forced his eyes open.

Candlelight was the first thing he saw. It dazzled his eyes with rainbow auras for a moment and spilled over the sleeping bodies of the other boys in the cage. He looked past them, focusing as well as he could through the fog of trauma that ruled him, to the figures outside the cage. By the flickering light Davy saw the naked witch, some kind of sheet draped over her head and shoulders, standing behind an equally naked child strapped to a chair in the middle of the star within a circle. The child's head had no hair on it. As Davy's eyes dropped, he thought for a moment that the witch had cut off this child's peepee, too, but then he realized it was a girl.

In the witch's hand was the thing that was making the awful noise that had woken him. It had a short round handle with a trigger on it, and a long, sharp, saw-toothed, double-edged blade extending out for more than a foot from the handle. The two rows of teeth moved opposite each other, sliding back and forth much like his father's hedge clippers only at a much greater speed.

As Davy watched in horror, the witch placed the whining saw against the girl's forehead and drew it back toward her. The saw screeched with an awful sound more shrill than a piece of broken chalk drawn hard across a blackboard. Bone dust and blood flew from the blade's jigsawing action. Blood ran over the tape on the girl's head and down her face like tears. The little girl's eyes widened. Her mouth dropped open and she drooled a thick line of spit. Held tightly by the gray tape, the rest of her body was becoming flecked with drops of blood, tiny skull splinters, and fragments of raw skin and flesh. Through it all the girl never uttered a sound.

It took only seconds for the saw to complete its path through the top of her skull, but to Davy Torrez it was an eternity. A scream of revulsion and horror built deep in his gut, travelled upward, bypassing his shock-silenced vocal cords, and exploded in his brain. Tears welled in his eyes and flowed freely down his face, matching the tears that welled in the eyes of the poor girl in the chair.

The saw came free of the back of the girl's head with one last screech, dotting the witch's flattened, wrinkled breasts with blood and bone dust. The scream in Davy's head grew louder. The witch turned the saw off and put it aside. She began to chant strange unintelligible words and placed her hands on both sides of the girl's head. As though she were lifting the lid of a cookie jar, the witch removed the top of the girl's head. Davy could see a glimpse of the top of her quivering, wet brain just above the bloody rim of her forehead.

The scream in Davy's head grew so loud it felt as though at any second it would blow the top off his head leaving his brain exposed to the air like the little girl's. Her eyes were still wide open, but had become bloodshot and glazed. Her face was streaked with blood that mingled with her tears, turning them red.

Something bright and silvery flashed over the little girl's ruined head. Davy pulled his eyes away from that horrible stare and looked. The witch held something metallic in her hand. Davy couldn't see it well at first because of the candle light reflecting off it directly into his eyes. He moved his head and saw what it was.

No! Please! Don't! a part of Davy's mind whispered beneath the scream that was reaching hurricane force between his ears. In her hand, the witch held a large silver spoon whose scooping end had been honed to dagger sharpness. The witch raised the spoon, holding it over the girl's head like a holy chalice, and intoned several incomprehensible words. She crossed herself with her left hand in a strange way, touching her forehead, breasts, and hips.

Licking her lips greedily, the witch dug the spoon into the little girl's opened skull. She jabbed and tugged; there was a sickeningly soft, wet sucking sound like something being pulled out of thick mud and the witch scooped a large spoon-ful of brains from the opened skull.

The girl's eyes widened farther than Davy would have thought was humanly possible, then rolled up into her head, showing only their whites. Her face twitched spasmodically, blood gushed from her nose, and her mouth opened and closed like a fish on land. The only part of her lower body that could move, her fingers, jerked convulsively. There was a farting sound followed by a soft spattering as her bowels and blad-der let go, flowing onto the chair and down her naked legs to the floor. A foul smell of rotten eggs filled the room.

The witch shoveled the gob of brains into her mouth, chewing slowly, relishing every bit of it, and swallowed. She smiled. Her lips and teeth were coated with a shiny bloody slime like gray Vaseline. She lapped the spoon and dug it in for another scoop which she pulled out and held toward Davy.

Want some? she asked in his head, and erupted into horri-ble laughter.

Reality snapped and Davy Torrez went into a tailspin falling deeper and deeper back into the protective black hole in his subconscious. As he fell, the scream of anguish in his head echoed around and around, accompanying him into the depths of unconsciousness where it went on and on and on.

CHAPTER 21

Oh, dear, what can the matter be?

Steve looked at the clock on his desk and sighed. It was 6 A.M. He'd been up since five trying to write but all he'd done was sit and stare at the blank paper in front of him and think of her. For the past month and a half, ever since he'd seen her that first day outside Roosevelt's Bar in Amherst, Steve Nailer had been haunted by the thought of, and desire for, the provocative young woman who seemed capable of crawling right inside his head and knowing all the dark, lustful secrets he kept hidden there.

It certainly wasn't helping his work. Here it was, late October, and he hadn't finished more than two lines of the first of four sonnets he was writing for the Dickinson Poetry Competition. The deadline was little more than a week away and he couldn't finish *one* poem, much less four. He was trapped in the middle of the worst writer's block he had ever experienced. He felt like he was stuck in quicksand; the harder he struggled for the right words the deeper he sank into frustration.

He tried everything he could think of to free his creative juices and get them flowing again. He began reading the works of the masters of the sonnet form, from Shakespeare to Theodore Sturgeon. He tried meditating, getting drunk—he'd even smoked pot on the advice of one of his fellow teachers at the academy—but nothing worked. Lately he'd taken to going for long drives in the surrounding countryside, but he found himself looking for the sexy young woman of his desires instead of thinking about his poetry.

Diane hadn't been much help, either. Steve was certain that a great deal of his creative stagnation was due to the fact that he hadn't been laid since they'd moved to Northwood. That was over a month without *real* sex, the longest he'd ever gone. Not that he hadn't had *any* sexual release. He was plagued with sexual dreams about the young woman, some of which ended in nocturnal emissions.

Invariably, after those dreams, which ran the gamut of sexual experience from oral and anal sex to bondage and worse, he was left feeling guilty, embarrassed, and more creatively barren than he had felt before. Never in his life had he dreamed like that. And what was worse, the shame and embarrassment had begun to wear off and, like some sicko pervert, he had actually begun to look forward to dreaming.

Steve couldn't figure Diane out lately. Since they'd moved, she had changed, and not for the better. Where she had once been an easygoing, loving woman and caring mother, she had now become a moody, brooding bitch who wouldn't let him touch her and who was equally cold to her own children. Even the terrible news of the disappearance of the Eameses' daughter Margaret and four boys from just around the corner on Route 47 seemed to have had no effect on her.

Poor Judy Eames must be insane with worry and despair, but Diane hadn't once gone over to talk to her and console her. Steve had thought those two were going to become the best of friends after that first night when they met, but since then Diane had wanted nothing to do with Judy, anyone, or anything. Several times they had been invited out to dinner and drinks by Bill Gage, another teacher at the academy whom Steve had become friends with, and his wife, but every time

Diane refused, using her pregnancy as an excuse, saying she was too tired or had morning sickness.

Her demeanor toward Jackie and Jennifer was no better. Steve had thought that when Margaret Eames and the other children disappeared so close by, Diane would once again become the caring, protective mother she had always been. He was wrong; nothing had changed. She didn't bother going to the bus stop to walk them home everyday and didn't care at all that Jennifer didn't even take the bus home anymore. Instead she walked home through the woods, sometimes spending hours out there alone doing God knows what and not arriving home until dark. Jackie, who was afraid for his sister, showing much more sense than his mother, had told him all about it. When Steve had brought it up with Diane, she had snapped at him, reminding him that they were *her* children and he should just butt out. When he tried to talk to Jennifer about it, she had acted just like her mother telling him to mind his own business. Angered and frustrated, he had.

He put the pencil down and stretched. From the bedroom across the hall, he could hear Diane whining in her sleep. It was a pitiful sound that she made often these days. Steve wondered what sort of terrible dreams she could be tortured by to make her cry out night after night. He pushed sympathy from his mind, telling himself that if she was going to play the part of an uncaring bitch, then he could be just as uncaring. Ignoring her whimpering, he got up and went into the bathroom to shower and get ready for work.

Roger Eames sat at the kitchen table in the gray light of dawn and smoked a cigarette. The ashtray on the table in front of him was overflowing with crushed butts. Unable to sleep, he'd been up since 2 A.M. chain-smoking in the dark, sometimes weeping softly. He'd quit smoking when Margaret was born but had started again since her disappearance. He

lit a fresh cigarette off the previous butt and stuffed the latter
into the full ashtray.

I didn't protect her.

The thought ran over and over in his mind like a broken
record. He took his glasses off, placed them on the table, and
put his hands to his eyes, massaging the bridge of his nose
and squeezing back the tears.

The last week and a half had been pure hell. Looking
back on it was like trying to remember a fever dream, a bout
of delirium. From the moment the call had come into work
for him from an hysterical Judy screaming that Margaret
was missing, his world had fragmented and turned into a
nightmare. Nine-thirty in the morning—that was the time he
had received Judy's frantic call, that was the time his world
had gone astray; that was the time he'd remember the rest of
his life.

The light grew a little brighter in the kitchen as day crept
across the fall sky, revealing the sink piled high with dirty
dishes, spilling over onto the countertop. The floor was a
mess, too, strewn with scraps of food left over from the few
meager meals he and Judy had managed to eat since Margaret
had disappeared. It was caked with dirty footprints from all
the police, reporters, and search party volunteers who had
tracked over it lately. The refrigerator and other kitchen ap-
pliances were similarly grimy, reflecting the general state of
the rest of the house.

It was amazing to Roger, who was normally a fastidious
man, how much dirt and dust could accumulate in just a couple weeks. He had made halfhearted attempts to pick up and
clean but had given up. What was the use? It was hard to
care about whether or not the house was clean when your
world was falling apart.

Roger took another cigarette out, lit it as before with the
stub of the one in his hand, and took a deep drag. He remembered reading somewhere, when he was trying to quit
smoking, that smokers have a subconscious wish to commit

suicide; they know the health hazards of smoking but continue to do so. With him, though, it was no longer a subconscious desire. With his little girl missing (he could not yet admit the possibility that she might be dead, even though, deep inside, he feared it was so and the knowledge was like a festering malignant tumor waiting to engulf him), he no longer cared about his health. If she was not found, then he no longer cared about his own life, either.

From upstairs he heard the soft creaking of the bed as Judy tossed and turned in fitful sleep. When it had become obvious that Margaret had disappeared and the police had to be called in, Judy had accelerated past hysterical, going completely to pieces. Their family doctor had prescribed Valium to keep her calm during the day and Seconal to help her sleep at night. Roger made sure she took them regularly, even if it meant she would develop a dependency, which seemed to be happening. In the past few days, Judy had started taking the drugs more often, sometimes mixing the Valium and Seconals. Roger looked the other way, telling himself that, if Margaret returned safe, Judy would kick the drugs out of pure joy. If Margaret didn't return, it wouldn't matter.

Roger stretched to relieve the pressure on his back from sitting too long and looked at the phone. He thought of calling the sheriff's office again. He'd taken to calling them every morning and several times during the day every day, especially since they'd called off the search parties. Roger had a feeling they were giving up on the investigation and he wasn't about to let that happen. He wasn't going to become one of those parents of missing children, existing like some kind of zombie in a living death, paying to have Margaret's picture put on milk cartons and hoping against hope that someone somewhere would come forth with information that would lead to her recovery. He would badger the police, hire private detectives (which he had already done), and do everything he could to find Margaret.

What else could he do? he wondered. He didn't know but

there had to be *something*, some piece of information that the police and private detectives had missed; some *memory* that was eluding Roger and, if remembered, would lead to Margaret's discovery.

He got up from the table and took a pencil and piece of paper from a drawer under the phone. For the hundredth time at least, he began to make a list of the facts concerning his daughter's disappearance.

Steve's first-period class was off the wall. Normally, they reserved such disruptive behavior for Fridays; Wednesday was a little early in the week for them to be so wild. Steve let them know it in no uncertain terms, coming down hard on them, giving several detentions and doubling the usual home-work load. They were reading, *'A Midsummer Night's Dream'*; he assigned the last two acts plus ten discussion questions to do overnight, and they could expect to be quizzed on it to-morrow.

The class, eleventh graders, moaned and groaned less than usual and still took awhile to quiet down. Strangely, Steve noticed that very few of them wrote the assignment down in their notebooks, a practice he required of them. He was about to instruct them all to do it, but then thought better of it. If they didn't do the assignment, he'd really nail them with the quiz tomorrow.

It was during second period, which was his free period, that he overheard something that would shed some light on his students' behavior. He was at his desk in the coaches' locker room in the gym, diagramming some new plays for the football team. Joe Conally, the athletic director, came in but didn't see Steve and went into his office, leaving the door open.

Steve and Conally had barely remained on speaking terms since Conally had laid his cards on the table and let Steve know that he was unwanted. Steve had made a point of staying out of his way and doing his job well, both as a health instructor and as coach. The varsity football team was five and one, with six games left to play against smaller schools that they should beat easily, which would get them a state super-bowl bid. Steve handed in his lesson plans for the health class on time and always made sure they were detailed with clear objectives and methods. He wasn't going to give Joe Conally any fodder for a campaign to get rid of him.

He'd thought things were going well, had even persuaded himself that Conally was begrudgingly aware of how good a teacher and coach he really was and had relaxed his drive to replace him. What he overheard next was to prove him utterly wrong.

"Mr. Turner?" Conally was on the phone and had left his door open. Steve could hear him clearly and his ears perked up at the mention of Mr. Turner, who was the chairman of the academy's board of regents. Steve was aware that Turner had been quite ill for a while, which was one reason Conally's attempts for a hearing on Steve's hiring had been thwarted.

"I'm calling about my request for a hearing on the Nailer matter," Conally said. Steve tensed. "That's great, Mr. Turner, I'm sure that I can prove to you and the board this was an improper hiring that did not follow union contract procedures. Yes, sir. I'll be there at eight sharp next Tuesday night. Yes, sir. Thank you, sir." Conally hung up the phone and left his office.

Now Steve knew why his students first period had acted so. Conally's son, Joe Jr., went to the school and was almost as bigmouthed and obnoxious as his father. Conally was not the type to keep anything confidential and must have gloated about Steve's impending dismissal at home. His son must have overheard and spread the information around the student population.

The rest of the day only confirmed Steve's suspicions. The students talked and fooled around, and no amount of threatening them with detentions or extra homework could quiet them for long. And from the way the other teachers looked at him and seemed to avoid him, Steve became convinced the entire school knew he was not long for the job. By the end of the day, he was hoarse from yelling, and very depressed. He cancelled all the detentions he'd given and called off football practice. When the final bell rang, he didn't even stay around for the forty-five minutes that teachers were contractually required to remain in the building. He got in his car and drove quickly away, as if by doing so he could escape his problems.

Roger Eames worked on his fact list all morning. By noon he had written down everything he thought was relevant to the day Margaret had disappeared. He was going over the list when Judy wandered downstairs, hair disheveled, dark circles under her eyes looking even darker because of her pasty complexion, and asked him if he had called the police yet. He lied to her, saying they had nothing to report. She stared dully at him, then took another Seconal and two Valium with a glass of orange juice and stumbled back to bed.

His list was useless. Roger stared at it until 2 P.M., tracing over what he'd written, underlining it, putting checks next to each item, but unable to see anything that might provide a clue as to what had happened to Margaret that morning. Frustrated, he crumpled the paper up and threw it in the direction of the wastepaper basket. It missed and landed against the cat's litter box, which had been pushed nearly all the way under the stove and out of sight.

Something clicked in Roger's mind.

Where is the cat?

A cold tingle ran down his back as he realized that he hadn't seen the cat since Margaret had disappeared.

No! It was before Margaret had disappeared. When?

He tried to remember. In all the confusion and emotion neither he nor Judy had thought once about the cat. Now he racked his brain trying to remember the last time he'd seen it. It had been at dinner the night before Margaret's disappearance, wasn't it? No, but they had talked about the cat then. He remembered he had mentioned to Margaret that he hadn't seen Puffin in a while. What had she said? *She'd look for her later.* Had she? Where?

The sheriff's department had decided, after searching the woods for several miles around Dorsey Lane and Route 47, and after dragging the river with no results, that Margaret had more than likely been picked up by someone at the bus stop before any of the other kids got there. But what if she had gone into the woods in search of her cat instead? If so, why hadn't the search parties turned up any trace of her?

What's in those woods? Roger wondered. He had never been out there. Except for the old couple, the retired undertaker and his sister, the Grimms, whom the police had told him about, Roger didn't know what else might be in the woods. Vagrants might have a shelter out there, or a gang of punk teenagers. No, he told himself. The police and volunteers in the search party would have found something like that.

What about the Grimms?

Roger vaguely remembered a deputy sheriff saying he had spoken to the sister and she had seen no sign of Margaret. Was that it? Yes, as far as he could remember. He had been so distraught by it all and distracted by Judy's hysteria that his memories were like trying to look at a photograph someone's holding by the side of the road as you drive by at fifty miles per hour.

What if the sister is lying?

The cold tingle ran down his neck again. Maybe I should check out the old couple myself, he thought. He knew it was a long shot, no matter how many tingly feelings he got that he was on to something, but at least it was *something;* it beat sitting around doing nothing. He got up from the table and started for the door, had a second thought, and went back to the table. On the pad of paper he left Judy a note:

Judy, have gone to Grimm Memorials.

                                                        Rog

    As Roger closed the back door, it created just enough of a draft to blow the paper off the table. It floated, then dipped and sailed backward under the kitchen table.

CHAPTER 22

Little girl, little girl, where have you been?

Diane was taking a hot bath when Steve got home. He let himself into the steamy bathroom and sat on the john. Diane was languishing, eyes closed, up to her neck in soapy water. Her swollen breasts and tummy floated just above the surface like newly formed volcanic islands.

"Diane," Steve started and stopped. He sighed. How was he going to tell her he was losing his job? "Babe, I . . ." he tried again to no avail.

Diane opened her eyes and glared at him for a moment. "Steve," she said frostily. "Can we continue this *after* I get out of the tub?" She smiled politely, but her eyes were sullen.

Steve could feel the hostility in her gaze. "Right! I should have known better than to come to you," he said between clenched teeth. He got up and stalked out of the bathroom and out of the house. Leaving rubber, he roared out of the driveway in the Saab and drove down Dorsey Lane.

On Route 116, going north toward Amherst, Steve drove faster, punching the pedal to the floor until the car accelerated to the same level as his anger. But the faster he went, the more the anger wilted, became frustration, desperation

and depression. His problems with Diane were just another
example of how badly he had screwed up his life. His writing was going sour—good-bye, college job; his job at the
academy was going sour—good-bye, house, car; his marriage was going sour—good-bye to the only person who had
ever truly loved him. What else could go wrong?"

Never take on more responsibility than you can handle,
he could hear his father's voice. Wasn't that what he always
said? And wasn't it Steve's failure to adhere to that rule that
had gotten him into all this trouble in the first place? He never
should have married Diane, that was the problem. He wouldn't
have had to take the crummy academy job if he hadn't married her and inherited an instant family. He wouldn't have the
debts hanging over his head that loomed there now, waiting
for the slightest tremor to make them fall.

He sighed. I fucked it up, he thought. I had it made, living
alone, going to school. I blew it. I shit the bed. Now he had
to figure out what to do about it. Without realizing it, he took
the Route 9 exit to Main Street, Amherst. He began running
through his options, which were few, and increasingly nonexistent.

Dr. Plent, the headmaster of Northwood and the man who
had interviewed and hired Steve, had stalled Conally until
now, but he was in Baltimore for a week attending a conven-
tion. He wouldn't be back to the school until the day *after*
the hearing, which seemed awfully convenient. It looked to
Steve as though Dr. Plent had decided to go to this conven-
tion because he knew a confrontation was coming and he
would lose it. Plent struck Steve as the type who would try to
avoid being present at his losses. Plent was a power game
player if he was anything. Steve knew the type; they were
everywhere in education.

Steve would have to face the board of regents alone. He
wondered if he should hire an attorney to accompany him,
then decided it would be a waste of money. If it came down

to violating union hiring standards it wouldn't matter how good a teacher he was. Conally would win and Steve would lose—*everything!*

"Damn, Conally, that shit! I wish I could change his mind somehow," he breathed as he pulled onto Main Street, passing the commons and driving through the lights at the intersection with Route 116. Like a balloon popping, all thoughts of Conally disappeared. There *she* was. He was driving past the place where he had first seen her and there she was in the doorway to Roosevelt's Bar and Grill, the seductress who gave psychic blow jobs.

She was wearing black leather pants and a tight, low cut red sweater. She was looking at him. She licked her lips, and ran her hand up her side, gliding it over her breast, giving it a little squeeze in passing before beckoning to him.

Steve nearly drove the car into a tree in his haste to park it. He finally found a spot twenty yards down and left it sticking crookedly out of the space. He jumped out of the car and ran to Roosevelt's.

She was gone!

I'm inside, the voice slipped into his mind with a sensation like a minor orgasm. Penis erect and raging, he rammed through the door and went in.

Roger Eames hurried along the dirt road through the woods. He passed the Nailers' property and broke into a run to Grimm Memorials.

I wonder why I've never been out here before, he wondered as he ran. It was funny because he remembered that one of the reasons he had liked the house when they'd bought it was because of the surrounding woods. He'd always liked hiking as exercise, and had done some cross-country running and skiing in high school and college. He had planned on doing both in the woods but never had. Now he didn't know why not. He guessed he'd just forgot about it, strange as that seemed.

He slowed to a walk as he reached the short, curving incline that led to the front lot of Grimm Memorials. The house looked deserted; there were no cars in sight. He sprinted to the front porch and went quietly up the steps. He tried the front door but it was locked. He was about to knock, then changed his mind. It might be better if he had a clandestine look around.

He crept to the nearest window on the porch and peered in. The glass was filthy and the drapes too heavy. Only a slim crack between them allowed him to see inside. The room was dark and there was some kind of wooden furniture with dust an inch thick on it close to the window. He checked the latch and found it open. With no storm window on, he easily slid it open.

The air in the house was musty, heavy with the smell of old leather, mildewing silk and velvet and something else he couldn't put his finger on. Roger didn't like it. He wrinkled his nose and breathed through his mouth. He didn't like what he bumped into either. It was a casket, open for display. Its red velvet lining was dotted with blobs of fuzzy black mold. He took in the rest of the room. It was full of coffins; all types and sizes. All rotting away in the darkness.

Looks like business is dying, he thought and giggled aloud nervously at his unintentional joke. He clapped his hand over his mouth and stood still for several moments, letting his eyes adjust completely before picking his way among the coffins to the door on the far wall. He reached it, quietly pulled it open a crack, and peeked in.

He could see a stairway and a black marble floor with a white marble pedestal supporting a large open book. The front door was to the left and against the back wall was a couch between two doors marked in gold letters: *Crematorium* and *Chapel*. Directly across from him was another door, open, but he couldn't make out anything within.

He started to open the door more and stopped. He heard a ticking sound getting closer. He just got the door silently closed again to the tiniest possible crack when, from out of the opposite door, came a giant black dog. Roger held his breath. He had never seen a dog that big, or that ugly. The thing was *enormous*. Its body rippled with muscles. Its head was conical in shape, with pointed ears, and was larger than Roger's own. Its mouth was as long as his forearm; its teeth as thick as railroad spikes. Its eyes were slanted and blood-shot. As Roger looked at him he had to fight down another case of the nervous giggles; it had just dawned on him that the black dog looked like Spuds Mackenzie on steroids.

The dog sauntered into the entranceway and sniffed around the marble pedestal for a moment before trotting up the stairs. When he could no longer see it or hear it, Roger opened the door and carefully crossed half the marble floor. He stopped and looked around. The dog was out of sight, but he knew if he made a sound the beast would be back in a flash. On tip-toes, he went to the door the dog had come out of. It opened on a narrow hallway, at the other end of which he could see a kitchen sink.

He went back to the middle of the entranceway, glancing warily up the stairs for any sign of the dog, and looked out the front door to be sure no one was coming. He went to the door marked Crematorium and eased it open. It led down a flight of stairs to another door at the bottom. Roger closed the door as quietly as he'd opened it. Being careful not to let his sneakers squeak on the smooth floor, he stepped over to the next door, marked Chapel. He turned the knob and pulled it slowly open. The door let out a thunderous squeak.

Roger froze and held his breath. For one wild, panic-stricken second he almost let go of the door and ran back the way he'd come in. He held out, though, overcoming the urge to flee and remained rooted, listening. After nearly a minute and no sign nor sound of the dog returning, he breathed eas-ier. Grabbing the doorknob with both hands, he lifted the door in its hinges to prevent it from squeaking again, and swung it open.

The room beyond was not as dark as the others. Opposite the doorway, two windows had no curtains on them and were open, allowing the cool autumn breeze to blow in, chilling him slightly. Light shown from another window to the right, on the back wall. The gray light of the cloudy day illuminated dingy brown walls and a floral-patterned rug fading on the floor. There were no other furnishings in the room as far as he could tell, but he could see only half the room from the doorway where he stood. Cautiously, he stepped across the threshold, from the marble floor to a wooden one, grimacing as the boards cried softly under his weight.

The room was much longer than it had appeared from the entranceway. The other end of the room was much darker than his end; the windows there were covered tight with the same type of heavy black drapes covering the windows in the coffin display room. He peered into the gloom and almost let out a surprised whistle at what he saw.

Against the far wall, in front of several rows of folding wooden chairs, was a large altar covered in molding red velvet. On top of it were six large black candles in silver holders and a large silver chalice set before a small open tabernacle. Hanging over the altar was what looked like a full-size wooden cross suspended from wires on the ceiling.

But it was upside down.

Roger took a step closer. The figure on the cross was *not* Christ. Roger took another step. The stench of rotten meat poured from the cross. The air was alive with the buzzing of insects. Roger stopped and put his hand to his mouth. The figure on the cross was a young girl.

Oh, God. No, please.

The body had been stripped of its skin. Its raw muscle was rampant with insects and maggots.

Oh no! Not Margaret!

Her feet and hands had been nailed to the cross, crucifixion style, only upside down.

Please not Margaret. Don't let it be Margaret.

What remained of her skin, mostly on her neck and face, was blue and crinkled. One eye was missing, devoured by insects, leaving a blood-encrusted hole. The other bulged grotesquely from its socket; the pain and horror written in it revealing that she had not died a quick death. Long, blonde hair fell from her head, nearly to the altar top.

Blonde hair! Roger screamed with joy. *It's not Margaret!*

His stomach revolted at the sight and stench of the fly-blown corpse and he nearly puked. He gagged back his revulsion and shock, clapping his left hand over his mouth in an attempt to filter out the smell. It didn't help.

Margaret's got to be around here somewhere, he thought. He just knew it.

God, please let her be alive.

He was about to turn and leave to search the rest of the house, when he noticed something below the cross, behind the altar. He could just make out the end of a dais, covered in black, a pair of small feet sticking out at the end. He ran to the altar, his mind barely registering the human heart sitting on a silver plate inside the tabernacle, and went around it. There was a small figure lying on the dais, covered with a black sheet embroidered with strange symbols from head to ankles. Hands trembling, he reached out and pulled the sheet off the head to reveal a pale face.

Margaret!

Roger's heart skipped a beat. He fell to his knees, grabbing her shoulders and drawing her to him in the dim light. As he picked her up he saw that her head had been shaved. When the top of it fell off, rocking back and forth on the dais like a bowl, showing skull bone and veins in an intricate network inside, Roger screamed. The sheet fell away from her body and he screamed again. Her body had been completely stripped of flesh, worse than the girl on the cross, right down to the bone in places. Roger staggered backwards, tripping on the sheet, and landed hard on his tailbone, sending jarring tingles of pain up his spine. Another scream erupted from his mouth, and he thought: *That's her heart on the altar.*

He had no time to think anything else.

From the doorway came a deep growl. The monstrous dog charged into the room. It leapt, jaws open, landing on Roger's chest, crushing him to the floor. His arms flailed wildly as the wind exploded out of him. The dog clamped its huge mouth on his neck; its teeth tearing easily through his flesh. With one snarling bite, it tore out his throat and his screaming voice with it.

CHAPTER 23

Ride a cock-horse to Banbury Cross
To see an old woman upon a white horse.

The interior of the bar was not well lighted. Its dark paneling and furnishings functioned only to dull further what little illumination there was. A long, oval, brass and oak bar was to the left. On the wall behind it was a long, brass-framed mirror, against which were arranged bottles of liquor and pyramidal stacks of glasses.

Steve glanced quickly around. All the stools were empty at the bar. The bartender was wiping glasses. He looked at Steve and nodded slightly, going on with his work. The right side of the room was a double row of high-backed wooden booths, only two of which were occupied by elderly couples finishing late lunches. To the back of the row of booths were double swinging doors leading to a kitchen. To the left of that was an archway and what looked like another room.

"You see a young woman, long blonde hair, just come in here?" Steve asked the bartender.

He looked up, thought for a moment, and shook his head. "Only person's come in in the last couple of minutes was an old lady. She went out back," he said nodding in the direction of the back room.

Steve gave the bartender an incredulous look. How could

the guy have missed her? Steve was sure she had come in here; he could feel her in here. He left the bar and went into the back room.

There she was sitting in the corner booth, the first of many that ran along the far wall. Three college guys, sitting at a booth near the door, were the only other people in the back. As Steve walked toward her, she looked up at him and smiled.

The tingling, orgasmic sensation grew, making him hot and bringing a fine flush of sweat to his forehead. He reached the table and hesitated for a moment. An instant of doubt, of guilt, made him ask himself what the hell he was doing. Then she licked her lips, her tongue wet and pink and running sensuously over her full lips and he felt it all over his throbbing cock. All doubts and guilt disappeared.

Not a word passed between them, words were unnecessary. She was wearing a dark miniskirt and a sheer white see-through blouse. The thought that she had been wearing slacks and a red, low-cut sweater when he saw her outside flashed through his mind for a second, but it was inconsequential; soon she would be wearing nothing.

He sat. Their eyes met. They kissed.

She was all over him. Mouth, hands, legs, she enveloped him with them. Kissing him greedily, her tongue slid between his lips, seeking out his tongue and sucking it into her own mouth. Her hands tore at his shirt, popping the buttons. Pulling it open, she ran her long nails across his chest, scratching him. She inserted her left leg between his thighs, rubbing her knee against his crotch. Her skirt rode up around her ass as she straddled his leg, rubbing her hot crotch back and forth against his thigh.

His hands went to work nearly as quickly. He tore the sheer blouse from her body as if it was made of wet tissue. She was wearing no bra, and her large, firm breasts swung free until his groping hands found them, squeezing them hard. She let out a loud moan and pushed his face into her chest, smothering him with her breasts. His hand slid down to her skirt, pulled it up, and searched beneath it. She wore no panties. He grabbed her firm cheeks and pulled her against the volcano in his pants.

Within seconds, she had his pants undone and off. Still holding her ass tight enough to leave his fingerprints, Steve lifted her onto the table. Her legs flew apart, wrapped around his head, and pulled him down on her.

Norm Carr walked into Roosevelt's and sat at the end of the bar. The bartender glanced at the clock even though he knew it was 3:30. Norm *always* came in at 3:30. Four boilermakers later, not to mention a shot of peppermint schnapps after for his breath, and he would be gone by five. You could set your clock by him.

The bartender drew Norm a Budweiser draft in a tall, frosted mug and poured him a shot of Jack Daniels. Norm sipped at the beer, drinking the head off it, and dropped the Jack Daniel's, shot glass and all, into the beer. It turned brown and foamed wildly, running over the top of the mug. Norm quickly brought the mug to his lips before more than a drop could escape, and downed the boilermaker in six gulps. He put the mug back on the bar, belched loudly (all parts of his daily ritual), and nodded to the bartender to draw him another.

As Norm prepared to drop the second Jack Daniel's into the beer, the three college kids came running out of the back room. Two of them were laughing hysterically while the other was making disgusting noises, as if he was going to be sick. The latter went to the bar and pointed back the way he'd come. "Gross!" he said. His two friends laughed harder, staggering against the bar stools and each other. "You gotta see it," one of them managed to say between guffaws.

Norm and the bartender looked at each other and the same thought crossed their minds: What are these college kids up to? They'd both heard of fraternity initiation pranks and suspected that now. Norm shrugged, dropped the shot glass into his beer and drank half of it before getting off the stool. The bartender shrugged and took off his apron. He'd go see what was up, but God help any of those kids if they had damaged his bar at all.

Steve was going to explode. She was tighter than a glove. He rode her like a prize bronco, building to the most incredible orgasm of his life. Not only did she have his cock inside her, she had his mind in her as well. Stroking and licking his libido, she was giving him the most intense pleasure he had ever felt. While she stroked his pleasure points, he could feel her exploring his mind, learning all of his worries and problems and telling him that she could make it all better if he just did what she told him to.

He came. He listened. He was conquered.

"Holy shit!" Norm Carr swore. He wiped the back of his hand across his lips. This was the most unbelievable thing he had ever seen. Next to him, the bartender gaped, his mouth open, his eyes nearly popping out of his head.

The scene before them was disgusting. The woman had to be at least eighty years old, maybe ninety. Her body was a pile of loose, wrinkled, brown-spotted bulges of skin. Varicose veins painted her knotted, thin-calved, thick-thighed legs, and ran up across her spongy, cellulite-filled stomach and her sagging, chapped buttocks. The skin of her arms hung like the skin of a chicken's neck. Her back was slightly hunched. Her breasts, also sprayed with rivers of dark purple veins, were long and flat, the nipples huge and callused. The guy on top of her didn't look to be more than thirty if he was a day, and he was humping her as if she was a nineteen-year-old beauty queen.

He had her spread-eagle on top of the corner booth's table

and was thrusting into her with machinelike regularity. His arms were around her, his hands cupping her wrinkled ass as if it were the tightest set of buns in the world. He lavished kisses on her neck, snaking his tongue into her hair-encrusted ear, and kissing down to her grotesque, wasted breasts. He licked the veiny skin like a child relishing an ice cream cone. He sucked each crusty nipple into his mouth, sucking so hard on them that they began to bleed. Twin trickles of blood ran down her bulging sides and dripped on the table top.

"You guys missed it," one of the college boys said. "A minute ago he was going down on her, *eating her out.*" His friend made gagging noises again and they all burst into laughter.

"You got to do something," Norm said to the bartender.

The bartender seemed not to hear; he just stood and gawked, oblivious to everything but the scene on the table. At first he thought he recognized the old woman as the one who used to come in a lot with an old man who looked enough like her that he had assumed they were related. In the past year or so, she had come in more infrequently, and alone. As he stared at her, he began to remember things about her that, for the sake of his sanity, he had repressed. There was something strange about the woman; whenever he'd seen her, she had looked *different*. Often it had been from one minute to the next; something subtle would happen to her face and she would change. Many times she had reminded him of people he had known in the past, and they weren't always pleasant reminders. Now, she was doing it again, shifting her image, changing into someone else. A pounding headache took up residence between his ears when he saw who she was becoming.

She was his ex-wife, Wanda. The bartender felt his balls tighten and his chest constrict. *Wanda,* that cheating tramp. *Wanda,* who had crushed him when he came home to find her at the end of a gang-banging train of six of his so-called friends. *Wanda,* who cleaned out their joint savings account of over twenty thousand dollars and left him alone, broke, and with hepatitis and a bad case of the crabs. A month later he had found out that she had also given him the clap. That and heartache were all she had ever given him. Now she was giving him more of the latter.

"You bitch," he whispered between clenched teeth and started toward her. She turned under the man porking her and looked at him. Her eyes, like headlights dazzling a deer in the middle of a road, stopped him cold. The inside of his head exploded in a flash of hot white light that burned everything out of his mind, leaving only her voice behind.

Guess what, Jake? Her words cut into his brain like a soldering iron into soft wood. *In addition to all the other fine gifts I left you with, there's one more: I gave you AIDS. l got it from gang-banging those three.* She nodded to indicate the three college boys. *Thought you might like to know that you're going to die a horrible, lingering death . . . unless, of course, you do something about it.*

The message sank into his mind like steaming dog shit into fresh snow; it made an ever-widening hole and left a hot stench behind. As the hole got bigger, melting away his rationality, and finally his sanity, Jake the bartender knew what he had to do.

Norm Carr was getting a hard-on. As incredible as that was, it was true. It had been ten years since his last one; right about the time that his wife Roberta went through menopause and began sleeping in another room, refusing to let him touch her. Norm had dealt with it by telling himself that he was too old for sex anyway. Sex was for youngsters who could have kids, not for sixty-eight-year-old men.

From what the doctor had told him about it, Norm understood that menopause was nature's way of telling a woman that her childbearing years were over. Since Norm was of the view that women were meant for only one thing, being mothers, he could understand Roberta's reaction when she lost the ability to carry out her purpose in life. The fact that they had never been able to have children only made it worse, he supposed.

From then on, Norm had kept his distance. He remained as kind and loving to his wife as a man of his limited emotional abilities could be, but left her alone and allowed Roberta time to get over it. He didn't know what else to do; he couldn't divorce her and didn't know what to say to make things better.

Since then, he had seen a lot of things that could have aroused him—what with all the stuff they got away with on TV these days, especially cable. Nothing had. Roberta had even felt like fooling around one night after she'd had a few drinks at her sister's house, but poor Norm had been telling himself he couldn't for so long by then that he really couldn't. Naturally, Roberta took it as a rebuff and a comment on her attractiveness. She could hold a grudge a *long* time, and things had gotten only colder after that.

But never *hard*.

Until now.

The sight before him was disgustingly obscene and grotesque but this was the time his cock picked to come back to life. The old woman hung her head back and looked at him upside down, her head bobbing from the force of her young lover's thrusts. She hit Norm's mind like a stone hitting water, sending ripples radiating outwards. In the splash, Norm could see himself standing up on the table, straddling the old woman's face. What's more, he could feel her gummy mouth actually slurping him in.

What the fuck? he wondered, feeling his penis become wet with her saliva.

Come and join the party, her eyes said into his brain. In their depths he could suddenly see something very dark and hungry; something so evil it quickly soft-boiled his hard-on and scared the ever-loving shit right out of him. He staggered and backed away, then turned and ran out of the bar.

Something had gone wrong. The Machine had fucked up. With all the power of her mind and the Machine, Eleanor called for Norm to come back, ordering him to return, but to no avail. This was the second time since the little girl had snuck up to her window that the Machine had failed her. She was starting to exhibit the same lapses that had affected Edmund just before his death. She was running out of time, just like Edmund did.

I would have had plenty of time if it weren't for you. Edmund sat in the booth to her right. He stared at their sweaty, churning bodies and let out a hiss of disgust. *Such manipulations, Eleanor. You never could do anything the easy way.*

Eleanor opened her mouth to answer, but he disappeared. Between her legs, Steve was thrashing and pumping her frantically. She gave an extra little boost to his libido and he detonated into an explosive orgasm. She had to hurry up and get this over with; Norm was getting away, and that could spoil everything.

"What are you going to do?" the disgusted college boy asked the bartender as they came out of the back room together. The other two were howling with derision at the guy who had just run out of the bar as though he'd seen the devil getting pumped on that table.

"Maybe that was his mother," one gasped to the other. That fueled their laughter even more and they nearly collapsed from the intensity of it.

"Are you going to call the cops?" the first one asked. His friends laughed themselves soundless at his question.

Jake went behind the bar and over to the cash register. He rang NO SALE and pulled out a gleaming .45 when the drawer opened. His first shot hit one of the laughing boys in the shoulder, spinning him around and slamming him into a wooden support beam. He looked at the tear in his shirt where the blood was oozing out. His laughter became choppy and his smile melted into a look of pain. Jake's second shot hit him in the chest and his laughter died with him. Jake's third and fourth shots were almost point-blank in the other two boys' faces. He made a new mouth, that wasn't laughing, for one of them where his eyes and nose used to be, and blew a hole the size of a silver dollar in the other's forehead. The latter's brains exited from the back of his head along with the bullet as both boys nearly somersaulted backward from the force of the shots. They lay side by side on the floor, flopping and twitching like fish out of water.

Jake's fifth shot was his last. He held the gun barrel under his chin, pointed up through his head at the ceiling, and pulled the trigger. The bottles on the bar tinkled under the rain of flesh and blood and bone. Flecks of his brain pattered across the glass of the mirror and up to the ceiling, leaving tracks that looked like some small animal had walked up the wall.

Shuddering, Steve finished his orgasm and collapsed, spent, into the booth. He felt as if everything inside him, his blood, breath, organs, muscle, *his life,* had been ejaculated from his aching penis. His balls felt shriveled to the size of raisins.

He looked at the young woman and realized he still didn't know who she was. *What's your name?* he asked her, and noticed he was talking with his thoughts.

Eleanor, she replied likewise.

When can I see you again?

*Bring your boss to my house tomorrow and I'll make sure
he doesn't fire you.*

But where do you live?

In the woods right behind your house. The young woman
touched his face and grinned. The grin widened when the
sound of gunshots came from the front room. They shook
Steve out of his post-orgasmic stupor and he sat up. The
young woman began to get dressed and he followed her example.

What was that? he asked, liking this form of communica-
tion. He pulled on his pants and zippered them.

We can leave by the back door, she answered, ignoring his
question. He didn't repeat it. He scrambled to finish dressing
as quickly as she. He tucked his ripped shirt into his pants
and hurriedly slipped his feet into his loafers as she went out
the back door marked FOR EMERGENCY EXIT ONLY.
Hobbling, his right shoe not completely on, he followed her.

Once outside in the alleyway to the left of the bar, she
threw her arms around his neck and kissed him lightly just
tickling his lips with her tongue. She looked deeply into his
eyes. *Bring him,* she commanded.

I will, Steve responded. He put on his watch and noticed
it was 4:15. He reached out to kiss her again and she wasn't
there. He glanced at his watch again, saw that it was now
4:30, and realized that he was back in his car and fifteen
minutes he couldn't account for had just passed in an instant.

Sam the Sham and the Pharaohs were singing, "Hey
there, Little Red Riding Hood," on the oldies FM 101 station
out of Northampton, but Norm Carr barely heard it. He was
concentrating too hard on trying to get his hands to stop
shaking. His palms, *his whole body for that matter,* were cold
and sweaty. He couldn't keep a grip on the wheel, nor his
mind off the old woman in Roosevelt's.

His balls ached and he felt sick to his stomach. The image of her grotesque body—the ancient, wrinkled flesh, the varicose veins like dead fingers under her skin—flashed repeatedly in his mind. And those eyes that had given him a glimpse of something horrible, like looking through a window into Hell, kept staring at him.

The wheel slipped in his grasp again as his pickup truck hit a bump. The vehicle swerved to the right, kicking up a little dust from the shoulder and nearly clipping a short sign that identified the road as Route 119 south. He glanced in the mirror as he pulled back onto the road, but didn't pay any attention to the black station wagon some distance behind.

Come and join the party. Her words echoed in his memory and he couldn't silence them. Had she really spoken in his mind? he wondered. He hadn't seen her lips move but had heard her voice as clear as a bell.

"Is that possible?" he whispered aloud.

Anything's possible. Her voice was back, no longer just a memory. He looked up. There she was, standing buck naked by the side of the road, her hand out and her thumb up like some kid hitchhiking. *Going my way?* she asked with a chuckle.

He jumped, the truck swerved, and he stepped on the gas, speeding by her. He looked back but she was gone. When he faced forward again, he let out a scream. She was sitting on the hood of his truck, legs spread wide facing him, giving him a nauseatingly close up view of her swollen purple vagina.

Norm yanked on the wheel hard, sending the truck swerving wildly into the left lane as he tried to shake her off his truck. He thought he had succeeded when she disappeared, but the next moment he was screaming again—she was in the truck, sitting on the passenger's side next to him. He could see her disgusting body in near microscopic detail. Blood flowed from her cracked nipples; between her breasts, sweat glistened on several, long curly white hairs. The smell of her was overpowering, a stinking mix of bad fish and stale chicken shit.

Gotcha! she shouted in his brain. She reached out a long, flabby arm, the arthritic fingers of her hand resembling claws, and grabbed him firmly by the balls. Norm let go of the wheel and screamed like a woman. The hand on his balls tightened. In reflex, his foot stomped the gas pedal to the floor. Norm Carr screamed again, not so much from the hand rupturing his testicles as from the sight of the bus his truck was about to plow into head on. It was the last sound he made.

The pickup truck and bus collided. Norm Carr shot forward. His chest was crushed by the steering wheel. His head went through the windshield where the broken glass separated it from his body. It sailed through the windshield of the bus like a cannonball, rolling down the aisle, before the bus flipped onto its side and skidded to a metal screeching stop.

Eleanor drove by the wreckage slowly, smiling. All was well again.

Don't count on it. Edmund was sitting on top of the smoking bus. He was looking at her scornfully.

"You're dead, brother," she said quietly, but firmly, and drove away.

CHAPTER 24

And all the pretty maids are plain to be seen.

Something was wrong. Eleanor knew it the instant she pulled into the lot at the front of the house. She got out of the hearse quickly and ran as fast as she could to the front porch.

A window was open.

She went to the front door, unlocked it and hurried inside. The chapel door was open. From inside, she could hear a wet, lapping sound. She went in and found Mephisto feeding on the still warm body of Roger Eames. The dog looked up at her, licked away the bloody froth that was dripping from his chops, and wagged his tail.

"Good boy, Mephisto," Eleanor said, praising her familiar. She crossed to the altar and patted the dog's head. He licked her hand and went back to work on the soft flesh of Roger Eames's neck and face.

Who is he? Eleanor wondered. Though she had heard his thoughts many times, him living so close, and had even probed his mind on occasion to keep him from hiking in her woods, Eleanor had never actually seen Roger Eames. At first she was afraid he might be a policeman, but he wasn't wearing a uniform. His proximity to Margaret's body suggested to Eleanor that he had perhaps come looking specifically for her—and found much, much more than he had bargained for.

Being careful not to disturb Mephisto, who could get downright nasty if his feeding was interrupted, Eleanor knelt by the body and went through his pockets. In his back pocket she found his wallet. She opened it and pulled out his license, nodding slowly as she looked at it. It was just as she'd thought. Somehow Margaret Eames's father had tracked her to Grimm Memorials. Eleanor wondered if he had come by mistake, but didn't think so. If he hadn't, he might have told the police, or someone else about where he was going.

There was only one way to find out.

Judy Eames woke from her drugged sleep and called out to Roger. When she received no answer, she dragged herself out of bed, put on her robe and slippers, and stumbled out of the bedroom to the top of the stairs.

"Roger?" she called again, her voice slurring his name. No answer. She had started down the stairs when there was a knock on the back door. She hurried through the living room and kitchen as quickly as her doped body would move. There was no sign of Roger in the house and she wondered numbly where he could be. She opened the back door, half-expecting to see Roger, but a tall, white-haired policeman stood on the step instead.

"Mrs. Eames?" the cop asked. Judy nodded. "Mrs. Eames, we've found your daughter."

Judy grabbed the edge of the door so tightly, her knuckles flared white. "Is she . . . Is she . . . ?" Judy stammered, unable to finish the dreaded question.

"She's fine," the policeman said, smiling. His teeth were bad. "Your husband's with her. I've been instructed to take you to them."

Judy nearly collapsed. For one horrible moment she thought this was just another version of the same dream she'd been having every night since Margaret's disappearance. But this time it was real.

"Oh, thank God," Judy exclaimed, nearly collapsing with joy, her voice thick with tears. "Thank you, dear God."

"I can take you to them now, ma'am," the policeman said.

Judy smiled at him, tears running joyfully down her face, and nodded. "Yes, yes please." She started out the door.

"You'd better get your car keys, ma'am. My partner had to go on ahead and your husband asked me to bring the car to him."

"Yes, of course," Judy said, as if his request made perfect sense. She never stopped to wonder how Roger had gotten to where ever he was; she was too overjoyed at getting her baby back to think of anything else. She went to the key rack on the wall near the kitchen table and retrieved the keys to their Volvo station wagon. In her haste to be reunited with her daughter, and with her eyes so full of happy tears, she didn't see her husband's note lying on the floor under the table.

"I'll drive, ma'am," the policeman said, taking her keys and holding the door open for her. "You're in no condition to." Judy readily agreed and anxiously got in the car.

When the policeman steered the car down Dorsey Lane and turned into the woods, Judy asked, "Where are we going? Where are they?"

"They're at the Grimm Memorials Funeral Home. Seems the old woman who lives out there discovered your daughter wandering in the woods. She must have hit her head or something and was lost. The old woman called your husband and he called us."

Judy didn't remember hearing the phone ring, but she had been so doped up that it didn't surprise her. But she couldn't understand why Roger hadn't woke her. She supposed he had been too excited to think of it, just as she would have been, or maybe he had wanted to surprise her. It didn't matter. The question of how Margaret could have been lost in the woods for nearly two weeks when search parties had combed the entire area nagged briefly at the back of her mind, but she pushed it away. That didn't matter either. All would be explained. All that mattered was that she was getting her little girl back. Everything was going to be just fine; she could feel it for the first time since this horrible nightmare had started.

Judy Eames's mind had been as easy to fool as taking blood from a sleeping baby. Before she had even left Grimm Memorials, Eleanor had probed her mind, found that she knew nothing of her husband's whereabouts. From there on it was child's play to don the image of the friendly policeman and capture Judy Eames's confidence. Now the obese woman in her bathrobe, nightgown, and slippers was Eleanor's plaything, her clay, her puppet, and she didn't even know it. She believed her thoughts were her own and she was completely unaware of Eleanor's presence.

"I haven't lost my touch," Eleanor mumbled, reassured by this easy conquest after so much trouble with Norm Carr. She steered the Eames's Volvo up the incline to Grimm Memorials.

"What?" Judy asked, her eyes still running with tears.

"Nothing," Eleanor said, smiling her policeman's smile. She brought the car to a halt at the foot of the porch stairs. "This is it," she said and got out, pocketing the keys.

Judy jumped out of the car and ran up the stairs. She never noticed that there were no police cars around and that the place looked deserted.

"Hold on there, missy," Eleanor said, stopping Judy with more than her voice. She hustled around the car and went up the steps to where Judy waited, breathless with anticipation. Eleanor opened the door and led her inside.

"They're in the chapel," she told Judy, pointing to it. Judy ran to the door and nearly exploded through it. Eleanor went quickly into the kitchen and returned. She stood outside the

chapel door and through Judy's mind, saw all that she saw
and felt all that she felt; from the joy of seeing Margaret
wrapped in a blanket, sitting at the altar, to horror and revulsion when she realized the Christ on the cross was a dead
girl. She ran to Margaret, embracing her, and the top of
Margaret's shaved head fell off, revealing a scooped-out cavity. Judy screamed then, and Eleanor laughed. Judy continued
screaming as the blanket fell away from Margaret, revealing
her butchered body. Her screams went up a pitch when she
saw the huge dog feasting on her husband's mauled corpse
directly behind the altar.

Eleanor relished it all, and waited. Seconds later, when
Judy came lurching out of the chapel, her face and mind
white and empty from shock, Eleanor was ready. She brought
up the long carving knife she had gotten from the kitchen
and rammed it right up to the hilt in Judy's heaving chest
until the tip of the foot-long knife stuck out between her
shoulder blades.

Judy's screams became gasps. She sank to the floor, still
seeing Eleanor as the friendly cop, and died.

You're really fucking it up, Eleanor, Edmund said, gloating. He was standing directly above her on the second-floor
landing, looking over the railing at her. Eleanor could see
the ceiling through his head.

*You're not going to make it. Too many people know about
you now. You've struck too close to home; you broke the car-
dinal rule.*

"I'll make it," she shouted defiantly. She bent over Judy's
body, grabbed the knife handle with both hands and pulled.
Judy's body flopped an inch off the floor and a big red bubble rose out of her mouth, but the knife didn't budge.
Eleanor reached out and popped the bubble with her finger,
flecking Judy's lip and face with tiny red dots.

*You can't keep them away. You're running out of time. The
Machine is dying and so are you.*

"I'll make it," Eleanor said again, grunting as she grabbed

the knife handle once more. She placed a foot on Judy's neck, and one on her stomach, and yanked. With a jarring bone-scraping sound, the knife came free, coated with blood and looking like a mechanic's nightmare of a dipstick. Being careful not to cut her tongue, Eleanor licked the blade the way a kid licks a knife her mother has just frosted a cake with.

The police are coming. They'll put you in prison where you'll rot.

"No," Eleanor gasped, out of breath from the effort of removing the knife. Her probe of Judy's mind had told her that Roger had never told his wife where he was going or why. If he hadn't told his wife, it was a pretty good bet that he hadn't bothered to call the sheriff, either. Even if he had, she could fix it with one phone call.

"Sheriff's office, Bureau of Missing Children, Deputy Vitelli speaking," the voice on the phone said.

Eleanor spoke into the telephone, and Judy Eames's voice came out of her mouth. "This is Mrs. Eames."

"Uh, yes, Mrs. Eames?" Deputy Vitelli answered with a hint of dread to his voice. He hated talking to the Eameses; hated the sad desperation in their voices, *especially* Mrs. Eames's voice. They were the case that he had been waiting for in his missing children investigation, and now that he had them, he wished he hadn't. Every time he heard the pitiful hope in their voices as they asked if there were any news, he despised himself for hoping to get a case such as theirs.

On all the other cases, there were extenuating circumstances that left doubt as to whether there was a serial child killer or cult working in the area; reports of which were what caused the county, after much heavy lobbying by women's groups, to create Vitelli's bureau in the first place.

The Hall boy's father was an abusive parent, and on the mother's admission, used to beat his wife and child. The wife hinted that she feared her husband had done something to the child, but he had been at work at the time. Vitelli guessed, and the sheriff agreed, that the boy had probably run away from home to escape his father's brutality. When the Eames girl disappeared, Vitelli had sought a connection between the two disappearances, but there seemed to be none; the Halls had moved months ago. He had added Jerry Hall to a list that had only the name of Stephen Lewis, the boy they'd found in the Connecticut River, on it, but the sheriff thought he was clutching at straws. And he had been. The women's groups were hounding the county, who was hounding the sheriff, who was hounding Vitelli to get results.

Every other case that had come up since then always had another explanation that suited the circumstance. The Torrez boy's parents were drug dealers. Vitelli had learned that they were into some very heavy debt to some mob-connected suppliers out of New York; real sickos, the kind of guys who would take a kid as payment, using him to make money in child pornography to get their money. The Lafleur twins' mother was insane, locked up in a private sanitorium. It was anybody's guess what she had really done with her children. Though Vitelli had assumed at first that she had thrown them into the Hadley River, their bodies were never found. Betty Boone and Timmy Walsh were obvious cases of a divorced parent abducting offspring. And the four boys who had disappeared the day after Margaret Eames had probably fallen into the river. They had been seen building a raft out of old two-by-fours the day before by another kid in the neighborhood.

The Eames case, and the case of the Lewis boy found in the river last year, were the only ones that had no explanation as to what had happened, other than that somebody, or *somebodies,* had kidnapped and, in the case of the Lewis boy, murdered a child. It was so ironic: now that he had the case that justified the existence of his bureau, he'd give anything for it never to have come into being.

"Has my husband talked to you today?" Mrs. Eames asked.

"Uh, no, ma'am," Vitelli answered, the question catching him off guard. He had been expecting her to ask, in that gut-wrenching, despairing voice with just a touch of hope to it—that made it all the more harder to listen to—the question she asked every day, whether or not her husband had also called: *Is there any news of my daughter?* He had been ready to give his standard noncommittal answer that was supposed to neither enhance, nor dash, a parent's hopes, but which was becoming old and hollow sounding of late.

"Oh. He was supposed to tell you that we're leaving today to go up to Vermont to visit with family and get away from things for a little while," she said softly, tiredly.

"I'm certain he hasn't called me, Mrs. Eames, but I think that it's a good idea for you two to have your families around you at a time like this. There's nothing you can do here. If we get any information, we'll contact you immediately. Why don't you give me a name, address, and phone number where you can be reached."

"Of course," Mrs. Eames replied.

Vitelli sat poised with his pencil over an index card for several seconds, then picked up the card and looked at it. "Okay, I've got it," he said, staring at the blank paper.

"Thank you," Eleanor replied, and hung up the phone. That would take care of the police at least for another few days, which was all she needed. After Halloween and the Harvest of Dead Souls, it wouldn't matter what they found out. All she had to do was get rid of the Eameses' car. Their bodies she could always put to good use.

On the other side of the house, away from the road, was a wide path to the river. She could easily drive the car over the skimpy underbrush and rig up a stick on the gas pedal to get it over the embankment and into the river. The Connecticut was swollen and running fierce from recent heavy rains; it would be awhile before anyone found the car there. The bodies were much more easily disposed of. Whatever Mephisto didn't eat would make a marvelous last meal for her captives. She thought hard for a moment, making sure she'd covered everything. Satisfied, she started for the door.

Don't count on it! Edmund laughed from the second floor.

Eleanor whirled. "Leave me alone! Why do you torment me?" she shouted. Edmund merely laughed at her. She knew the answer to that as well as he.

"You are *dead,* Edmund," she said vehemently, "and the *dead* stay *dead!*"

Then what am I? Edmund chuckled over the railing.

"An illusion, brother," she said, heading for the door with the keys to the Eameses' Volvo clutched tightly in her hand. "Just a guilty illusion."

Edmund's derisive laughter on her back didn't sound illusory.

CHAPTER 25

Friday night's dream, on Saturday told . . .

Diane Nailer sat at the kitchen table, staring at the wood grain with the blank gaze of the exhausted. She had expected to be very tired in the last few months of pregnancy, but she hadn't expected anything like this. She had never been this tired carrying Jennifer or Jackie. She had told Dr. Rice, her new obstetrician, about it on her visit last week, but he had explained it away as natural since her body was older now. He recommended plenty of rest.

Of course, that was the problem. She couldn't seem to get any rest, but she didn't dare tell the doctor that because then she would have to tell him about the dreams and her dead father coming to visit her. If she did that, her father would bring the baby-killing pain back with him. She would do anything to prevent that.

If only he would let her get some sleep.

Suddenly Diane burst into tears. What is wrong with me? Am I going crazy? she wondered. Ever since that day in the restaurant when her father had first returned from the dead to warn her to take care of the baby, she had felt her grasp of reality, her sanity itself, slipping slowly away. She was no longer in control of her life, her body, not even her mind.

Her father continued to visit her in her dreams, and she felt his presence like a cold draft when she was awake. Most of the time it was soothing to know he was nearby. She never thought twice about the fact that he had been *dead* for twelve years; it was as if he had never died. But, sometimes, she had moments of clarity, like now, when everything that had happened seemed like a horrid nightmare and she knew she was losing her mind. Those moments never lasted long though. Sooner or later she would hear her father's voice, or dream of him, and slip back into a state of sleepy submission.

She heard the front door open and Steve come in whistling. He came down the hall and into the kitchen, going directly to the refrigerator. His shirttails were hanging out of his wrinkled pants and he looked very sweaty. He took out a can of beer, popped it open, and drank half its contents in one greedy swallow.

"Hi, hon," Diane said softly. He ignored her and put the can to his lips again, drinking deeply. Diane knew she hadn't been very loving of late. But Steve *was* fooling around on her, wasn't he? In these moments of clarity, that seemed ridiculous; when her father was occupying her mind it was obvious to her that Steve was being unfaithful. Because of her father, she had become a world-class bitch. The thought that she hadn't been any better to the kids crossed her mind. She had all but forgotten about them; how could she have done that?

"Steve, can we talk?" she asked in a timid voice. She didn't know what she was going to say, but she had to try to explain what was happening to her.

Steve drained the can of beer empty and threw it in the sink. He belched loudly and sneered at her. "As usual with you, Di, it's too little too late. I've got better things to do."

"I know you're mad at me," Diane started slowly "and you have every right to be . . ."

"Ha!" Steve laughed with contempt and walked out of the room. He went upstairs to his study and slammed the door.

"Steve, wait. I need . . ." Diane got out before the pain hit the side of her head like a glancing blow. Tears sprang immediately to her eyes and she let out a sharp cry

It's all right, her father said softly in her ear. *You don't need him. Did you see his torn shirt? He's been with his lover again.*

Diane nodded slowly, her eyes glazing over, and felt the anger, resentment and hate for her husband and what he was doing to her well up inside her once again. When her father spoke again, his words were like heavy canvas curtains falling over her, weighing her down with drowsiness.

Think only of yourself and the baby. Nothing else is important.

"Yes," Diane said dreamily, letting herself become the center of the universe again. As her two children came in from outside, Diane ignored their greetings and turned her back on them, walking out of the kitchen and going upstairs to her room.

"She didn't even say hi," Jackie said, his voice quavering.

"She never says anything anymore," Jen complained. "It's like we're invisible. She doesn't care about us." *I don't need you,* she thought of her mother. Now that Grammy had come to live so close by, she didn't need anyone. Jackie, on the other hand, still needed his mother very much. He didn't like the idea of being invisible to her. Jen wished Gram would let her bring Jackie to see her; it would make him so happy, but she had said to wait until she was ready, so Jen had.

"One good thing about it, though," Jen said with a smile of sympathy for her brother, "is that we can do anything we want. They don't care."

"Like walking home through the woods every day?"

Jackie asked. He hated that Jennifer did that, and spent a lot of her free time out there. He was afraid for her, but she had shrugged off his concern, telling him that soon she would reveal a wonderful secret to him. Jackie didn't care about any secrets if they involved the woods.

Since Margaret and the four boys from around the corner had disappeared (he had heard on the bus radio that they were believed drowned in the river), Jackie had not wanted to go anywhere near the woods. He was sure that the woods, and maybe even the witch that Margaret and Jerry Hall *(who had disappeared too, don't forget)* had said lived out there, had something to do with their disappearances. So every day after school, he went right home and stayed close to the house, inside watching TV, or reading a book in his room, or going no further than the swings in the backyard.

Jennifer ignored his question and Jackie didn't repeat it. They had argued about it many times and she was still sore at him for telling Steve about her not taking the bus. He looked at the clock on the stove, noting that it was 4:30 and there was no supper cooking.

Jackie didn't know what was wrong with his mother— Steve had told him she was tired and moody because of the baby inside her—but she hadn't cooked supper for them in a long time. They'd had to make their own, eating sandwiches or cereal, unless Steve came down and offered to take them to McDonald's in Deerfield, or out for pizza, as he sometimes did.

"Ma cares more about her new baby than she does about us," Jennifer said.

Jackie didn't like it when she said that. He didn't want to admit it was true. It reminded him that he had always been his mother's baby, and now she had practically forgotten him. The thought saddened him to the point of tears.

Jennifer saw the look on Jackie's face and felt bad for him. "I bet if you went and asked Steve to take us out for supper, he would," she told him.

Jackie shrugged doubtfully.

"Come on. Go ask him," Jennifer prodded.

"He won't do it," Jackie pouted.

"He will if *you* ask him," Jen replied.

"You really think so?" Jackie asked hopefully.

"Sure, go ahead."

I knead you like dough
But you are full of razors
And my fingers bleed . . .

Steve stared at the haiku he had just written. A radical idea began to form in his mind. Since his incredible experience in Roosevelt's Bar that afternoon, Steve had felt the creative juices flowing once again. When he got home he had started right in on his sonnets, but instead, the haiku had popped into his mind.

He liked it; it reminded him of *her*. Though he knew little else about her other than her name and the ironic—since he'd been searching so madly for her—fact that she lived in the woods right behind his house, he felt as though he could trust her with anything, even his life. He felt he didn't need to know anything more—she loved him and was going to help him. Gone was the panic of just hours ago; she had given him a new perspective and had released him from the straightjacket of writer's block. It was only fitting that the first thing he should write would be about her.

He smiled now, remembering the intensely wild sexual experience he'd had with her at the bar. He had never done anything like that with Diane; she was too prudish. Though he had always thought he would remain faithful to Diane— he was not a good liar and was possessed of a strong conscience that usually dispensed guilt like an overactive gland— he didn't feel any guilt whatsoever about what he had done. He felt he was completely justified; Diane had blown their relationship, not him. And Eleanor was the best thing that had ever happened to him; he would be crazy not to grab her. Deep down, he knew his father would approve.

The door opened and Jackie stuck his head cautiously into the room. "Mum didn't make any supper again," he said softly. "We were wondering if you could take us to McDonald's," he added hopefully.

Steve turned back to his writing. "Not tonight. I'm too busy." When he didn't hear Jackie leave and close the door right away, he said, "And don't forget to close the door on your way out. " He had no time anymore for her kids; if she couldn't be bothered to take care of them, why should he? He was through bending over backwards to please her and try to make things work. He was free of her now that he had Eleanor, and he intended to make the most of it.

He sat back and stretched, raising his arms above his head, and reached his fingers toward the ceiling. It was just amazing how good he felt. He had ambition again, and optimism, was it all just because of an afternoon of hot sex with her? No, it was more than that. Eleanor did things to him that no woman had ever done before. It wasn't just the physical pleasure she gave him either; she did things with his mind. He felt as though she had drilled a deep well in his brain that had struck huge deposits of creativity that were heretofore undiscovered.

Not only had she given him inspiration, she had made all his other troubles seem trivial, inconsequential. Even Conally's vendetta against him seemed ridiculous and unimportant. It was clear to Steve now, thanks to Eleanor, that Joe Conally didn't have a case. Steve didn't know why he had worried so about it. Eleanor had made it all so clear to him with just a thought (her speaking in his mind seemed like the most natural thing in the world; the way true lovers should communicate) and she would do the same with Conally. She had taken everything she needed to know about Conally from Steve's mind and had shown him the perfect bait to lure Conally out to Grimm Memorials.

Bait? Lure? He didn't know why those words came to mind (after all she was just going to talk to Conally, and show him the folly of his ways, wasn't she?), but they were fitting somehow. The memory of the gunshots he'd heard in Roosevelt's came back to him, but he shrugged off the feeling of dread that came with it. That had had nothing to do with him, or her, he was sure of it. It probably hadn't even been gunshots at all, just the TV, or a car backfiring. He had nothing to fear from Eleanor.

I guess I've fallen in love with her, he thought, nibbling on his pencil. He certainly felt the same intense excitement and longing that he normally associated with falling in love, but his feelings for her went light years beyond that. He didn't just want her, he *needed* her; needed to serve her, worship her, even be dominated (in more than just a sexual sense) by her. This was unlike *anything* he had ever felt.

He went back to his writing and read the haiku over again. He liked the play on words resulting in double entendres: the *kneading* of dough meaning the attempt to change a person, and the *need* for dough in the sense of needing money; and the dough, or person, being full of *razors*, or cruelty, that cuts and causes pain; and in another sense, the dough rising, being full of *raises*, signifying rebellion against the attempts to knead, or need it.

It was unlike anything he had ever written. It was so short and neat. But what was exciting was that it suggested a totally new form to him; something that was sure to open the eyes of the judges and land him top honors in the Dickinson Poetry Competition, and a poet-in-residence professorship at Emily Dickinson College. Then he could tell Conally to shove it and Eleanor wouldn't have to bother with the likes of him.

Thesaurus by his side, Steve bent feverishly to the task of putting down on paper what was blossoming in his mind.

Jackie sat in front of the television watching "Wheel of Fortune." On the floor next to him was an empty bowl with a spoon in it. He and Jen had ended up with cereal for supper after all. He was getting sick of it. Now, as had been the case for some time, he was left alone in front of the TV. Everyone else was upstairs: Jen doing her homework in their room, Steve in his study, and his mother sleeping as usual.

I bet a monster could walk right in and grab me and no one would even know it, Jackie thought glumly. The idea chilled him and he looked warily at the night outside the windows. He got up and went into the front hall, checking the front door to be sure it was locked. He went into the kitchen and did the same with the back door. He was about to slide a chair over to the cabinet near the stove to see if there were any cookies left, when he heard someone coming down the stairs.

It was his mother. She lumbered into the kitchen, one hand on her belly, the other gliding over the countertop as if to keep her disproportioned body balanced. She went straight to the refrigerator, opened it, and hung on the door, looking over her culinary options.

"Hi Mom," Jackie said with forced cheeriness. "Me and Jen had Cocoa Puffs for supper," he added, looking for some response. There was none. Diane remained fixed on the contents of the refrigerator. "There's nothin' else to eat," Jackie explained.

Diane pulled a half-gallon carton of milk out of the refrigerator, opened it, and drank from the spout. She put it on the countertop after several gulps and retrieved the box of Cocoa Puffs from its cabinet along with a large mixing bowl. She poured the rest of the box of cereal into the bowl and added what was left of the milk, throwing both empty containers into the Tupperware trash barrel, which was already overflowing.

Jackie stared at the empty milk carton and gasped. Margaret's picture was on the back under the heading: HAVE YOU SEEN ME? Neither he nor Jennifer had noticed it earlier. He looked at her black-and-white face, frozen forever in a waxy cardboard smile. "Mom, *look!*"

Diane was too busy shoveling cereal into her mouth with a large soup spoon.

"Mom, it's Margaret's picture on the milk carton." He could almost hear the echo of Margaret's voice telling him that Jerry Hall had got his picture on a milk carton after he disappeared.

Diane shoveled more cereal into her mouth. "Not now, Jackie. The baby and I are hungry." Still spooning mounds of Cocoa Puffs into her mouth, Diane left the kitchen and went back upstairs.

She doesn't care what happened to Margaret, Jackie thought. And doesn't care what happens to me, either. Jackie walked over to the wastebasket. He reached out a trembling, cautious hand and touched Margaret's picture. What happened to you Margaret? Jackie thought. Did the witch get you?

He began to shiver, and tears filled his eyes. A long, slow sob rose from his gut, spilling from his mouth with a sound like a small buzz saw whining. His tears spattered on Margaret's cardboard face with a hollow, empty sound.

Seeking escape, tired and depressed, Jackie went to bed early. It didn't take him long to fall into a deep, forgetful sleep. Sometime after midnight, he dreamt that he awoke. At first, he didn't know what had awakened him. He could hear Jennifer snoring softly in the bed diagonal to his, and could hear the wind blowing in the branches of the tree outside, but neither of those things had woken him. It was some other sound.

There it was again.

A voice.

Calling his name.

Jackie.

He sat up in bed with the motion of a dream, slow and liquid. The moon was shimmering around the room as if it were underwater; its silvery light rippling and splashing. The wind was thrashing in the tree outside the window, giving it life to paw the side of the house and the window as if it were trying to gain entry.

Jackie threw back the covers. They made a whooshing sound like a wave hitting a beach. His feet floated off the bed as if weightless, followed by his legs. His chest and head came last, arms drifting apart, as he headed upside down for the ceiling. As he floated upward, body spiraling lazily, he looked out the window.

There was a boy climbing the tree.

Jackie twisted himself around for a better look and realized the boy wasn't climbing the tree, he was floating up the tree, just as Jackie was floating against the ceiling like a lost balloon. That boy could never *climb* a tree, Jackie realized as he watched him rise closer and closer; he doesn't have any arms or legs.

When the boy reached the window, and Jackie saw that he didn't have any clothes on, he realized it was an armless legless girl, not a boy; she didn't have private parts, like he did. It's Margaret come back, he thought with joy.

Is that you, Margaret? he asked, his thoughts speaking the words instead of his mouth.

No, the figure answered in the same manner. *Margaret's gone.*

Who are you then?

I'm Jerry.

But Jerry's a boy's name, Jackie said, giggling in his head.

I'm a boy.

Jackie bumped his head on the ceiling light and looked again at the figure in the tree. A feeling of dread wormed its way through his gut and up his throat.

Are you Jerry Hall? Jackie asked, dreading the answer.

Yes.

What happened to you? Did the witch get you?

Before Jerry could answer, Jackie was distracted by another noise from downstairs. It was the loud crying of a baby. When Jackie looked back at the window, Jerry Hall was gone.

The next instant, he was in the hallway, floating out over the stairs. He descended slowly, like a dirigible losing its lift, and landed softly in the front hall. The front door was open. The crying of the baby was coming from outside. His feet barely touching the carpet, Jackie drifted to the door.

There was something coming down the street, floating slowly, the same way he had floated down the stairs. It passed under the dark shadows of the trees and came into the dappling moonlight. Jackie floated through the screen door without opening it and settled on the front step. With a chilling sweat sweeping over his flesh, Jackie saw what it was. It took his breath away in a gasp, and made him want to become invisible, but it was too late for that. It had seen him.

The witch.

She was riding a straw broom. Her dress was long and black, billowing out around her as she glided through the moonlight. Her black silk hat was tall and conical, with a wide brim. Behind her on the broom sat a large glowing orange jack-o'-lantern with a hideously animated face that grinned at Jackie and winked evilly.

Jackie almost wet his pants.

The witch began to cackle and the sound froze Jackie's balls. She threw her head back, her pointy chin and long warty nose threatening to crash into one another, and cackled gleefully as she sailed by, not more than ten feet away.

Just when he thought he was going to faint from fear, Jackie saw something else. In the folds of the witch's long shawl he could see a tiny hand, then a cherubic face, for just a second, then the witch was by him, sailing eerily through the trees and into the woods, the jack-o'-lantern lighting her way with its ghostly aura.

A baby cried behind him. Suddenly Jackie was no longer outside, but in the living room. His mother was sitting in the rocking chair holding a baby wrapped in a blanket. Jackie went closer. His mother's blouse was unbuttoned and she was breast-feeding the baby. She held open her blouse and leaned forward so he could see the tiny mouth sucking hungrily and the look of serene security on its small face.

It was his face.

Suddenly Jackie knew where the baby in the witch's arms had come from: it was the baby that had been in his mother's stomach. The witch had it and he, like every other kid, knew what witches did with babies.

They eat them!

Jackie looked at himself snug in his mother's arms, and was secretly glad.

CHAPTER 26

Come when you're called.

Eleanor leaned heavily against the embalming table, listening to the sleeping sounds of the boys in the cage. Dried leaves and twigs were caught in her hair and her dress was caked with mud. She had awakened earlier to find herself in the woods near the river. The last thing she had remembered was rigging the Eameses' Volvo so that it had plunged into the river. She had just turned away from watching the last bubble break the surface when the pain rolled over her.

She had been submerged in pain in less than a second. It rode her like a runaway horse trampling through her chest, radiating out to her arms, legs, neck, even her toes, and drove her to her knees with every beat of her rapid firing heart. Rocks had torn through her dress, gouging her shins and knees but she hadn't felt it through the other pain. The other pain turned her mind first brilliantly white then darkest black. It twisted her head around as if it meant to break her neck. The pain had made her moan in agony; it ruled her, made her suffer, then mercifully had pushed her into nothingness.

She hadn't woken straight up, mind clear and completely in tune with the Machine the way she usually did. She woke slowly, aware at first of nothing except the mud and leaves in her mouth. There were no voices in her head, no awareness of her puppets nor the Machine. Everything was quiet.

Panic-stricken, Eleanor was sure that all was lost. The Machine had deserted her. The pain still ripped through her body and she was certain she was going to die. But then slowly, like the sound of a far-off train approaching, the Machine returned. It was very faint at first, and remained so for a long time, but it was still there, and that was all that counted.

Her puppets had had a spell of freedom from her control: the little mother'd had thoughts that could endanger the baby; the daughter had considered telling her brother, too early, about her grandmother in the woods; Steve Nailer had been feeling that everything was all right with his life; if she had allowed it to go on, everything she'd worked for could have been destroyed.

She needed the little mother to protect the baby—it was the most important part of the final ritual. And if the girl told her skeptic brother too soon about the gingerbread house and their grandmother, he might get suspicious. As for her lover Steve, if he felt that everything was okay, he wouldn't bring his boss Conally to her, and she needed him.

Something had to be done. The Machine was too weak, putting her at the verge of losing control over everything. She struggled to her knees, wincing at the pain of her scabbed-over kneecaps ripping open. Summoning every ounce of strength, she pushed her power, her life energy itself, into the Machine to boost it and bring it back. After a few seconds of this extreme exertion, Eleanor collapsed in the mud like a deflated balloon. The effort had cost her several more hours of consciousness, but the Machine went on.

When she'd finally woke, it took her nearly an hour to struggle to her feet. Her entire left side felt rubbery and numb and wouldn't respond right away when she tried to move. When she finally managed to stand, she had to limp slowly through the woods back to Grimm Memorials.

Eleanor stared now at the children in the cage but didn't

eally see them; she was too busy worrying about that awful apse of power. Never before had the Machine stopped running so completely. That it had, told Eleanor in the clearest erms possible she was living on borrowed time, because here was only one way the Machine could ever be truly silenced, and that was *in death.*

If I can hold on just a little longer, she prayed. She pushed herself away from the table and went to the wooden podium at the head of the pentagram on the floor. She ran her hand over the covering of the book that lay there and traced each dark letter of its title: *The Demonolatria.* It was in this book, which Edmund had brought home with him from college, that all the tenets of ancient ritual and worship she and Edmund had built their lives around were written. The cover and binding, Edmund had told her, were made of the cured skin of newborn babies and the contents were written in the nk of their blood. It was an ancient book, and according to Edmund, rivalled the secrets of the fabled *Necronomicon* itself.

Eleanor hadn't known or cared what he was talking about, it made no sense to her. But the *book,* the book was beautiful, and what it offered made beautiful sense the way Edmund explained it. It was a perfect way of life, the "ancient ways of the Wizards of Necromancy," as Edmund called it. It took her out of years of solitude, of living alone with her father, suffering his silent neglect and perverted abuse; spying on his crematorium liaisons with dead women until she had gone nearly mad. It wasn't until Edmund came back from eight years away—first at boarding school, then the university—that she was finally freed of all that and able to enjoy her power again.

Eleanor opened the book to a page marked with an old velvet bookmark. Here were written the Rituals of Preparation leading up to the final Ritual of Samhain on the Harvest of Dead Souls, which would bring her the eternal life Edmund had been cheated out of.

That you cheated me out of. His voice rang through her head. She ignored him and bent over the book.

There were five Rituals of Preparation she had to complete before Halloween when she would perform the final and most important ritual. As she read over the page she counted off the ones that were completed: She had skinned and crucified an innocent according to the rites of the Black Mass; she had defiled herself with her familiar, Mephisto; and she had eaten the live flesh and brain of an innocent, offering its heart up to the dark gods. The fourth ritual—the sacrifice of a good man turned evil (Steve Nailer), accompanied by the death of six innocent bystanders, would be complete as soon as Steve brought his boss to her and served out his purpose in her plans. And as soon as she collected five more boys (for a total of thirteen) for the fifth ritual, and continued feeding them according to the ancient dietary laws, she would be ready to make the final sacrifice and attain immortality.

You'll never do it all. You're running out of time.

Eleanor didn't look up. She refused to acknowledge Edmund's words. She had no time to waste arguing with a figment of her guilty conscience. Closing the book reverently, she limped from the crematorium, up the stairs, and out to her car.

Near Old Deerfield Village, an historic community museum on the other side of the Connecticut River, Eleanor picked up the scent of a child's thoughts in the night. They were faint at first, and she couldn't pinpoint where they were coming from—another sign that the Machine was failing and her lease on borrowed time was running out. She knew the child was close, she could smell him, but his thoughts were like a weak, intermittent radio signal.

Eleanor shook her head and rubbed her temples in an effort to clear her head and hear better. Suddenly, the child's thoughts blasted in her head unintelligibly for a moment, then disappeared, leaving a dull headache behind. But in that moment she had been able to make out one word, *Kansas,* and it was enough to give her a direction. The child was just down the street.

Eleanor drove forward slowly, trying to pinpoint exactly which house the boy was in. The Machine was louder now, but it wasn't filtering out the dreams and thoughts of other people in the neighborhood as well as it should. They interfered with her concentration and, try as she might, she couldn't block them out. Several times she was certain that she was outside the right house, only to receive a confusing signal. Finally, she pulled over to try and rid her mind of all intrusions completely. Ironically, when she did, she found she was parked directly in front of the correct house.

Eleanor turned off the hearse's engine and sized up the place. It was a small white ranch house with a screened-in side porch at the left end. Through a large bay window on the right side, she could see the flickering light from a TV screen dancing on the walls. Though it was after midnight, that was where the thoughts were coming from; that was where the child was.

Summoning her concentration again, Eleanor began to pick bits and pieces of information from the boy's head, but it was difficult, slow work. What normally took minutes, now took a half hour to learn: his name was Jason Grakopolous, he was six years old, and he had never been sexually defiled. He was a true innocent. She also learned that he was an only child, not too bright, and that his parents spoiled him rotten.

Right now, he was up far beyond his bedtime, watching a movie on video tape that he had *made* his mother buy him. After his parents had gone to bed, he had sneaked into the living room to watch it.

Eleanor smiled with satisfaction as she saw, through his eyes, the film he was watching. Maybe the Machine isn't failing after all, she thought. On the TV screen was a wrecked house with a pair of striped stocking feet sticking out from under it. There were two figures, one a girl in pigtails, the other a woman wearing a tiara and a fluffy gown, standing on a yellow brick road. The woman in the gown was speaking to the girl:

"Are you a good witch, or a bad witch?"

Jason Grakopolous pressed the stop button on the VCR's remote control, then the rewind button. He wanted to watch his favorite part again: the Munchkins. He ran the tape back, guessing when it was far enough and pressed stop again. He was about to push the play button when a flash of light outside the window caught his eye.

There was a bright light outside, descending from the sky and landing in the yard. Jason got up and dropped the remote on the floor where the play button was depressed. As he went to the window, the movie came back on at the part where Dorothy first opens the door on the land of Oz.

He looked out, but could see nothing there now. He was about to go back to the TV when he heard giggling from outside. He looked again, peering into the shadows of the yard, and listened carefully. *There!* Very faint and musical, like a burst of song from a bird, he heard the giggling again. It was coming from the backyard. He pushed his face against the glass, trying to see around the corner of the house, and noticed that the glowing light he had seen before was out there.

Jason left the window and ran into the kitchen. He threw open the back door and rushed out into the cold air. The backyard was empty. He turned round in a complete circle, searching for the light he had seen, and heard the giggling again coming from the bushes along the back fence. Proceeding on tiptoes, Jason crept to the bushes. Though the moonlight was bright, and the bushes weren't thick enough or tall enough to hide anything very large, he could see nothing.

A feeling like someone was standing behind him made him

turn suddenly. His eyes widened. Floating over the house was a small orange orb. It descended into the yard coming closer and growing larger as it did. It began to spin and glow brighter. When it was larger than Jason and only a few feet away, the bubble popped, and there stood Glinda, the Good Witch of the North.

The giggling from the bushes became louder. Jason turned and broke into a broad smile at what he saw. It was the Lollipop Kids and the Munchkin Mayor, emerging from the bushes, eyeing him shyly. Jason laughed wildly at them, having the last time of his life.

Glinda came toward him, her feet barely touching the ground. She smiled benevolently on him; he stared at her with anticipation. The Munchkins drew round, keeping to a respectable distance. Jason waited.

"Aren't you going to ask me?" Jason cried after a few moments. The Munchkins around him giggled, jostling each other.

"Ask me?" the Mayor said in his little toy voice.

"Ask me?" the first Lollipop Kid croaked in bass.

"Ask him?" the second one rasped in a baritone.

"Ask him what?" the third Kid squeaked in a tenor, the three voices achieving 78 RPM harmony.

"Yes," Glinda said. "What is it you want me to ask you?"

"The question you're supposed to ask Dorothy," Jason snapped, his spoiled temper flaring.

"But I don't see any Dorothy," Glinda said, her voice like large drops of water splashing into a pool. "There's only you here."

"Then ask me!" Jason demanded, ready to throw a tantrum if not obeyed.

"Ask you what?" Glinda quipped.

"Ask me if I'm *a good witch or a bad witch!*" Jason cried and stamped his foot.

"Why don't you ask *me?*" Glinda answered, her bubbly voice tainted with a hint of coyness.

"No! That's not the way it's supposed to go!" Jason bellowed. "You're Glinda, the *Good* Witch of the North."

"Am I?" Glinda cooed and laughed. It was no longer a pretty, musical sound. It was dry and cracked; a husky gravelly sound. A spot appeared on the front of her gown. It began to swell, spreading over the front of her dress like time-lapse photography of mold sliding over something dead, turning it black and wrinkled. The mold didn't stop with her dress. It crept up her neck, leaving it wrinkled and brown. More spots of mold suddenly sprouted on her face, erupting and spreading until the mold was everywhere.

Her skin was changing right before Jason's eyes. It went from milky youth to polluted old age, brown and wrinkled. It took on a greenish tint that grew stronger. Her eyes bulged, her blonde hair and eyebrows dissolved into inky black. Her nose grew long and hooked. Her chin narrow and sharp. On top of her head appeared a tall, black, wide-brimmed, conical hat.

Jason Grakopolous stared at the Wicked Witch of the West and felt all warmth evacuate his body. She towered over him, her robes flowing out behind her as if she alone was caught in a perpetual windstorm. Jason cowered before her.

A grunt to his left made him turn to see that the Munchkins were changing, too. Even faster than the witch's transformation, the Munchkins turned into the Flying Monkeys—the witch's private demons. Jason began to back away, but they surrounded him, pinching, and clawing him, and nipping his legs with their teeth. He tried to scream and a hairy paw was shoved in his mouth. It tasted like how a wet dog smells. They lifted him off his feet and carried him to the witch's open arms.

Jason Grakopolous's last thought before unconsciousness took him was a wish . . . for a bucket of water.

* * *

Eleanor realized she had trouble the minute she pulled into the yard. The children in the crematorium, except for Davy Torrez, were awake. She could hear their thoughts. The drugs had worn off and the Machine hadn't compensated in her absence. The children were awake and *aware* of the trouble they were in. They weren't talking, but they were thinking, and they were afraid nearly to the point of shock.

The drugs, with occasional help from the Machine, had been keeping them in constant somnambulistic oblivion where they'd be the least amount of trouble. Now, with the shock of the knowledge of their predicament, if she gave them drugs she could lose one of them to a coma or worse, but she had to risk it. There was too much to do, she couldn't afford to have them trying to escape or screaming for help while she performed the rituals. If she lost a few of them to comas, she'd still be all right as long as they lived for a few more days. There was nothing in *The Demonolatria* that said sacrifices had to be conscious during rituals. Eleanor just liked them that way. But she wouldn't get them *any way* if she let them screw things up.

As fast as her battered body would allow, she got out of the car, opened the back, and pulled out the large black sack that was sitting on the casket tray. It fell to the ground with a thud, but the boy inside never made a sound. Eleanor rubbed at the nagging numbness in her left arm and bent to pick the sack up. Grunting, her left arm hanging useless by her side, she slid it up to her right shoulder and swung it on to her back. She pitched backwards a few steps, momentarily staggered by the weight and the sharp ricocheting pain it brought with it, then plodded up the stairs, into the house, and down to the crematorium without stopping to use the gurney or the elevator. She was afraid to stop. If she stopped, she knew she might never get started again.

* * *

The boys in the cage heard the front door open upstairs and the heavy footsteps crossing above. They listened with a mixture of dread and curiosity. The twins wondered if Tweedle-dum and Tweedle-dee were returning. Timmy Walsh feared the evil Pied Piper and his rats. The brothers, Jimmy and Jeff, and their two friends trembled at the thought of *any* of the three bears returning. But all of them also hoped it was someone to rescue them.

The footsteps came down the stairs slowly and heavily. With each one the boys' emotions went up a notch. The footsteps stopped and the door slowly opened. By the dim light of the few burning candles, the boys saw a black blob float through the door. It was followed by a hunched figure. It carried the black blob to the metal table and dropped it. The blob hit the tabletop and rolled off, striking the stone floor with a thud. The black blob moaned. The hunched figure looked up.

In a collective response, each of the boys recognized the old woman before them as the last thing they remembered seeing before blacking out; and each of the boys felt their inside go hollow at the sight of her. She staggered to the large metal sink in the far left corner and filled a pitcher with water. As she turned back her eyes came into the light.

Suddenly, every boy in the cage was thirsty. Even Davy Torrez, deep in the caverns of oblivion, felt an insatiable need to drink. As the old woman brought the pitcher of water, they eagerly grabbed for one of the many dirty glasses or cups strewn around the cage from their previous meals and shoved them through the bars for her to fill. None of them showed fear of the old lady. All their attention was focused on getting water. They didn't even notice, or didn't care about, the milky color of the water, or the undissolved clumps of powder swimming in it and floating on top. They drank greedily.

When every cup and glass had been filled twice, and the boys had drunk everything, they began to drop, until the last one slumped against two others, joining them in sleep. Exhausted, wincing from the pain that each movement brought like a sledgehammer, Eleanor climbed onto the embalming table, and followed them.

CHAPTER 27

There was a crooked man . . .

Thursday morning at 9:30, Steve Nailer, taking a sick day from school, sat in the lobby of Hasty Hall, on the campus of Emily Dickinson College waiting with the four other finalists in the Dickinson Poetry Competition. Each was waiting for his fifteen-minute interview with the judges, when he would present and explain the work submitted for the competition. They had drawn numbers to determine the order of the interviews; Steve was fourth.

He was surprised at how calm and confident he felt. He was absolutely sure, *positive* that his piece would win. He could honestly say it was the most unique thing he had ever written, or read for that matter. He chuckled to himself. A month ago, hell, a *week* ago, he would never have felt this confident. He would have thought he was being too cocky to think that his poetry could be considered great. He'd always thought he had a fighting chance, but to think of himself as a shoo-in would have been out of the question. Ever since his meeting with Eleanor yesterday, all that had changed. All the insecurity and wimpiness had disappeared. He was a man in charge of his own destiny.

As he sat in the plushly appointed room, waiting his turn, he thought over his presentation and reread the poem.

ODE TO MODERN MAN

1.
The moon, the city,
Sewers smelling like dying
Mad dogs on the prowl.

2.
Rancid waste of life
Hear the dirge for Modern
Man;
Excremental noise.

3.
I pull the trigger.
Blood flies—burst water
balloon,
And walls shining red.

4.
Siren sound screaming
As I'm leaping down the
stairs.
In the street I'm gone.

5.
I saw your face bleed
Through the running
sewer's mess,
And in the concrete scum.

6.
My arms reach for you
I must teach them to
refrain.
But your eyes mock me.

7.
I awake all wet.
I think you are in my bed;
I try to explain:

8.
"I want you like dope.
I let you under my skin.
Too scared to mainline.

9.
"I drink you like wine.
You lift my head to new
heights,
But you stretch my neck.

10.
"I knead you like dough
But you are full of razors
And my fingers bleed."

11.
I look at my life
Seeing all of the dangers:
Good time—suicide!

12.
Where is there our life?
I'm a lost city dweller
Looking for his mind.

13.
I search in dead ends,
And peer into garbage
cans
Like a starving cat.

14.
Self-sufficient you!
Always cutting, and
burning
And running me through.

15.
Can't you see my cage?
Don't you know I can't
bite back?
Don't craze a captive!

16.
At the breaking point
I don't know what I might
do.
Whenever I sleep . . .

17.
I dream of murder—
Drinking your blood;
regressing
Into Modern Man.

As Steve was finishing a final few notes on his presentation, an elderly woman called his name and ushered him through a large, cherry-paneled door and into the Woodley Library to face the panel of judges. He strode purposefully through the door, taking in the room as he did.

The windows, three on the head wall, four each on the side walls, were high-arched, many-paned frosted glass, with no drapes. The walls were a rich cherry paneling above and around the tall cherrywood bookcases lining the room. The furniture was all dark wood, upholstered in dark brown, brass-studded leather. Several oriental rugs in dark blues and reds, and of varying sizes, covered the floor. At the right end of the room, directly in front of the windows, a long, gleamingly polished table had been set up. Behind the table sat three men and two women, the poetry judges, in high-backed, thickly cushioned, leather-upholstered chairs.

Steve carried his briefcase to the small round table and chair in the middle of the room in front of the long judge's table. He placed his case on the table next to a glass and pitcher of water and faced the panel.

"Good morning, Mr. Nailer," the college's president, Dr. William Harriman, greeted Steve. He was the chief judge on the panel, whose members were an assemblage of the top poetry professors from five Ivy League colleges in the Amherst area. "We've read your request to change your submission, Mr. Nailer," Dr. Harriman went on, "and frankly, we're puzzled. You were chosen as a finalist based on your proposal to write four sonnets on the seasons of New England, not to write Japanese haiku. If you had proposed this in the first place, you never would have been considered as a finalist. The competition is for poets working in traditionally accepted Western forms of poetry. Unless you have the sonnets you originally proposed, I'm afraid we'll have to disqualify you."

"But sir," Steve stammered, unprepared for this reaction, "you don't understand. This piece is an inspiration of genius that has not seen its equal since T. S. Eliot penned *The Wasteland*. Those sonnets were an unoriginal idea; *anyone* can write a sonnet. What I've done is marry Eastern structure with Western realism, redefining the face of modern poetry."

Dr. Harriman stared at Steve for several moments, then gave a little smirk. The other judges were looking at Steve and each other as if he had just been crude enough to fart loudly and blame one of them for it.

"I am truly awed to be in the presence of someone who ranks alongside T. S. Eliot," Dr. Harriman said sarcastically, "but you have violated the rules of the competition. Because you have not submitted the work you originally proposed, you must be disqualified."

Steve couldn't believe it. This couldn't be happening. "What? You can't do that!" Steve demanded.

"Oh, but we can, Mr. Nailer. If you had read the rules booklet we gave you, you would have seen rule number 31a, procedure 7, which defines the forms of poetry that are acceptable. Haiku, in any way, shape, or form, is not one of them. It doesn't matter how *brilliant you* might think this is; we cannot accept it."

Steve didn't know what to say. In an instant, his thick skin of confidence had been shorn, leaving his old vulnerable self raw and exposed again. He saw everything he had worked for going down the drain. All hope for a college position was gone and Conally was going to get him fired from the Academy. All optimism suddenly disappeared. Once again his entire life was one wretched failure.

He tried to speak, to plead with the judges, but the words stuck in his throat. Hot tears swelled in his eyes and drizzled down his cheeks. He choked out a few strangled words that sounded like sobs, grabbed his case off the table, and rushed out of the library, leaving Dr. Harriman and the judges bewildered and feeling sorry for him, when just moments before they had despised his egotistical arrogance.

Steve stumbled out to the car, his face wet with angry, self-pitying tears, and collapsed over the wheel. He was finished. Just like his father had warned. His only hope now was to hang on to the academy job, and the only way he was going to do that was if Eleanor could convince Conally to drop his grievance.

The thought of Eleanor made him feel better. If she could keep the academy job for him, he'd be home free. Even teaching there wouldn't be so bad if he was with her all the time. It would mean giving up his son, but he didn't care; having Eleanor had become the most important thing to him.

But what could Eleanor really accomplish with the hard-headed Conally? In answer, he thought of the effect she had had on him with her wonderful gift of getting inside his head and making him feel great. Could she do that with anyone? If she could, even Conally wouldn't be able to resist. But even if she couldn't, her beauty and sensuality might be enough to change Conally's mind. Steve suspected he was a lecher who would do anything for a beautiful woman in the hopes of some action. Would Eleanor go that far? Would he want her to? He didn't know. He'd just have to get Conally to her and trust her.

Steve stood in Conally's office that afternoon, staring at a photograph on the wall. It was of an old gravestone, etched on it was the epitaph:

> *Pause a moment, ye passerbye*
> *As ye are now, so once was I*
> *As I've becum, so ye shall be*
> *and remane throughout eternitee.*

The walls of Conally's office were covered with similar photos of graveyards and old headstones, plus over twenty headstone rubbings on rice paper. Headstone rubbings were Conally's hobby and the lure that Steve would use to get him to Eleanor.

When Conally came in, after the dismissal bell had rung, he frowned at Steve. "What are you doing here? I thought you called in sick today?"

Steve smiled apologetically. "Actually, I had an appointment." He didn't elaborate and Conally didn't ask about it.

"What do you want in here?" Conally asked gruffly.

"I was just looking at this photo. I saw a headstone just like this one yesterday."

Conally immediately became interested. He walked over to the photo and pointed at it. "You saw one *exactly* like this, spelling and all?"

"Yes," Steve said, smiling. "I thought I had seen it somewhere before, then remembered it was in this photo on your wall. The caption says the headstone is rare."

"Rare?" Conally cried incredulously. "There are only three that are known of. They date back to the 1600s. Where did you see it?"

"In the woods off Route 47," Steve explained. "There's a dirt road called Dorsey Lane Extension. I was hiking along that road when I came across an old graveyard behind an abandoned funeral home. Is it worth anything?" Steve asked innocently. He had once overheard Conally telling a visiting coach from the university that a series of numbered rubbings from that stone, if it was in good shape, could be worth five to ten-thousand dollars to a collector.

"Not really," Conally lied. He wasn't about to share this with anyone, especially Nailer. "It's worth a mention in a collector's magazine, nothing more."

"Damn," Steve said, feigning disappointment. "When I read this about it being rare, I thought I might get some money out of it. Oh well. " He shrugged and left Conally's office.

Perfect! he thought as he walked through the locker room. Conally's eyes had lit up like a kid's on Christmas morning. He had taken the bait, now it was up to Eleanor.

Steve hurried out to the parking lot, where he had parked close enough to Conally's car without danger of being seen by him, and waited for the athletic director to come out. He didn't have to wait long. Within minutes, Conally came out of the school, carrying a large black artist's valise and a small toolbox, and loaded them in the rear of his Jeep Cherokee. Steve guessed Conally kept rice paper in the artist's case, chalk and crayons in the toolbox.

When Conally drove out of the parking lot, heading toward Route 47, Steve waited until he was out of sight before following. There was no need to keep Conally in view, Steve knew where he was going.

Steve drove casually down Route 47, turning off at the

narrow entrance of Dorsey Lane Extension. The dry road puffed up dust around his car as he maneuvered it through the brightly colored woods. The leaves on the trees were in full autumn flame now, but Steve barely noticed them. He was too anxious to get to Eleanor's house. As he reached the open lot in front of Grimm Memorials, he saw Conally's jeep parked at the side of the house.

Steve parked in front and got out. He crept around the side where Conally's car was, but there was no sign of his boss. Steve ran quickly to the backyard. Conally came into view as he reached the rear of the house; he was in the graveyard behind the house, walking from headstone to headstone looking for the one he wanted.

Steve took a deep breath. He knew before he turned that Eleanor was next to him. She was dressed in a flowing white robe so sheer it was almost transparent. In the sunlight, Steve could see a clear silhouette of her incredible body. With her dressed like that, Conally would probably agree to killing his own mother if he thought he had a chance of jumping Eleanor's bones. Together, Steve and Eleanor walked out to the graveyard.

When he saw them approaching, Conally dropped his toolbox in surprise. He gave Steve a guilty look, but tried to cover it with a scowl. "What the hell are you doing out here, Nailer? Are you following me?"

"I'd like you to meet Eleanor, Joe. We lured you out here so we could talk to you about the grievance hearing next week."

Conally looked at them, his eyes lingering on Eleanor, and laughed. "You *lured* me? You goddamned little liar! I bet that headstone isn't even out here. You told me that just to get me out here, huh? Then you figure your bimbo of a wife here will show me a little ass, a glimpse of tit, and you'll be able to talk me out of anything. You insult my intelligence, Nailer." He knelt and began putting the spilled crayons and chalk back in the toolbox.

Steve called to Eleanor for help, but she was wandering away, head down as though she was searching for something in the tall grass between the headstones. "It's not like that at all, Mr. Conally," Steve pleaded, suddenly aware of what a stupid idea this had been. "You've got to drop your grievance. I can't afford to lose my job. I've got a wife and kids to support."

Conally sneered over his shoulder at Steve. "Tough shit! I *was* planning on asking for just a reprimand of Dr. Plent, and not that the board fire you, but after this little game, I'm going to get your ass booted out. You're history, Nailer." Conally grinned, obviously enjoying the look of panic on Steve's face, and stood.

"I can't let you leave until you've heard me out," Steve said, stepping in front of Conally.

Conally glared at Steve. "If you don't want to get hurt, I suggest you get out of my way," he growled.

Hold him! The thought hit Steve like a splash of cold water in his face. He jerked from the force of it. Before he knew what he was doing, he lurched forward, and grabbed both of Joe Conally's arms in a grip the strength of which astounded Steve, and Conally, too.

"Get your fucking hands off me before I break your arms," Conally swore, but the threat in his voice was minimal, giving way to fear.

Steve's hands tightened and Conally winced, dropping his toolbox and valise. Behind his boss, Steve could see Eleanor stepping around a tall marble monument. She was dragging something heavy behind her. Steve's hands clenched tighter, his fingers digging into the flesh of Conally's arms as if they had a mind and superhuman strength of their own. Steve couldn't control them. He could feel them crushing Joe Conally's arms and he couldn't stop them.

Conally's face was getting white. His forearms and hands had become numb. The muscles in his upper arms were being squeezed to a pulp. Any second the bones would snap. The pain was unbearable. All appearance of anger had left his face; only panic and pain remained.

Eleanor was just a few yards behind Conally now. As Steve watched, devoid of emotion, she struggled to lift the thing she had dragged out of the grass. As she raised it over her head, Steve recognized it as an old, rusted pickax used for gardening and landscaping.

Joe Conally began to whimper as the pain became so bad he nearly fainted. "Please," he whispered to Steve, but never got out another word. Behind him, Eleanor, pickax held unstably up, ran at him. There was a loud thud, a snap, and a quick squishing sound as four inches of the pickaxe's tip came through the front of Joe Conally's sweater, spewing blood all over Steve's pants and shirt.

Steve's hands kept tightening on Conally's arms, even though Conally's knees were giving out and he was gasping and coughing up gurgling wads of blood. His eyes rolled up into their sockets and his head began to jerk rapidly back and forth. Steve wanted to let go of him, but his hands refused to obey. He held Conally up, his hands still crushing the dying man's arms. Steve heard the bones splintering, and watched Conally's breathing slow and stop along with the flow of blood from his mouth.

Conally was dead, and still Steve couldn't let go of him. He felt as though his hands were embedded in the flesh of Joe Conally's dead arms. It wasn't until Eleanor stepped up to him and caressed his face that he was finally able to release his former boss. Conally sagged to the ground like a worn-out beanbag chair. The handle of the pickax hit the ground, propping Conally up for a moment on his knees as if he were begging. When the handle hit the ground, the spike through Conally's chest shuddered, and the last of the air that had been trapped in his lungs escaped in a soft moan. The pick slipped in his chest, squishing wetly. Slowly, his body teetered to the left, and fell as if in slow motion. He hit the ground without a sound at the foot of a narrow, thin old headstone. His dead face looked up at it and so did Steve. The gravestone had an epitaph written on it:

> *Pause a moment, ye passerbye*
> *As ye are now, so once was I*
> *As I've becum, so ye shall be*
> *And remane throughout eternitee.*

Steve read the inscription and began to giggle. Eleanor sidled up to him, wrapping her arms seductively around his chest, and slid them down to his waist, where she undid his pants. Steve's giggle grew into hiccupping laughter. Eleanor slid his pants and undershorts down around his ankles. Steve's laughter took on a taint of hysteria. Eleanor fondled his penis, blowing on it, before sliding her lips over its entirety.

Steve's hysterical laughter stopped abruptly in a sharp intake of breath. He arched his body, his head hanging back, and rode Eleanor's face. She drained the hysteria and memory of what he'd been a party to from his body and mind in a cataclysmic orgasm. By the time she was through, Steve had been driven to the ground where he lay leaning against Joe Conally's dead body. He didn't care; he wasn't even aware of the body there, nor had any memory of the murder. All he could see was her. All he could think of was her. She was everything. He was her slave; she owned him completely. He would do *anything* for her.

Disengaging her face from his crotch, Eleanor slithered up his body and kissed him. Looking deeply into his eyes, she told him what he must do. After several moments, she rolled off him and he got up.

His face blank, Steve went through Joe Conally's pockets until he found his former boss's keys. Lifting the dead man to his shoulders, he carried him into Eleanor's kitchen and laid him on the table.

Steve went out to Conally's jeep, got in the driver's side,

and started it. He backed it out, and drove it through the woods to the same spot where Eleanor had dumped the Eameses' Volvo.

When the Jeep Cherokee had been swallowed up by the swollen waters of the Connecticut, Steve hiked through the woods, back to Grimm Memorials. Eleanor was waiting by the front porch for him. He went to her. She kissed him deeply, and squeezed his aching testicles.

"I'll be back tomorrow with what you need," Steve said, his voice a dull murmur. He got in his Saab, looked at Eleanor, and drove away.

Eleanor stumbled into the house and up the stairs to Edmund's study. She went to the desk, where Edmund kept their supply of medicines and drugs, and slid the large bottom drawer open and rummaged around the pile of medicine bottles there until she found the supply of nitroglycerin pills. She fumbled the large bottle open, and popped a pill under her tongue. As she waited for it to work, she fell back into the chair.

The pain had begun galloping through her chest again when she'd lifted the pickax to kill Joe Conally. Only through a superhuman effort had she been able to finish what she'd started with Steve and send him on his way. Now the pain was so bad that her entire body ached. Nausea washed through her stomach and up into her throat with the taste of vomit. Her hands trembled and her skin crawled with a sickening feeling.

"Two more days," she gasped. In two days it would be Halloween, Samhain, the Harvest of Dead Souls, the only day of the year that the final ritual could be carried out.

Four more boys, Edmund said with a mocking chuckle. From the sound of his voice, Eleanor could tell he was standing by the fireplace, but she didn't look up. The pain was still so bad that she couldn't have if she'd wanted to.

Edmund chuckled some more. *Two more days, four more boys, and your ticker is ready to pop.*

Eleanor closed her eyes and tried to concentrate on slowing her breathing and the rapid beat of her tortured heart. Edmund was not to be ignored.

Hurts, doesn't it? His voice was strained as if speaking of it reminded him of how bad the pain had really been. *It'll get worse, Eleanor. Trust me. What's that? You don't trust me? But, Sister, you can trust me as much as I trusted you.* He laughed and it was a hollow, spiteful sound.

A fresh pain tore through Eleanor's chest, ripping her breathing to shreds.

You're not going to make it, Eleanor. You're pathetic. All you've ever been able to do is destroy. How fitting that now you are destroying yourself.

Another pill went under Eleanor's tongue. Her hands twitched and trembled on the arms of the chair. Her face was a pasty gray, her lips purple. Her eyes remained half-open, glistening wetly, pupils dilated. The room had begun to melt into a deep red fog of pain around her. The fog began to pulsate to the beat of her heart and the throbbing of the pain. She tried to hold on to consciousness, afraid the Machine would fail again if she blacked out, but the pain overwhelmed her. She slid into the depths of unconsciousness as easily as a drop of water into a pool.

When she woke she thought she had been out for only a few minutes. The pain in her chest was still clutching her insides in its clawed grasp, but she was breathing a little better and the red fog had receded to the periphery of her vision. When she walked to the window and parted the drapes, she saw that it was already dark, and the moon was high in the sky. She realized she'd been out for hours. She listened urgently and intently for the Machine. It was still running. It had continued running while she was out. The children were quiet; Steve was off on his errand; his daughter was a bird in the hand—all was intact.

"I can do it," she stammered, turning away from the window. Was that a snickering laugh she heard echoing faintly somewhere in the house? It didn't matter. She took a deep breath. Her head was clearer; she was feeling better. "Damn you to Hell, Edmund!" Eleanor muttered to the ceiling.

I'll see you there, came the reply, whispering out of the air.

A sharp pain bit into her chest. She staggered to the leather couch by the fireplace and lay face down on it. The pain wasn't as bad as before, but she was too exhausted to deal with anything. Within minutes she was sound asleep and remained that way all night and well into the next day.

CHAPTER 28

A diller, a dollar, a ten o'clock scholar!

Seventh period was Steve Nailer's eighth-grade health class and he awaited it anxiously all day. He had even dreamt about it last night and awakened that morning eager to get to school. Except for the sex, he was ignorant of the events of the day before. Eleanor was with him always now, living in his head, seeing what he saw, feeling what he felt, making him do her bidding. He didn't mind. Actually, he liked it. It was nice *not* to be in control, to not have any responsibilities.

The bell to end sixth period rang. Steve jumped in his seat as the students jostled out the door. His seventh-period class was at the other end of the school, making the walk from sixth to seventh period the longest of his day. Usually he took his time walking it, sometimes stopping to pick up a cup of coffee in the teachers' lounge. Today, though, Steve took a direct route to room 201 where the class was held. He arrived before any of his students, which had never happened before.

The period was interminably long. He gave them a test on personal hygiene, something he harped on with these particular students since most of them were entering or going through puberty. After the test he handed out a worksheet on dental hygiene and tried to correct the test he had just given. It was a ploy to pass the time so he wouldn't keep glancing at the clock every few minutes.

The final bell of the day rang. Steve stood, motioning to a small, brown-haired, thirteen-year-old boy who sat in the back. "Mark, come up here please. I wish to talk to you."

The boy looked longingly at his friends departing for their lockers, then the buses. He'd get the worst seat on the bus again, right behind the driver. Reluctantly, he walked up to Mr. Nailer's desk.

"Mark, I wonder if you could tell me how all of your answers on this test happen to be exactly the same as Rebecca Allway's, who sits next to you?" Steve asked him.

Mark looked genuinely puzzled. "I don't know, Mr. Nailer. Maybe she looked at my paper and copied off me," he said unconvincingly.

Steve shook his head. "I don't think so, Mark. Becky has an A average in this class, while you are a borderline C minus. I doubt she would need to copy from you."

Mark's puzzlement was quickly turning to fear. If he got accused of cheating, he'd get kicked out of the academy. His father would kill him. The worst of it was that he hadn't been cheating. It wasn't that he was above it if it was absolutely necessary, but this was just a health test. He had been ready for it, which, granted, was a rare accomplishment.

"But Mr. Nailer, I didn't copy from her. You can ask her! I wrote all my own answers. I *studied* for this test. Honest!" Mark pleaded his case. His face was getting hot and flushed and he could feel tears just waiting to spring.

Steve looked at him thoughtfully, knowing his hesitancy was giving the boy hope. "I'll tell you what, Mark. Becky's bus has probably already left, but she lives right down the road from me, so why don't you and I go over there and see if you are telling the truth?"

Mark didn't know what to do. If he had been cheating,

now he would have to admit it to avoid getting Becky in trouble. But he hadn't cheated, and he'd be damned if he was going to get blamed for it. He didn't want to involve Rebecca, but he had no choice. He had to prove himself innocent.

"Okay," he said defiantly. "Let's do that. I'll prove to you I didn't cheat."

Steve drove the Saab quickly down Route 47. He had a half hour before he had to get back to the school for football practice. As he drove, he thought about the strange disappearance of Joe Conally. Word had been all over school about it. It seems that Conally's wife had contacted the school, then the police, when Joe didn't come home all night. Steve, along with all the other teachers and many of the students, was questioned by someone from the sheriff's office. He'd told them he'd been sick the day before so he hadn't seen Conally for two days. He didn't mention that he had come in yesterday, because he no longer remembered having done so.

Steve smiled as he drove. He felt great again, strong and safe. The confidence he'd lost after his fiasco with the poetry competition judges had returned full volume. Eleanor had assured him that everything would be fine and it certainly looked as though she was correct. Conally's disappearance (gossip around the teacher's lounge was that Conally had a girlfriend whom he had run off with), just days before the hearing that would have got Steve fired, was an incredible stroke of luck. Steve sincerely hoped nothing had happened to his boss, but was ecstatic at the turn of events. And he had Eleanor to thank for it.

He slowed the car and made a left turn onto Dorsey Lane Extension and drove through the woods. Mark sat up, drawn by the fiery colors of the dying leaves, and looked around. "Are you sure this is the way to Rebecca's house?" he asked.

Steve smiled at him and nodded. "Trust me, Mark," he said.

When they pulled in at the front of Grimm Memorials, Mark was certain it couldn't be Rebecca Allways's house. Before he could say anything, Mr. Nailer was out of the car and walking up the porch stairs, motioning for Mark to follow. "Mr. Nailer," Mark started to say as he got out of the car, but Mr. Nailer disappeared through the front door without even knocking. "Mr. Nailer?" Mark called out again, getting no answer. He went up the stairs and crossed the porch to the open front door, peering warily into the gloom within. All he could make out was a black marble floor, some dim furniture, and a stairway. He stepped inside cautiously.

What is this place? he wondered, glancing around the room. He looked at the marble pedestal with its open dusty book atop it, and read the legend at the top of the page aloud: "Guests of the Dearly Departed." A chill of trepidation shimmied down his arms.

"Mr. Nailer?" Mark called out timidly. "I think we're in the wrong house." Behind him, the front door swung closed. Mr. Nailer had been standing behind it.

"It's the right house, Mark," Steve replied, his face hidden in shadow.

A door to Mark's right opened and Rebecca Allways stepped through it, smiling at Mark. Mark smiled back, blushing hotly with embarrassment: Rebecca Allways was completely naked. Mark knew he shouldn't look at her, but he couldn't help it. Her long brown hair hung over her round, milky white shoulders to the tops of her small, puffy breasts with their large pouting nipples. A fine black dusting of pubic hair showed on the little mound of flesh between her thighs. Mark felt his cock grow hot and hard as he eyed her.

"He's too old," Rebecca said to Mr. Nailer. Mark looked at her, then Mr. Nailer, in confusion.

"No, he can't be," Mr. Nailer replied, his voice sounding frightened.

"What are you talking about?" Mark asked, puzzled.

Do you play with yourself? The question shot into his

mind like a burning arrow. He spun toward Rebecca. *Do you beat your meat?* Another arrow. The thought questions were coming from Rebecca. Involuntarily, Mark found himself answering with a thought of outrage: *No!* He felt her mind enter his, exploring his memory like fingers flipping the pages of a book, learning everything about him. It was a horrible feeling having her search his mind like that, knowing all his private secrets and embarrassments. It gave him a headache and made his ears ring.

"Stop it!" Mark shouted loudly, clamping his hands over his ears. Her presence in his head was making him ill. The room began to spin as Rebecca walked over to him. She placed a hand on his crotch and leaned close to him. He heard a thick snuffling noise and realized she was sniffing him.

"Fe, fi, fo, fum," she mumbled close to his face. Her breath smelled like rotten fish and sour cabbage. Mark started to back away from her but she reached out and grabbed his arm.

He looked at her hand; it was the hand of an adult, with long boney fingers ending in dirty, sharp nails. The skin of her hand was a mottled brown with veins and tendons showing through. Her knuckles were wrinkled, swollen knobs.

"He's not tainted yet, but he's close," Rebecca said to Mr. Nailer.

Mark's throat dried up and he choked on a swallow. Rebecca's soft white arm was growing to match her hand. The wrist and forearm stretched and kept stretching. Her skin turned a rough brown covered with rows of tiny, scaly wrinkles. Age spots blossomed like dead flowers between the wrinkles. The flesh under her upper arm and elbow sagged loosely like empty sacks. Her gnarled hand tightened on him as he staggered back, fighting to get away, trying not to look at what was happening to the rest of her body but unable to help it.

It was swelling. With gushing, wet snapping sounds her body was swelling, inflating. Her legs cracked and grew, pushing her torso up a foot. Her stomach bulged and squished, the skin rippling, puckering, and becoming rumpled with cellulite. Her rib cage danced against her tightly stretched skin like xylophone bars. Her breasts ballooned, the nipples erupting like tiny novas to envelop the entire end of each breast. With a tight hissing sound, her breasts began to deflate, wrinkling down into long, flattened slabs that looked a little like half-empty water bottles. Her neck, too, vibrated with growth, pushing her head up several inches. Its skin crawled with change; scars, wrinkles, age spots, and blemishes flourished there. A double chin grew, hanging under her jaw, and another one grew below it. The chins, and her entire neck, began to shrivel like the neck of a turkey.

Mark's mouth opened and his brain signalled *scream* to his vocal cords, but his voice had fled in terror. He tried to look away, but his neck wouldn't turn. His eyes remained clamped on the grotesquely changing Rebecca. She now towered over him. As bad as the changes had been to her body, the effects on her face were more horrible.

Her cherubic, wholesome skin disappeared, pimpling and pulsating until it resembled rubber being stretched a hundred different ways. Her slightly pouting, pink lips cracked, grew longer and thinner and darkened to a deep purple. Two long white hairs and one black one grew out of the end of her chin. A mole popped out on her cheek and sprouted a long, curly, black and white hair. Her cute, upturned nose, seemed to slide toward him, growing long and thin, the nostrils flaring large and wide. Her fine blonde eyebrows burst into growth like dried brush into flames. Her wavy, long blonde hair curled gray then white, as though a wave of bleach were passing over her head. It became stringy. It hung over her forehead in disarray to her eyes, which had once been big and blue but now became squinty and black and milky with age, the skin around them puffing and wrinkling.

Rebecca was gone. She had evolved into an ancient hag whose grip on his arm was so tight he began to whimper.

She dragged him across the room to the door marked Crematorium. Mark looked desperately back at Mr. Nailer for help, but he was turning away, going out the door as if nothing were wrong.

"No!" Mark screamed, his voice returning in panic. "No! No! No!" he continued screaming as the old hag dragged him through the crematorium door. He tried to grab at the door knob and jamb, but she pulled him off them and down the stairs. He bounced from step to step, on first his side, then his back, as he tried to squirm away. She held on to him relentlessly.

At the bottom of the stairs, she pulled him through another doorway into a candle-lit room and across a stone floor. He didn't have a chance to look around. She grabbed his head by his ears and drew his face close to hers. Her breath reeked like something dead, but he didn't smell it for long. Her eyes enveloped him and he disappeared into the ocean of her mind like a wrecked ship going down. The world became varying shades of green and gray before blackness settled in.

CHAPTER 29

Billy, Billy, come and play . . .

Eleanor bustled out of the house, her left leg barely limping, and got in the hearse. The sun was dipping behind the browning leaves, giving them a momentary flash of their former autumnal beauty. There was an hour of daylight left at least, but that couldn't be helped. She'd decided to strike while she felt good. If she waited until darkness, which was the safest time, she might not be conscious or strong enough. Tomorrow was Samhain. She had to be ready. If she missed it, she was dead.

She was feeling a rare interlude of relative freedom from pain—the constant squeezing of her heart was reduced to steady eruptions of sour, flaming heartburn and a tug every few minutes. The Machine was running strongly again, though still not completely up to peak. But it was good enough to get her to tomorrow night and the final ritual. After that, she'd have plenty of time to rest and let the Machine regain its former splendor.

"Three more to go," she whispered to herself as she backed the hearse out from the side of the house and onto the road.

Unlike the other night, when she'd driven at random until she'd discovered Jason Grakopolous watching TV, she knew

exactly where she was going now. When she was driving
home the other night with her catch neatly stashed away in a
coffin in the back, she had picked up the dreams of a small
boy like a stray radio signal. She was able to pinpoint it and
remembered it. She drove there now.

The house was in an ideal location. It was in a neighborhood in Deerfield where the houses were large and spread
apart. The backyards all bordered on the densely wooded
foothills of Mount Sugarloaf, which dominated the skyline.

Eleanor parked the hearse next to a small park at the end
of the street commemorating victims of the Deerfield Massacre.
The house she wanted was just a few down on the left. She
turned off the engine and relaxed behind the wheel. She began
pushing the tendrils of her thoughts throughout the neighborhood, weaving the fabric of the Machine into the area
until no one would see what she was doing; no one would
hear.

The boy was playing in his back yard. His father had built
a sandbox for him that was huge. Right now it was filled
with every truck he owned and he was busy pushing them
around as he built a city of sand. Eleanor probed his mind
quickly and bluntly; there was no time to be subtle. The tugging pain in her heart had begun to accelerate, and the burning feeling was spreading to her arms again.

The boy was filling a yellow Tonka dump truck with sand
when he heard high-pitched singing:

"Tra la la."

He looked up and heard it again.

"Tra la la."

The boy stood and looked toward the trees. The singing
was coming from there. The voice sounded like a little girl's.
Leaving his trucks and sand city behind, the boy climbed out
of the sandbox and started across the wide lawn to the trees.

The singing continued, fading for a second now and then
as if the singer was passing in and out of earshot. As he followed the sound, the boy realized the singer was walking

through the woods on the trail that ran from the small park down the street, past the row of houses, winding eventually all the way to the top of Sugarloaf. He had walked that path with his dad several times that past summer and knew it well.

He ran to the large elm tree nearest the edge of the woods and slipped around it onto the path.

"Tra la la."

The singing was coming from not too far ahead. The boy ran in the direction of the sound, moving swiftly along the path, jumping over exposed tree roots and fallen trees and branches. There was something familiar about the voice. He couldn't quite put his finger on it, but he knew he had heard the voice somewhere before. The fact that he couldn't remember where was driving him nuts and egged him on harder to find the source.

Several times he thought he was close. The little girl's voice sounded just ahead of him over a small slope in the path or just beyond a bend of trees and overgrown bushes, but each time he pushed on, he found nothing. It was almost as if the voice was teasing him, playing with him, luring him on. It was annoying and, combined with the elusive familiarity of the voice, was fast becoming maddening.

The boy ran faster in an attempt to catch up with the singer. Though she continued to elude him, he was glad she wasn't heading for Mount Sugarloaf. His father wouldn't let him go that way on the path unless he was with him. If the singer kept on the path, the boy knew he could catch her at the park where the path came out of the woods.

It wasn't too much farther now, and the boy pushed on doggedly. Just through a ravine, up and over a leaf-covered embankment, and the path descended to the small, tree-dotted park. The singer's repetition of the same three notes was starting to annoy him, also. He wanted to catch up to her to tell her to shut up, as much as he wanted to find out who she was and why she sounded so familiar.

The boy ran down the path into the park. The grass around the stone monument to settlers who had died in an Indian uprising was carpeted with brightly colored leaves. Brilliant reds, yellows, and oranges painted the ground and danced along, pushed by small gusts of wind.

The boy ran into the middle of the park, glancing every-where. The park appeared empty and the voice had stopped. He walked over to the stone monument and heard a shy gig-gle from behind a nearby tree. He turned and caught a glimpse of something red. "Who are you?" he called.

There was another giggle before a little girl stepped around the tree and smiled shyly at him. "I'm on my way to my grandmother's house," the girl said in a squeaky, Betty Boop voice.

The boy's mouth dropped open in amazement. He stared wide-eyed at the little girl wearing the red cape and hood tied up under her chin and knew why she had sounded so fa-miliar. Last weekend his father had brought home a video-tape of classic Tex Avery cartoons. One of them, called "Swingshift Cinderella," had started with Little Red Riding Hood being chased by a jazzy-looking wolf in a zoot suit and spats. Eventually, in the cartoon, the wolf dumped Red Riding Hood to chase after a blues-singing Cinderella who drove a long sports car.

The boy had loved the cartoon, laughing wildly at it and watching it over and over again. Now, Red Riding Hood stood before him. That in itself was amazing, but what was really incredible to the boy was that she appeared exactly as she had in the video—*she was a cartoon!* Just like the title char-acter in his favorite movie, *Who Framed Roger Rabbit?*, Red Riding Hood was a walking, talking, three-dimensional, real-life cartoon.

"You want to come with me, big boy?" Red Riding Hood said in a pouty voice and with a seductive sway of her hips. "My boyfriend will be along any minute to give us a ride. Whatcha say? Wanna?" she asked coyly, winking at him.

The boy didn't know what to do or say. He was dumb-founded. He knew that what he was seeing couldn't be so—his father had told him cartoons, like Roger Rabbit, weren't real—but here was walking, talking proof.

"Whatsa matter, honey? Cat gotcha tongue?"

The boy gave her a goofy smile. Whatever was going on, he liked it. This was *neat!*

The sound of a car engine drawing close caught Red Riding Hood's attention. "That must be my beau, now," she said in her funny voice. A cartoon car pulled up at the curb just a few yards away and the door flew open. Out popped the Big Bad Wolf, just as the boy had remembered him from the cartoon. He was decked out in a yellow and green pin-striped zoot suit. A huge, gold watch chain hung from his vest pocket and his bushy, cartoon tail stuck out of the seat of his pants. He flashed a large, toothy smile (one of his teeth was gold and sparkled brightly in his mouth) and laughed a deep, soulful laugh.

"Hey baby! What's cookin'?" he cried in a raspy, jive voice.

Red Riding Hood blushed and giggled. "Hiya Wolfie," she squeaked. She ran across the park and threw herself into his arms. They kissed and bright red hearts flew from their meeting lips and sailed around their heads before popping like soap bubbles.

"Wolfie, this is my new friend. He's comin' to Grandma's house with us," Red explained, pointing at the boy.

"Okay, dollface. Whatever you say," the wolf replied, motioning to the boy. "Hop in, pal. There's a real gasser of a party goin' on down at Granny's pad. We'll have a blast."

The boy laughed loudly. I'm in a cartoon, he thought gleefully. He nodded his head rapidly, still too overcome to speak, and ran to the Big Bad Wolf's cartoon car. The wolf stood by it, holding open the driver's door as Red Riding Hood climbed inside. The boy followed.

Suddenly everything was different. The outside of the car

was long and balloonish, the way a cartoon car should be, but the inside was like any other *real* car. Everything was dull and drab. He had gone from a colorful, bright world to a cold gloomy reality in a matter of seconds.

The boy looked around for her but Red Riding Hood was gone. The Big Bad Wolf was getting in and the boy turned to ask him where Red was. Like the car's interior, the wolf was no longer in cartoon form, either. The inside of the car filled with the smell of dirty, wet fur, like a dog left out in the rain. It was overpowering and gagged the boy.

A long, furry gray, *real* arm with a huge paw tipped with deadly looking claws grasped the steering wheel. A massive, pointy-eared head, with eyes glowing an ember red over a long snout and mouth hanging open to reveal a dangerous array of saliva-coated teeth, ducked into the car followed by a massive, fur-covered body. The wolf's eyes fixed on the boy, and his long, sharp mouth curled into a grin. He reached out a brutish, clawed paw and put it on the boy's head.

"Th-th-th-that's all f-f-folks!" he growled in an ugly imitation of Porky Pig.

The boy collapsed on the seat.

CHAPTER 30

You shall have an apple.

Jennifer walked home through the woods, searching frantically for the path that led to her grandmother's secret glen and gingerbread house. Everyday that she could, since she'd first discovered Grandma living in the woods behind her house, Jennifer had walked home from school, taking Dorsey Lane Extension to the candy house where she whiled away the hours listening to Gram tell stories that painted beautiful images in Jennifer's mind. Two days ago, that had changed. Walking home, crossing Jackie's troll bridge, the path was no longer where it should have been, and Jennifer couldn't find the gingerbread house, or her grandmother.

At first, she had rushed home to tell Jackie, against Gram's orders, all about it so that he could help her look. But just as she'd been about to tell him she'd got the overwhelming feeling that she shouldn't; that if she did, Gram might *never* come back. Instead, she had gone back into the woods and searched, and continued searching every day, on her way home from school every afternoon, and after supper. It was difficult to believe that her grandmother would desert her like this but the more she searched and couldn't find her, the more it seemed that way.

It had ruined Jennifer's entire week. Gram had promised to help her make a wonderful Halloween costume of Cinderella's ball gown to go trick-or-treating in, complete with glass slippers. With Halloween tomorrow, she had nothing to wear. Without Gram, Jen didn't even feel like dressing up, much less going trick-or-treating. She'd end up staying home with Jackie, who *never* went trick-or-treating because he was too scared of all the kids in costume.

Frustrated, Jen sat on a tree stump and tried to retrace mentally the steps she'd taken that first day she'd discovered Grandma's house. She was certain she was going in the right direction, but instead of coming out on the secret place with its glimmering candy house, she came out of the woods to find only the ugly, old Grimm house, which as far as she knew was deserted. She was going to have to face it; Grammy was gone. At the sadness of that thought, a sigh rose in her and climbed until it reached a sob. Tears weren't far behind and soon she was wallowing in self-pity.

Jackie got off the bus and ran home as fast as he could. He did that everyday, but today he did it out of excitement rather than fear. Today had been his best day ever at school. Today he'd won the first-grade spelling bee over all the other students from all five first-grade classes at Pioneer Regional. In his backpack he had the engraved plaque he had been given for first place.

He was so excited he hadn't once thought about the fact that tomorrow was Halloween, the one holiday in the year that he *didn't* look forward to. He had never really liked the idea of dressing up like a monster or a ghost, which was what Jen had always wanted to be. He had liked getting candy, but when he heard his parents talking about how some people put razors and bad drugs in candy to hurt kids, Jackie had stopped liking even that part of it.

Right after school, he had raced out to the parking lot to tell Jennifer, but she had already gone, off to her stupid woods. He had been very disappointed. He was dying to tell someone and show off his trophy. He'd shown a couple of kids on the bus, but they hadn't seemed impressed. He couldn't wait to get home to show his mother. Maybe, because he'd done something really good, she'd pay some attention to him.

He flew through the front door. "Hey, I'm home," he called. After a quick glance in the living room, then the dining room, he ran down the hall to the kitchen. All the downstairs rooms were empty. He turned and ran back through the hall and up the stairs. A quick perusal of the second-floor rooms showed that he was alone in the house. Looking sadly at his plaque, Jackie sat at the top of the stairs, fighting back tears of self-pity.

He heard a noise, a loud creaking, like someone stepping on a loose floorboard. It came from his parents' room. Jackie leaned back, looking through the open doorway where he had a view of the head of his parent's bed and the closet beyond it.

The closet door was opening.

Jackie tensed, his stomach muscles clenching in fear. Something was in the closet, and it was *coming out!* It's the *Bad Person,* he thought immediately. A deeper, nastier thought told him it was the witch on a broomstick from his dream. His sense of survival screamed for him to run, but his feet wouldn't react.

The door swung open slowly, as if it was yawning. Jackie couldn't pull his eyes away. The thing inside began to shuffle out. Cold fear constricted Jackie's throat.

It's the Bad Person! It's the witch. It's the Bogeyman. It's . . .

His mother. She crept out of the closet, dressed in a long cotton nightgown that clung tightly to her swollen stomach. She tiptoed to the bed and slipped under the covers, being very quiet.

A hot burst of tears flushed from Jackie's eyes. Why was she in the closet? Jackie wondered, knowing the answer but not wanting to admit it could be true. He got quietly to his feet, went to the bedroom door, and stepped in.

His mother was sitting propped up on a pile of pillows, a box of chocolates in her lap. She looked at Jackie with mild surprise when he walked through the door. The look quickly became one of annoyance.

"Why were you in the closet?" Jackie asked her. She picked up the chocolate box, chose a piece, and popped it into her mouth. "Why were you in the closet?" Jackie demanded this time, growing angry.

"Jackie, please," Diane said in a bored voice, "Mommy doesn't feel well. The baby and I need our rest."

"You were *hiding* from me," Jackie cried, his voice thick with betrayal. Tears gushed from his eyes and his bottom lip trembled.

"Please, Jackie, just go away and leave me alone!"

"I'll go away," Jackie shouted in a bawling voice. "I'll go away and never come back!" He turned and ran out the door and down the hall into his room, slamming the door behind him.

"Good riddance," Diane whispered sullenly and turned her attention back to the box of chocolates.

Steve dismissed football practice early, which was standard procedure the day before a game, but that wasn't why he did it. He couldn't care less about football these days; all he wanted to do was get back to Eleanor. He told his assistant coach he would be in charge for the game because Steve had something personal to attend to and couldn't make it. The assistant was more than happy to agree. He'd thought for a long time that he was a better coach than Steve and now was his chance to prove it.

Steve left the school quickly and drove to Grimm Memorials via Route 47 and the Dorsey Lane Extension. The smooth high he'd been on since the last time he'd seen Eleanor was wearing off. Like a junkie, he was in dire need of another fix. Nothing mattered except seeing her again. He didn't even care anymore that he had been thrown out of the Dickinson Poetry Competition. He no longer needed that, or anything else, as long as he had Eleanor.

He parked the Saab behind the hearse at the side of the house. Though the back door was closer, Steve went around to the front door so as to avoid Mephisto the dog. The rope that secured him was frayed and Steve didn't like the looks of it, or the overgrown, ugly, pit bull.

"Eleanor, it's me," he called out as he stepped through the door. He was so finely tuned to her that he could feel her presence immediately. She was very close by. He heard footsteps from the other side of the crematorium door just before it opened and Eleanor came out.

She looked radiant. Her long blonde hair cascaded over her bare shoulders, shimmering as it caught the light. She was wearing a low-cut peasant blouse showing her ample cleavage and just a hint of nipple over a flowing black skirt. Steve went to her and embraced her, urgently seeking her lips with his own, thrusting his tongue into her mouth like an erection. He found a long, white hair in his mouth when their lips parted. He noticed several more on her skirt. He picked the hair off his tongue and made to brush the others off her, but when he reached for them, they were gone, as was the one in his hand that he had just taken from his mouth.

Eleanor ran her hand up his thigh, cupping his testicles, squeezing them gently, and he forgot all about the hairs. Her other hand ran over his face, as if writing on it. "There's something I want you to do for me, lover," she whispered in his ear, giving it a little lick.

Steve stood limp with ecstasy as she massaged his balls and his brain. His head bobbed up and down in agreement.

"Bring me to meet your stepchildren. If we're going to break up their family, I ought to at least explain to them why. I'm *very good* with children." As she spoke she worked him over with her mind, stroking his libido, and her hands—one moving over his face, the other working his crotch until he peaked, moaning and thrusting his hips against her hand and shuddering with delight.

Jennifer walked slowly through the field and into her backyard, going to the rusted swing set and sitting on one of the swings. She couldn't understand why her grandmother had left her; everything had been so perfect with her living in the woods. Jennifer didn't know what she was going to do without her.

What happened to her gingerbread house? she wondered. Had it burned down? Had Grammy moved it? Or had Jennifer just dreamed it? The latter thought had persisted as she'd searched for the path and Grandma's house, but until now it had seemed stupid. She *knew* Gram had been living in the woods; she could not have dreamt it. But now, with her disappearing so suddenly and completely, Jen was not so sure.

She began swinging slowly when she noticed their car passing on the dirt road through the woods. Steve was driving and someone was in the passenger seat. Wondering what he was doing in the woods, Jennifer jumped from the swing and ran around the house to the front just as Steve pulled the Saab into the driveway.

Steve got out of the car and smiled at her. "'Hi, Jen. There's someone here that I want you to meet." The other person got out of the passenger's side and came around the car.

Jennifer couldn't believe her eyes. It was Grandma. She

had come back. Jennifer ran to her arms and hugged her. "Where were you, Gram? I thought you left me!"

"Hush, now," Grammy cooed. "It's all right. I had to go away for a little while, but now I'm back. Everything's going to be fine."

"Where's your brother?" Steve asked Jennifer.

"Upstairs, I guess," Jen answered, clinging to her grandmother.

Jackie was stuffing a pillowcase full of clothes and toys, the latter outweighing the former, when Steve walked in on him.

"What are you doing?"

"I'm running away," Jackie grunted tearfully.

Steve suppressed a laugh. "Before you do, big guy, there's someone downstairs who wants to talk to you."

Jackie gave him a suspicious look.

"I'm not going to stop you," Steve said, his arms and hands held up in a gesture of innocence. "You can run away any time you want. Just come and say hello now, then you can go."

Jackie let the pillowcase fall on the bed. He didn't really want to run away, but after what his mother did to him, he felt that he had no other choice. He doubted that there was anyone downstairs; he figured Steve was just trying to talk him out of it. But that was okay; Jackie wanted to be talked out of running away. He just didn't want Steve to know that.

"Okay, I guess," he grumbled after a moment's hesitation on. "But I *am* going to run away."

"I believe you," Steve said. He took Jackie's hand as they left the room and went downstairs. When they walked out the front door, Jackie couldn't believe his eyes.

"Oh, Jackie! I'm so sorry!" His mother was standing on the lawn, one arm around Jen, smiling at him with love the way she used to.

Jackie shook his head and looked at her again. There was

something different about her—*she was no longer pregnant!* She was skinny again and pretty. There was no baby that was going to take his place. He realized something must have happened (in the back of his mind the memory of his dream rose for a moment, then sank again). His mother must have had a "messy carriage" like she'd had once before. Jackie didn't care what had happened, and needed no explanations. His mother was back.

"Please forgive me, honey. I've been terrible lately, I know. But now everything's going to be like it used to." She held her other arm out to him.

Tears of happiness sprouted from his eyes as he nodded joyfully. Jackie ran to her and hugged her. Jackie looked up at his mother and she caressed his face.

"You're still my baby, Jackie," she cooed lovingly. She bent down and picked him up, cuddling him close. Her blouse was unbuttoned and Jackie could see that she wore no bra. Her breasts were exposed. She cradled Jackie in her arms and brought his face to her breasts. "You're still my baby, honey."

Dreamily, Jackie opened his mouth as his mother inserted a nipple between his lips. A wave of pleasure passed through him as he sucked greedily at her beautiful breast that was all for him. Carrying him as he fed, his mother turned and went back to the car, getting in. Jen and Steve followed, with Steve starting the car and backing it out of the driveway.

Jackie was in Heaven. He curled up in his mother's arms and sucked the sweetest milk he had ever tasted from her breasts. The road they were travelling on was bumpy, but he didn't care as long as he could remain suckling, happy and secure, at her rounded breasts. He drank hungrily from one, then the other. It was such a wonderful feeling that he felt like he was floating.

In the back seat, Jennifer looked happily at her brother

wrapped snugly in Grammy's arms and sighed. Everything was going to be great now, she just knew it.

The car came to a halt and Jackie felt cool air on his face as his mother opened the door. Suddenly, the milk from her breast grew hot, then scalding and took on a foul taste. He opened his eyes and spit up a runny blue gel. It was followed by a scream.

The tit he was sucking at was not the same one he had put in his mouth. It was bulbous, the skin green and covered with pimples and hairy moles. He glanced in panic at the other one. It was the same. The nipples were purple and spiny; sharp enough to cut his mouth.

He looked up and nearly dumped in his pants. He was sucking at the breast of the troll he'd seen at the bridge in the woods. Her long red hair hung like kinked wire from her huge, scabby head. Her pointed ears and horns stuck up through her hair like mountain peaks. Her wide red eyes leered at him and her mouth opened in a hideous smile revealing a wall of teeth parted by a gray, saliva-coated tongue.

Jackie screamed again and squirmed in the troll's arms, trying to get away, but the creature held on tight. Jackie managed to twist his head away, but found himself screaming louder at what he saw when he did. A short distance away was a small house that Jackie recognized immediately. Its roof was brown and thick and hung low. Its walls were white and creamy. Its fence was candy-striped. It was none other than the gingerbread house from "Hansel and Gretel" and Jackie knew who lived there.

Dry laughter brought his head around again. The troll was gone. In its place was a wrinkled old witch grinning at him.

"Aren't you a nice fat one," the witch said in a terrible voice.

Jackie fainted from sheer terror.

* * *

Jennifer followed her grandmother and Jackie into the gingerbread house and watched as Gram placed Jackie in a cage with a bunch of other boys. She never wondered why her grandmother would be doing such a strange thing; she just kept on smiling happily.

Steve Nailer didn't hear Jackie's screams. He remained in the car, as Eleanor had told him to, and listened to an old Chuck Berry tune turned up loud on the radio. He didn't turn it down until Eleanor came back and got in the car again.

"The children are fine," she said as he leaned over and nuzzled her ear, giving her tit a little squeeze as he did. "Now I want to meet your wife. We've got to make this a clean break." She put her hand on Steve's lap and rubbed. "It'll be easier if we do it together."

Diane Nailer got out of bed and lumbered down to the kitchen. She opened the refrigerator door, hanging on it while she leaned over to check its contents, and had a sharp contraction. She straightened, breathing deeply, and patted her belly. That was the second contraction in less than two hours. By her doctor's count, she was a week overdue, but on her last visit to him on Monday, he'd said there was nothing to worry about and everything was fine.

The baby moved suddenly inside her, kicking painfully against her side. "Are you hungry, too?" she spoke to her stomach and the baby inside. "Why don't you come out and get something to eat, then?" She reached into the fridge and pulled out a package of sliced processed cheese and carried it to the counter. She tore at the package with her teeth, getting it open, and proceeded to fold and wolf down several slices.

She was taking the package of cheese upstairs with her

when the front door opened and Steve came in. Diane retreated back to the kitchen, but Steve followed her. "Diane, there's something I have to tell you, and there's someone I want you to meet," he said.

"Maybe later, Steve," she mumbled around a mouthful of cheese.

"No, Diane, now!" Steve said adamantly. He went to the back door and opened it.

"Steve . . ." Diane protested until she looked out the door and saw her father standing on the back step. Diane dropped her handful of cheese, and ran to the door, pushing the screen open and waddling out to him.

"Daddy!" she squealed happily. "I'm so glad to see you," she cried embracing him. "I've been taking care of the baby just like you told me to."

"Good child," Daddy said soothingly, patting the back of her head. "I brought you something like I used to. Remember?"

Diane stepped back and looked at him with happy expectation. He reached in his pocket and produced a large red apple. "For you, bambina. An apple, just like old times."

Diane took the fruit with both hands and caressed it as if it were gold. She smiled a sweet and innocent little girl smile at her father and brought the apple to her lips. Just for a second, before she bit into the fruit, the image of a tall, white-haired old woman looming over her father flashed in her mind. Instantly, it was gone and she was sinking her teeth into the fat apple, feeling the juice squirt into her mouth and run down her chin. She swallowed, and choked. A piece of the apple was lodged in her throat. She spit chewed pulp from her mouth and coughed, hard and dry. There was no intake of breath. Her mouth was gaping, her eyes wide.

Diane staggered, and nearly fell, but her father reached out and steadied her. She was growing dizzy, lightheaded, and her legs felt nonexistent beneath her. The trees and sky began to slide away from her. She reached out to empty air, and her father caught her with one hand under her waist and the other over her mouth. Just before she slipped into unconsciousness, Diane wondered why her father held a handkerchief in the hand over her mouth.

CHAPTER 31

My little old man and I fell out.

Steve didn't know what had happened. One minute Diane and Eleanor were standing on the back step, talking, and the next Diane was lying on the ground immobile. Steve rushed out to where Eleanor knelt, taking Diane's pulse with one hand and feeling her belly with the other.

"She fainted," Eleanor explained. "Pick her up. We'll take her back to my place. I can take care of her there."

Steve saw no reason to argue. He slipped an arm under his wife's neck and the other under her knees. He lifted her carefully and carried her to his car in the driveway. Being careful not to bang her head on the door frame, Steve placed her gently on the backseat. Eleanor slid in beside her and put an arm around Diane's shoulders to keep her from falling over. Steve got in, started the car, and drove them back to Grimm Memorials.

"Carry her inside," Eleanor instructed Steve as he lifted Diane's body out of the car. Eleanor held the front door open for him. "Down there," she said, guiding him through the entrance hall to the crematorium door, which she also opened for him. She followed as Steve carried Diane down the stairs.

"Put her over there," Eleanor said, pointing to the leather reclining chair set up in the middle of the ritual pentangle.

Steve carried Diane to it and lowered her softly.

"Perfect," Eleanor said, smiling. She pulled Steve away from the table and kissed him deeply. "Take off your clothes," she whispered in his ear.

"But, Diane . . ." Steve began to protest.

Eleanor unbuttoned his pants, reached in, and grabbed his penis. "She'll be fine," Eleanor breathed, licking her lips, turning Steve to putty in her hands.

He undressed quickly, tearing his clothes from his body in his haste to get at Eleanor. When he was naked, he went to the wooden podium where Eleanor was reading from a large book and grabbed her breasts.

"Wait," she said, turning to him. "There's just one more thing I have to do." In her hand she held a Ball jar with a thick, tarry substance in it. She dipped her finger in the jar and began painting odd-looking symbols on Steve's chest and face.

Steve laughed. "What's this?"

"You'll see," Eleanor cooed, painting with one hand and masturbating Steve with the other. "I've got something for you."

Steve waited anxiously, his penis erect and throbbing from Eleanor's stroking, while she finished painting him and went to the strange-looking metal table a few feet away. "Hurry," Steve urged her.

Eleanor took a long knife from the table and turned. She opened her mouth to speak, but only a gasp came out. A grimace of pain clenched her face. She leaned against the embalming table, clutching at her chest with both hands. Her mouth opened in a low, guttural moan and she doubled over, curling to the floor almost gracefully.

Steve ran a hand over his brow. He felt suddenly dizzy

and sick, like he was coming down with the flu. He lowered his hand. There was a red substance on it that looked like blood. He rocked on his heels and had to reach out for the leather recliner to steady himself, and saw his wife unconscious.

"Diane! Oh my God!" Steve cried looking at her. She didn't appear to be breathing. (*Is that why he had blood on his hand?*) He looked around for help from Eleanor and saw the room clearly for the first time since entering: the huge crematorium furnace low on the far wall, a roller-topped feed table in front of its door; the metal embalming table with its gutters and collection bottle, the wooden podium with the large book open on it, the pentangle painted on the floor around where he stood, the hundreds of black candles everywhere in the room, and the large cage, from which a stinking odor of shit and urine was coming. It was filled with small boys, his stepson Jackie one of them, lying unconscious around a filth-ridden toilet.

"What . . . What's going on here?" Steve stuttered. He felt like Rip van Winkle just waking from twenty years of sleep. A wave of dizziness washed over him again and he staggered back, grabbing at the metal table. He hung his head, trying to take deep breaths when he looked down and saw Eleanor.

She was old—hideously old. Gone was the sexy, seductive siren he had fallen in love with. In her place was a gnarled, wizened old hag who reminded him of the Weird Sisters in *Macbeth*. For a moment, Steve tried to convince himself that it was someone else, but it was no use. She was lying right where Eleanor had fallen. He didn't know how, but it was her all right.

"Oh my God," Steve mumbled, his expression a mixture of revulsion and fear.

One of the boys in the cage woke from his stupor with a loud scream that jerked Steve around. He stared at the boy who screamed and realized it was Mark Thomas, a boy in his Health I class. A picture of Joe Conally with a pickaxe through his chest blew through Steve's mind.

What have I done? he wondered. Mark screamed again and looked around. A boy next to him awoke and began to scream. Another woke sobbing. "What have I done?" Steve shouted loudly, overpowering the voices of the boys in the cage. They became aware of him and stared.

"Mr. Nailer! Help me!" Mark Thomas cried when he realized who Steve was. He hadn't recognized his teacher at first since he was naked and had the intricate patterns of red lines painted on his face and chest.

Steve ran to the cage door, his once-aroused cock now gone limp, and grabbed the bars with both hands, trying to yank it open. It was no good. He ran back to Eleanor's body and rifled her pockets looking for the keys to the cage. They weren't on her. Behind him, Mark Thomas urged him on with pleas to hurry, and more of the boys awoke in tears, or screaming with wild terror. "Sssh!" Steve hissed at them. He couldn't hear himself think. He had to find some way to get that cage door open.

He began searching the room for something to pry the door with when he caught the glint of candlelight reflecting off a large brass keyring hanging on the wall several feet to the right of the cage. The long silver skeleton keys on it looked to be the perfect size for the cage's lock. Steve ran to the ring, reaching for the key, but he never made it.

Like a marionette being jerked to its feet, Eleanor got to her knees, then stood. Mark Thomas opened his mouth to warn Steve, but Eleanor silenced him, and the other screaming boys, with a glance.

Steve turned at the sudden silence and saw Mark and the conscious boys staring in terror at something behind him. Steve himself never had time to turn. Eleanor was at his back, thrusting the knife she'd taken from the instrument cart up into the back of his neck and into the base of his brain. He died almost instantly, his eyes bulging, blood gushing from his nose with the force of a sneeze. He crashed against the wall face first, and slid to the floor.

The room was quiet except for the soft squishing sound of the blood still gushing from Steve's nose. Eleanor stood over Steve's twitching body and rolled him over onto his side. With a great deal of effort, she removed the knife from his neck and proceeded to castrate him.

As she worked, Steve's lips opened and a glob of blood slipped from his mouth. She looked at the children in the cage, trying to send them back to sleep, but she didn't have the strength. Instead, she was the one to succumb. The room began to fog up as the never-ending pain rose out of control again.

Keep the Machine going, she repeated to herself, over and over as the fog swallowed the room and her. From somewhere above in the vast house, she could hear the loud brayish laughter of Edmund mocking her. The sound pierced her flesh like a cloud of exploding glass, amplifying the pain in every fiber of her body and driving her to the floor where she collapsed onto Steve Nailer's still warm body, her hands clutching his bloody, severed manhood to her chest.

Imagine a dry riverbed. Imagine standing on it. Imagine a river roaring through. Imagine the river's name is Pain.

Eleanor felt that river rage through her and carry her away. She was swept through chasms of torture and canyons of hurt. She rode the Pain, and became submerged in Pain. It swirled around her and through her and pulled her down, burying her deep within herself.

In the depths of her pain ridden existence, she saw light and swam through the river to get to it. The closer she got to it, the less the river tugged at her. She kept kicking, pushing toward the light until it collided with her eyes and she surfaced in a room full of ghosts.

It was the night of Edmund's and Eleanor's thirteenth birthday. It was also the night Edmund was to leave for boarding school. They were in the front waking room, saying good-bye. His bags were all packed and sitting in the front hall. A carriage sat out front, ready to take him to the Springfield train station where he would just make it in time, five hours later, to catch a rail for Boston and the Patrician School for Boys. Eleanor was crying and pleading with him not to go.

"I have no choice," he said to her. "Father is making me."

He may have had no choice, but Eleanor knew he was not sorry to be going. She saw it in his face, half-lit by the gas lamps on the wall, and read it in his mind. He was happy to be escaping from the lonely, boring confines of Grimm Memorials. He was going out into the world where he could really use the Machine. Eleanor even detected a hint of gladness that he was escaping from her, also.

She didn't think it was fair of him to leave her behind with their father, who almost never spoke to her anymore. By that thirteenth birthday, Eleanor had a very good idea of what had started their mother's madness long before either of them had been born. With Edmund around, her father's neglect was merely annoying. With him gone it would make her as batty as her mother had been.

The first time she had ever felt hatred for Edmund had been at that moment when he walked out to the carriage and climbed in to be carried off to a new world of adventure, condemning her to a living Hell. It was that moment which was to be the spark of all that happened later.

As Edmund rode off, with never a look back, the scene slid sideways, changing color and brilliance. It shifted to later that same August evening. She lay in her bed staring out the window, crying softly into her pillow, when her father crept into the room. She watched him approach by the feeble glow of the hall lamps turned low.

He reached her bedside and knelt next to her. Without a

sound, he reached up and began massaging her budding breasts with both hands. He pinched her nipples through the thin cotton nightshirt and grabbed a handful of the material in each hand. With a quick tug he created a tear at the top. One quick motion and her nightshirt was laid open to reveal her naked breasts the size of small apples with the nipples indented, and the tuft of dark hair floating out from between her legs.

Eleanor never moved as he bent over her and began licking her skin from her toes to her neck, then back to her crotch where he buried his face and went to work on her with his greedy mouth. This wasn't much different from the games she'd played with Edmund to pass the time; games they had made up after continuing to spy on Father and his dead mistresses.

For the rest of the night Father played with her and Eleanor never voluntarily moved a muscle. He moved her around, manipulating her to whatever position his desire to put his thing in her called for, and she remained near catatonic, not caring what he did. Not even pushing his fishy-smelling thing in and out of her mouth and making her drink a sour-tasting liquid from it could bring her out of it.

After that night, Father's nightly visits to Eleanor's room became a part of their regular silent routine. And every night she lay unmoving, uncaring, as he did whatever he wanted to her.

The bedroom scene blackened and faded, melting away as she sank into nothingness. At the bottom of the river she again plummeted through, there was another light, pulling her like a magnet. She swam through it and immediately knew where she was and what day it was.

She was in the kitchen the day Edmund returned from Housatonic University after being away from Grimm Memorials for most of eight years. He had managed to get himself invited to a classmate's summer residence seven out of the eight years he was away, first at boarding school then the university, and had gone on a solo secret vacation somewhere the other summer. He had returned home three times in those years, once for a weekend, the other two times just overnight. Not once had he written to her, and on his visits home he lied to her. Now he was home to stay, a certified mortician and medical examiner, ready to take over Father's business. In spite of all that he had done to her, she awaited his arrival anxiously.

Eleanor stood by the stove, watching a pot of water boil. Not wanting him to see her, she'd run in there from the front hall, where she'd been watching out the door, when Edmund and Father rode up in a motorized hearse that Edmund had convinced, with a little help from the Machine, a rich friend to buy for him. It was the first one Eleanor had ever seen.

She heard him come in the front door and call to her. She felt the presence of his mind, as she had for the last hour as he'd gotten closer and closer to Grimm Memorials, only now it was actively seeking her out. It led him to the kitchen.

I'm home, Edmund's thoughts reached her as he swept grandly through the door. *Ta da!* he tooted, spreading his arms in presentation of himself.

Eleanor didn't turn around. She continued staring at the simmering water and kept her mind quiet. From out back she could hear the chugging of the motorcar as Father drove it around the house and parked it in the barn.

Aren't you glad to see me, Eleanor? Edmund asked. She shrugged. He crossed the kitchen and placed his hands on her shoulders, turning her around. *What's wrong?* She kept her eyes down and said nothing. Edmund persisted, coaxing her with his thoughts until she gave in.

You left me alone here. Tears came next as all the pent-up anger, hurt, and loneliness she'd been collecting since he'd left came welling to the surface. Without a spoken word between them, she conveyed it all to Edmund, playing it in his mind for him like a silent movie, complete with every sordid detail from the first night he left her, through all the years of abuse and degradation she'd suffered under her father from then on. As it poured from her, she wept, until she grew weak and collapsed into her brother's arms. He embraced her and soothed her.

It's all right now, he reassured her with soft mind whispers when she was done, exhausted. *Things are going to change now. I've learned so much! That's why I haven't been home. I had to use every moment I was away to learn everything I could so I could come back and teach you, and give you what I had without you. And such knowledge I have gained! Now we can start together and live for power and pure pleasure.*

He grinned fiercely and his eyes widened. *I've gained the powers of Hell, and the secret to immortality itself!*

The word immortality echoed in Eleanor's head as she floated through the pain, rising to semiconsciousness. Somewhere—at times they sounded near, then far away—several children's voices were crying for help. Eleanor tried to open her eyes but they felt nailed together. She tried to move, but the air was like glue and she stuck to it. All the while, the pain burned throughout her entire being, becoming heavier and heavier until it was immense. It became the river again and carried her away until nothing else existed.

CHAPTER 32

What is the news of the day?

Jackie woke to the sound of many voices, and the rancid choking stench of stale shit and urine. His head hurt. He rolled over and gingerly felt the bump on his head, wincing at the pain. "Help! Somebody help!" a voice was wailing nearby. Other voices were sobbing. Two voices very near him joined in crying for help several times before stopping. "It's no use," one of those voices said. "No one can hear us." Groaning with the pain in his head, Jackie sat up and looked at the speaker.

The boy was taller and bigger than Jackie, obviously older. He had brown hair, large brown eyes, and a face spattered with many freckles. Jackie looked past him, to the other boys in the cage. Against the bars, farthest from him to his left, a pair of twins, dark-haired and red-eyed from crying, were clinging to each other as they huddled near a filth-stained, lidless toilet. They had been yelling for help, also, but stopped when the older boy said no one could hear them. Against the bars to the left of the twins was Timmy Walsh from school. The memory of the Pied Piper and his rats flashed in Jackie's head, making him wonder what had happened to Betty Boone.

As far as he could tell, there were only boys in the cage. Timmy was crouched, arms wrapped around his knees, hugging himself, and rocking on his heels, not looking at anyone. Beyond him, Jackie recognized the four boys who lived on Route 47 from the pictures that had appeared in the newspaper after they'd disappeared. They were supposed to have drowned in the river. On the other side of the cage two short boys, one blond, the other brown-haired, stood with their backs to him, grasping the bars in their hands and staring out at the candlelit room. In the rear corner nearest him, a dark-haired, dark-skinned boy was slumped unconscious.

For a few minutes all the boys were quiet. Jackie's still-dazed eyes slowly took in the rest of the room, eventually settling on the nightmare vision of the old woman sprawled over his naked stepfather, Steve, who had a stream of dried blood frozen in mid-flow coming from his mouth and nose and a slow steady trickle coming from the horrible gash where his private parts should have been.

Jackie couldn't see much of the old woman slumped over Steve, just the top of her head, her long white hair splayed out in all directions, and her bony, age-spotted hands at the ends of her black-sleeved arms laid out to the sides. What he could see, he didn't like. She looked like the witch from his dream, the witch who had carried him here. This must be the gingerbread house, he thought.

He looked away from the witch and saw his mother sprawled on the reclining chair set in the middle of the circle within the star painted on the floor. He let out a yell. "Mom!" he cried. All the boys in the cage looked at him as he leapt to his feet and flung himself against the bars, arms reaching out to his unconscious mother.

"Mom, wake up!" Jackie cried. She gave no response. It was no use. She was out. Maybe she was dead. Jackie gulped back a panic of tears and slid to his knees, his head resting against the bars.

"Is that your mom, kid?" the older boy asked Jackie.

Jackie nodded his head, fighting back tears, unable to speak.

"I think she's still alive," the older boy added. "I saw them carry her in here. If we could wake her up we could get out of here."

Jackie looked at the boy, then his mother, then Steve. "That's my stepfather," he heard himself say ridiculously, as if he was pointing out his skateboard or his bike and not his stepfather *who lay naked on the floor with his private parts cut off and blood flowing from his nose and mouth and eyes wide open, staring at some faraway spot on the floor in front of him.*

The shock of it settled into him.

It was the older boy's turn to look upset. Tears formed in his eyes. "He was my teacher," he said brokenly, adding angrily, "he brought me here!" He looked away, fists clenched until his knuckles turned white.

"What does she want?" one of the boys, a redhead, spoke up, asking in a trembling voice. No one said anything. They avoided looking at each other for fear of seeing the same sense of terror they felt reflected on another face.

The older boy thought for a few minutes, then shrugged. "It doesn't matter," he said in a low voice, as if speaking his thoughts aloud. "She's dead. Someone will come and find us, or the kid's mother will wake up and get us out. We'll get out of here somehow. We just have to wait and be patient. There was a girl with the old lady when she brought you in, I think," he added, pointing to Jackie, "but she left. Maybe she'll come back."

"Jennifer!" Jackie cried. "That was my sister Jennifer." His mother turning into a troll then the witch flashed before his eyes and he trembled with a fearful chill. But what had happened to Jennifer? Hope surged in him and he jumped to his feet.

"Jennifer!" he shouted as loud as he could. He repeated it several times, most of the children joining in. After several minutes, and no answer, they stopped yelling and Jackie slumped again to the floor.

"My name's Mark Thomas," the older boy said, sitting next to Jackie and introducing himself.

"I'm Jackie Nailer," Jackie answered in a dull whisper.

Mark looked around the cage at the other boys, some of whom had begun to cry again, then looked out at the bodies of the old woman and Mr. Nailer. "Who is she?" he asked.

Jackie glanced sideways at her through the bars and tried to speak, but a sob rose into his mouth instead of words and he couldn't.

"She's the Wicked Witch of the West," a pudgy boy behind them said.

"No, she's the Big Bad Wolf!" another boy spoke up. Suddenly all of them began talking at once, gibbering about what each of them had seen the old woman as.

"Whoa! Wait a minute," Mark said, standing and holding up his hands for quiet. "One at a time. You first," he ordered, pointing at the pudgy boy who'd spoken first. "What's your name?"

"Jason Grakopolous," the pudgy boy said, resentful of being ordered around by Mark.

"Who did you say she was?"

"The Wicked Witch of the West," Jason replied belligerently, as though this were the hundredth time he had to repeat it. "I was watching *The Wizard of Oz* on TV and Glinda the Good Witch landed in my backyard with the Munchkins, then she turned into the Wicked Witch of the West."

Mark looked doubtfully at the boy, who stared sullenly back at him, then pointed to the redhead next to him. "What about you?" he asked.

"My name's Jeff Best. This is my brother Jimmy, and our friends Bobby and Danny," he said quickly before his voice began to falter. He continued haltingly, as if he doubted his own words. "She was the Three Bears. We found Goldilocks, too." A sob escaped his lips. "She was dead," he finished, giving way to silent tears. His brother slid over next to him and put his arm around Jeff's shoulder. The friend he had introduced as Danny, nodded over and over in shock while the other boy, Bobby, sucked his thumb and stared into space.

"She was Tweedle-dum," one of the twins, the smallest and obviously youngest boys in the cage, said from his perch near the stinking toilet. "And Tweedle-dee," chirped his brother who was lying on the floor, clinging tightly to his brother's legs. When Mark asked them their names, they jumped and clung to each other like frightened chimpanzees in a zoo and refused to answer.

"She was a cartoon," a little voice piped up from the far side of the cage. A little, brown-haired boy stood up, a half smile on his face. Everyone looked at him, but no one laughed at what he had to say. "First she was Red Riding Hood, then she was the Big Bad Wolf like in the cartoons my dad showed me." He paused, a look of fear entered his eyes. "Then the cartoon Big Bad Wolf became the *real* Big Bad Wolf," he finished, his voice hoarse with terror.

The boys looked at him and each of them knew that sound; knew what it felt like. They all grew very quiet, each caught up in memories of their own personal nightmares.

"What's your name?" Mark asked the boy who said he had seen the Big Bad Wolf.

"My name is Billy Schmidt. I live at 200 Old Deerfield Road. My telephone number is 887-7550," the boy replied like an automaton. Mark couldn't help but smile at him and one of the other boys giggled.

"How about you, Jackie?" Mark asked, gently. "What did you see?"

Jackie looked around at all of them and was afraid to speak. He didn't care what anyone else had seen; he didn't care who they thought the old lady was; she was the witch, like the one from his dream and the story Jennifer had read to him. He had begun to doubt that she was really dead, so if they kept talking, they might wake her up.

"Come on, Jackie, tell me," Mark coaxed.

"She was my mom," Jackie whispered. "Then she became a troll, then a witch. Alright? I don't think we should talk no more. We might wake her up."

The boys looked from Jackie to the old woman and felt the sense of terror that had been wearing off grow bright again. They had all been too ready and willing to believe that the old woman was dead. Jackie's mere mention of the possibility that she wasn't made them all cringe.

"I'm pretty sure she's dead," Mark said, after looking at her body for several minutes. "I saw my grandfather have a heart attack when he died and the old lady looked just like that. I'm telling you she's dead."

Jason and Jeff crept to the bars and looked out at her gray, lifeless face and were ready to believe him again. They all were. Believing she was dead was easier than fearing she would awaken. They were safe now and wanted nothing to intrude on that.

Mark stepped over Jackie and Jerry and crouched in front of Timmy Walsh who sat in a fetal position against the left wall of bars, hugging his knees. He stared at the floor avoiding everyone's eyes.

"What happened to you?" Mark whispered.

Timmy put his hand over his eyes and began to tremble.

"Hey, it's okay. It's alright," Mark said, reaching out for him. Timmy screamed and retreated from Mark's hand.

"His name is Timmy Walsh," Jackie whispered after a fearful look at the witch. "He's in my grade at school. I saw him and Betty Boone get carried away by the Pied Piper."

"What about you?" redheaded Jeff asked Mark.

"I don't know," Mark said, embarrassed. "I thought she was this girl in my class, but she wasn't." He blushed and looked away. "Boy, that toilet stinks. Is it backed up or something?" he added with a nervous laugh to cover his embarrassment.

The rest of the afternoon and into the evening, the boys talked softly about school, or family, and what their mothers and fathers were doing and how they would be coming any minute to save them. Twice they heard a dog barking and they all began yelling, except for Jackie who kept his eyes on the witch for any sign of life. Each time it was nothing and they yelled themselves hoarse.

By the time the light in the basement window grew dark, the boys had lapsed into an uneasy silence. By the eerie glow of the many candles still burning, the boys dreamed of rescue, listening intently for any sign of it, while keeping a wary eye on the old woman. The candle flames cast flickering shadows that played easy tricks with their vision. More than once one of them thought they saw the old woman's body move, or worse, they saw the dead guy beneath her move. They drew instinctively closer together in the middle of the cage, all except the dark boy who was still unconscious in the corner.

The night wore on and the candles burned out one by one, until they were left in darkness. The smaller boys tired first and fell asleep. But soon all of them, exhausted from fear and the aftereffects of the drugs they didn't know they had been given, were dozing. They slept fitfully until the early hours of dawn.

Eleanor opened her eyes and mouth at the same time. She vomited soundlessly and blinked. She looked at the body she was lying on top of. It was her father lying dead at the bottom of the stairs where he had ended up after Edmund had pushed him.

Liar! Edmund screamed.

Eleanor raised her eyes just enough to see him standing

in shadows under the gray light streaming in the window. She could only see part of his forehead and nose.

Does lying help you forget the truth, Eleanor? Edmund asked, a mocking tone to his words. *Why can't you admit the truth?*

Edmund, help me, Eleanor thought desperately. He laughed disgustedly and vanished, sucked up by the shadows. Eleanor remained still for a few moments, sucking air into her lungs. Edmund can't help me, she thought. He's gone. Dead.

The pain in her chest was lighter, but not as light as it normally was after an attack. Usually, an attack relieved the pain for a little while, but this time it hovered on the edge of becoming a full force attack again. The Machine was almost silent. She could hear the boys in the cage dreaming fitfully, free of the Machine's influence. She also registered that Diane's drugged sleep was wearing off. The only person the Machine still retained control of was Jennifer, who had returned to her empty home, ready to carry out her grandmother's wishes.

By the light in the room, Eleanor could tell the night was almost gone. It was October 31. Halloween. Samhain and the Harvest of Dead Souls. Ritual day. The day she gained immortality. She just had to keep the Machine running a little longer and she'd be home free.

Despite the pain, despite Edmund, despite everything, she had to make it. With a slow and steady effort, still clutching Steve Nailer's bloody organ in her hand, she raised her head, moved her arms, and pushed off the stiffening body of her former lover, getting to her knees.

CHAPTER 33

And if she's not gone, she lives there still.

Jackie was the first to see her. He was sleeping curled up against Mark's hip. The dirty gray dawn light seeping through the window played across his eyelids and woke him. At first, he didn't remember where he was. He thought he was home in his room. He yawned, blinked, and was about to roll over and go back to sleep when he saw the silhouetted figure rising slowly in the dim light. He thought it was Jennifer until he realized the figure was too tall to be his sister. Suddenly, he became completely aware of his surroundings and the memories of what had happened the day before.

He sat up. The figure was rising over the dead body of his stepfather. His mother was still on the chair in the middle of the room, so there was only one other person that it could be.

"The Witch!" Jason Grakopolous screamed as he woke and saw Eleanor, too. The rest of the boys came awake, some of them screaming with fright, others crying loudly. Only Jackie and Mark remained quiet, never taking their eyes off the old woman who rose unsteadily to her feet.

"Quiet!" the witch hissed in the direction of the cage. The very act of speaking seemed to give her pain and she grimaced. The crying boys behind Jackie immediately ceased their loud wailing but continued sniveling softly.

The witch teetered a moment, one hand grasping at the wall, the other clutching something bloody to her chest. Her eyes closed, and the pained grimace on her face deepened to a scowl. The old woman straightened, her hand fell from her chest, and she tossed the bloody thing she'd held there into the circle at the foot of the chair holding Jackie's mother.

With a gasp Jackie saw what it was.

The witch shrieked in pain and for one hopeful moment, Jackie thought she was going to collapse again, maybe even die. He wished it, demanded it, shouting it in his mind: *Die! Die!*

The witch's eyes opened, and she looked directly at Jackie. *You'd like that, wouldn't you?* Jackie wasn't sure if he'd heard her with his ears or his mind but her voice made his bowels clench with fear. She let go of the wall and moved forward, stepping on Steve's corpse, which emitted loud simultaneous burps and farts under the weight of her body. She ignored the foul, pungent odor that rose from the dead man and staggered to the cage.

The boys moved back until they were huddled at the far end of the cage, but none of them took their eyes off her. She stared at Jackie until he looked away in terror, on the edge of pissing in his pants. Slowly, she looked at each of the boys, staring them down in turn.

"Thought I was dead, didn't you?" she croaked in a hoarse whisper. *Not yet, my pretties,* she giggled in their heads. She turned, went to the chair, and secured the arms and legs of Jackie's mother with the leather straps that hung from the front and from under the arms. When that was done she leaned against the chair resting for several moments before pushing herself up, crossing to the door, and going slowly through it and up the stairs.

* * *

"You said she was dead," Jeff, the redhead, whispered fervently to Mark when they could no longer hear her footsteps.

"I thought she was. She looked like she was, for Christ's sake," Mark whispered back.

"Shhhh! She'll hear you," Jackie said fearfully. Those eyes were still with him, looking inside him and turning his guts to Jell-O. He had wanted to yell at the witch, tell her to leave his mother alone, but he couldn't. He was ashamed of his cowardice, but the last thing in the world he wanted was for the witch to look at him again with those monster's eyes, and he didn't want her to return now.

"She can't hear us," Mark said. "She's out of ear shot."

"She can hear everything," Jeff said in a soft voice. They all considered that, and though no one said so, they all knew it to be true. They remained quiet for several minutes before Mark spoke up again.

"What does she want with us?" Mark wondered aloud.

"She's the witch, like in 'Hansel and Gretel,'" Jackie said in a frightened voice. "She wants to eat us up."

They grew very quiet again at that until one of the twins began to whine in a long, painful tone, tears dripping from his face. His brother soon joined him and within seconds so did most of the other boys in the cage. Only Jackie, Mark, and Davy Torrez, unconscious in the corner, didn't cry, though Jackie came very close. He had begun to wonder what had happened to Jen and, when he did that, he felt like crying because he got a real bad feeling about her.

Mark watched their hysteria build and knew he had to do something. "Quiet!" he whispered at them as loud as he dared. He stood up and shushed them with his hands. "She'll come back if you don't stop it," he threatened. That was more effective.

"She's not going to eat us. Someone is going to come and find us. This many people, grown-ups, too, can't disappear without the cops or somebody finding out." He didn't believe his own words, but he was doing a pretty good job with the others because they quieted, though they were still visibly frightened.

"If she isn't going to eat us up, what does she want?" Jackie whispered faintly, falling in with the other's wanting to believe Mark rather than his own instincts.

"She's probably holding us for ransom," Mark said. It was possible, but he didn't really believe it, either. The fact that Jackie's stepfather had helped the old lady until she killed him, and that Jackie's mother was there, knocked out on the chair, discounted *his* being held for ransom. Mark looked around at the boys thoughtfully. Though none of them were dressed nicely enough to appear wealthy, he couldn't be sure.

"Are any of you guys rich?" Mark asked softly.

The boys looked at him uncomprehendingly.

"You know what I mean. Are your parents rich? Anyone?"

No one answered. The boys looked at each other questioningly. Finally, Jason Grakopolous raised his hand as if he was in school. "I'm rich," he said quietly, but with a touch of arrogance.

Mark looked at him suspiciously. There was something about Jason that he didn't believe. "What's your father do?" Mark asked.

"He's a foreman in a big factory."

Mark smiled. He knew the kid had been lying; foremen aren't rich. As far as Mark could see, only he, himself, came from *some* money. His father was a computer engineer who had started his own software company, and his mother was a psychiatrist, but they weren't superrich like the families of some of the kids at Northwood Academy. If kidnapping for ransom was the motive here, why didn't Mr. Nailer kidnap a wealthier kid, Mark wondered. But even if Mark was to be the object of ransom, why kidnap the other kids? And why bring his wife and stepson here? These questions alone ruled out kidnapping for ransom as a motive.

Mark looked through the bars at Mr. Nailer's corpse. Only the top half of his body was in the growing square of yellowish gray light climbing in the window. Mr. Nailer's face had turned a bad color—a mix of purple, blue, and black, making it hard to see the lines painted on his face. Only one, a squiggly line on his cheek that reminded Mark of a spider, could be seen clearly.

Mark looked at the symbol, did a double take, and looked at the floor outside the cage where the star was painted inside the circle. The same symbol that was on Mr. Nailer's face was painted at the upper left point of the star.

That, Mark thought, is the key. Though he wasn't into it himself, he knew several kids at the academy who loved heavy-metal rock. It was on their T-shirt and jacket decals, which were usually reproductions of their favorite group's logo or latest album cover art, that he had seen the same star inside the circle with the corresponding symbols before. He also knew that it was a satanic symbol.

Mark gulped nervously. He had seen the TV talk shows— *"Geraldo," "Donahue," "Morton Downey Jr."*—do programs on Satan worshippers.

They killed people.

Eleanor staggered up the stairs, into the entrance hall to the stairway, and leaned on the railing for several minutes. Outside, Mephisto was barking rabidly; Jennifer was approaching the house with the thirteenth sacrifice for tonight. Straining, she pushed herself up and started for the kitchen, then stopped.

I've left the ether in the crematorium, she realized. There was no time to get it. Jennifer and the last sacrifice were coming in the back door.

CHAPTER 34

Who caught his blood? I, said the fish . . .

Jennifer woke just before 5 A.M. She sat up and immediately got out of bed. She was fully dressed, having slept in her clothes so she'd be ready first thing in the morning to carry out Gram's wishes. She went out of her room, down to the front hall closet where she put on a heavy coat, woolen gloves, and a woolen watch cap pulled over her ears. Slipping out the front door, she ran across the street and into the woods opposite the entrance to the road that led to Grimm Memorials.

On one of the first days of school, Jennifer had overheard Greg Roberts, a boy in her class, tell some other boys that he went fishing every Saturday morning in the Connecticut River behind his house. Since the boy lived a few houses down Route 47, Jennifer knew approximately where his fishing spot was likely to be.

She made her way past birches, and oak trees, stepping over and through the thick laurel and ivy underbrush until she stumbled upon a path. She followed it, hearing the rushing sound of the river getting closer as the path wound constantly to the left. Soon she was walking along the top of the riverbank, ignoring the beautiful river scene and keeping her eyes peeled for Greg Roberts. She found him downriver, sitting at the tip of a long, flat boulder jutting out of the top of the riverbank like a nut wedged in a piece of candy.

"Hi!" Jennifer called, waving.

The boy glanced in her direction, but didn't return her greeting. He looked around to see to whom she was waving.

Jennifer ran down the path to the boulder. She walked out to the edge and sat next to Greg. The river rushed directly below them. "Hi, Greg," Jennifer tried again.

"Oh, uh, hi," Greg muttered. He wound his reel a little and looked off upstream.

"You remember me don't you? We're in the same class, Mrs. Reinbold's?" Jen asked.

"Mm," Greg grunted noncommittally.

"What are you fishing for?" Jennifer asked him.

"Trout," Greg replied out of the side of his mouth.

"I know a much better place to catch trout than this crummy spot," Jennifer said as if she had one up on him.

"This is the best place," Greg replied. He wasn't going to let a girl say she had a better spot than his.

"I caught one this big." Jennifer held her hands out nearly two feet apart to show him.

He laughed at her. "I'll bet," he said sarcastically.

"I can prove it," Jen said in defense. "I have the fish at my grandmother's house right near my spot upstream from here. I caught it yesterday."

Greg looked at her doubtfully, but her claim to proof had him intrigued.

"I'll show it to you," Jennifer challenged.

Greg looked at the river, then his fishing line. The fish certainly weren't biting *here* this morning, that was for sure. He figured it couldn't hurt to see if she was telling the truth. He was wrong.

"Okay. Show me," he said, calling her bluff.

Jennifer led the way back along the path upstream until it wound away from the river and she could see the gingerbread house through the thinning trees. "That's where my grandmother lives," Jen said, pointing proudly to the gingerbread house.

"It looks deserted," Greg Roberts remarked, looking at Grimm Memorials.

Jennifer glanced at him and wondered if he was joking; couldn't he see the curl of smoke coming from the solid milk chocolate chimney? She smiled awkwardly at his comments and led him on through the woods.

"I hope that dog doesn't get loose," Greg said. Mephisto had heard them coming through the woods and was barking ferociously at them. Lunging against his leash, he frantically tried to break free and attack them.

Jennifer laughed. Greg had such a strange sense of humor. There was no dog at Grandma's.

They came out of the woods on the right side of the house, several yards down from Mephisto. Oblivious to the dog, who was in a frenzy at their being so close, Jennifer led Greg around the side of the house to the back door.

"Your grandmother lives here?" Greg asked incredulously, looking at the size of the place and the cemetery in the back-yard.

"Yes. It's beautiful, isn't it?" Jennifer said, sounding to Greg like a member of the Addams family for liking such a weird place.

Jennifer led Greg into the kitchen and offered him a seat at the kitchen table. "Have some candy," she said pointing at the wall.

Greg Roberts sat down and looked at her like she was crazy; there was nothing but wall where she was pointing. He looked around with distaste at the rest of the dingy room with its ancient black stove and filthy sink. To Greg, this place looked like somebody's *dead* grandmother should be living there. It was creepy.

"So where's this great fish?" Greg asked uneasily, want-ing to see the damn thing and get the hell out of there. The place gave him the willies for certain.

Jennifer went to a tall freezer in the far corner of the room and took out a foil package about two feet long. She placed it on the table in front of Greg.

Greg gaped at the size of the package. *It was true!* He couldn't believe the size of it. Anxiously, he began to open the foil wrapping. As he peeled it away, he thought the fish had a funny shape, and color for trout. He ripped more foil off.

Trout didn't have fingers, or a hand and wrist.

He tore away the rest of the foil. A whole severed arm, from shoulder to fingertips lay on the foil in front of him. He let out a yell and jumped up, backing right into Eleanor. She swung a heavy, cast-iron frying pan at him, striking the back of his head and knocking him senseless to the ground.

CHAPTER 35

Pussy-cat ate the dumplings, the dumplings . . .

"Shhh! What's that?" Jackie asked. The room was filling with a loud electronic humming, that stopped suddenly with an airy, blowing sound. Moments later, he heard the witch's footsteps on the stairs. "She's coming back!"

All of them scrambled at once to the back of the cage, as far as possible from the door as they could get. Without realizing it, they collectively held their breath when the old woman entered the room.

Eleanor lumbered into the crematorium, her left leg dragging, the pain making her vision thick, and went to the casket lift, which she had just sent down from the chapel with Greg Roberts inside. She unlatched the lift door and slid it up. Using the casket gurney, she lifted Greg out of the elevator and wheeled him to the cage.

She got the key from the wall, opened the cage door, and wheeled the gurney and its human cargo inside. She pulled a lever and the table holding Greg Roberts collapsed. He fell heavily to the floor and rolled off the table in front of the others.

Eleanor gave them a cursory glance, just enough to provoke a cold sweat, wheeled the gurney out of the cage, locked the door again, and placed the gurney next to the embalming table. From the instrument tray she removed a large brown bottle of ether and a white cloth. She opened the bottle and, keeping her face turned away, splashed some ether on the cloth. The cloth went over Jackie's mother's face. Eleanor held it there for less than a minute before tossing the cloth back on the cart and limping to the crematorium door, and back upstairs.

"Mom!" Jackie called as loud as he dared to his mother when the witch was gone. She didn't respond. He started to call her again, but no sound came out of his mouth as he choked up with emotion and nearly burst into tears. He stood against the bars, his hands clenching them tightly, and stared sorrowfully at his sleeping mother.

The sweet sound of metal chopping through meat reached Eleanor's ears as she climbed to the entrance hall. The pain bearing down on her drove her to the leather couch, where she lay popping *bomb pills* and praying for the pain to decrease. After a few moments, she felt the nitroglycerin taking effect on her heart rate, slowing it, but it couldn't touch the pain. "I need something stronger," she whispered to the couch cushion. And she knew where she had to go to get it.

Halfway up the stairs to the second floor Eleanor was sure she would never make it. The next thing she knew, she was standing outside Edmund's study, her hand on the doorknob. There was a loud crackling noise in her head, and she didn't know how she'd got there. She had no memory beyond stopping on the stairs and wrapping her arms around herself as Pain River swept her through a nasty set of rapids.

She pushed through the door and hobbled inside to the

large oak desk in front of the fireplace. In the third drawer on the right, Edmund kept a cachet of army surplus field medic supplies. At one time the drawer had been filled with plastic-wrapped syringes, each filled with a pain killing dose of morphine. Edmund had picked them up on the blackmarket, trading two young boys to a CIA agent, who planned on giving them as a present to an Arabian prince for inside information on a terrorist group. Edmund had accepted five hundred of the morphine packets for each child. In the bottom of the drawer, only two remained.

Eleanor looked at the two syringes and remembered Edmund's last attack. Doctor Phelps had given him morphine then for the pain. It was the morphine that had been Edmund's undoing. The morphine not only dulled the pain, it had dulled his mind. But like Edmund, Eleanor was at the point where she had no choice: take it or die.

She pulled a packet out, clutched it in her aching hands. She couldn't tear it open. Her hands were too feeble to separate the plastic at the dotted line. After all her effort, she was going to die, all because of a vacuum-sealed plastic bag. She lay her head on the desk top and sobbed. The pain was so bad she almost wished she *could* die.

You'll wish it soon enough, Edmund promised from nowhere and everywhere.

No! Eleanor answered. Summoning the last of the strength that was left her, she shoved the packet in her mouth. With her teeth, and her will, she tore the plastic open and released the drug-filled syringe. She popped the cap, pushed the needle into her forearm and pressed the plunger. The syringe fell to the floor as Eleanor slumped over, head on the desk, waiting for the morphine to tame Pain River.

And waited. Some more. Still the river went on and on. Eleanor had been waiting for the initial rush to hit her and carry her away, the way it always had the many times before that she and Edmund had used the army surplus morphine packets for pleasure, but this time, the drug came on slower.

Gradually, Eleanor began to notice a feeling of apartness from Pain River. Instead of submerged in the waters of Pain, she stood on the riverbank, getting soaked from its spray—but not swimming in it; not drowning in it. The crackling noise in her head subsided to a steaming hiss.

Sleep came then, pulling her under, leaving the Machine to limp along on its own. She slept for a short while. When she woke, the swollen waters of Pain had retreated to the size of a stream. For the first time in days, she actually felt hungry.

Snatching up the last morphine packet, she stuffed it into her dress pocket and stood. Her limp left leg felt stronger. Moving slowly, enjoying the simple act of walking without being a pack animal to killing pain, Eleanor went to the open study door and took a deep breath. There was a wonderful smell coming from the kitchen.

"I cut the meat and added it to the stew, Gram," Jennifer said. She stood on a chair at the stove, stirring the contents of a large black pot that sat on the front burner. "It's almost done."

"Good girl," her grandmother replied, smiling as she came into the kitchen. "When it's ready, we'll feed our guests." She patted Jennifer on the head as she went by her. She took a bottle of Cuervo Special Gold from a shelf by the stove and took a long, hard pull from it before heading for the table, where she scooped up several of the fingers lying there and began to gnaw on them in between swigs of tequila.

There's thirteen of us, Mark thought. He had noticed their number when the old woman brought the last kid in. Unlucky 13. He counted them over again, for something to do, and wondered why the old woman was collecting just boys.

The boy the old woman had just left began choking. He

was still out, lying on his back just inside the door. He was having trouble breathing. Suddenly he vomited. It gushed up out of his mouth, running down his chin, and sank back into his mouth. The boys nearest him made disgusting noises and moved away. Mark jumped up and dragged the boy to the side of the cage and turned him over so that his head was next to the bars and he was puking outside the cage.

This kid is in bad shape, Mark thought as he took his hands from the boy's head and saw the blood. The boy had a deep four-inch gash in the back of his head. With a sick feeling, Mark realized he could see bone: the boy's exposed skull. Mark bent over him and put his ear to the boy's back. He was barely breathing and his heart was hammering like a drumroll.

He's going to die, Mark realized, if he doesn't get help. Tugging at his cotton, tab-collared shirt, Mark ripped a sleeve off, rolled it up, and applied it to the boy's head. He wished he could do more for the boy, but he didn't know what else to do other than what he had already done.

"She's coming back," one of the boys whispered loudly. Mark listened, and could hear footsteps on the stairs, only this time it sounded like more than one person was coming. Mark left the makeshift bandage pressed to the boy's wound and, on his knees, scrambled back to the others huddling together in the rear.

The second the door opened, Mark felt the cold, numbing tendrils of the old woman's mind probing into his, and felt an overwhelming desire for food. A second later, a delicious hot smell hit him as the old woman and a young girl carried trays stacked with bowls, two loaves of bread, two large pitchers of milk, and a big black pot of steaming stew.

In the rear corner of the cage Davy Torrez's ego was coming up for air, climbing up from the depths of shock-induced oblivion to reality. A number of things triggered it: the presence of the witch in the room; the sound of the boy's voices; and especially the smell of something hot and meaty. His starving body responded and his stomach growled. His mouth watered with faint memories of Sunday dinners. He began to breathe deeply. He floated upwards, out of total unawareness, into the normal levels of sleep. The memory of Sunday dinners grew stronger and became a dream.

He saw himself sitting at the kitchen table. His mom was pouring milk into Flintstones jelly glasses. Davy's father came to the table and placed a fat, perfectly cooked turkey on the table. Davy's mouth watered as his father rubbed the knife and fork together before carving the bird.

As metal sliced through meat, Davy looked at the turkey again, seeing it for what it really was—a headless child's torso cooked to a golden brown, hands and feet cut off, arms and legs trussed, with stuffing popping out of its neck and rectum.

Davy tried to scream, but his father grabbed him by the neck and shoveled steaming gobs of human meat into his mouth.

"Jennifer!" Jackie cried loudly. He felt the witch poking his mind with the same burning hunger for food that Mark and the others felt, but it wasn't enough to contain his joy at seeing his sister alive. She smiled at him and concentrated on carrying the tray to the cage. Jackie yelled again and the witch gave him a look that froze his vocal cords. She followed Jennifer into the room and put her tray down on the embalming table.

Jackie backed away from the front of the cage, but never took his eyes off his sister. She wouldn't look at him, keeping her eyes down on the tray in front of her. The witch retrieved the key from the wall and unlocked the cage.

Never looking up, Jennifer placed the tray she was carrying, inside. The witch followed with the other tray and placed it on the floor next to Jen's. The witch gave them all a glance. Jackie, along with the others, heard the command, *Eat,* in his head as though it was a thought of his own, then she had his sister by the arm and was leading her out, locking the cage, and taking Jennifer upstairs with her.

The boys rushed the food, scrambling over one another in an attempt to grab *anything* to eat. For most of them, it had been more than two days since they'd eaten last. Even without Eleanor's influence they would have eaten almost anything served them; now they couldn't get it fast enough. With all of them greedily pushing and shoving, no one was getting much of anything, and they were in danger of spilling and losing everything.

Mark saw this and, though he was so hungry it would have been easy to knock the smaller boys aside and take what he wanted, he made the boys take turns with him dishing out the food and the boys lining up. "Take it easy. Stop pushing, you're going to make me spill it," Mark complained grufffly.

Besides the fact that he was starving, too, Mark was glad there was food. The boys had been hovering on the edge of full-blown hysteria ever since the old lady's revival and this was getting their minds off her for a while. Even Jackie, who sat crying his eyes out in the corner over his sister not noticing him and helping the witch, finally came around and helped Mark by pouring a glass of milk for each boy as Mark filled their bowls with stew.

When all the boys had some, Mark dished out bowls for Jackie and himself. Jackie declined his, saying he wasn't hungry. The truth was he couldn't bring himself to eat anything the witch had touched no matter how hungry he was. Mark shrugged at his refusal and poured Jackie's portion into his bowl.

"Want some milk?" Jackie asked Mark.

"No," he replied. "I'm allergic to it."

As Jackie watched and his stomach gurgled noisily, Mark and the boys devoured all the food.

Acting from reflex, Mark took his bowl to Davy Torrez and the new boy with the head wound, and spooned stew into their unconscious mouths.

Davy Torrez's smothered dream screams triggered his rise toward consciousness again and he left the level of sleep. He became aware of his body and the hard floor beneath him. The smell of hot food was all around him. He could taste it, making his stomach gurgle against his will. He could hear spoons scraping on dishes and the slurping of small mouths drinking. He could hear murmuring voices and the sounds of eager chewing.

With a great deal of effort, Davy began to move his lips.

Jason Grakopolous and Jeffrey West were fighting over the last bit of stew left in the pot. Mark intervened, splitting it up between the two of them, then finished his own bowl. Jason took his stew to the far corner, near the unconscious dark-skinned boy, and shoveled it into his mouth, keeping a wary eye on the others.

Suddenly he jumped, and looked at the boy lying near him. "He just said something," he explained to the others.

Jackie and Mark both got up and went over to the boy. Jason moved away from them, hugging his bowl to his chest, and continued eating. Jackie leaned over the boy and put his ear to the boy's mouth.

"What's he saying? Does he want some more to eat?" Mark asked, kneeling next to Jackie.

Jackie listened carefully, his head nodding a little, then looked up at all of them. "He says don't drink the milk. The witch put something in it to put us to sleep." He and the others looked at the empty glasses and two empty pitchers. One of the twins began to cry. Jackie bent over again, holding his breath as he listened to the faint words coming from the boy's mouth.

"What!" Jackie gasped. He listened some more, then started to get up, but fell over, landing hard on his rump and sat there dazed, as if he'd just had the wind knocked out of him.

"What'd he say?" Mark asked anxiously.

"Don't eat the stew," Jackie mumbled. The boys looked at their bowls.

"Why? Is it drugged, too?" Mark asked, sniffing at one of the boy's empty bowls.

"No . . . ," Jackie said hesitantly. "He says . . . He says . . . it's made out of . . . a . . . a . . . *kid*. A kid . . . who . . . was in here before us." Jackie's voice went up an octave. "He said . . . the . . . the . . . witch . . . *cut the kid up and made stew out of him!*" He began to cry, sobbing out the words. "That's what she wants with us. I told you. She wants to *eat us up!*"

Realizing what Jackie had just said, Jason Grakopolous gagged and threw his bowl to the floor. The thick brown liquid splattered and several large pieces of meat rolled out of the bowl. One of them was the tip of a finger, the fingernail still intact.

Eleanor leaned on Jennifer as they went up the stairs to the second floor. Though the pain was far away, she was exhausted. Everything was ready. All she needed now was some sleep before the night's work would bring her immortality. Clinging to Jennifer for support, she steered the girl to the bedroom and brought her to the bed.

"Are you all right, Gram?" Jennifer asked, looking at her grandmother's tired face.

"Yes, dear," Eleanor answered. "I just need a nap. Come lie down with me for a while." As Jennifer sat on the bed, Eleanor took her face in her hands and kissed her forehead. With the kiss, she slipped into Jennifer's mind. *Later,* she in-

structed, *you'll know when, I want you to take your mother
home and call the doctor. No matter what else happens, you
must be sure that she gets to the doctor's.* Eleanor gave the
command a little kick, burying it deep in Jennifer's mind,
and laid the girl beside her on the bed.

"Sleep now," she said softly, her arm around Jennifer's
shoulder. "Sleep," she crooned, and felt herself drifting off
into a sleep alive with dreams of memories.

*"Another heart attack," Dr. Phelps says to her. They are
standing outside Edmund's bedroom. "I might have to put
him in the hospital, but I don't think he should be moved
right now. Tomorrow, after he's rested and is a little stronger,
we'll see how he's doing." Dr. Phelps reaches in his black
bag and produces a small brown pill bottle.*

*"This is a more powerful nitroglycerin. He's to take one
whenever he has pain in his chest or arms. I've given him
morphine, which should help the pain for a while. If he doesn't
get overexcited or do anything strenuous, and takes his medicine, he should be fine. But knowing your brother, you'll
have to watch him like a hawk."*

The dream shifted and she was in Edmund's bedroom.

*She stands at the foot of the bed, staring at Edmund,
whose pale face barely juts above the blankets. His eyes are
closed and next to him on the bed lies* The Demonolatria.
*Something the doctor told her comes to mind and she looks
at the pill bottle in her hand. He'd told her that Edmund's
heart problem was congenital, and that since they were
twins, she probably had it, too.*

*"Running out of time," Edmund croaks from the bed. It is
early October of last year and he has been planning for*

*Samhain all year. Now his eyes are bloodshot slits and his
lips barely move when he talks. "I've got to perform the
Rituals of Preparation, Eleanor. You've got to help me."*

*"Yes, Edmund," she says soothingly and looks at the pill
bottle again. She slips them in her dress pocket and goes to
his side. "I'll help you, Edmund, but first you need your
rest."*

*When Edmund has succumbed to the morphine and sleeps,
disconnected from the Machine and unable to hear her
thoughts any longer, Eleanor leaves the room and returns to
her bedroom. Under the mattress she hides the nitroglycerin
pills and lies on the bed. Several hours later, and after much
concentration by Eleanor, Edmund wakens in pain and calls
to Eleanor to bring him his pills.*

*Eleanor lies in the darkness, listening to his voice grow
fainter, and his mind grow dimmer, until both stop altogether.*

CHAPTER 36

For want of a nail, the shoe was lost . . .

Eight of the thirteen children in the cage had dropped off to sleep, empty glasses stained with milky residue by their sides, or still clutched in their hands. Add to that the boy with the gash on his head, and the boy who had just told them of the stew and milk and who now had relapsed into unconsciousness, and only Mark, Jackie, and Jeff West were left awake. Since Jeff had already drunk half of his glass of milk, he too was nodding. Though he was putting up a valiant effort to stay awake, within minutes of the others, he, too, keeled over, lying on top of his sleeping brother and joining him and the others in slumber.

The drugged milk had had a domino effect on the boys who'd drunk it. At first, after hearing Davy Torrez's utterances and seeing the truth of what he'd said in the amputated, cooked finger end on the floor, they had all sat in horrified, incredulous silence. Mark had been the first to react, crawling to the stinking filthy toilet and jamming his fingers down his throat in an attempt to make himself puke. He was only partly successful, spitting up a little of the stew, but not much. Some of the others had followed his lead but most of them were already starting to topple over into slumber. First one slumped over, then another, and another, falling into each other and collapsing in a rough line.

Jackie and Mark sat alone in the cage, watching the sleeping boys, and found themselves almost wishing that they, too, had drunk the drugged milk. At least then this nightmare would be over.

Mark and, in a less articulate way, Jackie, felt as though reality had been nudged. Mark visualized it as reality being this big box set up on a table. Somebody—or *something,* he couldn't even be sure that the old lady was *human* anymore— had just bumped into the table and moved the box. It was not a pleasant feeling.

If this crazy old woman was eating children, then suddenly anything was possible. What had previously been a scary and dangerous situation had just become something out of a horror film or a nightmare. But even the scariest, grossest horror film or the worst nightmare couldn't even begin to compare to this because, like it or not, this was for real, for keeps, for life or death.

The severed finger on the floor mesmerized Jackie until he could stand looking at it no more. He pulled off his sweater, one his mother had knitted for him, and threw it over the finger. Getting on his knees, he made the sign of the cross and clasped his hands beseechingly towards the ceiling. "In the name of the Father, the Son, and the Holy Ghost. Please God, get us out of here. I promise I'll be good. I'll never be bad again. I'll never fight with Jen. I won't bug my mother . . ." He burst into tears at the mention of his mother and was unable to continue his prayer. He curled up, hugging his legs to his chest and pleading softly, "Please . . . please . . ."

Mark wiped tears from his own eyes and got up. He began pacing back and forth in the small clear area in front of the bars, racking his brain for some way out of this mess. As he walked, he kept staring at Jackie's sweater on the floor. Suddenly he had an idea. He went to the right wall of the cage and looked through the bars at the keys hanging on the wall. He estimated that they were ten feet away. He took off his belt, then his shirt, and looped the one sleeve left on it through the buckle and tied it with a bulky knot.

"Give me your shirt," Mark whispered to Jackie. He was shivering slightly and goosebumps had risen on his bare chest and arms.

Jackie stopped crying and looked at the half-naked Mark as though he were crazy.

"Come on. Give me your shirt. And get the shirts and sweaters off the other kids so I can tie them together. Maybe I can hook the keys and get them and we can get out of here," Mark explained hurriedly as he began removing Jeff's shirt.

Jackie looked at the keys on the wall, then at Mark tying Jeff's shirt to his, making a clumsy rope, and saw a glimmer of hope, maybe even an answer to his prayer. He immediately took off his shirt and gave it to Mark. He started to take off his undershirt also, but Mark stopped him.

"Help me get the shirts and sweaters off the others first," Mark told him. "That should be enough."

They worked quickly; thoughts of the old woman returning too soon urging them on. When they had removed five shirts—none of the boys other than Mark wore belts—Mark started spinning them tight, the way he would a wet towel to slap someone with, then tied them to the makeshift line.

Eagerly, Jackie continued removing clothes from the sleeping boys, all except for the boy with the cut head and Davy Torrez, whose pajama top was caked with dirt and dried vomit, and piled them next to Mark. Five of the nine boys, besides Mark, wore long-sleeved shirts and sweaters, which Mark tied sleeve to sleeve. Other than Davy Torrez, Jason Grakopolous was the only boy wearing pajamas, the top of which was also long-sleeved. The twins wore sweaters over short-sleeved soccer shirts.

A pile of laundry lay at Mark's feet by the time he tied the last shirt on. "Go to the other side and listen for her coming back," he directed Jackie, who immediately did as he was told. He stood with his head turned, his ear toward the door listening, but also watching Mark's attempts at the key ring.

First, Mark wound all the clothes up into a bunched coil in his hand, then pushed his arms through the bars as far as they would go. Holding the end of the shirt rope in his left hand and the coil in his right, he swung the latter a few times to build momentum and let it fly. It went a few dismal feet; the coil of shirts never unwound.

Mark hauled the shirts in again, winding them looser this time. Again he swung them: 1, 2, 3—he let them go. The shirt uncoiled this time and the line reached the wall but it was way off target to the left of the key ring. He reeled the clothes line in for another attempt and tried to stay calm and patient.

With each throw Jackie's heart surged and he felt a jolt of hopeful excitement. With each miss he sagged against the bars, expelling air and wincing as the dagger of dread in his stomach cut a little bit deeper.

Mark continued his attempts at the ring for hours. Several times he had to stop when Jackie thought he heard something. They both listened intently each time to every sound in the house above them. When he'd satisfied himself that the old woman wasn't coming back, Mark returned to casting his line, and patiently reeling it in.

Though he kept at it faithfully, he began to see that it was useless. He should have seen it sooner, but it had felt so good to have hope, to have a plan, to have a *chance,* that he had ignored the obvious: The keys were on a large metal ring that was hung on a thick nail driven at an upward slant into the wooden support beam along the wall making it nearly impossible to get the ring off the nail with the sleeve of a shirt or sweater as he was trying to do.

Useless, or not, Mark kept trying, partly to keep Jackie's hopes alive so he wouldn't cry, and partly because he didn't want to give up his own hope without making the best attempt that he could. After an hour, the line became heavier, and after several his arms felt like stone. He struggled on for another hour, numbly throwing the line out and reeling it in without even thinking about what he was doing, then he had to stop and rest.

"Let me try for a while," Jackie said, coming over and kneeling next to Mark who sat slumped against the bars.

Mark, at first, shook his head no, then reconsidered. It would give Jackie something to do. He handed Jackie the clothes rope, but after half an hour, Jackie too gave up. None of his throws had gone very far.

"You can try it again after you rest, huh Mark?" Jackie asked hopefully, sitting cross-legged next to the older boy.

Mark shrugged, but couldn't bring himself to tell Jackie that it was hopeless. If he did, the kid would lose it and start bawling again. If that happened, Mark knew he wouldn't be able to control himself and would follow suit. And they were never going to get out of this unless he could stay in control and think.

Every problem has a solution, his father always said. *The trick is to remain calm and patient and think through all of your options.* In this case, though, that way led to trouble because one of the options was surely a nasty death after which they would be chopped up for stew.

Mark shrugged into a slouched position with his chin resting on his chest and pulled the pile of clothes over his chilly, naked chest. The only outcomes to this situation that he could see, other than the one he didn't want to even think about, were: someone would rescue them; the old woman would have another attack and die; or somehow they could attack her and escape the next time she opened the cage door.

Thinking out loud, Mark explored the chances of being able to attack the old woman. They had no weapons, but Mark figured that if he or Jackie could somehow hide behind the door, they could slam the door bars on her head when she came through and maybe knock her unconscious.

It sounded like a dangerous plan to Jackie, and Mark

knew it was a long shot. There was nowhere for either of them to hide behind the door without being seen. Still, talking about it and planning diversions helped them both pass the time for a while.

Sometime in mid-afternoon, Mark and Jackie dozed for about an hour. They woke hungry, but the memory of the stew and a rising stench in the room like bad farts and boiled cabbage that came from Jackie's ripening stepfather turned their stomachs and killed their hunger quickly.

Several times Steve's corpse made hissing and gurgling sounds and once, actually burped. Mark and Jackie both giggled nervously at first, each thinking the other had done it, until they realized the truth when they smelled the foul wave of air that washed over them from the body's direction. Their smiles quickly disappeared.

"Maybe you should try to hook the key again," Jackie offered when the room began to lose the light. "It'll be dark soon."

Mark didn't answer for a moment, but then shrugged off the pile of clothes and got up. "Sure, what the hell. I haven't got anything better to do." As he got up, his foot kicked a spoon and another idea popped into his head. Picking up the spoon, he bent it and pushed the handle through the loose knitting of the sleeve of a sweater at the end of the clothes rope. It wasn't real secure, but it just might be enough to hook the key ring and slide it off the nail, Mark figured. With renewed hope he began tossing the line, with the spoon hook on the end, at the key ring again.

On his thirteenth try (he was keeping count to break the monotony) the sleeve of the sweater got caught on the nail. "Damn!" Mark swore. He had just missed getting the spoon through the key ring. Now the sweater was stuck, the nail poking right through the fabric. To make matters worse, as he tugged on the line, trying to free the sweater, the spoon slipped out of the sleeve and fell, clattering, to the floor. "Double damn!"

Mark was getting scared now. If he couldn't get the sleeve off the nail and the old lady came back, she'd know what he had been up to and he might become stew a lot sooner than he thought. In desperation, he began tugging forcefully on the sweater with all his might. With a ripping, squeaking sound the sweater came free of the nail at the same moment that the nail came free of the wooden beam. The key ring fell to the floor, bounced off dead Mr. Nailer's ear, and landed next to his head.

"You did it!" Jackie nearly shouted, trying not to look at Steve.

"Shhh!" Mark hushed. "I haven't got it yet. You're going to give us away." Though he chastised Jackie, Mark was just as excited. He couldn't believe he had actually knocked the keys from the wall. Now he had to calm down and figure out some way to get the keys within reach of the cage.

He pulled the clothes in and threw them again. After a couple of tries that landed on Mr. Nailer's discolored face, Mark got the end sweater on the keys and tried to drag them across the floor. The sweater wasn't heavy enough to pull the ring along and slipped off it as soon as he tugged on it. He realized he needed something heavier that would sit on the keys and drag them along.

Mark looked around the cage for something heavy enough. The stew pot was too big and heavy to fit through the bars; the spoons they had eaten the stew with were too light. He kicked one of the spoons with his sneaker. *His sneaker!* That was it! Perfect! His sneaker would definitely be heavy enough. He sat down and untied his sneaker, a size 9 Converse Larry Bird All-Star basketball shoe, and slipped it off. He tied the laces to the sleeve of the sweater at the end of his makeshift rope and stood for another try.

The sun was setting, throwing the room into dusky shadows. Mark could just make out the keys on the floor next to Mr. Nailer's head, whose eyes were open, staring forever at the floor. Mark cursed himself for wasting so much time doing nothing when it had been light in the room, but that couldn't be helped now.

Mark coiled the line, liking the heavy feel of his sneaker on the end and gave it a good toss. He overshot the keys. The sneaker hit the wall and fell, bouncing off Mr. Nailer's body, which squished a little when jostled. Mark pulled the line in quickly and tried again. This time his sneaker landed hard on Mr. Nailer's face. Mark pulled it off quickly, revealing a large, purple bruise in the soft, ripe flesh of Mr. Nailer's cheekbone. Miraculously, the sneaker landed right on the key ring when it fell off his former teacher's face.

Mark began pulling the line in slowly and could hear the keys scraping along the stone floor as they slid toward him. In a sudden surge of excitement, he pulled the sneaker in faster, and lost the keys.

"Don't go so fast!" Jackie cried harshly. He had resumed his lookout station at the front of the cage.

"Shut up!" Mark shouted back. He wrapped the shirts up again and tossed the sneaker.

"Bull's-eye!" Jackie cheered five tries later, his voice threatening to become louder than a whisper. With a loud *ka-chink!* the sneaker had landed on the key ring.

"Shut up, I said," Mark whispered nervously. Moving as slowly and steadily as possible, Mark began to pull the sneaker back, and heard again the scrape of the keys on the stone floor. Four feet later the scraping stopped, the sneaker pulled free, leaving the key ring behind. But they were halfway. A couple more tries and he would have it.

Two hours later, he was still trying. Now that the keys were closer, instead of becoming easier to hit, they became impossible. The room grew steadily darker, and Mark grew anxious, rushing his shots. Soon he couldn't see the key ring at all and had to throw blind at where he guessed he remembered it to be lying. He hit it once, but the key ring got pushed away and he lost it completely.

For the next hour, no matter where he threw the sweater,

he came up empty. Eventually it got so dark that he could barely see his hand in front of his face. Hope of snagging the keys began to fade.

As the night wore on, the heavy, drugged breathing of the other boys seemed louder in the darkness and made Jackie nervous. He was so scared of the dark that they seemed to drown out all other noises except for the *clop!* and drag of the sneaker across the floor as Mark searched for the key ring. The two together were so loud that Jackie couldn't tell if he heard the witch coming back or not.

Another hour passed while Mark searched in vain for the key ring. Suddenly, Jackie thought he heard a creaking sound from the ceiling. At the same moment Mark let out an excited gasp of joy. Jackie forgot all about the noise or keeping watch and scrabbled across the cage to Mark's side.

"I've got it," Mark exclaimed through clenched teeth, resting his head against the bars for a moment. "I didn't even know I had them until I started pulling the sneaker in. I almost lost them."

He giggled nervously and took a deep breath. Getting down on his knees, he began to pull the line in slowly and again heard the sweet sound of the keys moving across the floor. With only a sweater left to go, he lost them again. He quickly dropped to his stomach and reached both hands through the bars as he groped the dark floor for the keys.

Jackie followed Mark's example and helped him.

"Damn it," Mark swore softly. He couldn't find them. They had sounded so close, but he couldn't find them anywhere within the area of his reach. He must have been mistaken about where he'd heard them stop. He pulled his hand in to try the sneaker again, when his fingers brushed against the keys. They were lying right up against the base of the cage. He grabbed them and pulled them in.

"You got them!" Jackie cried, so excited he forgot to be quiet. He listened to the sound of the key ring jingling in the dark and thought it was the best sound he had ever heard.

"Yeah," Mark said, breathless with excitement. Getting up quickly, he felt for his sneaker, untied it, and put it back on. In the dark he couldn't remember which shirt on the rope was his so he left it and slid along the bars until he reached the cage door.

"What about the others?" Jackie asked, following Mark to the door. He was sticking close to the older boy in the dark, keeping a hand touching his arm at all times.

"We can go get help," Mark whispered. "We won't make it if we try to wake them up, or take them with us." Mark selected one of the four keys on the ring and reached carefully between the bars with it. Doing it backwards, he inserted the key into the lock. It didn't fit. He pulled the key out and, working with his arms outstretched between the bars, selected another one. It fit, but didn't turn. He tried the third. The ring slipped out of his hand and fell to the floor.

"Oh no!" Jackie sobbed.

Mark dropped to his knees, both arms still through the bars, and began to search frantically. Agonizing minutes later, with Jackie whimpering in his ear all the time, Mark found the keys again. "Got 'em!"

Jackie, keyed up beyond his wildest limits, began to sob with joy.

Mark put his arm around him in the darkness. "Hey! It's okay, kid. We're going to get out of here, but I need you to be brave, okay? You got to stay brave or you'll never get out."

Jackie sniffled his assent and choked back his tears.

Mark tried the last two keys. Neither of them fit. "What the heck?" he whispered to himself.

"What's wrong?" Jackie asked, the dread creeping back into this voice.

"None of the keys fit," Mark explained. "They worked for her," he added, bafffled.

"I bet they're magic keys," Jackie despaired, his voice full of defeat. "You can't use the witch's magic keys."

"That's stupid," Mark said, but suppressed a chill. He tried all the keys again, then tried them upside down. The last one slid in this time. "Shhh!" he cautioned Jackie and turned the key. The lock tumbled, and the door opened.

"This is it," Mark whispered urgently. "Come on," he said to Jackie, and swung the door all the way open. Mark stepped out of the cage.

Jackie groped in the darkness for Mark's hand and couldn't find it. "Wait!" he whispered loudly. He was too scared to follow and too scared to be left behind.

The lights came on, filling the room with blinding light. Jackie put his arm up against the harsh light and backed away quickly from the cage door. The witch stood in the doorway. Behind her, Jennifer followed like a puppy.

Mark was just outside the cage door. He tried to get back in the cage, but he bumped into the open door as he backed up and it swung closed with an ominous sound. He lost his balance and stumbled back against the bars.

The witch, her arms reaching, her clawed hands seeking, charged across the room and grabbed for Mark's throat. He ducked under her arms and tried to run to the door, but she caught the back of his hair and yanked him back to her.

"Jackie! Help!" Mark screamed, his voice warbling with terror, as the witch got her hands on him.

Jackie didn't move. He was paralyzed.

The witch's hand closed round Mark's throat. He squirmed and kicked wildly in an effort to get away. One of his wild punches got lucky and caught the witch in the stomach. The air went out of her in a gasp. She staggered back. Mark tried to lunge away, and she nearly lost him, but managed to grab him by the hair again. She pulled him around hard and whipped him into the bars of the cage. Mark hit the bars face first, his nose crunching against them and spewing blood over his mouth and down his chin. He collapsed senseless at the witch's feet.

Jackie trembled as the witch fixed him with a baleful glare. She was clutching at her stomach, gasping for breath, but she made him cringe under her stare.

"You boys have been naughty," the witch wheezed. With each word from her mouth, she changed a little in Jackie's eyes. By the time she reached the word "naughty," she had become the she-troll: massive head; pointed ears; mottled skin; long neck; flat, leathery breasts; yellow eyes and fangs as long as brand-new no. 2 lead pencils. The hideous creature grinned.

"Pay the troll." Jackie remembered its voice only too well. "Treat me to dinner," it groaned hungrily.

Several of the boys behind Jackie let out frightened cries, aware of the witch's presence even in their sleep, and the troll cackled shrilly. "Come, my kittens," it crowed. "It's time. Time. Hickory, dickory, dock!" It cackled again and in the blink of an eye turned back into the witch.

Still clutching her stomach, she shuffled over to the cage. "You're going to wish you'd drunk your milk, little kitten," she said, leering at Jackie.

Mercifully, Jackie swooned with fright.

CHAPTER 37

Cry, baby, cry . . .

Eleanor tried to straighten up, but she couldn't. The pain wouldn't let her. With the help of the morphine, she'd been doing so well. She'd woken rested from her sleep, the Machine strengthened, and was ready to start the rituals that had to culminate in the final sacrifice at exactly midnight.

The little brat who now lay bleeding at her feet had nearly ruined everything. His punch to her stomach had reawakened her old friend Pain River, which was threatening to break through the morphine dam containing it and become a raging torrent again, this time carrying her away forever. It kept her bent, like a knee to her back. Her wind was returning, and the soreness in her stomach from his kick was fading, but the pain in her chest, neck, and arms had become so bad again that she couldn't straighten up completely.

She scuttled over to Mark's body and kicked him viciously in the back. It was all his fault. Just for causing so much trouble, he would be the first sacrifice of the fifth ritual. She bent over cautiously, not wanting to aggravate the pain in her chest any further, and grabbed Mark by the hair. "Girl!" she bellowed at Jennifer.

"Yes, Gram?" Jennifer replied, running eagerly to Eleanor's side.

"Bring that contraption over here," she instructed, pointing at the casket gurney by the embalming table. Jennifer did as she was told while Eleanor drew the last packet of morphine from her pocket and tore at it with her teeth. Her hands shook with pain as she removed the syringe cap and eased the needle into her arm.

Relief was quicker and stronger this time, and didn't make her feel as tired as before. Within minutes, she was on her feet, cranking the gurney down to pick up Mark's prone body. "Take his legs and help me slide him on," she instructed Jennifer, who happily complied. Together they picked Mark up, placed him on the gurney. Eleanor buckled the straps and lifted the boy waist high. She pushed the gurney to the embalming table, released him from the straps and rolled the boy onto it.

With the same gray tape she'd used on Margaret and Betty Boone, Eleanor taped Mark's hands together. She pulled off his sneakers and socks and did the same with his ankles. Producing a large pair of shears from the tray, she cut Mark's pants away from his body until he lay naked. She strapped him to the table.

Eleanor turned her attention to Diane, her little mother, the most important one. She went to the reclining chair, Jennifer following like a shadow, and checked Diane's pulse and eyes. She seemed satisfied with her condition and began to cut the maternity slacks and sweatshirt from the pregnant woman's body.

"Replace and light all the candles," Eleanor told Jennifer as she worked the scissors. She pointed to the shelf where a box of black candles and kitchen matches sat. "We're going to have a Halloween party."

"Goody," Jennifer exclaimed happily. She went eagerly about her chore, replacing each candle carefully, cleaning off the old wax when it got in the way, and lighting them.

While her helper replaced the more than one hundred candles in the room, Eleanor stirred a jar of baby's blood and painted the ritual symbols on Diane's swollen vein-webbed belly.

Jackie swallowed. His dry throat closed up on him like a fist. He choked and coughed. He came out of his stupor, became aware of his surroundings. Disjointedly in jagged, fearful flashes, he remembered where he was and how he'd got there. Each memory assaulted him, jolting him a little bit more awake.

Groggily, he saw Jennifer replacing candles. She was working her way slowly toward the cage, replenishing the holders strewn on shelves and the floor stands surrounding the circle where his mother was.

"Jen," Jackie mumbled. He shook his head and rubbed his face with his hands. His head hurt and everything inside him felt like it was caught in a whirlpool—his mind, his stomach, his heart. He was reeling in shock from the horror of the situation.

"Jen!" He cried again, louder. He glanced warily over at the witch and stifled a shriek: The witch was doing something to his mother. He flushed hotly with embarrassment as he realized that his mother was naked. The witch was bending over her, painting her naked belly with funny symbols, like the ones on his dead stepfather's dark blue face and mottled chest.

Jackie watched the witch and realized she wasn't hurting his mother. He could see his mother's chest—he flinched at the memory of suckling those breasts and seeing them turn into the witch's—rising and falling with her breathing. She was all right, for the time being at least.

Where's Mark? Jackie wondered. The witch blocked his view of the embalming table. Quietly, he got to all fours and crawled to the edge of the cage. He put his face between the bars and called to his sister again as loud as he dared. "Jennifer!"

Jennifer looked at him without pausing from her work, and smiled. "Hi, Jackie," she said pleasantly, as if nothing in the world were wrong.

Jackie stared incredulously at her. She was smiling a goofy smile that was like a slap in the face of his terror. "What's wrong with you?" he asked her, his voice whining. "Help me get out of here," he pleaded.

Jennifer smiled and shook her head as if Jackie had just said something very foolish. She replaced another candle, struck a match, and held it to the wick.

"Jennifer, please!" Jackie whispered, his voice unsteady, on the verge of tears. "Please, Jen, help me. Help me get out of here."

Jennifer stopped a moment and gave her little brother a stern look. "Shame on you, Jackie. We're Grammy's guests. We can't leave now. That would be rude." She turned back to the candles, dismissing Jackie's absurd idea. She left Jackie sobbing against the bars, arms outstretched, pleading soundlessly, and went to the candles set up on the stands on the edge of the circle and star on the floor around their mother.

The witch finished painting his mother's bulging belly, went to a shelf on the wall, took down a pocket watch on a chain, and hung it on the wooden podium. She went to the metal table behind her and Jackie saw Mark.

"No!" he choked out, tears springing to his eyes. He turned his face away, unable to look at Mark's battered face and naked body. "Jennifer. Help us. *Please!*" Jackie pleaded too loudly.

The witch paused from painting Mark's chest in the same way she'd painted Jackie's mother's and looked at him. *Give it up, boy!* the witch spoke inside his head.

Jackie recoiled at the touch of her voice, scampering to

the back of the cage and huddling there. The hopelessness of the situation was pushing him closer to the edge of insanity. He peeked out at the rest of the unconscious boys in the cage and felt a deep, compelling urge to join them, to also be unconscious to the horror unfolding around him.

He wanted to scream in the worst way, just to let it out. A scream had been building inside him for a long time, welling up and threatening to boil over and out of him in a never-ending howl of fear and anguish. In a last-ditch attempt to stifle the scream that would surely bring the witch, Jackie stuffed the knuckles of his right hand into his mouth and bit them.

"That's a good boy," the witch croaked from the head of the table. She was undressing. "No screaming," she said with what was almost a gentle smile.

Jackie watched her in terrified fascination while Mark woke and began moaning and sobbing. "Mark," Jackie cried, and flinched at the sharp look the witch gave him.

"Jackie," Mark said thickly, blood spitting from his mouth, "help me." His nose and cheekbones were swollen and purple with bruises. A nasty gash across the bridge of his nose sent blood into his eyes and down his cheeks. His lips were split open, the top one mashed brutally. He choked a moment, then spit out two of his teeth.

"God helps those who help themselves," the witch croaked and burst into shrieking laughter that set Jackie's teeth on edge.

"No," Mark groaned in pain as she leaned over him.

The witch laughed louder. She was naked now, her clothes piled at her feet. She ran one hand caressingly over Mark's bruised face. Her thumb pressed down on the gash across his broken nose and he screamed until he blacked out.

Giggling with delight, the witch picked up a long knife.

* * *

Eleanor curled the knife handle into her palm and took a deep breath. The pain was still with her, hovering above and around her, but the morphine was doing its job keeping it dammed up. Now that she was actually getting down to the business of the final rituals, she felt a surge of renewed strength in both herself and the Machine. She felt like nothing could stop her now.

Don't bet on it! Edmund's voice came out of the air behind her.

Shut up, Edmund. You're only in my mind. You're dead and you can't stop me. No one can, Eleanor resolved strongly. Edmund laughed, but the sound was faint and faded away in the face of her confidence and determination. Eleanor smiled. Edmund's ghost was beaten. She knew now, irrevocably, that it had been her own guilt all along that had resurrected him.

She went around the table to the wooden podium and placed the knife on the open page of the book. Her confident smirk turned to a cruel sneer as the brat on the table woke screaming again. "Enough dawdling," she murmured. Time was getting short.

She ran the point of the knife in her hand down the page of the book like a pointer ticking off the four Rituals of Preparation she had already completed. She looked over at the crumpled corpse of Steve Nailer. He was beginning to smell very bad. He had almost ruined everything. If Eleanor hadn't woke up when she did, it would have been the end of her. Her eyes drifted from Steve, over the twelve boys in the cage and the naked screaming brat on the table next to her.

It was time to start the fifth ritual.

Jackie watched in tears as the witch made Mark scream. He tried to block out the sound with his hands but couldn't.

He tried humming a loud monotone to block it out, but it regressed into a mumbled *no no no* over and over again.

The witch turned away from Mark and went to the wooden stand with the big book on it and bent over it as if reading from it. Jackie was about to try and get Jennifer's attention again when the witch turned around, looking at him and the other boys in the cage. Her awful stare drove him to huddle behind the slumped bodies of the twins and fat Jason Grakopolous. As he trembled there, hoping against hope that the witch would decide to just leave him alone, he peeked over Jason's arm.

The witch was bending over and and removing from a cabinet against the wall a large fire-blackened stoneware bowl with the same symbols that she had painted on the others, including herself, carved into it. She placed the bowl on the floor between his mother's outstretched legs and went back to the cabinet.

In horrified disbelief, Jackie watched as the witch dropped a pulpy, raw, human heart and his stepfather's bloody private parts into the bowl. She followed those with what looked like a wrinkled brown sheet cut in the rough shape of a body, with arms and legs.

Jackie whimpered and trembled uncontrollably. There was no end to this horror, it just went on and on. The witch knelt in front of the bowl, as if praying over it. She rose slowly and went to the huge metal door set in the wall to the right of the cage. In front of the door was a low conveying table, the top of which was a series of black, hard rubber rollers. To the left of the door was an instrument panel with dials, a small spoked wheel, and a large lever.

Jackie didn't know what the metal door was to, but he was sure it was nothing good. When the witch pulled the lever and turned the wheel, making the door open to reveal a space about as large as a pantry, Jackie discovered he was right. The witch turned a dial and long jets of blue flame roared from dual rows of four pipes running up both inside walls. A wave of heat rolled through the room, making the candle flames dance madly.

It's an *oven!* Jackie thought.

The better to cook you with, my dear, the witch answered in his head. Jackie put his hands to his ears and crawled away to the far side of the cage, where he curled up against the bars. But, try as he might, he couldn't keep from watching the witch.

A big part of Jackie's mind just wanted to retreat, recede into numbing shock, but another part wanted to stay conscious, *wanted* to know what the witch was doing. If he didn't stay awake and sane, he wouldn't see an opportunity to escape if and when it showed itself. If he let shock take him, he was dead meat.

The witch turned the dial again and the flames dwindled to candle points. She picked up the stoneware bowl and placed it on the roller-topped conveyer and pushed it into the oven. Spinning the small wheel, and releasing the lever on the instrument panel, she closed the oven door. She turned the dial controlling the flames up for a few minutes, then lowered it and opened the oven door again.

With a pair of large metal tongs that she took from a narrow space in the wall below the oven door, the witch removed the bowl from the oven and replaced it on the floor between Jackie's mother's outstretched legs. The bowl had a fresh layer of black soot on it and its middle was red hot with a dull glow. A crackling, sizzling noise came from inside it, accompanied by a foul smoke. The room filled with the rancid smell of fat burning.

"No-o-o," Mark wailed, thrashing his head wildly back and forth, making the pain in his head explode. The old woman was approaching him, knife held up like an icon over her head. She crossed to the table where he lay and stood over him, eyes closed, mouth mumbling, knife slashing invisible symbols in the air over his body.

"Mommy!" Mark screamed as loud as the pain in his face would allow. The old woman's wrinkled, grotesque body so close was more than he could bear. Her flabby, malformed breasts flopped against her skin with every swing of the knife. The sour, pungent smell of her body sweat trickling from under her arms and breasts washed over him, filling him with nausea.

The knife dipped lower. The old woman's mumbling chant began to rise. "Mommy, please save me! Mommy, Mommy, Mommy," Mark pleaded. All rational thought had deserted him. He was reduced to an incoherent babble, reverting to an infantile pleading for his mommy.

The old woman's voice rose, her unintelligible words running together at a fever pitch. Mark's garbled cries for his mother speeded up, too, matching the old woman's cadence. The knife was barely an inch over his body now, squirrelling back and forth and around as if the woman was mixing the air over him.

The blade touched Mark's skin and he let loose another loud scream, more in terror than in pain. His cry was answered by a scream from Jackie whom Mark could just see sobbing in the corner of the cage. Behind the old woman and to the side, just within Mark's vision, Jackie's sister, Jennifer, stood smiling placidly.

The knife blade began to scratch his skin, tracing over the symbols the old woman had already painted there, raising beads of blood on his chest and stomach. His screams grew more frequent and he thrashed his bound body madly against the straps in an attempt to free himself.

"Shut up!" the old woman bellowed loudly between chants. She brought her balled-up left fist down hard on his nose and bleeding mouth like a judge hammering his gavel. Again and again she pummelled his face. A bright red explosion of pain burst in Mark's head, followed by swirls of white hot light spinning into a growing cloud of blackness.

The last thing Mark Thomas saw, as he was slipping into the black cloud forever, was the knife raised high over him, falling fast, plunging toward his naked chest. He mustered one final, pathetic scream, and died.

CHAPTER 38

What are little boys made of, made of?

Deputy sheriff Ken Vitelli felt like a fool. He stood just outside the sheriff's office, his hand on the doorknob, his head hanging in embarrassment. He knew everyone in the station had heard the sheriff bawling him out yesterday because he hadn't put surveillance on Steve Nailer after the disappearance of Joe Conally. Since then, and with the abduction of Mark Thomas, who had last been seen in Nailer's company, Steve Nailer had become a prime suspect in the investigation of missing children in the area. And now he had disappeared.

As if that wasn't bad enough, the sheriff had just called him in again to rake him over the coals some more for not getting a forwarding address or phone number from Judy and Roger Eames before they left town. Everyone in the station house must have heard—again!

Ken had been sure he had gotten the address, but when he'd pulled out the paper he'd recorded it on to show the sheriff, the paper was blank. The Eameses' proximity to Steve Nailer seemed now to be a primary lead in the disappearance of their daughter. The sheriff had called him an idiot and a clod and charged him with sloppy policework.

Vitelli didn't think the sheriff was being fair, but that

wouldn't keep his fellow workers from staring or cracking jokes about him. As he walked across the station house to his office he could already hear sniggering laughter and was certain that it was at his expense. He went into his office and quickly closed the door behind him.

"I'll show him," Vitelli muttered to himself. He went to the coat tree in the corner, removed his hat, gun belt, and jacket, and put them on. He pulled the visor of the hat low to one side, pulled open the door, and swept the station house with his best steely gaze. When he was certain none of his co-workers were going to stare or laugh or make snide remarks, he walked to the dispatch desk and told the dispatcher that he would be over at the Nailers' house in Northwood.

It was the most horrible sound Jackie Nailer had ever heard. He'd heard it just for a second as Mark had screamed for the last time, but he would remember the sound for the rest of his life. It was the sound of steel plunging into flesh. It was a sound he immediately wished he would never hear again. But he knew wishes rarely come true.

The witch was methodically slicing open Mark's chest. Blood spurted onto her flabby chest and sprayed in her face. Blood ran into the metal table's gutters, running down to the bottom where Jackie watched it drip into the big glass jar at the base of the table. The witch licked blood from her lips as she worked at pulling the knife through Mark's body, sometimes sawing at a particularly tough obstruction.

After his initial scream of terror, Mark had quickly subsided into a low gurgled moaning. At one point, while the witch was sawing through a difficult spot, blood bubbled out of Mark's nose and mouth, running down his cheek in a thick red line like a clown's painted mouth gone berserk. After that he grew silent and his feeble thrashing ceased altogether.

Jackie blacked out for a moment then. He woke curled into a fetal position, retching against his knees. The witch was still at it, working the knife. Blood had stopped spurting from Mark's wounds now that his heart had stopped beating, but the witch was dripping with it. Blood painted her neck, chest, and face, dripping from her chin, running down her flat, elongated breasts and from her grossly large, excited nipples. She was grinning fiercely as she worked, her nostrils flaring as she breathed heavily. Her teeth were stained red with Mark's blood, which she kept pausing to lick from her fingers.

Jackie wanted to scream and keep on screaming, but couldn't bear to have the witch turn her blood-spattered visage his way. He clapped both hands over his mouth, fighting down the terrified, high-pitched whine and nauseating bile that were building in his throat, just waiting for a chance to erupt, and rocked himself back and forth.

The witch stopped cutting. She pulled the bloody knife from Mark's body and held it aloft once more. Streams of blood ran down her arms from her red, soaked hands and she again made invisible symbols in the air over Mark's corpse while chanting in a strange, foreign language. When she had finished her chanting, the witch handed the bloody knife to Jennifer, who stood serenely by.

To Jackie's horror, the witch thrust her hand into Mark's chest. There was a thick, squishing, *awful* sound that was almost as bad as the sound of the knife cutting Mark's skin. The witch tugged at something several times before finally pulling her hand free of his chest with a loud *plop!*

The bile in Jackie's throat surged into his mouth, hot and bitter, when he saw what the witch had removed from Mark's chest and now held aloft as if it were something cherished.

Mark's heart quivered wetly in her hands like a blob of thick gelatin. The witch spoke several weird words reverently, then brought Mark's raw, bloody heart to her mouth and began eating it.

* * *

This was the second time in twenty-four hours that the sheriff had bawled Vitelli out. Ken Vitelli mulled over that. Soon he began to fume. Yesterday it had been because he wasn't moving fast enough on the investigation, letting Steve Nailer get away; today it was for not getting a forwarding address from the Eameses.

Contrary to what the sheriff thought, Vitelli had begun to suspect Nailer might know more than he was saying about the Conally disappearance. As far as Vitelli was concerned, the sheriff was just using him as a scapegoat, dumping him with the blame for Nailer's getting away when Vitelli wasn't even officially investigating the Conally disappearance. Yesterday, when Vitelli had mentioned that to the sheriff, pointing out that it didn't come under the heading of his special bureau created to look into the disappearances of children in the area, the sheriff had made it official and dumped the Conally investigation on him, also.

The thing was, it wasn't even his fault that Nailer had slipped away. Vitelli had been asking all the teachers questions about the athletic director and had told two of his best men to talk to Nailer, keep an eye on him, and not let him leave the building before Vitelli had a chance to talk to him, yet they had let him slip through their hands.

Vitelli hadn't thought it was a very big deal at the time; he figured he could talk to Nailer later at his home. But when Mrs. Thomas notified the sheriff's department that her son, Mark, hadn't returned home from the academy yet, and a classmate came forward to relate that Nailer had kept the boy after class, Nailer had become the prime suspect in his investigation of *all* the recent disappearances.

When the men sent out to his home reported that his car was gone, and the house open as if someone had left in a hurry, Vitelli had become certain that Nailer was his man and was on the run. The only problem was that no one knew where Steve Nailer had run to, taking his family with him. An APB had been put out on their car, and surveillance of the major highways in the area had been doubled, but still nothing had turned up.

As far as he was concerned, Vitelli thought he had done a pretty good job with the investigation so far, especially considering the fact that he was putting in nineteen hours a day on it. It wasn't fair for the sheriff to get on his case just because of a couple of little mistakes.

He pulled the gray and blue sheriff's department cruiser on to Dorsey Lane and drove slowly past the Eameses' house. The driveway was empty and the house was dark. Though his main reason for driving out there at this time of night was to look around the Eameses' house to try and find some clue to where they went in Vermont, Vitelli decided to first look around the Nailers' house. His men had gone through the place yesterday afternoon when they'd come to pick him up, but after they'd let him slip through their hands at the academy, Vitelli had lost some confidence in them, to say the least. They might have overlooked some vital clue just as they had overlooked Nailer walking out of the building right under their noses.

He parked the cruiser in front of the Nailer house and got out. Like the Eameses' place, the house was as dark as the night sky. Taking a high-powered flashlight out of the glove compartment, Vitelli got out and went up the walk.

Jackie hung his head over the small puddle of bile that had surged from his mouth and tried not to listen to the terrifyingly gross sound of the witch munching on Mark's heart. Jackie wouldn't have thought it was possible, but *this* was a sound worse than steel cutting flesh. This was a sound that lifelong nightmares are made of. It was enough to make Jackie wish he was dead.

The sounds stopped. Jackie didn't want to look up but curiosity (*killed the cat, his mother always said*) got the better of him. The witch was holding what remained of the heart over her head with both hands and was walking around the perimeter of the circled star where his mother lay unconscious, strapped to the reclining chair. The witch continued her strange chanting, circling his mother six times before stopping at the head of the recliner and holding her bloody prize out over his mother's head. Slowly, the witch lowered her arms and began feeding the remains of the heart to Jackie's mother.

A severe contraction brought Diane Nailer to the brink of consciousness. Her head felt like it was filled with heavy, lead ballbearings, and her eyelids felt nailed down. She was cold all over. There was a strange restrictive tightness in her wrists and ankles that kept her from moving. Within minutes another contraction tightened her abdomen with pain. She started to cry out, but there was something in her mouth and she was chewing it. It tasted salty and had a metallic aftertaste. It was also tough to chew. She managed as best she could and swallowed, but before she could say anything another piece of the stuff was pushed between her lips.

Another contraction began, stronger than the last one. With a start, she realized she was in labor. Where was Steve? He was supposed to be there with her, coaching her through her breathing exercises. She knew she had seen him not that long ago, but couldn't quite remember when or where. The ballbearings in her head kept rolling around, making her thoughts a jumbled mess. She vaguely remembered having seen Steve in the kitchen, and there had been someone else there, too; someone she hadn't seen in a long time.

The contraction lessened and with it went some of the heaviness in her head and eyelids. She blinked, and opened her eyes. Blurry shadows and flickering lights wavered above her. Steadily, everything crystallized, becoming clear like an instant photograph that develops right before your eyes.

Her father stood by her side. In his hand he held a bowl of cut-up apples. He was feeding her pieces, one by one, smiling benevolently and filling her with a deep sense of peace.

"You're fine," her father said, his rich Italian accented voice like soothing music to her ears. It made her want to just float away and sleep. Just before she sailed completely away into happy oblivion, Diane Nailer wondered why her father's apples tasted like raw meat.

Deputy Vitelli tried the front door. It was locked. With his flashlight, he peered through the front windows into the darkened living room and dining room. He went around to the back of the house and swore when he saw the back door open. His men had told him the door had been open when they'd checked the house yesterday, but Vitelli thought they would have had the sense to close it. He swore again at their stupidity and started for the door when he heard a sound from inside the house.

Quietly, he upholstered his gun and crept to the open door. A scurrying sound came from within, then a loud thump. Vitelli gave a quick glance inside, sweeping the kitchen, and entered the house in a crouched position, ready to fire. Moving from the door to the stove he listened again to the scurrying sounds. They were coming from upstairs.

Vitelli went down the front hall, his back against the wall, his gun held up in front of him so that he was ready to drop and shoot if necessary. He gave a quick glance to the two front rooms, then cautiously started up the stairs. In the upstairs room with two student beds in it, Vitelli found the perpetrator of the noise—a couple of squirrels.

Vitelli laughed as the squirrels ran away from him, finding hiding places in the dark. It looked like his men had been right. From the way the house looked, it seemed Nailer and his family had left in a hurry. It didn't appear that they had taken their clothing or luggage, or any personal hygiene items since their closets and dressers were full of clothes, and deodorant, toothpaste, brushes, and other needed items were still in the bathroom medicine cabinet. The only thing that was missing was some clue as to where Nailer had gone.

Vitelli left the Nailers' house, closing the back door behind him, and went to his squad car. Since it was such a nice night, he decided to walk to the Eameses' house. Clicking his flashlight back on, he started up the street.

The witch dropped Mark's freshly amputated private parts into the red-hot bowl on the floor. She knelt, praying over them as they sizzled, caught fire, and filled the room with their awful smell. Jackie continued to watch numbly as she revved up the oven, put Mark's body on the collapsible table on wheels, and transferred him to the conveyor table in front of the oven.

She pulled the lever and spun the wheel to open the oven door, and pushed Mark's torn and bloody body inside. She closed the door again and turned up the flame. After a few minutes, which seemed like hours to Jackie, she turned the flame down and opened the oven door again.

Mark's body was gone. All that remained was a bulky pile of bones and ashes.

The witch reached under the conveyor belt, below the oven door, and pushed something metallic back and forth. As she did, most of the pile of Mark's ashes in the oven collapsed, then disappeared. A moment later the witch withdrew her hand from under the oven and table.

As she turned, Jackie saw that she held a small, square metal drawer. It was filled with Mark's ashes. She scooped the bones out of the oven, into the drawer, and carried them to the star/circle around Jackie's mother. With a new set of mumbled incantations, she began sprinkling Mark's remains along the perimeter of the circle.

When she finished, she replaced the drawer under the oven and turned toward the cage. "One two, buckle my shoe," she said, cackling merrily.

CHAPTER 39

1 2 3 4 5 6 7, all good children go to heaven.

Jackie couldn't get far enough away from the front of the cage. The witch unlocked the door and Jackie scrambled over the bodies of the unconscious boys, retreating to the corner where he huddled by Davy Torrez's side.

The witch, her face and entire front of her body stained with drying blood, looked at him and chuckled. "You didn't drink your milk, did you, boy?" she croaked. Jackie shook with every word. "You won't grow big and strong if you don't drink your milk," she added and laughed loudly at what she obviously thought was a good joke. Suddenly she grew very serious. "You should've drunk your milk, boy," she said in a threatening voice. She swung the cage door open and shuffled inside, pulling the collapsible gurney behind her.

The witch grabbed the newest boy, the one with the head wound, Mark's makeshift bandage still stuck to it, by the collar of his shirt. She dragged him onto the table and pulled it up to the carrying position. "I'll get to you yet, my little kittens," she whispered to the sleeping boys and Jackie. She pushed the gurney out of the cage, locking the door behind her.

Jennifer came over and helped the witch transfer the boy's

body to the metal table with its bloody gutters. Mark's blood had barely filled the bottom of the large collection jar at the base. The witch slapped the boy's face, then grabbed his wrist and held it the way the nurse at the doctor's office did when she took Jackie's pulse. After a few moments, she dropped the wrist and reached for her large scissors. She began cutting away the boy's clothes.

Jackie lay against Davy Torrez and watched Eleanor go through the same procedures with the new boy as she had with Mark. This time, though, there was no screaming when the knife traced the painted symbols on him nor when it ripped through his chest. When the knife went into him, the boy merely gasped and let out his last breath like a sigh.

Jackie put his hands over his face and wept.

Ken Vitelli stood in front of the Eameses' house for several moments before going to the door and knocking. He tried the door and found it locked. Following the same procedure he'd used at the Nailer's house, Vitelli flashed his light in the windows and worked his way around to the back of the house.

He went to the back door, taking out his wallet and removing a plastic credit card. He grabbed the door knob as he was about to insert the card between the door and the jamb, but the door was unlocked. A sense of dread filled Vitelli. If the Eameses were in Vermont, why was their back door open? It was just like the Nailers' house. Vitelli removed his gun and proceeded into the house with caution.

He went through the house slowly, methodically checking each room upstairs and down. The Eameses' house, which was an exact structural duplicate of the Nailers' house, was similar in another way. All the closets, bureaus, and cabinets upstairs were full of clothes and items one would normally take on an extended trip. In the closet of the master bedroom he found a complete set of luggage. On the night table in that same room he found an address book. He sat on the bed and opened it shining his flashlight on the pages as he searched for a clue to where the Eameses were.

Mrs. Eames had told him she was going to Vermont he remembered, but, embarrassingly, that was all he could remember. He had no memory of her giving him a name of a town she was going to, or of any relatives through whom she could be reached. He was sure she *had* given them to him, he remembered writing them down, for Christ's sake, but when he had pulled out the card to show the sheriff, it was blank. The memory of what he'd written there had dissolved like the bottom of a Styrofoam cup left too long with station house coffee in it. There were no Vermont addresses in the book, but he pocketed it anyway to check through all the names later and try to track the Eameses down.

Vitelli went downstairs and looked around. He turned up nothing but more evidence that the Eameses had left on their supposed trip in a hurry. The television and radio were plugged in. A timer to turn on the living room lights automatically had not been set. A pack of cigarettes and a personalized silver lighter left on a coffee table, and winter coats (certainly mandatory wear in the cold autumnal wilds of Vermont) still hanging in the hall closet convinced Ken Vitelli that something was amiss.

He went into the kitchen and opened the refrigerator door. The smell of sour milk floated out to him. The fridge was by no means full, but it did contain items, like a full bottle of soda, a half-empty gallon jug of milk, and a bottle of orange juice, less than half of it gone, that were perishable.

Vitelli didn't know about the Eames but whenever he and his went on a trip they took any half-empty bottles of soda or milk with them to drink on the road rather than leaving them to spoil. Of course, he had to consider that the Eameses were still very distraught over their daughter's disappearance, but he couldn't believe that they could be so distraught as to go a long trip without any luggage or clothes.

In the refrigerator light playing across the kitchen table, Vitelli noticed a long pad of yellow legal paper. He went to the table, sat, and shined his light on it. There appeared to be a list scribbled on the paper, but he couldn't make out the handwriting; it was so cramped as to be nearly illegible.

Playing his flashlight around the room, he located the light switch on a wall near the back door and turned on the fluorescent light over the table. He went back to the paper, glancing at his watch as he did. He was into some heavy overtime tonight. He knew he'd better produce something to justify it the way the sheriff was acting lately.

The first word at the top of the list appeared to be a name. He could make out the letters *Marg*—before the scribble became undecipherable, and assumed that to be *Margaret,* which made sense since that was the Eameses' girl's name. Next to the name was a date, which looked like either October 14 or 19. Vitelli realized it was the nineteenth, the day Margaret Eames had disappeared. The next word written under the name and date appeared to be Thursday, though it could be something else, too. Vitelli had always thought *his* handwriting was bad, but this was the worst he had ever seen.

Vitelli got up from the table and went to the cork board hanging on the wall next to the telephone. He checked the calendar pinned there and confirmed that the nineteenth had indeed been a Thursday. He went back to the table and looked at the paper again. He couldn't make out the next two words, though he guessed that one of them might be *moving* or *morning.* The fifth word in the list was written larger and clearer. It was another name, *Puffin,* with triple question marks after it. Below that was written: *Where is Puffin???* It was underlined twice. Vitelli assumed correctly Puffin was a pet, either a dog or a cat. The next word was a clearly written, *police!* Next to that was something about woods.

The last item was written so hastily that he couldn't read it at all. It was two words and each was capitalized, the first with a *G* or a *J,* and the second with an *M* or a *W,* suggesting it was another name of someone, or something. Vitelli mused over the name, but could make neither head nor tails of it. He finally gave up and folded the paper, pocketing it for further analysis at the station.

Vitelli yawned and got up from the table. He stood stretched, and noticed something he should have seen before: a black-leather, phone-number record book lying on the counter next to the wall phone. He went to it and picked it up. He began flipping through it when he noticed another piece of paper on the floor, under the table. He got down on his knees and reached under for it. After banging his head twice on the underside of the tabletop, he grabbed it and pulled it out. It was in the same illegible handwriting as the paper on the table, but not as bad. At least he could read this:

Judy, Have gone to Grimm Memorials.

Rog

Grimm Memorials! Vitelli looked at the name, his lips pursed in thought. His men had checked that place when they were searching the woods for Margaret Eames. They'd reported that a nice old lady lived there and she hadn't seen any sign of the girl. He realized now that he had never asked them if they had looked around the place.

If Roger Eames had gone to Grimm Memorials, where was Mrs. Eames? Did she find this note before or after she called him, or at all? If she did find the note, did she go there, too?

"Curiouser and curiouser," he muttered absentmindedly. "I guess I'll take me a look at Grimm Memorials," he said with a grunt and headed for the door.

"Five, six, pick up sticks!"
The witch was back. Jackie cowered against the bars hiding his face, but peeking between his fingers at her. He prayed

she wouldn't come for him. Her terrifying voice filled the cage as she counted off her victims with the glee of a schoolgirl. Her horrible figure stood in the doorway of the cage, surveying the boys like a butcher in a slaughterhouse.

She was an even more hideous sight now, covered with six layers of blood from head to toe. It caked on her hands and arms with the ashes of the six dead boys and mingled with her sweat, becoming liquid again and running down her body as if it were she that was doing all the bleeding. Her face was something out of a nightmare. Fresh blood smeared her lips, but the rest of her face was a dried mask of reddish black blood. Only the whites of her eyes shown, making them more horrible to behold than before. Bloody sweat dripped from her nipples as she went to work over the sleeping twins, rolling the shorter of the two onto the collapsed gurney.

The oven behind the witch was working furiously. It roared like a strong wind each time it was fed the sliced remains of another boy. The room was stifling hot with the heat their burning had produced, and the circle of ashes and bones around Jackie's mother had grown taller. The arched oven door was glowing a dull red. Tiny wisps of smoke rose from it and seeped from around its edges into the room. It curled against the ceiling, mingling with the smoke from the candles until there was a thick cloud of stinking smoke hovering lower and lower in the room. The air began to smell like burnt hamburger and hot metal.

The witch grunted as she put her hands under the gurney and lifted. The collapsible legs, that looked to Jackie like an accordion, straightened and snapped ramrod straight when the body was as high as the witch's waist.

When is she going to take me? The thought terrorized Jackie as he huddled, trying not to look at the witch's face.

I'm saving you for last, my kitten, the witch said in his head a second later.

Jackie shuddered, crying out at the presence of the witch

in his mind; then she was gone, preoccupied with locking the cage door and wheeling the boy, with the help of zombie Jennifer, to the bloody metal table. But the feeling of her remained, like a greasy residue that will only wash off with scalding water and steel wool.

Jackie tried to draw completely into himself once again, driven to escape by the witch's invasion of his mind, but the twin on the table woke screaming as the witch strapped him to it and began cutting away his clothing. None of the six boys between Mark and this twin had screamed as the witch made quick work of them. Each of them had drunk too much of the drugged milk, or were too deep in shock to react except to groan, or fart hideously when the witch drove her knife into them.

The screaming had an odd effect on Jackie. Instead of pushing him closer to the edge of total shock, it snapped him back to the realization that sooner or later the witch was going to get to him. Mark's words: *"If we lose control, we're dead!"* echoed in his mind. *Mark's dead!* the part of him that wanted to give up and veg out, reminded. But they had *almost* escaped, too. *(Almost is only good in horseshoes and hand grenades, his mother always said.)* Jackie knew with sudden certainty that *no one was coming to save him.* If he wanted to live and get out of there, he'd have to do something himself.

The twin's screams ceased suddenly. The witch grabbed the knife stuck hilt-deep in his chest and began cutting, splashing herself with a fresh coat of blood, and chanting her strange words.

Jackie tried to think of something to get him out of this mess. Mark had said something earlier, before devising his plan to get the keys, but Jackie's short-term memory had been shocked until it had fragmented, letting his mind handle only pieces of the horrors that had befallen him, instead of the whole, terrifying, mind-destroying dose at once. That combined with the fact that Jackie hadn't listened very well to anything anyone had said before because he had been too busy listening for the return of the witch and being terrified, made it difficult to remember what Mark had said. It might have been something about a weapon.

The witch was at the reclining chair, feeding his mother. Jackie tried to blot out the smacking, chewing sounds she was making as she ate the revolting meal. He looked outside the bars for something within reach that he could use as a weapon. From where he was crouched, he could see the right side of the floor outside the cage. There were a couple of tall brass candle stands nearby, but Jackie doubted he could get them in the cage without the witch noticing. A smaller one he might have had a chance with, but there were none close enough on his side.

Quietly, so as not to draw the witch's attention, Jackie crawled to the other side of the cage. A loud, airy roar made him jump. The witch had just spun the wheel that opened the oven door. Jackie froze in horror as he watched her feed the twin's body into the oven. His hair ignited from the pilot flame and went up around his head like Fourth of July sparklers. The witch pulled the lever and the oven door slammed closed with a resounding clang.

After removing and sprinkling the ashes around the star/circle, she turned and came toward the cage.

Jackie skittered to the rear left corner and cringed there, ready to fight tooth and nail should the witch come near him. He tensed, wild-eyed and certain that she had heard his thoughts of a weapon. She unlocked the door, pushed it open, and wheeled the gurney inside, but she barely glanced at him.

She can't hear *every* thought, Jackie realized. Or maybe she can but she just doesn't pay attention to them, like when Jen would do her homework in front of the TV. Maybe if he just kept his thoughts quiet, they wouldn't disturb her.

The witch rolled the gurney over next to the second twin and lowered it. Jennifer had followed her into the cage this time and helped roll the body onto the gurney and lift it into its upright position. With Jen at the foot of the table and the witch at the head, they wheeled the twin's body out of the cage. As she went through the door, the witch grabbed it and pulled it shut behind her. It closed with a crash that shook the whole cage. Jackie could feel the bars vibrating against his back.

The door!

The crash of metal on metal rang in his ears.

The door is heavy! Mark had said they could use the door as a weapon!

The witch turned quickly and fixed him with a curious gaze. Jackie's skin turned clammy cold with the certainty that he had let his thoughts get too excited and the witch had started paying attention to them. After gazing at him for what seemed a hideous eternity, she locked the door and told Jennifer to help her put the body on the bloodsoaked metal table.

Jackie relaxed a little, then stiffened. The memory of Mark's plan to slam the door on the witch wanted to charge full of excitement through his head, but with great will, he tried to suppress it. *Don't think about it.* He took a deep breath and let it out slowly.

Somehow, he had to keep his thoughts hidden and still plan the act and muster the courage to carry it out. He began counting the bars in the cage, starting with the one he was leaning against, and ticking them off in his head as he slowly slid from one bar to the next until he was in a position along the left wall of the cage to run at the back side of the door when it opened.

CHAPTER 40

Hark, hark, the dogs do bark!

Deputy Vitelli was excited. The more he thought about it the more it seemed to him that he was really on to something. He trotted back to his car, got in, and started to pick up the radio mike to report in what he'd found. On second thought, he decided to check Grimm Memorials first, just in case this was a wild-goose chase. He didn't need to give any of the clowns at the station more fodder to ridicule him.

He started the cruiser and turned on the headlights. He drove to the opening of Dorsey Lane Extension and guided the cruiser onto the narrow dirt road. He drove slowly, the road was just wide enough to permit a car. The headlights barely illuminated the twists, turns, and ruts of the dark road before him. With no street or house lights, and the thick trees overhead blocking out any moonlight, the road and surrounding woods were black as pitch.

In his excitement, Vitelli had to fight the urge to drive faster. He definitely did not want to wrap the cruiser around a tree or rip up the chassis by bottoming out on the bumpy road—that certainly wouldn't do much toward soothing things with the sheriff. He continued on carefully, at times slowing to a near halt as he maneuvered the cruiser through several deep ruts and over large bumps until the road opened up at the front of Grimm Memorials.

Vitelli parked the car near the porch steps and got out, leaning against the door as he looked up at the dark house. The smell of garbage burning wafted over him and he wondered where it could be coming from. He looked up and saw smoke coming out of a chimney at the top of the house. Except for that, the place looked deserted; worse, it looked haunted. Every window was dark. Vitelli could half imagine ghosts looking out at him, eager for him to enter.

He shook the feeling off and closed the car door. The three-quarter moon lit the front of the house well enough for him to notice tire tracks going around the side of the house. Clicking on his flashlight, he started round to investigate.

Jackie crouched in the left front corner of the cage, head down, feigning shock but actually very aware of what was going on. Outside the cage, the witch tossed the second twin's private parts into the hot, smoldering bowl on the floor and prayed over it as before. Her voice rose and fell, running on with its litany of unintelligible words. When she got to her feet, she wheeled the twin's body to the oven and fed it in. More smoke, thick and black, seeped into the room.

"Forty-two, forty-three, forty-four . . ." Jackie was counting the candles in the room now in an effort to keep his thoughts hidden while he waited for the witch to finish sprinkling the bones and ashes and return to the cage for another boy.

When she finally did, he tensed, ready to leap.

The witch unlocked the door and pushed it open. She leaned wearily against the iron jamb and waved at Jennifer to wheel the gurney in. The witch came through the door on the other side of the gurney, keeping it between her and the door as she helped to guide it in, making it impossible for Jackie to slam the door on her. He'd have to wait until she was leaving.

The witch and Jennifer put the unmoving body of Timmy

Walsh on the gurney and lifted him. As they wheeled him out of the cage, Jennifer went first, and the witch last. Jackie got ready to leap. He was going to lunge against the door and smash it into the old witch. He was going to crush her with it, knock her out with it.

He was ready.

He was going to do it.

Do it now!

Do . . . do . . . *nothing!*

No matter how much he wanted to, he was too scared to do it. His legs wouldn't respond. He tried forcing them to push him forward but they were paralyzed with the fear of what she would do to him if he failed.

She'll do it to you anyway, sooner or later, stupid, he told himself. He gripped the bar with his right hand, pulling himself up to make the lunge when the witch looked at him, freezing him in terror.

"Nine, ten, big fat hen," she said playfully, as if talking to an amused child. Jackie fell back into the corner. The witch closed the door and locked it. "Girl. Get over here and help me," the witch bellowed at Jennifer who eagerly ran forward to assist. Together they transferred Timmy Walsh to the metal table.

Jackie relaxed a little and counted candles again. He began psyching himself up for the next time the witch came in the cage. By the way she was still happily going about her gruesome business, Jackie guessed she was still ignorant of his plan.

He cowered through the dissection of Timmy Walsh, trying not to think that his failure to act had cost Timmy his life, holding onto his sanity by the barest thread of hope that his plan would work. He glanced at his sister several times, hoping to see some spark of the Jennifer he knew instead of the mindless robot the witch had turned her into, but he was disappointed. He could expect no help from her. He hunched tighter into himself and waited.

There were only two boys left before the witch got to him: the boy in the corner who had warned them about the milk and the stew, and redheaded Jeff Best. That meant he had two more chances to escape, but if he did and blew it, he knew the witch would not give him another try. If he was going to do it, he had to do it right the first time.

Too soon he heard the sizzle of Timmy Walsh's private parts in the burning bowl and smelled the wretched stench of human flesh melting. When the oven door opened, he felt a blast of heat from it and heard the screech of the metal door as the witch slid Timmy's destroyed body into the oven and closed the door. He watched as the witch walked around the circle, sprinkling Timmy's ashes and bits of charred bone over the other boys' burnt remains.

As she finished, the witch approached the cage, her bare feet slapping against the stone floor. Jackie raised himself cautiously from his crouch.

The witch retrieved the door key from the nail on the side of the podium where she'd also hung the pocket watch. She slipped it into the lock, and turned it. Jackie readied himself to lunge against the door as soon as she stepped inside. She pushed the door open and paused a moment before entering. "Girl, bring the gurney over here," the witch growled at Jennifer.

"Yes, Gram," Jennifer said pleasantly, and obediently pushed the gurney into the cage. The witch followed right behind her.

Jackie slumped. Jennifer was blocking the way. He watched as the two of them picked up Jeff Best and slid him onto the collapsed gurney. Together they lifted the gurney to the up-right position, and Jennifer pushed it out of the cage, the witch by her side helping her. Again, Jennifer was in the way.

There was just the dark-skinned boy in the corner left. After warning them about the milk and the stew, the boy had lapsed into a mumbling stupor that had quickly regressed into total unconsciousness again. When the witch came for him would be Jackie's last chance to catch her off guard with the door. Theoretically, he knew if he missed this chance he'd have one more, when the witch came for him. But he was afraid that with her attention focused solely on him, he'd be unable to pull it off. And once she got her hands on him he wouldn't be able to do anything except go insane with fright.

Whatever happened, he couldn't let the witch get her hands on him. He'd rather run and jump into the oven and burn alive than have that happen. The next time she came in the cage would have to be the moment of truth.

Ken Vitelli walked around the long black hearse parked next to Steve Nailer's Saab and shined his light in the windows of both cars. He tried the hearse's doors and found them locked. The Saab was open but there was nothing inside that could be considered a clue.

He left the cars and walked a ways to the back of the house, shining his light on the headstones in the cemetery and on the surrounding trees. The place looked so thoroughly deserted except for the hearse and Nailer's car that Vitelli doubted he'd find anyone inside. He glanced at his watch, noting that it was after eleven, and started back to the front of the house.

Jackie waited and watched. Blood spurted from Jeff's body as the witch cut into him, and ran down the table's gutters to where it trickled into the collection jar. The jar was three-quarters full now with the blood of eleven children. The rest of their blood was splattered on the floor and on the witch. More sprayed on her now as she worked the knife through Jeff's body. It squirted in her face and up her arms onto her shoulders and chest. It mingled with her sweat and ran in rivulets over her skin. She licked it from the corners of her mouth and from her ashy fingers.

Jackie watched, seeing the horror, but not seeing it; concentrating instead on counting the candles *(125, 126)* and keeping his mind free of everything else until the moment was right. A couple of times the witch paused from her debauchery and stared at him quizzically, but each time he weathered her gaze and kept on counting.

She eventually went back to her grisly task, removing Jeff's heart and wolfing down half of it. She finished her portion and smacked her lips as if she'd just eaten the tastiest treat on Earth. Clots of blood and tissue slid down her chin as she took the rest of the heart to Jackie's mother.

Again he heard the disgusting slavering and chewing. Again, he had to witness the witch removing her victim's private parts and throwing them into the smoking, sizzling bowl, fat bubbling over onto the floor, before she fed the body into the oven. For the last time, Jackie hoped, he watched the witch ring his mother with the burnt remains of a dead child.

It was time.

Jackie took a deep breath. His arms and legs trembled. The old witch brought the keys to the door and unlocked it. Jackie crossed his fingers. Jennifer pushed the gurney up to the cage door. *No, Jen,* Jackie thought, fearful his sister would get in the way again.

The witch pushed the door open, and stood half in the doorway, motioning for Jennifer to push the gurney in. Jackie knew he couldn't let her; she'd get in the way and ruin everything.

"Jennifer!" he screamed as loud as he could. She came to an abrupt halt, jerking her head toward him as if it were an effort to move it of her own free will. The witch, too, turned on him, but by then it was too late.

As soon as he screamed, Jackie lunged forward, diving at the door bars, his arms outstretched. He hit the door hard with both hands, jamming his wrists, and spraining the left one badly. The door swept closed on the witch.

She tried to get her arms up and duck out of the way, but couldn't. Two iron bars caught her full on the right side of her face and head, sending her crashing into the iron door jamb. She let out a grunt and a pained moan, then collapsed, sliding to the floor in a crumpled, blood-caked heap in the doorway of the cage.

Jennifer Nailer took a sudden deep breath, coughed and staggered dizzily away from the cage door. Her eyelids fluttered, and her glazed, bloodshot eyes cleared. She felt as though she had been submerged in water and forced to hold her breath until it burned in her lungs, ready to explode. Now she surfaced to the real world. She gulped in air, coughed on the smoke and the foul odor in the room and tried to steady herself. She looked down. In the doorway of the cage lay an old, blood-drenched naked woman.

Where's Grammy? was her first thought, followed closely by: *Where the hell am I?*

"Jennifer!" a familiar voice cried.

She looked up and saw her brother lying on the cage floor, holding his wrist as if in pain. "Jackie," Jennifer asked in a confused voice. "Where's Grammy? Where's the gingerbread house?"

"Jen," he cried, getting to his knees. "Are you okay?"

"I think so," she said tentatively, unsure if she really was. She felt so strange; like she had just woken from a beautiful dream of flowers to find herself standing in a pile of garbage. Just a moment ago, she was positive her grandmother had been by her side, healthy and sane again after all these years. Jennifer had been helping Grammy bake in the kitchen of the gingerbread house.

How she suddenly got in this hot, smokey, and horrible-smelling dungeon, she didn't know. The gingerbread house was gone, Grammy was gone; in her place was this grotesque, bloody, apparently dead, white-haired old woman on the floor. It made her nauseous just to think about it.

Jackie got to his feet, still holding his wrist, and walked to the doorway. He never took his eyes off the old woman on the floor. "We've got to get out of here, Jen," he said in a half whisper.

"But where's Grammy? How did I get here?" Jen asked again, panic showing in her voice.

Jackie started to answer her, then stopped and stared at the old woman again. He stepped cautiously closer to her crumpled body lying in the doorway. He jumped over her quickly, landing and dancing away from where she lay as if it were a pit infested with spiders. He ran to Jennifer and burst into tears as he wrapped his arms around her. "Jen! I'm so glad you're all right," he blubbered. "I was so scared . . ." he carried on.

"What happened to Grammy?" Jennifer pleaded suddenly with him, grabbing his shirtfront with both hands.

"She's not here," Jackie sobbed and tried to calm down. "She was never here. It was the witch," he explained through intermittent tears and hitches of breath. He looked in the direction of the old woman on the floor when he said witch. "She had you in a spell."

"A witch?" Jennifer said, doubting if she had heard him correctly. "A spell?" Jackie nodded. Jennifer started laughing.

"Don't laugh!" Jackie hissed. "You thought Grammy was living in a gingerbread house in the woods."

Jennifer stopped laughing. It was true. The nausea in her stomach did loop to loops with the realization of it. She had visited Grammy in a gingerbread house! She had *believed* that Grammy had built the house just for her and Jackie!

Jennifer staggered from the impact of the impossibility of those things. Grammy was in a nursing home in Boston, crazy with Alzheimer's disease. And had she really thought that a house could be built of gingerbread? The memory of Grammy throwing a Halloween party for a bunch of Jackie's friends and of her and Gram baking something blurred in her mind, becoming vague with disbelief.

Had she really done those things?

Somewhere beneath those benign memories, dark ones lurked, pushing their heads up to the light of her conscious mind just long enough for her to catch a fleeting glimpse of them. Images of monster bears and blood-soaked children and the faint sound of screaming showed their faces and then were submerged again by her mind's defenses. Moving in a daze, Jen slowly put her arms around her brother.

He looked up at her, eyes streaming with tears. "Jen, it was awful. The witch killed everybody, cut them up, and ate their hearts. She burned them in the oven and you helped her!"

Jennifer glanced at the furnace with its huge, smoking hot door against the wall, then at the unconscious boy lying in the back corner of the cage. Where *had* all the boys gone? Had she really done what Jackie said? The memories flitted before her mind's eye, showing her the horrible truth. She had helped this bloody old woman lift the bodies of the boys in the cage and then had stood by as if watching a game of Pin the Tail on the Donkey while she mutilated them.

Another memory rose and Jennifer whirled around, afraid of what she might see; those fears were confirmed. Her mother was lying naked, tied to a reclining chair, her chest and stomach painted with bloody symbols, blood and gobs of raw tissue hanging out of her mouth and running down her chin.

"We gotta get out of here," Jackie said urgently, grabbing her hand. He gave a fearful look back at the witch. "We gotta get out of here before she wakes up." He started for the door, pulling her by the hand, but she wrenched her hand free of his and ran back to her mother's side.

"Mom, wake up!" Jennifer whined through tears. She shook

her mother's arm and patted her face lightly, but the only movement her mother made was to open her mouth. Jennifer thought her mother was trying to talk, but quickly realized she was doing something else. Her teeth were blood-stained and dirty with trapped shreds of raw meat. Gobs of the stuff filled her cheek pockets and she pulled it between her teeth now and began chewing.

Jennifer thought she was going to be sick. The foul odor of her mother's breath almost made her faint and she had to move away from her.

"The witch did something to her," Jackie said in a nervous whisper behind her. "But we gotta get outta here and get help before the witch wakes up." He grabbed her hand again.

That was when Jennifer saw her stepfather near the wall by the window. She let out a short, high-pitched gasp, then lost her breath completely as though she'd been punched hard in the stomach. She hunched over, stomach hitching as she tried to inhale and couldn't.

Steve's eyes were wide open, staring intently at the floor. His lips were pulled back into a rictus snarl. His skin had turned blue-green with large dark purple bruises on his neck, face, and back. As she looked at him, unable to breathe, unable to take her eyes off him, Jennifer noticed something else, too. There were tiny dots on his face and naked back and arms; and the dots were moving. The cracks in the floor around his face and body had all erupted with tiny anthills as a legion of red ants lay claim to the body. They swarmed over him, and built a city around him.

She saw one crawl across his open eyeball and felt the room spin and her legs go limp.

"Oh God!" she finally croaked out—it sounded more like a burp than words—and took a huge breath. "Oh God," she repeated a little louder, tears streaming down her face. *"Oh God!"* she screamed again, backing away, shaking her head.

"Come on!" Jackie bawled at her. He was crying and

frantic to get out of there. He yanked on Jennifer's arm with all his might. Like a rag doll, Jennifer let herself be led out of the crematorium.

Deputy Vitelli breathed through his nose, no longer able to stand the awful stench of whatever was coming out of the Grimm Memorials' chimney. He approached the front door cautiously, trying to be as quiet as possible. He peeked in the small round windows in the top of the massive double front doors, but they were too grimy for him to see anything. Holding his flashlight with his left hand, he tried the door with his right. It was locked. He moved along the porch and noticed the first window was open. Keeping his back against the wall, he slipped to the window, crouched and looked inside.

The heavy drapes blocked his view. Carefully, he lifted the nearest side open and peered inside. There was a large piece of furniture near the window, but he could see little else beyond. He flashed his light inside and felt his throat become a little more dry as he looked at the moldy, velvet-lined coffin. The room was full of them. They smelled like rot.

That's perfect for this place, Vitelli thought with a silent, nervous chuckle. He wondered, if he knocked at the door, would Lurch answer it? Suddenly that didn't seem so funny. For a moment he considered calling in some backup, but then chided himself for being a coward. If this was going to be a big breakthrough in the investigation, he wanted it all for himself so he could prove to the sheriff and the other jokers at the station that they were wrong about him.

Ducking his head and holding both sides of the drapes open, Deputy Vitelli stepped over the sill and into the room. The smell inside was worse than what it had been from the window. It was heavy and cloying, almost liquid in his nostrils. He blew the smell out and covered his mouth with his hand. There was more than just the smell of mildewing fabric and rotting wood here. There was a smell that Vitelli had experienced only once before: the time they'd pulled that mutilated kid from the river. It was the smell of rotting human flesh.

Vitelli crossed to the door, a cold sweat capping his brow. He grabbed the doorknob and pulled it open. A moment later he flashed his light out into the entrance hall, noting the marble podium and the doors marked *Crematorium* and *Chapel*. He slipped through the door and crept to the marble podium. There was a door to his left, but the stench of wasted flesh came strongest from the door marked Chapel.

He started toward it when he heard a sound that froze him. It was a loud crack. A moment later there was another one. They were coming from behind the chapel door. He noticed it was open just a bit.

Vitelli freed his .38 from his holster and clicked off his flashlight. He returned the latter to his belt, and held the former upright in the ready-to-fire position as he crept to the chapel door. Holding his pistol with both hands, Vitelli nudged the door open with his knee. The sickening smell of death rolled over him and he gagged. He pulled out his handkerchief with his left hand and held it over his nose and mouth.

The room was dimly lit by waning moonlight. He immediately saw two tall windows with no curtains on them, but could see little else. There was another sound as he stood in the doorway. It was the sound of wet lapping, and a snuffling sound. Vitelli stepped into the room, wincing at the stink the handkerchief was doing little to relieve, and looked around. The sound was coming from the other end of the room, to his left. Something huge hung from the ceiling at that end that looked like a weirdly placed cross beam.

A loud crack from the darkness ahead made Vitelli jump. There was something moving at the foot of a long, high table beneath the cross beam. Two eyes glowed at him for a moment as he moved sideways through the room. He stopped. He stood, not moving a muscle, and stared in shock at the horror before him.

A dog the size of a lion was crouching over something hideous. The dog lowered its massive head and took what appeared to be a human rib cage in its mouth, cracked several ribs open, and began lapping out the marrow.

Vitelli wanted to puke. His eyes, grown accustomed to the dark, showed him the rest of the dog's meal, or what was left of it. Both legs were gone except for two stumps of bone hanging off the hips, and only one arm remained attached to the shoulders, which still had chunks of rotting flesh clinging to them. One side of the arm had been ripped clean of meat down to the bone. The hand had been chewed off and lay a few feet away, palm up, fingers curled slightly, as if waiting for a handshake. The ribs the dog was working on were still attached to a backbone at the end of which was the gnawed remains of a human head. The face was turned, as if looking back at Vitelli. The eyes were gone, hollow black holes shown through the leathery skin of the upper part of the face. The bottom part, everything below the nose except the upper teeth, was gone, also torn away. Vitelli recognized the jawbone, with its bottom set of teeth, lying above the head. The rest of the head was wasted flesh, the ears gone, skull showing through over the eyes and at the crown. Vitelli couldn't tell who it was by looking at the face, but the blond hair was the same color as Roger Eames's, as were a pair of glasses lying nearby.

The dog, too involved in cracking open the ribs, hadn't seen him yet. Sweating every move, he slowly backed up. As he did, he looked up at the weird cross beam and almost screamed. The flyblown corpse of a child was nailed to the beam, which Vitelli realized was an upside-down cross. The blackened, wasted face stretched in an eternal shriek and long blonde hair still hung from the shriveled scalp.

Sickened, he pulled his eyes away. His foot hit the doorsill and he backed over it, through the door to the entrance hall again. With images of himself on the nightly news telling how he single-handedly captured the ring of childnappers, he fought the urge to call for reinforcements.

Vitelli backed to the stairway and looked up, seeing nothing but shadowy hallways leading away in two directions from the second-floor landing. Behind him was a door with a short corridor leading to another room. He slipped quietly down the corridor and into the kitchen.

The smell of decomposing flesh was strong here also. Vitelli pulled out his flashlight and looked at the room. The wooden table against the back wall was covered with what looked like dried blood. A severed finger lay on the table while the bones of several more littered the floor under it. To his right was a refrigerator and a large, bulky gas stove that had a vat of some spoiled, stinking substance in it. To his left a large restaurant-type freezer stood to the ceiling against the wall. Vitelli pocketed his gun, went to it, and opened it.

Faces stared out at him, their hair in disarray, eyes wide, but glazed, mouths stretched open bigger than mouths should be. Judy Eames's head sat on the third shelf; around her, on the other shelves, were more heads: a white-haired old man, Joe Conally, and Jerry Hall. On the lower shelves were foil-wrapped packages, one of which had been torn open and not rewrapped. It contained a man's frozen penis and testicles.

Vitelli closed the door quickly and leaned against it, fighting down the nausea that threatened to bring up dinner, lunch, *and* breakfast. *That's it!* He'd had it. There was no way he could handle this alone. He was going to have to forget the glory and call in reinforcements. And if anyone ever asked why he did, he would lie, not admitting he couldn't go on because he was scared shitless.

Vitelli turned to leave the kitchen and heard footsteps, like someone running up stairs, somewhere in the house. He pulled his gun out again and ran back to the entrance hall. The footsteps were coming from behind the crematorium door. Vitelli crouched and brought his gun up.

"Hold it!"

The boy shrieked, jumping as Vitelli spoke and stepped out at them. The girl looked out of it, like she was in shock or on drugs. Vitelli recognized them as Nailer's stepchildren and lowered his gun. "Where's your father?" Vitelli asked quietly.

The boy and girl began to cry. The boy, whining loudly, pointed back at the crematorium door.

"Alright. Come here. I'm going to put you in the squad car and call for backup," Vitelli said quietly, holstering his gun and motioning with his hand for them to move. As they crossed the room to him, the massive, man-eating dog in the other room began barking loudly at the voices it heard. Seconds later it came charging out of the chapel, straight at the Nailer kids. Vitelli screamed for them to get out of the way and tried to get his gun out again. The kids just got clear, diving at the foot of the stairs, just as the dog leaped.

Vitelli got his gun out just as the dog hit his arm. He was knocked backwards into the wall next to the kitchen door, the gun flying out of his hand. The snarling creature went straight for his throat, but missed, clamping on to his face instead. Vitelli screamed into the monster dog's cavernous mouth as the canine's teeth tore his cheeks from his face and gulped them down. Vitelli's teeth and gums were exposed in a hideous grimace.

The next bite found his neck, crushing his windpipe and severing both his jugular and carotid arteries as the dog's saber teeth ripped through muscle, flesh, and tendons. Blood sprayed in all directions like water from a punctured garden hose. It began to spurt in pulses, squirting blood to the beat of his dying heart. The dog, its head and coat covered with shimmering droplets of blood, held on to Vitelli's neck, drinking the hot blood spurting into its mouth.

* * *

Jennifer screamed when Jackie screamed, his alarm setting off the reflexive action in her. Jackie grabbed her arm, backing up the stairs in terror. It was Jackie who, as the dog released the policeman and began lapping up the flood from his neck that had slowed to a weak, bubbling flow, heard the footsteps coming up the crematorium stairs.

"The witch!" He gasped, his voice squeaky with fear. The dog, settling down to an earnest lapping of the still-twitching policeman, who lay on top of his gun, was between them and the front door, and the door to the kitchen was much too close to the horrible animal for Jackie to even consider trying for it. Since he'd only been in the entrance hall and crematorium, he didn't know what was through that door, it could be a dead end. Realizing there was no other route of escape, Jackie grabbed Jen's hand and began pulling her up the stairs to the second floor.

CHAPTER 41

Here we go round the mulberry bush . . .

Eleanor opened her right eye. The left one wouldn't respond. It felt as big as a grapefruit and throbbed intolerably. The throbbing pain went straight down the left side of her face. It lodged in her cheekbone and crushed her jaw. The pain picked up again in her arm, rendering it useless. She could feel broken bones rubbing and wanted to faint with the pain every time her arm was moved or even touched. She couldn't feel her left hand.

Eleanor looked at the floor for several moments, then at the base of the cage, trying to comprehend where she was. The return of the sharp, burning pain in her chest, cutting through all the other pains her injuries had brought reminded her. She was in the crematorium. Whom with? *My little kittens.* But one of the kittens had claws.

Grunting, and cradling her broken arm as best she could, Eleanor rolled to her right side before she had to stop for a breather to let the pain subside. She wondered how much time she had left and looked at Edmund's pocket watch, requiring a painful lift and twist of her head to see it where she'd hung it from its chain on the side of the podium. The watch face was smeared with blood—she realized she must have rubbed against it—but she could see enough to guess. She had less than an hour left until midnight. So little time to perform the last two sacrifices of the fifth ritual and complete the sixth. So little time to live.

She took a deep breath and struggled to her knees. The pain expanded but she fought it, going beyond the limits of normal endurance. She had to. She'd come too far to lose it all now to mere pain. As she grabbed the cage's iron door jamb with her right arm and pulled herself to her feet, she had to concede that what was rioting through her body was no mere pain. This was pain that went beyond the River Pain. This pain rivalled the universe itself. This was pain that deserved respect.

She reached her feet, and leaned against the cage, her breath rattling in and out of her. Her left arm hung limply at her side, jangling with intense pain at having been moved when she stood. The pain brought on gray waves of unconsciousness like a storm rolling in off the sea, but she fought them off.

As the waves receded, she became aware of voices. She heard them with her ears, and faintly, like an echo in her head, with the Machine. She closed her eyes and listened. It was the brother and sister *(Wait till I get my hands on him!)* and another person . . . a *policeman!* At that moment she heard Mephisto bark and charge out of the chapel.

Pushing herself away from the cage, Eleanor staggered across the room to the door. Pain bombarded her with every step, but she went on. Each step up the crematorium stairs was a world of pain, but she made it to the top. She pushed open the door.

Mephisto glanced up menacingly from his meal until he saw who it was. He wagged his tail and went back to lapping the blood from the dead policeman's ripped face and neck.

"Good boy," Eleanor wheezed with pain. She stood in the doorway at the top of the stairs, holding onto the doorknob with her right hand so that she didn't go plummeting down

the stairs. Where were her little ones? She cast about for
them with the Machine. It was as weak as she. It took her
several long, painful minutes to find them, upstairs somewhere; she had trouble pinpointing exactly where.

She stepped away from the crematorium door and the
room began to spin. She fell back against the wall, twisting
her body, so as not to hit her tortured left arm. It screamed
with pain at the motion anyway. She leaned against the
couch for support while the pain had its way with her, then
summoned every feeble ounce of strength she had left. She
staggered away from the couch, crossing the entrance hall to
the stairs in a sideways roll of limping steps and grabbed
hold of the newel post like a drowning victim reaching for a
hand. At the bottom of the stairs, she slid to her knees, and
leaned forward, resting her head on the fourth step.

It was no use; at the moment, she could go no further. She
closed her eyes and began to breathe deeply, trying to blot
out the pain, and revive the Machine. Her body couldn't go
after them just yet, but the Machine could.

"Maybe Grammy's in the backyard," Jennifer said softly,
her voice shocked and distant. "Can we go see?" she whispered to Jackie.

"Shh!" he shot back, harshly. They were creeping along
the left hallway from the second-floor landing, which was
still visible behind them. Though he had not heard the footsteps coming up the crematorium stairs following them yet,
Jackie was more scared than before. He could feel something, something in the air; a feeling that the air was expand-
ing, growing, becoming *alive*. He began to feel like the very
air itself could eat him—*just like the witch!* Suddenly Jackie
could feel her all around him as if her obscene arms were
wrapping him in their deadly embrace once again.

The darkness ahead of them didn't seem empty anymore.
Jackie hesitated. He looked at his sister, then into the

darkness ahead. A pair of eyes flickered in the shadows for a moment. He began to back up, pulling Jennifer along with him. The eyes reappeared again for a second, moving toward them. Jackie began to backpedal faster. Jennifer stumbled along at his side.

The eyes came out of the darkness and a face was revealed. Jackie smiled with happy relief at first, until the head came fully into view. It was shaved. The top of it was slightly askew, not aligned with the rest of the face. Dried blood crusted along a line at the top of the forehead.

It was Margaret.

Jackie gulped. The air became thick and heavy and hard to move through. Margaret kept coming. The more he saw of her, the more he wanted to run. Her face was bloated and streaked with vertical lines of blood running down it from the horizontal cut across her forehead. Her eyes were vacant, dead. A line of dried blood ran from both nostrils and from the corner of her mouth down to her neck; that was where her blue-tinted skin ended.

The rest of her body was like one of those Human Body glass models that Jackie had seen once and hated immediately. Her insides were exposed and rotting. The skin and most of the meat had been flayed from her body, exposing bone and shreds of muscle that were putrefying and rotting away. There were gaping cavities in her chest and stomach and Jackie realized that, like the Tin Man, she didn't have a heart.

Jackie backed himself and Jennifer all the way to the landing. Margaret walked out of the darkness on her raw legs and decomposing body. She smiled at him and spoke to Jennifer.

"Hi Jen," she said sweetly in a voice that Jackie immediately recognized as the witch's.

"Run Jen!" Jackie yelled, making a dash for the other hallway and pulling Jennifer with him.

"Grammy!" Jennifer cried. She pulled her hand free from

Jackie's. "It's only Grammy, Jackie," she said to him and went back.

Jackie watched in horror as his sister wrapped her arms around dead Margaret's stinking remains and kissed her on the cheek, knocking the lid of her head off. It bounced on the floor and rolled around and around like a dropped quarter before spinning to a halt.

The witch is playing games with us. The thought was a crystal-clear revelation for Jackie, like a flashbulb going off in a dark room, freezing everything perfectly in the light for a second. He'd just been wondering what had happened to Margaret and whether or not the witch still held her captive. The witch had heard his thoughts and was able to make him see her, forcing him to retreat back to the stairs where she was probably lying in wait to grab them. She had made Jennifer see Grammy, and now it looked like his sister was back under the witch's spell.

"It's not Grammy," Jackie yelled at Jennifer, trying to jar her out of her trance. "It's the witch! Don't look at her," he urged, but it was no use. Jen was lost to him. A creaking sound behind him made him turn. He was near the top of the stairs. The witch was crawling up toward him, clutching the banister with her right hand and taking each step on her knees.

Here we go round the mulberry bush, the mulberry bush, the mulberry bush, the witch sang off key in his head.

Jackie shrieked, stepping away from the stairs. Margaret's skinned and rotting hand clutched at his shoulder. He turned, saw Margaret's bloated, overripe face, and shrieked again. He pulled away from her, shaking his shoulder free of her clutches and ran headlong down the other hallway.

"Jackie, come back!" Jennifer cried after him.

Halfway down the hall, Jackie saw a door and ran to it. He pushed it open and ducked inside. He stood against the door, catching his breath and wondering what he was going to do now. In the dim moonlight shining through the window, he could see an old, dust-caked, four-poster bed in the corner and a large dresser against the near wall.

Jackie ran to the window and yanked it open. The swollen wood screamed as frame and sash rubbed hard against each other. Jackie stuck his head out, the night air was cold, but felt good after the heat and stench of the crematorium. The window was about thirty feet off the ground over the side of the house where the family Saab and the witch's hearse were parked. It was definitely too far to jump, but running down the side of the house, right next to the window was a drainpipe that Jackie thought he could climb down. He didn't want to, but knew he had no choice.

He put his knee on the sill and leaned out to grab the drainpipe when he heard a whispery, scuttling sound above him. He craned his head up for a look and gasped. Scrabbling down the side of the house above him was a black spider the size of a horse. Its onyx eyes gleamed in the moonlight and fixed on Jackie's head. Its foot-long mandibles dripped with poisonous drool as they opened and the witch's voice came out, croaking, "Itsy-bitsy spider went up the water spout."

Jackie pulled his head quickly in and slammed the screaming window shut. A small black spider skittered across the glass, leaving a trail of silk. "The witch again," Jackie whispered. Outside the door, he heard footsteps approaching down the hall.

Jackie looked about frantically for a weapon. The only thing handy was a small, glass perfume bottle on the dresser next to him. He grabbed it and made ready to whip it at whatever came through the door.

The knob turned slowly.

Jackie gritted his teeth.

The lock hammer clicked and the door opened a crack.

Jackie's bowels clenched so tight in fear they hurt.

The door started to open.

Jackie raised the bottle.

A stream of warm air blew in from the door.

Goosebumps blossomed on his arm.

The door opened. The light came on. The witch, dried blood caking her body, streaking her legs, the left side of her face swollen and bruised purple, stepped into the room. Arms reaching, clawing hands clutching, she rushed toward Jackie.

He threw the bottle with all his might. It struck the witch in the forehead, and passed right through it as her head, then the rest of her body, became transparent and disappeared.

The room was empty as before. The door was closed. The light was off. Jackie still held the perfume bottle in his hand. The witch was gone, but there were again footsteps in the hall.

In an exact replay, the footsteps stopped outside; the door opened; the light came on; the witch charged in; he threw the bottle; the witch disappeared.

The room was dark and quiet again. The bottle was back in his hand.

And there were footsteps in the hall.

They stopped.

The knob turned.

Door opened.

Lights came on.

Witch charged in.

Throw the bottle.

Witch disappeared.

Footsteps in the hall.

The scene played over and over. The gruesome, murder-bent witch charging in; the gruesome murder-bent witch disappearing. Each time, Jackie thought he was going to crap his pants. Each time, after he threw the bottle, his arms flailed, fighting off empty air.

Jackie was helpless. He was like a kid on LSD captivated by a strobe light. The repeating scene held him enthralled in abject terror because he knew that one of these times the witch would be real and there would be no escape.

The scene began to play faster, like a film run on fast-forward. Jackie began to cry and the tears helped break the hypnotic effect of the scene. He stopped throwing the bottle and dropped it. He turned to the window, but the small spider weaving its silk web across the glass dissuaded him from trying it again. It didn't matter if he knew it wasn't real, he hated spiders and couldn't face that big one again, real or not. Any second now, he knew the witch coming through the door would be the real one. He had to do something. The panic of terror spurred him to courage. He let out a yell and charged the witch as she came through the door again.

She looked surprised, then disappeared.

Jackie dashed into the hall and looked back toward the landing. The witch was on the top step. Jennifer was reaching down, helping the witch to her feet. "Jen! No!" Jackie cried with renewed tears.

Jennifer didn't turn to look at him, but concentrated solely on helping the witch. When she was on her feet, hanging on to the newel post as if she'd fall over without it, the witch whispered in Jennifer's ear. She nodded and turned, walking toward Jackie.

"Come with me and Grammy, Jackie. She's come to take us away with her," Jennifer coaxed.

"She's not Grammy!" Jackie screamed at her.

"Yes she is," Jen replied calmly with that maddening, vacant smile plastered to her lips.

"That's not Grammy," Jackie sobbed, backing away from Jennifer. "That's a *witch!*" he shouted.

"You and your imagination," Jennifer clucked. "Don't be silly. How many times do I have to tell you: There are no such things as witches," she lectured. "Now stop being such a big baby and come with us." She reached out her hands to him.

"Stay away from me, Jen," Jackie said pleadingly, backing up some more. Behind his sister, the witch stood hunched over, wheezing in pain, her left eye swollen closed but her right one watching every move they made.

"I just want you to come with me and Gram and be happy."

"No!" Jackie choked out. He turned and ran away from his sister, down the hall and around the corner into darkness.

Eleanor was on the verge of collapse, but the Machine was humming strong. For the first time in days, she was certain that if she did lose consciousness, the Machine would roll on, keeping things under control. It was ironic that here she was, weak to the point of collapse, in the worst physical shape she'd ever been in, on death's doorstep, and the Machine was running like old times. It was as if the immense pain within her had helped her become detached from her physical body and more completely immersed in the Machine than she had ever been before. At times she felt as if the Machine was feeding on her life's energy itself.

The Machine was strong again. Growing stronger every moment.

Eleanor knew that the only thing that could stop the Machine now would be her death, which would be inevitable if she couldn't get that damned boy back.

As Jennifer returned to her at the top of the stairs, Eleanor let go of the newel post and grabbed Jennifer's shoulder with her good hand. Using her as support, Eleanor turned and looked back down the stairs. She pursed her lips and let out a low whistle. Below, Mephisto stopped dragging the policeman's body into the chapel and responded to his master's call. He padded quickly up the stairs, head raised inquisitively, waiting for instructions.

CHAPTER 42

Alabone, crack a bone . . .

Jackie felt his way along the wall through the darkness. There was a window at the end of the hall, but since it was on the side of the house away from the moon, it glowed only dimly, revealing its own outline and little else. Jackie glanced back every few seconds to be sure neither Jen nor the witch were creeping up on him. He knew the witch would be after him soon, and he didn't know what to do. He was totally alone, and more scared than a six-year-old should ever have to be.

The witch had Jen in her spell again. His mother lay down in the crematorium, waiting for whatever horrible thing it was that the witch was going to do to her. He thought of his stepfather Steve, and his short-lived friend Mark, and tears flooded his eyes. Not for the first time nor the last, he wished this was all a nightmare that he could wake up from.

A giggle slipped from the darkness ahead. Jackie froze against the wall. He stood there, listening, and straining his eyes into the darkness. Gradually, he became aware of a dim glow from a door ahead and to the left. It was partially open. Another giggle came from beyond the door. It sounded like a child's voice.

Maybe it's another kid the witch kidnapped, Jackie thought hopefully. He crossed the hallway quickly and quietly. He leaned in and peered around the door, but couldn't see much. A dark, cane-bottomed wood chair sat in the corner and a writing desk was just inside the door, against the wall. The light flickered, as if from a candle, and cast shadows on the furniture and walls.

Jackie looked at the two pieces of furniture and realized there was something strange about them. They were not regular size. They looked like children's furniture, similar to a desk and chair he had owned when they lived in the North End. Jackie pushed the door open slowly. He hoped it wouldn't creak and miraculously it didn't. The door silently swung wide.

The room was filled with small furniture: a table, a leather-upholstered captain's chair, a small bed. Sitting on the bed was a young, dark-haired woman of exceptional beauty, with skin so pale it was luminous. *Snow White!* Jackie thought immediately. He heard the giggling again, but it wasn't Snow White giggling.

Jackie looked beyond the bed to the dark shadows of the far corner. There stood the seven dwarfs, all bunched up close together. This can't be real, Jackie thought. It's got to be . . . *the witch.* As Jackie stared at them, he realized these were no Disney dwarfs—no Grumpy, Sneezy, or Dopey. These dwarfs were for real: mutant miniature old men with long beards and tough wrinkled skin.

The one in the front, a muscular, thick-necked, ugly thing, giggled. The sound was no longer childlike. His laughter was bad, what Jackie's mother would call a *dirty* laugh. The sound bit into Jackie, making him shiver and snapping him back to his senses. It was then that he noticed that the thick-necked dwarf, and all the others, were naked.

The ugly one in front was fondling his private parts as he stared lecherously at Snow White. Jackie looked at her on the bed and winced. She was pulling her blouse open, revealing firm white breasts topped with cherry red nipples. Jackie looked at her face, noticing something he hadn't before. Her face was lewdly made up with too much mascara. There were bright red rouge spots on her cheeks and thick red lipstick on her mouth. She looked at Jackie and winked. She opened her mouth and ran her tongue slowly over her lipstick-stained teeth.

"Come on in, Jackie," Snow White said in a lusty voice. She beckoned to him with a crooked finger.

Jackie felt a powerful urge to obey her command. His legs actually began to move forward, propelling him into the room before he realized it and pulled back. Snow White laughed obscenely when he backed away.

From the other side of the room, the lead dwarf grunted and charged the bed. The rest followed him. They converged on Snow White, pushing her back onto the bed swarming over her with probing hands, tongues, and privates. One of the dwarfs shoved his fat head between Snow White's legs and she let out a loud moan. Two others squeezed her breasts with their tiny hands while the leader sat on her head, straddling her face with his stubby, muscle-bound legs and pumped his long, dirty-looking thing into her mouth.

Jackie fled the room and the horrid sight. The sound of Snow White's ecstatic moaning and the evil grunting of the dwarfs chased him down the dark corridor. As he turned a corner a huge shadowy form rose before him. Red eyes gleamed malevolently out of the darkness at him.

"You're going the wrong way, sonny." The voice came at him thick and mean and familiar. It was a woman's voice, but it wasn't the witch's voice. He had heard it before.

"And, you forgot to pay the troll!" the horrid voice snarled.

The huge head loomed over him and he could see the wide, bulging brow over the cruel eyes and flat nose. The troll's mouth opened, emitting a smell like moldy fish, and revealed upper and lower rows of jagged, sharp teeth.

The troll! She's come back for me. Jackie thought in a

panic. He tried to control himself. "It's not real," he whispered, his lips barely moving. "It's the witch."

The troll laughed and the stench of her breath grew stronger.

"You're not real," Jackie spoke up with uneasy courage.

"Wanna bet?" the troll hissed at him and came closer.

It's not real. It's not real. It's not real, Jackie repeated over and over again in his mind. The troll was coming closer. Jackie backed away. *This is just Anna Lucy Nation. It's just the witch. She is making me see things like I did back in the room.* He had charged through her image then; he could do it now. If he could only muster the courage.

The troll grinned at him and a long gluey string of drool ran from the corner of its mouth and hung slowly to the floor. Its body came into the shadowy light of a curtained window Jackie had just passed, and he saw its dead-looking skin and its flabby, thorny breasts.

Jackie tried to overcome the mind-numbing terror of the beast in front of him. He thought, not unusually, of Steve, the only father-figure and model of courage Jackie had ever really known, since his real father had died when he was three. He thought of something Steve had said to him the first day they moved into the new house when Jackie had been so scared of the big trees and the forest.

People are afraid only when they don't understand something, Steve had told him. *If you know what something is, then you don't have to be afraid of it anymore. Fear is ignorance! Knowledge is strength.* Jackie hadn't been sure at the time exactly what Steve meant, but now the words filled Jackie with a sense of courage.

I don't have to be afraid of this troll, he told himself, because I know it's really just the witch making me see something that isn't really there.

The troll stepped closer. Its long black tongue slithered out of its mouth, licking its thick, chapped lips with a sandpaper sound. Its dead breath was overpowering but he held his ground, legs trembling, but holding. He could smell its body now, too; a rancid bad cheese smell. The troll reached out its arms for him.

Jackie counted to three, took a deep breath and ran straight at the troll.

Her mouth opened wide, and she roared with a sound a lion would make if it could laugh. Her claw-fingered hands swept out of the darkness, closing in on him. He felt her hand, all leathery and sharp, fall on the back of his neck squeezing it tightly. Her ravenous mouth lunged for him, her foul breath panting in his face. The teeth were closing, he would be ripped to—

The troll was gone.

Jackie stumbled forward in the darkness. His heart beat so hard in his chest, he had to stop and drop to his knees for several deep breaths. He began to tremble in small, quick tremors in different parts of his body. First his head shook. Then his legs. The right side of his face. He giggled hysterically at the sensation. The tremors and giggles grew until his teeth were chattering and his giggling sounded like weeping.

He had run the gamut from terror to hope and back again and again. It left him feeling like he'd been kicked in the stomach several times. He crouched on the floor holding his belly, giggling and trembling, feeling like he was going to puke his guts out, but he didn't care.

He had hope again! He knew he could beat the witch's power over him because he knew what it was. Just plain old Anna Lucy Nation, the lady who wasn't there. *Knowledge is strength.*

The sound of a clock ticking in the darkness brought Jackie out of his bout of hysteria. Jackie peered into the darkness in both directions and could see nothing in the dim light but the corner he'd just come around. The clock ticked louder and faster. Another sound became apparent. It was a snuffling, panting sound.

Whatever it is, Jackie thought, steeling himself, it isn't real. It's just the witch.

Just as the huge thing came around the corner, Jackie realized it was not Anna Lucy Nation again.

This was for real.

Very real.

The dog turned the corner and Jackie understood what the ticking-clicking noise was. He started running. He could hear the dog picking up speed behind him. Jackie ran to a door on his right. He clutched at the knob but his suddenly sweaty hands slipped off. He could hear the dog's growling now, and the loud, getting louder, *thup, thup thup* of its paws, which he had mistaken for a clock, on the floor.

Jackie grabbed the knob again and turned it—the wrong way.

The dog's breath was coming fast and furious. Its deep growl rose to a frenzied pitch.

Jackie turned the knob the other way and pushed. The door opened a fraction of an inch and stopped with the loud squeak of a rusty hinge sticking.

He looked fearfully over his shoulder. The dog was loping out of the darkness, running low on its long legs, its bloody mouth open, its tongue dangling pink and wet to one side, its teeth baring to reveal gleaming white fangs ready to rip his throat out the way it had done to the policeman who'd come to save them.

Jackie threw himself against the door. It shrieked in protest but skittered open, tumbling Jackie inside. He landed on his right hip, just inside the door, and tried to kick it closed behind him as he fell.

The dog stuck its head in and nearly got his foot before Jackie kicked it in the head. He slid to his back and kicked furiously with both feet on the door. It slammed on the dog's intruding snout. It yelped in pain and withdrew. Jackie kicked the door again with both feet and it closed.

Jackie jumped to his feet and stood against the door, his ear to the wood listening, but could hear nothing. Suddenly his head bounced off the door as the entire thing shook in its hinges. There was a pause and the door shuddered again. Jackie could hear the scrape of the dog's claws on the wood each time it jumped against the door. The way the door was shaking, Jackie didn't think it would stay up too long.

He put his back to the door and surveyed the room he was in. The dog hit the door again, jarring Jackie's vision for a moment, then he saw that the room was a small one. There was a Singer sewing machine opposite the door with a low table next to it. Against the walls were naked dress dummies. To his right was a door, and another was near the far left corner.

Just before the dog struck the door again, Jackie ran to the far door and opened it. It was a closet.

The door behind him let out a resounding crack. Jackie ran to the other door and pulled it open. It was a large room. Jackie ran in, slamming the door behind him. The room was lit by several heavy-shaded floor lamps against the walls. The windows were tall and heavily draped, the walls covered with bookshelves stacked to the ceiling like in the school library. In the middle of the room was a wide, wooden desk with a high-backed leather chair at it. Against the back wall was a great flagstone fireplace. A braided rug was on the floor in front of it, as were several leather armchairs and a small sofa.

Jackie ran to the windows, but they were too dirty for him to see anything through them. He tried to open one, but it was too large and he could not budge it. He knew he had to get down to the first floor anyhow if he was ever going to get out.

He ran to the desk with another idea, but there was no telephone. He frantically searched the entire room but could see no phone anywhere. He went through the drawers looking for anything to help and found a long, thin, silver letter opener done to look like a sword. Jackie pulled it out and clutched it in his hand.

The sound of voices approaching drove Jackie to dive

under the desk where he crouched, looking under the bottom edge. A door opened and several people came into the room; three ladies and two men and they were all wearing strange clothes. Though Jackie could only see them from the shins down he could see that the women were wearing shimmering, ballooning gowns of silk that reached all the way to the floor. The men were wearing tights and leather shoes, the toes of which were pointed and curled up.

"The foot that fits this glass slipper shall be the foot of the next Queen, for the Prince will wed her on the morrow," a very English accented man's voice proclaimed.

"It will fit my foot!" a high-pitched squeaky voice answered. The women sat on the sofa by the fireplace and the two men knelt in front of them. One of the women offered her foot, but when the man tried it on it was too big.

"Just a moment," an older woman's voice said. Two of the women got off the couch and came near the desk, their feet just inches from his face. The older woman whispered to the other: "Cut your toe off; when you are Queen you will have no need to walk."

Jackie shoved his hand in his mouth, biting down on his thumb as a hand with a knife came into view and began slashing and sawing at the big toe of one of the feet. The sound of the knife grinding through bone set Jackie to shivering. The toe came free of the foot and blood spurted right in Jackie's face.

He let out a yell and backed out from under the desk. The room was empty. He touched his face and found it dry. It was the witch again. He'd been thinking that the fireplace in the room looked like the one he'd seen on TV on "Fairy Tale Theater" when they showed "Cinderella."

He stood and a scrabbling sound caught his attention. It sounded like tiny pebbles and grains of sand falling on a hard surface. He looked around, unable to pinpoint its location until he saw a puff of soot mushroom out of the fireplace. A rock fell from the chimney and bounced into the room. There was a loud scraping sound and a grunt just before a short, fat man with a white beard and a red suit dropped out and waddled into the room with a sack over his shoulder.

Santa Claus had seen better days. His suit and hat were moth-eaten, his boots ripped and muddy. His eyes were bloodshot and rheumy; his beard, stringy and greasy. He had a large canker sore on one lip and was missing his front teeth.

Suddenly Jackie recognized who Santa really was: the person he'd *always* associated with Santa Claus.

When he was three, a few Christmases ago, his mother had taken him to see Santa Claus at Faneuil Hall. On the way, he had seen a street person in a red bathrobe and ski hat dragging a large pillowcase filled with his belongings. Jackie had thought that the vagrant was Santa and had been afraid of him. Santa looked so mean and dirty and scary that Jackie had started to cry. He'd also had nightmares after that, of the scary Santa climbing down his chimney to carry him away in his sack. Ever since then, Jackie had never completely enjoyed Christmas because he always thought of that incident sooner or later.

"Ho, ho, ho," Santa coughed more than laughed. He plopped his bag down on one of the armchairs and winked at Jackie. "Have you been a good boy?"

Jackie didn't answer.

"I know who's been naughty or nice," Santa crowed in a cracked voice. He opened his sack and looked in it. "Let's see what we've got for you."

Jackie found himself taking a step forward in anticipation without thinking.

Santa rummaged around a bit and finally seemed to have found what he was looking for. He pulled it out.

Jackie screamed. In Santa's hand was a freshly severed human head, the head was Jackie's. He looked at himself decapitated, the blood still dripping from the torn flesh of his neck like gutter overflow, and felt his stomach plummet. Waves of hot and cold sweat rolled over him and he felt dizzy. The room began to spin as he backed away in search of escape.

"Merry Christmas!" Santa said, smiling. Jackie could smell his alcohol breath and B.O. all the way across the room. It increased his nausea dramatically.

The eyes of Jackie's decapitated twin opened and stared balefully at him. Jackie let out a shriek that the bloody head echoed and ran to the door at the other side of the room.

"Here. Catch," Santa called after him, swinging the head by the hair and tossing it to him as he pulled open the door and slipped out into the corridor again. He heard the head thump against the other side of the door and roll away on the floor. His stomach rolled with it.

Gritting his teeth, he realized he was back in the hallway. He tensed, looking left and right for any sign of the dog. There was none. Keeping his back to the wall and clutching the letter opener firmly in his grasp in front of him, Jackie slid along the wall to the right. A few feet on, he stopped. He thought he had heard something. He peered into the darkness behind and in front of him, but could see nothing. He listened a moment longer, then went on.

There was a quick rush of air in the hallway and suddenly the dog's massive head, the mouth yawning and the teeth snapping, was just inches from his face. It had been lying in wait; invisible in the dark. Instinctively Jackie put up his arm, warding the dog off and the animal's leg knocked the letter opener out of his hand. It clattered away in the darkness. The dog sprawled in the shadows beyond him.

Jackie rolled to his feet and ran in the opposite direction, but his legs felt like they had been tied together. Behind him, he could hear the canine getting up and following. Jackie tried to run faster but his knees didn't want to bend. He felt like he did at Hampton Beach trying to walk against the incoming waves.

The sound of the dog's breath and the clicking of its nails on the floor grew louder and louder until Jackie felt its paws hitting his back left shoulder. He was flung forward by the dog's weight, and its teeth caught on his T-shirt, tearing it across his back. Jackie sprawled into the darkness, smashing into the base of the wall with the shoulder the dog had just hit. He bounced off the baseboard and lay still.

His shoulder was burning with pain so badly, Jackie almost wished the dog would hurry and rip his throat out and put him out of his misery. But it seemed the dog had other plans. He walked over to Jackie's prone body, sniffed it, and grabbed his injured shoulder firmly in its mouth and picked him up. Jackie screamed with the pain and blacked out for a second. The dog began to drag him down the hallway. Jackie screamed again, drowning in a dark black hole of hot acid pain. He sunk into unconsciousness again but rose back to the pain. Through it all he managed to realize that the dog was taking him to the witch.

Jackie opened his eyes and gritted his teeth against the torturing pain in his shoulder. He hung limply from the dog's mouth as it dragged him along on his stomach, his left shoulder clamped firmly in the canine's mouth. He could feel its breath on his neck; it smelled of dead flesh. Jackie glanced around for some way to escape, but when he moved his head, the pain in his shoulder intensified.

Just as he was fainting away, giving into the pain, giving into the witch, ready to give it all up, he noticed the glint of something metallic for a moment on the hallway floor a short distance ahead. The dog dragged him nearer and Jackie realized it was the letter opener he had dropped when the dog first attacked him.

With a supreme effort, his shoulder sending white-hot lightning bolts of pain through his entire body, Jackie twisted and reached out with his free arm. He just barely grabbed the end of the handle, pushing it along a few inches until his fingers closed on it and he could pull it in.

Jackie's fingers fumbled with the opener for a moment, and he almost lost it again, but then managed to grip it tightly in his free right hand. Striving to keep conscious through the pain that every move he made and every step the dog took brought to his shoulder, Jackie tried to twist around to stab the dog in the chest.

It was no use.

The dog held his shoulder so firmly, and the pain was so bad, that even if he could reach the dog's chest with the letter opener he would not be able to put any force into thrusting it into the dog.

All seemed lost again. Jackie began to cry, but instead of giving up, he began to get angry. Tears streaming down his face, he yelled and flailed wildly with the letter opener, trying to make the dog let go of him. The dog growled and shook Jackie back and forth like a rag doll, making him scream from the pain. The pain blotted out everything and he felt like he was caught in a whirlpool, being dragged down into an evil blackness. And within that blackness, Jackie knew the witch was waiting for him. If he blacked out now, he would waken to the witch's embrace.

With one last ditch effort Jackie twisted his body against the pain and swung the letter opener in a wide arc, stabbing upward with all the force he could muster. The ensuing pain was excruciating. The black whirlpool sucked him in and, gratefully, he let it.

He woke to a strange sound, part scream, part gargling. He was lying on his right side, with his legs crossed and his hurt shoulder throbbing. He realized the dog wasn't dragging him anymore when something large and black rushed by him. There was a loud crash and he craned his head to see what was going on.

The dog was a few feet away, dancing madly round and round as if chasing its tail. It crashed into the left wall, bounced off, and jumped sideways across the hallway, crashing into the opposite wall. It slumped to its side, its paws clawing at its head, and Jackie saw why. The letter opener was sticking halfway out of the bottom of the dog's mouth. The dog clawed at it as blood stained its teeth and tongue and gargled in its throat. It whined so shrill that it sounded like a girl screaming.

Jackie moved his feet, felt the pain in his shoulder shake him again, and tried to crawl away.

The dog let out an inhuman growl of rage and pain and, fixing its eyes on Jackie as the source of its torment, pounced on him.

Jackie felt himself moving as if he were in slow motion. He rolled onto his back, sending another spear of pain through his shoulder, and held up his right arm to ward the dog off. The dog lunged and Jackie's forearm hit the bottom of the letter opener, ramming it up into the dog's head where the point pushed out of its left eye with a gush of blood and white pulpy tissue as it pierced the eyeball.

The dog went over him, gyrating madly and convulsing as it jerked its head around wildly and clawed at the handle of the letter opener sticking out of the bottom of its mouth. It tried to turn and bite Jackie, but it couldn't get its mouth open wide enough with the opener stuck through it. It smashed into the wall several more times, then charged head first into a closed door and collapsed on the floor a few feet from Jackie. Bloody foam bubbled from its mouth as its thrashing grew feeble. Its breath rattled loudly and it blew blood from its nose. Its good eye rolled up into its head, showing only white. The dog's legs twitched, and its head jerked once more before it settled almost peacefully into a pool of its own foamy blood and lay still.

Jackie's shoulder hurt worse than anything he had ever felt; even worse than the time when he was four and his Cousin Danny had slammed the car door on Jackie's fingers, breaking two of them. This pain was ten times worse than that.

Jackie lay on the floor, sobbing, and looked fearfully back

at the dog. He cried harder. He had always liked dogs; they were one of the few things he had never been afraid of. He had always thought he had a special way with dogs. Never would he have thought of hurting or killing one, or of one trying to kill him. Never in a million years.

The tears kept coming. Once they started, Jackie couldn't stop them. He cried for the dog and he cried for the pain; for Jennifer and Mark and the other boys; for his mother and Steve. He cried especially for himself because he was hurt and scared and tired; he just wanted to go to sleep and forget everything.

Several minutes later, he was all cried out. His shoulder was becoming numb, which was a vast improvement over the excruciating pain, but it also became very stiff, along with his left arm, hand, and ribs. With some difficulty and a flaring resurgence of pain in his dead shoulder, Jackie struggled to his feet. Leaning heavily against the wall with his good side, Jackie slid down the hall, away from the dead dog.

He didn't know how long he'd been walking, wincing at the dull pain throbbing through his entire left side, drifting in and out of awareness of his surroundings, when he came to a corner and turned it. He found himself in a short hallway that led to a narrow stairway going up into the house. To the right, a short distance ahead was another, wider stairway that went down to the first floor.

Before Jackie could take another step, the air on the stairs leading down danced with minute sparkles like a cloud of dust made suddenly visible by a beam of sunlight. The very air began to take shape, forming into something huge. The air swelled and bulged, turning as black as boiling tar. Fire suddenly erupted from the middle of the seething mass, blossoming toward the ceiling, and the form emerged in hideous detail.

Its ears were batlike, wide and pointed. The scales of its

head were green razors crusted with barnacles. Its eyes were crocodile eyes, cold and deadly. Its snout was long and supported a mouth studded with foot-long teeth. Above the teeth, two wide nostrils spouted licks of flame and puffs of black smoke. Its body was something like that of a stegosaurus, a picture of which Jackie had in a book at home. Spiny green razor-sharp fins made a ridge down its back to its long, twitching spiked tail. Its neck was long and its legs short.

It snarled at him, its forked tongue slithering from its mouth. A billow of flame erupted from its nostrils and travelled up the hallway to within inches of Jackie.

He could feel the heat from the flame on his face.

"You're not real," he mumbled defiantly at the dragon.

The dragon's mouth curled into a frightful mockery of a smile. It spoke and its lips moved like a human's. "If I'm not real, how come you're sweating?" the dragon asked him in a hissing, growling voice.

It was true, the blast of flame had made him break out in a sweat. Jackie looked disbelievingly at the dragon. *It couldn't be real. It just couldn't.* Another blast of flame poured from the dragon's snout, driving Jackie back from the heat of it. The hairs on his arms singed while at the same time the wallpaper along the hallway and the paint on the stair's banister began to peel, smoke, and bubble. Jackie's shoulder throbbed from the heat.

Jackie backed away from the dragon. This isn't real, he told himself. It's the witch. If she could make him see things that weren't there, couldn't she also make him feel things that weren't there? Of course. But it didn't make the heat from the dragon's flame any less hot knowing it.

The dragon crawled to the top of the stairs. Its long claws scraped on the wood like fingernails on a chalkboard. The sound ran over the back of Jackie's neck like a cold ice cube being rubbed there. The dragon's head swung back and forth, low to the floor. Another cloud of flame shot from its nose and rolled down the hallway, blackening the floor and setting the wallpaper to burn where it had peeled away from the wall.

Jackie felt the heat of the flames and again told himself they weren't real. This was just like before. If he charged the dragon, he could run unscathed through the flames and the dragon itself and get downstairs to freedom. His worst enemy was fear, and he had to conquer it.

Taking deep breaths, and psyching himself up to do it by repeating, *It isn't real!* over and over again, he started forward.

The dragon began to shrink.

Jackie stopped in his tracks and watched as the dragon grew smaller and smaller, losing its shape and changing, metamorphosing into something else, something on two legs that was not much taller than Jackie.

It was Mark Thomas.

Jackie groaned, the sound thick and hurtful in his throat.

Mark was standing naked at the top of the stairs, his stomach still painted with the witch's bloody symbols. His chest was laid open to reveal a blood-oozing, wet cavity where the witch had removed his heart. More blood ran from a wide gash between his legs where his private parts should have been.

"Give it up, Jackie," Mark said with a sad smile. "You can't get away. Come with me and we'll be friends . . . *forever!"*

Mark stepped toward Jackie, arms outstretched for an embrace. "Come on," he pleaded, "have a heart." A sick smile crossed Mark's face and he chuckled.

Jackie couldn't stand this. It didn't matter if he knew whether it was real or not, he just couldn't take it. In a panic, he dashed back down the hallway to a door on the left. With his good arm and hand, he grabbed the doorknob and flung it open.

A huge, smiling wolf looked into his eyes. It was dressed

like Robin Hood and sat at a wooden dinner table. A drop of blood clung to one long, sharp tooth. On the plate in front of the wolf were the cooked remains of something in a red cape and hood. On the other three plates set at the table were pigs, roasted brown in tiny, charred business suits, legs up and apples in their mouths. One of them wore gold-rimmed glasses.

"Come join me," the wolf said, leering. "Plenty for everyone."

Jackie backed away and ran to a door on the opposite wall. He opened it on a bedroom that looked normal. Just as he was about to dash inside, the window in the room burst inward, glass flying everywhere. Jackie stared, dumbstruck, as a branch of a vine as thick as a redwood tree filled the room. Through the broken window's frame he could see a skinny boy was on the vine, climbing down. He glanced up, then quickly jumped through the window into the room.

"Hide me!" he begged of Jackie. A moment later, a huge body climbed down the vine and a giant face appeared at the top half of the broken window. A massive hand and arm reached over the viny branch, through the window, and grabbed the skinny boy. With one quick squeeze of the giant hand, the boy was squished to a bloody pulp, his head popping like a squeezed grape.

Jackie slammed the door and stumbled down the hallway. Just ahead, a naked Snow White came out of another room, stumbled, and fell. The dwarfs, following hot on her heels, fell upon her immediately. This time, sex was not their object. Now they carried chains, knives, and clubs. They began beating Snow White, who screamed in agony at the bite of their weapons into her too-white flesh.

Jackie looked away, but there was Santa the derelict standing in another doorway, Jackie's decapitated head swinging lazily in his hand.

Jackie spun around, in his terror barely even aware of the pain the movement brought to his shoulder, and saw Mark coming down the hall. He held his beating heart in his cupped hands like an offering and opened his mouth wide to show his private parts stuffed into his throat.

Jackie, teetering on the edge of hysteria, looked around wildly. Everywhere, the hallway was coming to life with horrible images.

From the narrow stairway that went up to the next floor, a giant toad hopped forth, croaking: "Kiss me!" Its long tongue rolled out of its mouth. Jackie could see half-digested insect parts stuck to it.

From behind Mark, a unicorn trotted into view, a screaming baby impaled on its spiral horn.

The air in the hallway began to dance with spirals of light. Tiny winged fairies, like Tinkerbell, began to flit around Jackie's head, yanking his hair and nipping at his ears and neck with stinging little needle-sharp teeth. He swatted at them with his good arm the way he would at bothersome insects.

From the walls themselves, more apparitions appeared: the Pied Piper, rats climbing over his body; the Three Bears, each gnawing on a different part of Goldilock's torn body, their teeth as pointed as their ears; the Big Bad Wolf, picking the shreds of a red cape and pork flesh from between his teeth with a long claw; a horde of elves and leprechauns, each looking evilly deformed and demented as they advanced on Jackie.

Jackie was surrounded. Every way he turned there was a new horror waiting for him.

Santa was joined by the troll who was tying a napkin around her neck as if in preparation of a meal.

The dwarfs stopped their mutilation of Snow White and advanced on him. Behind them, a giant, grizzly looking rabbit, with long spiked teeth jutting from its mouth, hopped into view. It carried an Easter basket filled with gray eggs. The eggs began to crack open and spiders and snakes slithered out.

Panic and fear built in Jackie to the exploding point. He

whirled around, looking for escape and shrieked at what he saw coming around the corner behind him.

It was the witch's dog, letter opener still stuck through its head, blood pouring from around its point showing through where his left eye should have been. The dog was on a leash. Holding the other end was the walking corpse of Jackie's stepfather, Steve. "Come on, Jackie," he gurgled. "It's time to go home."

"No!" Jackie screamed and ran away from the horrible sight. He swatted at the fairies with his good arm and shoved elves, leprechauns, and dwarfs out of his way. Screaming, "You're not real!" at the top of his lungs, he plunged through the apparitions of the Easter Bunny, Mark Thomas, the unicorn, and the giant toad.

He reached the top of the wide stairway to the first floor and didn't stop. Wincing with pain at every step down the stairs, Jackie descended to the kitchen. Behind him, the howls of outrage and sounds of hot pursuit suddenly faded.

Jackie ran into the kitchen and slipped in blood. He fell hard on his butt, the pain in his shoulder imploding deep to the bone with the jolt. He saw the back door and, knowing he was so close to escape, struggled painfully to his feet. As he pushed himself off the floor, Jennifer walked in.

"Stay away!" Jackie gasped in pain.

"It's okay, Jackie," his sister said excitedly. "Look, the witch is dead and I got Mother free."

Behind her, on the floor of the short corridor to the entrance hall, lay the witch, her eyes open, the pupils rolled up into her head, and a thin line of blood running from her mouth down her chin. Jackie saw his mother, still naked, her left arm hanging limply at her side, standing in front of the dead witch. She looked dazed as she stepped into the kitchen, but managed a weak smile at Jackie.

"Mom!" Jackie sobbed with joy. He limped to her, wrapping his good arm around her waist, and buried his face in her belly. Likewise, she drew him near with her right arm and hugged him. Pain shot angrily through his arm and shoulder with her hug, but Jackie didn't care anymore. The nightmare was finally over. He cried and held on to his mother, enjoying her embrace despite the pain.

She hugged him tight.

And tighter.

Jackie was having trouble breathing. His mother was holding him so tight he couldn't lift his face from her belly. His shoulder was going beserk with pain, leaving him faint and nauseous. Suddenly, the realization that he had *never* heard Jen call their mom "Mother" before popped into his head.

Managing to pull his head away from her long enough to suck in a gasping breath, Jackie looked up at his mother and screamed.

The swollen, bruised and blood-encrusted face of the witch stared down at him with a malevolent smile.

"Bad boy," Eleanor scolded. She threw Jackie hard against the cabinets along the wall. Blood spurted from his nose. One of the cabinet handles caught him in the stomach, knocking the scream out of him in a gasp. She quickly picked him up and swung him by his bad shoulder, head first into the large upright freezer in the corner by the door. His breathless cry of anguished pain was abrupt, as was consciousness.

With her good right arm, Eleanor picked him up by the ankle of his left foot and dragged him out of the kitchen. His head thumped loudly on the doorsill and the door swung back, slamming into his side, cracking his ribs. She dragged him into the entrance hall, across the cold marble floor, to the crematorium door.

She opened it and started down, pulling the limp Jackie behind her. He bounced heavily from step to step, breaking his left arm, separating his left shoulder worse than it was, and fracturing his collarbone. At the bottom of the stairs,

Eleanor dragged him across to the cage and flung him against the bars, breaking his other arm, his right leg, and both his hips. Jackie collapsed to the floor on his back, his head turned back at Eleanor, eyes glazed.

Eleanor stood over him, breathing heavily and fought the urge to kick the little brat. He had nearly spoiled everything. Now she had less than fifteen minutes to complete the sacrifices before midnight and the consummation of the final ritual. She had to work fast, despite the intense pain in her face, chest, broken arm, and just about every place else on her body, all thanks to the brat who lay at her feet.

Again she got the urge to kick him and keep on kicking him, but she stepped over him instead and went into the cage to get Davy Torrez. Halfway there, she had to stop and lean against the bars while a wave of pain and dizziness swept over her. The beating she had given Jackie had taken its toll on her as well; her body was a pulsating mass of pain and exhaustion.

"Girl! Get that thing in here," Eleanor wheezed at Jennifer, who stood quietly near the crematorium door. Jennifer did as she was told, pushing the gurney around Jackie's limp body and into the cage where she collapsed it. Eleanor used her foot to roll Davy Torrez's upper body onto the gurney while Jennifer lifted his legs and swung them on. She pushed the lift lever, raising the gurney to its upright position, and with Eleanor by her side, leaning on her for support, wheeled him out of the cage to the embalming table.

Eleanor didn't bother removing Davy Torrez's clothing. There was no time. She cut his filthy pajama top open with her knife and yanked his bottoms down enough with one hand to reveal his genitals. Dipping her fingers in the jar on the instrument table, she hurriedly painted his chest while quickly chanting the accompanying words. In less than a minute, she had the symbols done. She picked up the knife, sprawling it over the boy's chest as she traced the symbols, cutting deeply in places in her rush.

Davy Torrez never made a sound. As soon as Eleanor laid her hand on him, his mind had completely disintegrated in terror and disappeared. There was no Davy left to feel the pain, much less cry out.

Eleanor finished the chant and the tracing of the symbols with the knife. She raised it over the boy's bloody chest and let it fall, plunging it into the center of the circle of symbols she had drawn on his chest. The child flopped twice, expelled air in a long sigh, and never took another breath. While she cut his chest open, his left hand and right leg twitched.

CHAPTER 43

Put it in the oven for baby and me.

A ten-ton pile of hurt was jumping on Jackie's body. It trampled his legs, crushed his hips and back, and drummed through his head. The hurt was so bad that he wanted to cry, wanted to scream; but this hurt was beyond crying, beyond screaming. This much hurt *had* to be close to dying.

He tried opening his eyes and found that they were already open. All he could see was a billowing gray cloud with a swarm of needle-shaped lines of light coursing through it. Slowly the gray began to fade into a blurred mass. Something was moving to his left, but he didn't think he could turn his head to see what it was. Directly ahead, and above him, was a row of tiny, bright lights.

The hurt jumped harder sending him wading into the gray cloud again. When his vision returned, the room came into sharper focus. He was able to make out the oven with its roller-topped conveyor belt ready to feed it. Someone was standing near it. He squinted and realized it was Jennifer.

Where's the witch? Everything came back to him at once, doubling the pain he already felt.

I'm right here, the witch said in his mind.

Jackie winced, stiffening involuntarily, driving the pain in his body to new heights.

I'll be with you in a minute.

The witch's horrid cackling came from his left. Jackie also recognized the sound of the knife cutting deep into flesh and knew what the witch was doing.

Jackie looked at Jennifer. She was staring vacantly in his direction, not seeing him at all. He blinked at her, trying to get her attention, but she didn't notice. While the witch's voice rose with hoarse chanting, Jackie tried to speak.

"Jen," he thought he said, but no sound came out and he wasn't sure if his lips had even moved. He tried again and produced a whisper that shook him with a pain so intense it brought the gray cloud back momentarily. His sister remained unmoved.

"Jen," he managed to say louder, and cried out at the hurt that stomped him when he spoke. A loose tooth fell out of his mouth and bounced on the floor near his head. "Help me, Jen," he croaked, whining and groaning.

He could hear a sizzling noise and knew the witch had tossed another set of private parts into the burning bowl. A second later he smelled them burning. He couldn't see what she was doing but knew by the sounds coming from behind him that she must be feeding the heart to his mother.

Jennifer blinked and looked at him, giving him a goofy smile. "Help me, Jen," Jackie pleaded again. The words came out of him in painful, mucous sobs.

"Shut up, boy," the witch rasped from nearby.

"Please don't eat me. Please don't eat me. I didn't eat your gingerbread house," Jackie cried, the pain making him delirious.

Cackling laughter spilled from the witch like hot lead in Jackie's ears. "You're my own little Hansel and Gretel, aren't you?" the witch said gleefully in her raw voice. "I like that. My little Hansel and Gretel," she mused.

"Please don't eat me. Please don't eat me," Jackie continued to mumble.

"Gretel!" the witch called to Jennifer and cackled with delight. Jennifer ran to her, crossing in front of Jackie and passing out of his line of vision. She came back into it a moment later pushing the blood-dripping gurney with its mutilated cargo past him to the oven. The witch followed and together they placed the last boy on the conveyor belt. The witch opened the oven door, and she and Jennifer slid Davy Torrez inside. Closing the door, the witch turned up the dial that controlled the jets of flame. Smoke poured from the seams of the door, adding to the sooty cloud already hanging low in the room. After a few minutes of anxious waiting the witch, coughing harshly, removed the ashes and bones and spread them around the circle with her right hand. The left one hung useless and shuddered with each coughing spasm. When she was done, she advanced on Jackie.

"Jen, please," Jackie pleaded with all the feeble force he could muster.

"Quiet, Hansel. Your time has come. You're plump enough for me," the witch cackled. Her feet crossed to directly in front of his face and he felt a hand grabbing his hair. She picked him up that way and dragged him over to the gurney.

Jackie let out one short, pain-filled scream, then was silent.

What's going on?

He was enveloped in grayness, but this was not the pain-induced grayness of unconsciousness that he had felt before; this was something else. It was thick and sooty. It smelled horrible, like bacon burnt to a crisp. It swirled around him. He looked at himself and realized it was swirling through him as well; his body was transparent and he was floating inside the grayness. For a moment he thought there was someone else floating by his side, but when he looked, all he saw was the cloud.

The grayness grew sparse and parted for a moment. Jackie saw a room, and realized he was floating near the ceiling. This is like my dream, he thought. The grayness around him was smoke. It was pouring from a large arched metal door below and to his left, set into the wall, and from hundreds of candles set around the room. Jennifer was standing near it. He started to call to her, but noticed some-one else in the room. It was his mother, naked and tied to a reclining chair in the middle of a star within a circle that was painted on the floor and enclosed with a ring of ashes. Near her, bending over a naked boy on the table was . . . the witch!

Suddenly it all came back to Jackie. He cringed at the memory of what the witch had done to him, but realized he no longer felt any pain. The unbearable hurt that had been destroying him was gone. It had left his body.

The witch moved away from the table and Jackie realized why he felt no pain—His naked, broken body was lying on the table below him, his torn clothes crumpled around him. The witch returned with a jar and began painting squiggly lines in a circle on his chest.

She's going to kill me, Jackie thought, but giggled. I think I'm already dead, he answered himself. No, that wasn't true. He didn't know how he knew that, but he did. He was close to death, but he wasn't there yet. If the witch continued, though, he knew he soon would be. He thought he should do something, but the desire to just remain there and float was great.

The witch looked up at Jennifer and a strange thing hap-pened. Jackie became aware of tentacles of light like living things stretching from the witch's forehead to Jennifer's fore-head. The same beams of light also went from the witch's head to his mother's. Each rod of light was like a twisting snake, pulsating with surges of colors that ran back and forth between the witch, Jennifer, and his mom.

They're under her spell, he thought. That's what that is. I'm seeing the witch's spells over them. He looked at his transparent body floating above his real one and realized something else, too. The same lines of living light very subtly filled him also, but were unconnected to the witch or anyone else.

I've got to do something, he thought. I've got to connect with Jennifer like the witch is and make her help me. But how?

In the back of his mind he heard the witch cackling and calling him and Jennifer Hansel and Gretel.

Jackie laughed.

"Jennifer."

Jennifer looked up and saw her grandmother standing before her, leaning over her. My, *what big eyes you have,* she thought with a giggle, but said, "Yes, Gram?"

"Mom said you were supposed to take care of me," her grandmother said.

Jennifer laughed at Grammy saying such a funny thing, and in such a funny voice. "Yes, Grammy. I will," she giggled some more, wondering what kind of new party game Grammy was playing.

"Yes," Grammy said, as if reading her thoughts. "We're going to play a game. Now listen carefully."

Jennifer leaned forward, listening intently as her Grammy explained the game. The party was going wonderfully; a game would only make it better. Jennifer tried hard not to laugh as she listened, but it was difficult because Grammy's voice sounded so funny. As she listened, Jennifer wondered why Grammy would want to disguise her voice to sound like Jackie's.

* * *

Eleanor worked furiously, painting Jackie's chest with the bloody circle of power symbols. She had less than four minutes left to sacrifice him and prepare herself for the final ritual. Out of the corner of her eye, as she worked, she saw the girl get up and walk toward the podium.

"What are you doing, my little Gretel?" she asked chuckling. She liked the idea the boy had put in her head. It was fitting.

What do you think I'm doing? Edmund's voice came back at her. It set off a chain reaction of pain inside her, exploding through her chest, out to her arms and up into her head worse than any previous pain had been. She staggered from the force of it. Her erratic heartbeat became like thunder in her ears. She leaned over Jackie's body and puked blood onto his stomach.

You're finished, Eleanor, Edmund said when she looked up. He was standing at the podium, *The Demonolatria* in his hands. He strode to the crematorium furnace with it. *No!* Eleanor pleaded. *I'll die without that!*

Why should I show you mercy that you never showed me, or anyone else? Edmund ranted. *It's time to face your lies, Eleanor! It was you who killed Mother with your dreams, not I. It was you who made Father come to your room and rape you. All those years you had me fooled thinking you were the victim; thinking you were weaker than I. But the truth was you were much stronger, wasn't it? You were so strong that you were even able to use the Machine on Father and keep it from me. You were so strong you were able to make me kill Father and think it was my idea. You were so strong that you were able to hide your plan to get rid of me. And I was stupid enough to think that I could hear all your thoughts.*

"You left me!" Eleanor screamed out loud in pain. Remaining bent over Jackie's body, she slid the length of the table and tried to walk. "You were going to perform the rituals and leave me again."

Now you're leaving, Edmund said, opening the furnace door.

"No, you can't," Eleanor gasped, staggering away from the table.

Why not?

"Because you're not real!" Eleanor screamed in a hoarse whisper.

I'm not? Edmund asked, and tossed the book into the oven.

Jackie blinked his eyes as he regained consciousness. The smell of vomit and smoke was thick in his nose. He twitched his nostrils trying to block it out. They, and his eyes were the only part of his body that moved. He had a vague memory of a weird dream, but all that remained of it was the sensation of no pain anymore; he could feel nothing and could move nothing below his neck.

His head lay turned to the left and, across the room in his horizontal line of vision, he could see Jennifer standing next to the oven door, holding up the witch's big book. Suddenly the witch came into view screaming in a hoarse, garbled voice.

Jackie couldn't believe his ears. Something had happened while he was unconscious; the witch, of all people, was accusing Jennifer *of not being real!* Suddenly he remembered something else about his dream, that it had something to do with a fairy tale.

Before he had time to think of what the tale was, Jennifer threw the witch's book into the oven. Jackie cheered in his head. Suddenly it came to him, brought back by the memory of the witch's voice: *You're my little Hansel and Gretel.*

The witch let out a gasping shriek and staggered to the

oven. She climbed over the side of the conveyor belt and reached into the oven for the book. *Go for it!* Jackie shouted to Jennifer in his head and hoped the witch heard him.

Jennifer ran at the witch and gave her a hard body block in the rear with her right shoulder. Grunting, the witch sprawled into the oven, her wrinkled, flabby ass and veiny legs hanging out, splayed on the conveyor belt. Jennifer reached out and released the lever and wheel that closed the door. It came down with a heavy crunching thud on the back of the witch's waist.

Jackie could hear the sizzle of the hot door melting into the witch's skin as she screamed in the oven. She began to squirm, frantically trying to pull herself out of the oven. Jennifer hesitated a moment, then reached over and turned the dial that powered the flames to full.

Fire shot out from under the door, licking up around the witch's naked legs and butt. She let out a scream horrible beyond words. Her legs and feet began to kick wildly as the skin on them began to cook, reddening and bubbling with blisters. The witch's screams rose, climbing higher and higher without pause for a breath until they reached an hysterical barking, gasping, laugh/screaming that seemed to go on forever, echoing like thunder in Jackie's head before it finally faded and died away. The convulsions of her legs and feet, which at first hammered frantically on the melting rubber top of the conveyor belt, the skin peeling from them under the assault of the flames, soon followed suit, diminishing to feeble sporadic twitchings.

Yes! Yes! Yes! Jackie thought with vengeful joy.

Jennifer staggered and nearly fell over from a sudden feeling of dizziness. She put her hand to her eyes and reached out to steady herself, but touched something hot. She opened her eyes and looked at the oven and conveyor belt next to her. There was something stuck in the oven door and it was burning with a horrible stench and clouds of black smoke as its skin blackened and bubbled under the flames shooting out from the half-open oven door.

Those are legs, Jennifer realized. She backed away nauseous at the sight. She turned around. Her mother was behind her, naked and strapped to a leather reclining chair, her legs outstretched, her feet tied to metal stirrups. Her head was moving back and forth and her eyes were blinking.

Gasping, Jennifer saw her brother lying broken and bloody on the metal table to the right of his mother. He was naked, too, and looked to be in terrible shape, but Jennifer ran to her mother's side first, and began undoing the straps.

Jennifer had no immediate recollection of what had gone on in the crematorium, but she did know that she had to get her mother out of there. For some reason, that was the most important thing she had to do. It didn't matter how hurt Jackie was, even if he was dying, Jennifer had to get her mother and the baby to safety.

As Jennifer undid the leather thongs holding her mother to the chair, her mother moaned, and a gush of brown, fishy-smelling fluid came from between her legs.

Jackie was drifting, losing sight of the room every few minutes, then slipping back into it again. Every time he did, he looked at the smoking, burning flesh of the witch still stuck in the oven to be sure she was really dead. Her legs were blackening, torched by the flames still shooting out through the billows of black smoke from under the half open iron door. Only her ankles and the soles of her feet remained white. Her calves were bright red and covered with blisters. Her blackened thighs and buttocks had cracked open. Melting fat ran through the fissures and sizzled as it dripped from her body.

She was really, really, most sincerely dead. Dead as a doornail. *Dead Meat!* The last thought sobered Jackie's joy as he drifted on the edges of reality. He had seen too much Dead Meat this day. With all that had happened, he thought it might have been better if the witch had killed him first so that he wouldn't have to live the rest of his life with the terror of her inside him. He knew that if he lived, and that prospect was getting dimmer as he began to find himself drifting on the ceiling for seconds at a time, he'd never forget this; it would haunt his life forever.

He was floating again, slipping into the gray cloud when a loud moaning noise, like a rusty iron gate closing slowly, snapped him back to consciousness.

The oven door was moving. With a screech, it dropped an inch, making the witch's legs shudder. A second later, the door let out a loud, iron shriek and slammed closed, chopping the witch's charred body in two and shutting in the flames and most of the smoke. The witch's cooked buttocks and seared legs remained lying on the conveyor belt, streams of black smoke spiralling gracefully upward from her melted flesh.

Suddenly Jackie couldn't breathe.

The witch's legs moved!

Suddenly, Jackie was sure he would never breathe again; if he did, it wouldn't be a sane breath. He wanted to scream but knew if he started he wouldn't stop until he had screamed himself crazy.

The witch's cracked, burnt, and crispy legs, *were moving.* The knees slid forward, the kneecaps sticking to the table's melted rubber rollers and pulling off, remaining there. The witch's shriveled, charred ass rose into the air. Smoking, bubbling blood and grease ran from it, down her torched and splitting thighs.

She's coming back for me! Jackie screamed silently.

The witch's charcoaled legs and ass began to sway as the gray cloud returned for Jackie. The right leg lifted, leaving half its shin on the table to keep its kneecap company and off balance, the rest of her toppled. Her cooked remains fell off the conveyor belt onto the stone floor, trailing smoke like a shot-down airplane and spattering hot, sizzling grease and bloody fat in a wide arch on the stone floor.

When she fell, so did Jackie, toppling over into oblivion.

CHAPTER 44

And now my story is done.

"It's all right," a voice said.

Jackie groped toward it. Suddenly, the gray fog he lived in grew dark.

"You're safe now."

Who was speaking to him? It seemed very important that he should know. Why it was important, he couldn't grasp. But the cloud grew darker.

"I'm just going to take a little of your blood."

The witch!

Jackie opened his eyes.

She was back.

Standing by the bedside.

Needle in her hand.

Leaning over him.

"Just a little of your blood."

He tried to pull away but nothing worked. His arms, legs— his entire body was disconnected from his brain.

The witch changed. She became a nurse, smiling kindly and looking at him with genuine pity in her eyes. She changed again. The charbroiled remains of her burnt body from the waist down stood by the bed. Behind her on the floor, the horrid, fire-blasted upper torso walked in on its arms, her huge, fried-egg eyes with their lids burned off searching for the rest of her body.

Jackie woke to the sound of a television and the dull throb of pain that was like a giant hand squeezing his body tightly every few seconds. The news was on. He opened his eyes but could see nothing. After several minutes of blinking his eyes—that still being the only part of his body that he could move—he began to notice a light, dim and flickering; the sort of light cast by a TV screen. Either it was a small set, or he was too far away from it, but it didn't illuminate his surroundings very well. All Jackie could make out was a ceiling and a pipe with a curtain on it going around where he lay.

He was concentrating on trying to move his head when he heard his name on the television. Straining to hear, he listened to the news commentator tell how men from the county sheriff's department had discovered him, Jennifer, and their mother at Grimm Memorials, after answering Jennifer's phone call for help. Though they gave some of the grisly details, police were still discovering bodies and did not yet know the whole story of what had gone on there. Jackie wanted to speak to get someone's attention to tell them what happened, but something else the commentator said recaptured his attention.

"The most bizzare aspect of this horrifying discovery is that in her will, Eleanor Grimm, the woman who committed these atrocities, left her entire estate, worth half a million dollars, to the unborn son of the woman she kidnapped, and whose husband she murdered—Diane Nailer. Police are baffled as to Eleanor Grimm's motives other than that she was involved in some kind of occult worship that involved human sacrifice and cannibalism. There has been some speculation by authorities that she may have belonged to the coven of

drug-running satanists responsible for similar atrocities in
Mexico and Texas last year . . ."

Jackie couldn't believe it. Why would the witch do that?

Diane Nailer put the car in neutral as she sat at the red
light. She glanced in the rearview mirror at the baby, little
Steve, sitting in his car seat cooing at his fingertips. Jennifer
sat next to him, watching him, but not playing with him. She
did that a lot, Diane realized. Jennifer would sit and watch
the baby, but not play with him or talk to him. She'd have to
ask her psychiatrist about that; he had warned her that Jen
and Jackie would probably need counseling, too.

The light turned green and she put the car in gear again
after a few prodding horns from the cars behind her. She
smiled wearily to herself at the thought of seeing a psychiatrist. Before Grimm Memorials she had thought having a
shrink was a luxury of the rich. Now she knew that if you really needed one, it was a luxury that you paid for with more
than money; you paid for it with your well-being, your spirit,
your very soul.

At first, Diane hadn't needed any help. When the police
and ambulance finally got to Grimm Memorials, after Jennifer
called them, she was well into labor. She delivered little Steve
in the ambulance on the way to the hospital at 12:33 A.M.,
November 1.

All her attention that night, and in the days that followed,
was focused on the baby. It wasn't until nearly a week later,
when she was strong enough that her doctors allowed first
the police, then the media to interview her, that anything else
could occupy her mind. That was when she finally learned
what had happened at Grimm Memorials, and felt her sanity
trying to slip away.

Her last coherent memory, before giving birth in the ambulance, had been of going out to lunch with Steve, back in
September, the first day of school. She was, not surprisingly,

shocked to learn what had happened in the two months since then to her husband and the children that the old lady the papers were calling a witch (using her son Jackie's description of her) had killed.

She was so shocked, in fact, that after a week of questionings and interviews, as she sat in her hospital bed with a copy of the *Boston Herald* in her lap with three-inch headlines blaring the length of the front page: MODERN-DAY HANSEL AND GRETEL THWART DEVIL WORSHIPPING WITCH, she shrieked and blacked out for three days. That was when her doctors transferred her to the psychiatric ward.

She would have remained there for years, at least, maybe more, if her doctors had not allowed her to see little Steve. When she held him, felt his need for her, she strengthened and knew she had to get out of there. She dealt with all that she had been told and had remembered in the only way her mind could: she forgot.

Except in her sleep.

She'd been out of the hospital only a week when the nightmares had started, memory returning in dreams livid and horrifying. That was when she'd started seeing the psychiatrist. Now, two months since the Hansel and Gretel murders, as the papers labeled them, she felt like she was finally making some progress in dealing with all that had happened.

Sometimes she felt guilty about the seventy-five dollars an hour she paid the shrink, but then remembered that she didn't have to worry about money, would probably never have to worry about it again. Thanks to Steve's life insurance and (she didn't like to think about it) the money and property the old Grimm woman had left little Steve, she and her children looked like they were set for life.

As she steered the Saab into the parking lot of the hospital where Jackie was still laid up, she told herself that it didn't matter where the money came from or even how much there was. Money was unimportant; it was only useful. It would help her get her children away from the media limelight so that they could salvage something of their lives and live like normal people again; at least as normal as money could buy.

That was what gave her hope. That, and little Steve were what kept her going.

Jennifer sat in the back seat of the Saab, next to the car seat holding little Steve. She and her mother and the baby were going to the hospital. Today was the day Jackie got part of his upper-body cast cut off.

It had been a little over two months since Halloween at Grimm Memorials, but the media hoopla was already dying down and it wasn't even mentioned on TV anymore. Jennifer was glad. Every time she heard the story Jackie had told the news people, she felt sick. Though she didn't remember much, Jennifer knew she had done, or helped do, some terrible things. Jackie had never once mentioned that fact to anyone. He told the police and reporters that she had been a captive just like him, and had even made her out to be the hero because she had pushed the old woman into the crematorium oven. Now she owed him.

She patted the small lump in her pocket and thought about what Jackie had told her, about what he wanted to do. She looked thoughtfully at little Steve and frowned.

"Did you bring it?" Jackie asked his sister after he got rid of their mother by telling her the doctor wanted to speak to her before they removed the cast.

"Yeah, I brought it. But this is stupid. This isn't going to prove anything," Jennifer argued.

"I don't care," Jackie replied, jutting his jaw out over the top of the body cast that he was dying to get out of. "What did you bring?"

"A piece of liver."

"Good. Do it."

As Jackie watched intently, Jennifer took out a quarter-size piece of aluminum foil and unwrapped it, revealing a glob of dark red, bloody meat. Taking a deep breath, she went to the baby, still in his basketlike car seat, which their mother had placed on the other bed in the room while she went to find the doctor.

"It's no good. He's sleeping," Jen said, leaning over the baby. There was relief in her voice. Before she could straighten, little Steve opened his eyes and looked at her.

"Do it!" Jackie urged.

Trembling, Jennifer held out the raw meat to the baby.

My tale is done, there runs a mouse, whosoever catches it, may make himself a big fur cap out of it.

—the Brothers Grimm

Please turn the page for a sneak peek of
R. Patrick Gates' new novel
GRIMM REAPINGS
coming soon from Pinnacle Books!

Thirteen years later . . .

"Hey! Hurry! It's coming on!"

Jackie Nailer brushed the unevenly chopped, green-tinted blond bags out of his eyes enough to take measure of himself in the bathroom mirror. In the community room, his girlfriend, Chalice, continued to urge him to hurry up. Jackie ignored her and looked deeply into his eyes. What *was* that look he saw there, far within his dilated pupils? It was *something*, something *different*. And when had he first noticed that odd something deep within the black holes of his pupils?

Why right after meeting the witch, yes, thank you very much.

Even after thirteen years just the thought of her brought a cold clammy *liquid* feeling to his bowels and he felt the urge to vacate them. Which brought him right back to the problem at hand, staring into his eyes and trying to figure out how *crazy* he was, was just another method of procrastination. What it really came down to was: Did he *really* want to do this?

You should have thought of that before you signed the contract and took the network's money, his hindsight voice told him. Jackie shook his head and watched his hair flop back and forth.

It's over and done with, he mentally told himself. *Why shouldn't I profit from what happened? Jen has!* But then Jen didn't remember *anything* that had happened at Grimm Memorials thirteen years ago, while Jackie couldn't forget it. It had been tough enough when the cameras from CBC had shown up and he had actually sat down with *the* Barbra Waters and looked at photographs and video from the police and trial files on the Grimm Memorials case. Looking at his six-year-old face, peering out at him so frightened, looking from the past, had brought it all rushing back at him. All that he thought he'd managed to deal with, after thirteen years of counseling, came rumbling back on great big painful emotional wheels.

Like every other sappy guest of Barbra Waters, Jackie had cried.

He pushed the embarrassing memory from his mind and thought again of those photos of his childhood self. He looked much different now, and not just because of the punk haircut with its green tint and the rings piercing his left nostril and both ears. Thirteen years had passed after all and he had grown up. He had matured physically over the last two years and now nearly resembled the adult man he would become. His eyes, which had diminished a little in their blueness, made up for it in their largeness, which gave him a puppy-dog look girls could not resist. Add to that his straight, small nose, full lips, and square jaw and he was one of the best looking boys on campus. If he didn't do his best to always hide it, that is.

"Jackie! Come on! It's starting!"

Do I really want to watch this? he mentally asked his mirror image. Chalice certainly did, as did her crew, several other Goth types she'd brought along with her. Jackie regretted now telling Chalice about the TV special; she'd spread it all over campus. Not that it wouldn't have happened anyway—but it would have (*should* have) happened after the fact, not before, which ensured that a lot more people on campus would be watching the special than normally would have. Chalice and her crew would have certainly seen it; it was right up their alley: a Barbra Waters Halloween special about the gruesome mass murders that had taken place thirteen years ago at the now infamous funeral home known as *Grimm Memorials.*

Sighing, Jackie resigned himself to the fact that he was going to have to watch the program with his girlfriend and her friends. He slouched into the living room and slid over the back of the decrepit couch, landing slumped against Chalice. He tried to do it unnoticed, but it didn't work. Every eye in the room, all of Chalice's friends, were on him, every expression the same frozen half-smile, the same unsure look in every eye bespeaking of each person's discomfort laced with anticipation. Of course, when he looked directly at any of them, their expressions changed, their smiles broadened, became full, but remained phony.

There was a commercial on for feminine hygiene spray that showed a mother and daughter at the beach sharing quality time over the subject of battling pussy odor. One of Chalice's friend's made a comment: "Now if they were selling canned *sweat* I might be interested!" To which the others laughed. Jackie half-heartedly joined in, though he didn't get it. He was too nervous to think about anything beyond the tv program that was about to reveal his bizarre past.

The commercial ended and the scene changed to a long shot of Barbra Waters, host of "It Was ? Years Ago Today!" the CBC news program that reveled in revisiting natural disasters, strange crimes, and bloody mass murders. Waters sat, shuffling papers, at a desk on a tastefully decorated set, the background of which was an aerial shot of a peaceful New England town, complete with a white steepled church spire nestled between the gently sloping, breast-shaped, tree-covered hills flamboyant with autumn colors. A title, "Season of the Witch," appeared in large, Gothic-style letters in the upper right corner of the picture. The Donovan song of the same name, with the title and chorus line reaching a crescendo before fading, played in the background. As the camera drew closer, focusing in on Waters, she put her papers down, looked directly into the camera and the living rooms of millions of Americans, smiled her trademark slightly buck-toothed smile, which was also the cause of her trademark—and much-ridiculed—lisp, and began speaking.

The same joker as before (for the life of him Jackie couldn't remember her name) said, "She sounds like Elmer Fudd," and got another big laugh. Jackie didn't join in this time, nor did he bother trying to fake it. His mouth had gone dry and his right leg was jiggling madly. When the laughter died, he heard Barbra Waters warning parents that the show's content might not be suitable for children.

"Well I guess that leaves me out!" Joker-girl commented and got up to leave. Surprisingly, few people laughed. Chalice and several others shushed her. Chalice grabbed Jackie's hand, squeezing it reassuringly and giving him a smile and wink, before turning her attention back to the screen. The gesture had the opposite effect, making Jackie more uncomfortable than he already was, and he didn't know why. He liked Chalice a lot. He hoped she still liked him two hours from now.

The program went on, but he found it hard to focus. The faces and reactions of the others in the room, especially Chalice, were too distracting. She was watching the screen intently, shaking her head every now and then and clucking her tongue in disbelief. Suddenly, Jackie heard Barbra Waters speak his name, and he became aware that every other eye in the room was on him. The screen was showing his first communion picture—him dressed in blue shorts with a white shirt and blue, clip-on bow tie, his white socks pulled smartly up to his knees over his brilliantly shining black patent leather wingtips.

Jackie glanced at the others and all eyes avoided his, returning immediately to the screen. Blushing so hotly that he knew his pale complexion was glowing bright red, he mumbled, "I need a drink," rose, and stumbled from the room into the kitchen as quickly as possible. There, he slumped against the refrigerator and banged his forehead slowly on the freezer door.

Why did I agree to be on that show? he wondered. If he hadn't agreed, maybe Jen wouldn't have done it either. Without either of them, or his mom, they couldn't have done the show.

Yeah, right!

After having met the producers of "It Was ? Years Ago Today," Jackie had known they were going to do their story with or without his and Jen's input. He had had the choice of staying out of it or helping and getting some money out of it. At the time, $1200 had seemed like a lot.

"I've sold my privacy, my anonymity, for twelve-hundred bucks," he muttered to the refrigerator between head butts. *For a lousy twelve hundred dollars I've made myself into a walking freak show.*

"Hey, if you need to have your head beat in I'd be glad to do it for you."

Jackie rested his head against the freezer door and smiled weakly at Chalice, standing in the kitchen doorway. "Actually," he said, "you could be a bigger help if you'd stand behind me and kick me in the ass while I knock my self sense*ful*!"

Chalice laughed but looked puzzled. "Don't you mean sense*less*?"

"No, I mean sense*ful*, 'cuz if I'd had any sense to begin with I wouldn't have agreed to do that stupid TV show. It represents everything that I despise about TV. The only programs worse than that one and its ilk are the reality shows."

"Aw, come on. What's the big deal? So you might become a minor celebrity on campus for a while. What's wrong with that? Think of all the hotties who are gonna wanna bang you cuz they see you on TV."

Jackie mentally winced at Chalice's mangling of English

grammar and managed a "very funny" smile for her. "I doubt anyone will think of me as a celebrity after this—more like a freak. I might as well go on tour with Lollapalooza."

"I could go with you," Chalice said, a mischievous grin on her face as she sidled up to Jackie, put her arms around him, and nuzzled his ear. "I'm double jointed, in *all* the right *joints*," she whispered and winked sexily when Jackie, wide-eyed, turned to stare at her.

He and Chalice had got to the heavy petting and occasional oral sex part of the relationship, but for reasons she kept to herself, she was reluctant to consummate it. Despite the severe Goth look, she was a very pretty girl. Jackie couldn't be sure, but he thought she might even be beautiful. He had yet to see her without makeup, which was always excessive, or without the many piercings that decorated her face. She was five foot five and a hundred pounds, with shoulder-length hair that looked like someone had hacked at it with a hatchet, leaving some parts short, others long, and most of it hanging in her face. The hair could be any color, depending on her mood, from orange to green, purple, red, or yellow, to the jet-black she presently sported. Her eyebrows were pierced with three rings each and she wore a stud in each nostril. Her ears were rimmed with studs and tiny hoops from top to bottom. She had a tongue stud and a lip ring. Her nipples were pierced and ringed, as was her belly button.

And this was all that most people saw. Add to it her stark white complexion, intense, intimidating eyes, and scowling expression, and most people probably thought her ugly. It was the effect she was going for, and she was very happy to have succeeded. She liked nothing better than to run into a bunch of "straights," as she called non-Goth types, and freak them out with her look. Jackie couldn't wait until they spent their first complete night together so that he could see what she really looked like without the costume. So far, she'd only let him have peeks—but what peeks! Though he still hadn't admitted it to himself—much less to her—he had fallen in love with her.

"Oh?" Jackie said, matching her mischievous smile and raising an eyebrow. "And exactly *what* positions can you double your joints into?"

She giggled throatily and licked the side of his face from his jaw to his eyebrow. "If you're lucky, I'll show you later, and you can bet it'll double *your* joint in size.

"Mmm," Jackie said, licking his lips, "But can you *smoke* a joint while you double your joints and, vis a vis, mine?"

"I can smoke *double* joints while doubling my joints and watching your joint double." She smirked, proud to be able to match his word skills in this little game they'd randomly developed and played often and spontaneously.

"But," Jackie said, always ready with another come-back, "can you smoke double joints while doubling your joints and watching my joint double *while* in *Dublin* chewing *Dubble Bubble* bubble gum?"

Chalice opened her mouth once, twice, and burst into raucous laughter. "No, I can't, you *retard*!" She punched his arm.

"That's good," Jackie told her in a mock-serious tone, "because the person who could do all that would . . . *rule the world*!" He said the last with a flourish, raising his right arm, index finger pointed up, like a fleshy exclamation point.

"You are such a dork," Chalice said sweetly. "I'm sorry to use such lame-ass, eighties disco terminology, but it truly is the only word that fits you to a tee. *Dork* from the Latin, *Dorkus Erectus*."

"Then that would make you a *dorkette*," Jackie immediately quipped.

Chalice roared at that, too, and sputtered out, "I could play Radio City Music Hall as a double-jointed dorkette." Her amusement was cut short by the voices of her friends from the living room.

"It's on!"

"Jackie, you're on! Chalice! He's on!"

Chalice looked at him and touched his face gently. "It'll be cool if you let it be," she said and took his hand, leading him back to the couch, back to watching his childhood exposed like the guts of the cadavers old Eleanor Grimm had worked on all those years.